# City of Death

ALSO BY LAURENCE YEP

*City of Fire*
*City of Ice*

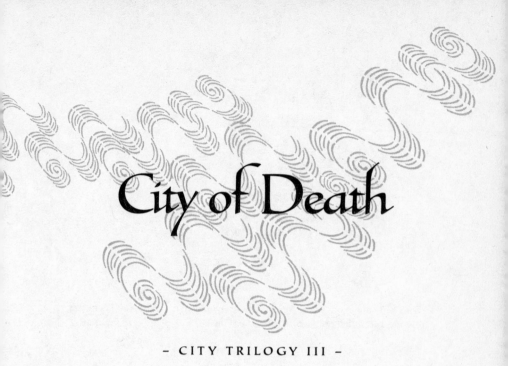

# City of Death

## - CITY TRILOGY III -

## *Laurence Yep*

A TOM DOHERTY ASSOCIATES BOOK
NEW YORK

CITY OF DEATH

A Starscape Book
Published by Tom Doherty Associates, LLC
175 Fifth Avenue
New York, NY 10010

www.tor-forge.com

ISBN 978-0-7653-1926-5 (hardcover)
ISBN 978-1-4299-9664-8 (e-book)

First Edition: February 2013

Printed in the United States of America

0  9  8  7  6  5  4  3  2  1

2921

*To Jackson, who will have his own adventures*

# Guide to Pronunciation
## of Kushan Names

*Árkwi* (Ark-wee). Lord Tsirauñe's griffin.

*Klestetstse* (Klays-tayts-tsay). More often shortened to Kles (Klays). Scirye's lap griffin, a gift from Princess Maimantstse.

*Koyn Encuwontse* (Koin En-coo-wōn-tsay). Iron Beak.

*Kwele* (Kway-lay). Lady Sudarshane's griffin.

*Lady Miunai* (Mee-oo-nai). A Sogdian lady near the Arctic Circle.

*Lady Sudarshane* (Soo-dir-shi-nay). Scirye's mother.

*Lady Tabiti* (Tuh-bee-tee). A legendary Sarmatian warrior chief.

*Lord Resak* (Re-shak). A spirit of the Arctic.

*Lord Tsirauñe* (Tsee-rou-nay). Scirye's father.

*Māka* (Mo-kuh). An aspiring sorceress.

*Nishke* (Neesh-kay). Scirye's older sister.

*Nanaia* (Nuh-nai-uh). A goddess.

*Nanadhat* (Nuh-nah-dat). The princess's steward and a relative of Princess Catisa.

*Nanayor* (Nuh-nuh-yoar). A captain in the vizier's personal troop, the wolf guard.

*Oko* (Oa-kao). A Pippal who once served with Nishke.

*Pärseri* (Pir-say-ree). A ratlike creature called an akhu (Ah-koo).

*Prince Etre* (Ay-tray). Kushan consul.

*Prince Tarkhun* (Tur-koon). A Sogdian prince near the Arctic Circle.

*Princess Catisa* (Ka-tee-si). A Sogdian princess.

*Princess Maimantstse* (My-mun-tsuh-tsay). Cousin of Scirye's father.

*Rapañ̃e* (Ruh-pun-nyay). Scirye's clan.

*Sakre Menantse* (Suh-kray May-nun-tsay). A name for the Kushan Empire meaning "Blessed of the moon."

*Sakre Yapoy* (Suh-kray Yuh-poi). Another name for the Kushan Empire meaning "the Blessed Land."

*Scirye* (Skeer-yay). Mistress of Kles.

*Riye Srukalleyis* (Ree-yay Sroo kull-lay-ees). City of Death.

*Tarkär* (Tur-kir). Kles's clan.

*Tute* (Too-tay). A lynx and friend of Māka.

*Upach* (Oo-pak). An ifrit, a desert spirit who happens to live near the Arctic Circle.

*Wāli* (Wo-lee). A Pippal who once served with Nishke.

*Warmapo* (Wir-mi-puh). A griffin captain.

# City of Death

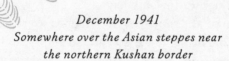

# 1

*December 1941*
*Somewhere over the Asian steppes near*
*the northern Kushan border*

## Scirye

"How fast do storms come in here?" Bayang the dragon asked, staring at the dark gray clouds boiling rapidly toward them from the east. The misty wave rolling toward them was at least a mile across and two miles long, and their shadows plunged the mountains beneath them into an ominous twilight.

Scirye and her companions were sitting on a great triangular wing that had been woven magically from straw, and Scirye tugged at a strand of her red hair as she wondered how long the flimsy mat would last in a tempest like that.

Suddenly the wing lurched upward. "Ho, fear not, lumplings," boomed the great wind, Naue. For a wind, he was fairly pleasant company, except for a bad habit of boasting.

In Hawaii, they had saved the goddess Pele and, in return, she had helped them on their quest by summoning the Cloud Folk to weave the straw wing they rode on now. She had also charged the powerful zephyr, Naue, to carry them on their quest, and he had faithfully carried them to the Arctic and now into Asia. "No little drizzle can stop Naue the magnificent. He will just carry you above it."

As Naue picked up speed, the sound of their passage rose to a high keening, and perhaps they would have been blown off the mat except for the magical frame of woven straw. The frame was little more than woven poles set upon four upright ones so that it resembled the sketch of a house, but its enchantment protected them as efficiently as brick walls would have.

Behind Scirye, the snow-covered steppes stretched like a huge sheet of cotton batting. It was so vast, so empty, so harsh. It had shaped her ancestors, the Kushans, into a warrior race as hard and sharp as steel. She had never appreciated just how tough they must have been—she knew that she herself could never have survived there.

Somebody as weak as she had no place chasing Badik the dragon and his employer, Roland, who was one of the richest men in the world. Worse, when they had stolen an ancient Kushan treasure and killed her sister, Scirye had been so blinded by rage that she had rashly asked the powerful goddess Nanaia to help her get her revenge. Now there was no question of dropping the pursuit because Nanaia always expected people to keep their word—or else.

Scirye's palm itched at the mere thought of the goddess, and she glanced at the glove covering it. There was a faint glow from Nanaia's mark, the number 3, though they could only guess what it meant. Scirye might have felt more reconciled to the bargain if the goddess had made it clear what She wanted Scirye to do.

Scirye and her friends had already survived a trip through the molten insides of a volcano and the sinking of an island to the freezing Arctic wastes, but their greatest trials were just ahead.

Her green eyes gloomily watched the mountains pass underneath them. Snow covered the mountains' shoulders and the steep black slopes looked as if some giant monster had raked its claws through the earth.

On the other hand, Scirye's lap griffin, Kles, had grown up in mountains like these, and the excitement of his homecoming had made her parrot-sized friend chattier than usual, eyes bright, eagle-shaped head jerking from side to side, and lionlike tail twitching as if he wanted to take in everything.

Upon her shoulder now, he fluttered his wings and crowed excitedly, "The Astär Mountains, the roof of the world." Astär meant arrow in the old tongue, and the sharp peaks did look like arrowheads. "Home! We're home, lady. We—." He dove suddenly, pinning a two-inch-high badger against the mat near a pouch. "Stay out of the supplies!"

The head of an indignant Koko wiggled up between two of Kles's claws. His round head seemed to be all gray fur except for the large, shining black eyes—made to appear even larger by the rings of black fur.

His round ears wriggled indignantly on top of his head as he piped in a barely audible voice, "I just wanted a snack. Transformation is hungry work."

Another miniature Koko kicked the griffin's haunch. "Don't be such a pill. When we're this size, it won't be more than a nibble."

"Yeah, you'll never notice it, you big bully." A third Koko pounced on Kles's tail and began trying to pull the griffin off his prisoner. More tiny Kokos joined him in yanking at Kles until the exasperated griffin let go of his captive and swept his forepaws behind him, bowling little badgers left and right.

The air hummed as Leech floated over on his flying discs, his brown hair rippling about his head. He was a human boy about Scirye's age, and he had joined her quest when Badik had killed his friend Primo. "I thought you were trying to transform into a tiger?"

A dozen Kokos scratched their heads. "So did I," they all chorused.

"Will you re-unite?" Kles snapped. "One of you is bad enough."

"Keep your paws crossed that this works." When the miniature badgers began muttering and making passes, their outlines shimmered. Immediately they began running toward one another, merging until there was a single, much larger badger again. "Whew, that's a relief," he said, rubbing his fur vigorously. "But I itch all over now."

As Leech squatted to scratch his friend's back, he asked Kles and Scirye, "How much further to the City of Death?"

"We find a peak called the Black Diamond and turn east," the griffin explained.

Koko gave a shiver. "So why do they call it the City of Death anyway? Is it full of skeletons?"

"It was where Yi the Archer killed a terrible monster who was destroying the countryside," Kles explained. "The grateful people built a temple in his honor, and so many pilgrims visited it that a city grew up near it. Many centuries later, the Kushans and griffins stopped an army of Huns there, but at great cost. Neither the defenders nor the invaders survived, and no one goes there now."

"Except Roland and Badik," Scirye said.

"Yes, except them," Leech agreed. "But we'll stop them."

Roland and Badik were heading there, where they hoped to find the last part of an ancient super weapon that would be capable of destroying a sun. They already had the bow of the fabled archer Yi, as well as the special archer's ring, for which they had killed Scirye's sister, Nishke, and injured her mother, Lady Sudarshane. Now the thieves were hunting for the arrows.

Suddenly Kles's fur and feathers began to fluff out and Koko began to scratch more furiously than before. Scirye's own skin began to tingle as if a thousand ants were running up and down over her.

"I think that storm is moving even faster now," Bayang said.

The roiling storm swallowed up the land as it chased after them like an angry gray tidal wave.

## 2

## Leech

Wheeling around, Leech saw that the storm cloud had arched upward to intercept them, its sides churning and writhing like a giant panting worm.

Sitting at the wing's apex, Bayang dug her claws into the interwoven straw and tightened her grip on the straps that steered the wing. "That's no normal storm cloud. Everyone sit down and grab hold of the wing. And that especially means you, Leech."

"But—," Leech began to protest.

The tip of Bayang's tail whipped about the boy's wrist and held him firmly in place. "I don't want you going to check out the cloud. Now sit!"

As Leech obediently stepped off the discs and restored them to his armband, the inner voice in Leech's head complained, *Why do you let her boss you around?*

Leech couldn't bring himself to call the Voice, Lee No Cha. Long ago, Lee No Cha had been a boy who had killed a dragon prince and then used the hide to make a belt as a gift for his father. For that horrific crime, Lee had been executed by his own family and had been hunted down in subsequent lives by the dragons.

That earlier self was dead. He was the real one, but Lee No Cha existed somewhere in his memories and had awakened when Leech had discovered the magic in his armbands—the very same devices that had killed the dragon prince.

Bayang was supposed to kill Leech before Lee No Cha could rouse, but when Leech had saved her life, the dragon had made her peace with him. But that was because she assumed he was different from that earlier self. If she knew that Lee No Cha had not disappeared, the dragon might decide he was a danger to her kind after all and go back to trying to assassinate him. But Leech was more afraid of losing Bayang's friendship than he was of losing his own life.

Raised in a San Francisco orphanage where he'd been bullied, Leech had not had any friends until he'd run away and met Koko, who disguised his badger form in a human shape. A man named Primo had befriended them, but he had died fighting Badik the dragon. Since then, his circle of friends had expanded to include Scirye and Kles, but he'd come to depend upon the tough, smart Bayang the most.

So the voice was a double-edged weapon: Leech needed its advice for flying and fighting, but it was also a threat.

*She's gotten us this far,* Leech replied and, plopping down on the woven surface, grabbed some nearby straps that had been placed strategically about the wing. But would Bayang stay his friend if she knew Lee No Cha had awakened inside him?

Scirye sat down as well and took hold of another pair of straps. "Do you think this is Roland's work?"

Kles, her lap griffin, landed on her shoulder and slipped inside her coat. "He might have set patrols as a precaution. Or it could just be our bad luck. The mountains are very old and full of magic. And there are monsters here that go back to the creation of the world."

"Monster or Roland's slave, nothing can catch Naue," the wind bragged and he flew even faster and higher.

*Thunk-a thunk-a-thunk.*

"That sounds like a drum roll," Leech said.

A bolt of lightning suddenly shot from the cloud to blast the mountain beneath it, the light temporarily highlighting the curling mist of the storm.

*Boom!*

More and more lightning bolts crackled from the cloud's belly so that it resembled a giant centipede climbing rapidly after them on fiery legs.

"Ho, so you want to play tag with Naue? Then so be it," Naue boomed.

And the next moment Naue banked sharply until he was zooming toward the cloud.

"No, no, go away from it!" Bayang shouted.

But the wind ignored her, and as they rushed toward the face of the cloud, the inky strands writhed like charcoal snakes.

Naue roared with laughter as he plowed through the cloud, whipping it into smoky tendrils. Their straw wing bucked and rolled as Naue twisted and turned, tearing the storm to shreds.

And yet through Naue's merriment the drum roll deepened until it was a steady booming.

"Ha, that will show it," Naue announced as he finally circled away.

"Who's that?" Leech asked.

It was as if a huge ball of dark cotton had been ripped apart to reveal an inner core, a rough gray oval about ten feet long like a huge bar of soap. And upon the disc a creature danced on two stubby legs. He looked like a squat man but his skin was blue and tusks rose from his lower jaw. From his shoulders hung a wide strap of drums and in his hands were the bones he used to beat them.

Bayang swore an oath in an old dragon tongue. "What's a lord of thunder doing here? He belongs in China."

The strange lord brought both sticks down upon one drum, and the next instant there was a flash of light. The gold flecks in Bayang's green scales shone as a bolt streaked from the drum across the sky and through Naue.

*Boom!*

"Aiee," Naue cried out in agony and shock, as if this was the first time the fleshless creature had felt pain. "Naue hurts!"

The sudden flash made spots dance before Leech's eyes, and the smell of ozone tickled his nose.

*Boom! Boom! Boom!*

Naue screamed as each beat of the drums shot lightning bolts through him. It was all they could do to hold on as the wind whirled about, trying to escape, but the lightning was relentless. Too late, Bayang realized that their wing marked where the invisible Naue was.

"Naue . . . can . . . not . . . keep . . . together," the wind gasped.

Though the lightning could not destroy the air that made up the wind, the energy was making it hard for Naue to keep his currents together. It was like unraveling the threads that make up a piece of string.

Naue bellowed in torment, and suddenly the wing was spinning earthward as they fell out of the injured wind's grasp.

# 3

## Bayang

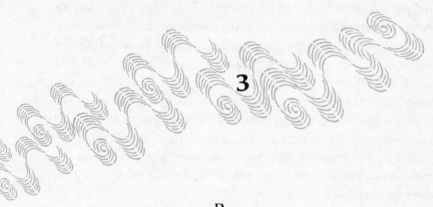

With a ripping noise, a large scrap of the wing fluttered away and then more and more pieces whipped after it.

"The wing's falling apart," Koko yelled in alarm.

"Tell me something I don't know," Bayang said grimly.

The long trips and abuse had taken their toll upon the wing's woven straw. Through the numerous holes, Bayang could see the earth waiting for them three thousand feet below.

Bayang clenched her fangs in frustration. If only she could fly her friends to safety under her own power, but she had injured one of her wings fighting Badik. She tried to unfurl them anyway, but pain shot instantly through her back from the half-healed wound.

Their only hope was to land the straw wing before it disintegrated. Her eyes searched the mountains below for a soft landing spot, but it was one fanglike mountain after another. And then she saw the silvery oval that must be some frozen lake in a bowl formed by the mountains.

She yanked at the left strap, trying to angle the wing toward it, only to have the strap tear off in her paw. Sometimes all you can do is trust your instincts, her old flying instructor, Sergeant Pandai, had told her, so she threw away the useless strap. Then she dug the claws of her left forepaw deep into the woven material itself and began to pull.

If she had used all her strength, she probably would have torn a whole section from the weakened wing, but instead she used a steady tugging. Bit by bit, the wing began to point toward the oval.

All Bayang could do was hope there was enough snow on the lake to cushion their landing and that the ice was thick enough to take their weight.

Above them, Naue had stopped screaming. Bayang hoped the wind was still alive and had gotten away.

Unfortunately, the thunder lord could now direct his attention solely at them. A streak of dazzling light sizzled the air near them and her scales tingled with the electric charge.

*Boom!*

The lake rose toward them quickly. It looked about a mile long and about half that in width. Wisps of snow drifted across the top.

Even as she began to try to ease the nose up, something made her jink to the right. A lightning bolt shot past, just burning the port side.

*Boom!*

Her muzzle wriggled as smoke tickled her nostrils and she felt the warmth as the wing's edge caught fire.

*Boom!*

"I'll put out the fire." Twisting her head, she saw Leech begin to free one gloved hand from the strap. The little fool was making it so hard to keep him alive.

"Keep hold of the wing," Bayang snapped. "Leave this to me."

And she used her tail to beat at the flames—gently, of course. Too much force and she'd break the wing up herself. As she put out the fire, she felt the flames char her scales.

*Boom!*
*Boom!*
*Boom!*

Lightning bolts shot all around them and somehow she managed to dodge them. But that distracted her from the landing itself.

Suddenly the lake was looming before them. With no choice, Bayang hauled at the wing, trying to nose it up. There was a terrible ripping sound and then she was tumbling through the air, her feet entangled in fragments of woven straw. And behind her, the hatchlings and Koko were shouting.

The next moment she was rolling tail over head over a layer of snow covering the lake. As she finally lay dizzily looking up at the sky, she thought, *Thank Heaven there was a cushion of snow.*

Then she raised her head to look for her friends. Scirye was a few yards away on her right with Kles fluttering over her as he tried to pull her upright. Leech was rising on all fours as he shook his head groggily.

Leave it to Koko to land on a bare patch of ice. Every time the badger tried to get up, his paws slipped so that he went muzzle first back onto the lake.

Of the wing itself, there were only shreds floating about in the breeze. It had served them well.

Bayang shook the patches of woven straw from her paws and then rose on her hind legs.

"Lady, are you all right?" Kles asked as he hovered anxiously over Scirye.

Scirye sat up groggily. "I think so, as soon as things stop whirling around. Did you always have three heads?"

Her griffin clicked his beak. "That's a nasty bump you got from the crash. One of these days Bayang is going to surprise us with a soft landing."

The dragon rose, shaking off patches of woven straw. "And if you were bigger than a canary, Kles, you wouldn't have to depend upon me."

Kles's fur and feathers both ruffled so that he swelled half again his size. "I'll have you know that—."

But Scirye had seized his tail and given it a tug. "We should be grateful Bayang got us down alive."

Suddenly the air grew dark as a shadow covered them. Bayang looked up at the creature floating overhead, the bones in his hands poised over his drums.

"What did we ever do to you?" Leech demanded, already reaching for the decorative discs on an armband that would become his flying discs with a simple spell.

The lord of thunder ignored him as he looked about the fallen comrades. "You're just as strange a group as Lord Roland described you," he said in Chinese. "It's hard to believe you're a threat to him. But he asked me to keep watch for you anyway just in case he really hadn't killed you."

Koko had managed to crawl from the ice onto the snow. "Speak American, will you?"

The man frowned. "I don't know what you said, but I don't like your tone. Don't you realize you're addressing the great and famous lord of thunder?" Annoyed, he brought the bones down upon the center drum. Lightning shot from it toward Koko. The next instant, snow and ice geysered into the air with the cold lake water that had lain beneath them.

*BOOM!*

Ears ringing, Bayang hoped the hatchlings could hear her. "Head for cover!"

"Oh, you'll be dead long before that," the thunder lord sneered and began a rapid tattoo upon his drums.

# 4

## Leech

Leech had just worked the transformation spell for his
flying discs even as the first lightning bolt shot down.
He felt the lake's thick surface vibrate beneath him as
the bolt smashed in front of him. Blinking his eyes to clear away the
spots dancing before them, his groping fingers found the discs and
he climbed on. Steam plumed from the crater in the ice, but the
drops were quickly freezing. Though each of them had a magical
charm to protect them from the cold, it must have been overwhelmed. Leech himself was shivering. "K-K-Koko, you okay?"

"Y-yeah," his friend stuttered through chattering teeth as he
sprawled on the ice. The frozen drops of spray had transformed
his fur into a coat of diamonds. "But I'm going to turn into a
K-K-Koko-cicle soon."

Suddenly Leech heard an urgent shout in a language he didn't
recognize. Twisting his head around, he saw a girl of about eighteen
jumping up and down on the lakeshore and beckoning to them. She

was dressed in a robe patched together from dozens of bits of cloth on top of which she had sewn silvery crescent moons and stars. As she bounced about, the moons and stars sparkled so that she looked like a rainbow about to explode.

Behind her was a wagon even gaudier than her robe, with swirling patterns painted in bright reds, yellows, blues, greens, oranges, and purples. Hundreds of tiny mirror chips glittered even in the gloom. In bright daylight, the wagon would dazzle the eyes.

"We have to get off the lake," Scirye said as she struggled to her feet with Kles's help.

Leech managed to stand up, but Koko kept flopping on his muzzle.

Ice crunched as Bayang dug her claws into the frozen lake and shoved herself forward on her belly. "This is no time to clown around!" Picking up the badger, she flung him onto her back like a sack of flour.

The ominous drumming grew louder as the lord of thunder dove toward them.

There was no time to think, only time to act if he was to buy some time for his friends. *All right.*

As he rose into the air, the Voice complained, *How come you're listening to me now and not when I warned you about the dragon?*

The smell of ozone stung his nose as he pulled off the other armband. *Because these are the only times you make sense,* Leech responded.

*I'm only saying what you're feeling in your heart,* the Voice said.

Leech ignored the Voice as he spat on the armband and shouted, "Change!" Immediately it began to tingle as the ring expanded with a musical chime. About twenty inches, the metal ring was as light as a feather and hard enough to smash through walls.

On the cloud above him, the lord of thunder looked surprised. Perhaps when the dragon had not used her wings, he'd thought himself safe in the air. The last thing he'd expected was a human to attack him.

Leech soared higher and faster, the sheer joy of flying temporarily replacing his fear until a bolt sizzled past his ear. His hair literally stood on end in the electrically charged air. And his eyes were temporarily dazzled by the flash, so he could see nothing.

*Loop! Loop!* the Voice said urgently.

Though Leech practiced every chance he got, he was still just learning how to fly. Instead of arching upward in a loop, he began to corkscrew through the air instead, just managing to miss the next bolt that whizzed by.

He tried to straighten his course but only wound up plunging toward the lake.

*You're moving through the air, not standing on the ground,* the Voice shouted. His frustrated tone reminded Leech uncomfortably of Bayang when she coached him. *Make your center of balance lower.*

Leech bent his knees but he still spun out of control toward the lake.

*Lower!* the Voice screamed.

Beneath him, he saw the horrified faces of his friends. And when the lord of thunder was finished with him, they would be next.

*Let me handle this,* the Voice said.

With dismay, he realized that Bayang had been right: he was still only a beginner at flying . . . but the Voice was not. The Voice had enough skill to take on the lord of thunder, but if they survived, what would happen afterward? In the Arctic, the Voice had taken over and its violent rage had made him as much a danger to Leech's friends as his enemies.

What if the Voice decided to attack Bayang after he dealt with the thunder lord? *How do I know you won't try to attack Bayang after we take care of the thunder lord?*

*You don't,* replied the Voice. *But if you don't let me fly right now your friends will die.*

There was no choice. *You do it,* Leech said and then warned, *But I won't let you harm my friends.*

As he surrendered to the Voice, he felt himself squatting so low that his knees almost touched his chest. Wrapping his arms around his body, the Voice straightened out his legs in a deliberate fashion. No longer out of control, he veered upward again. *See? Don't fight your motion*, the Voice coached. *Guide it instead.*

Even though it was his ankles that crossed over each other, Leech felt like a spectator. He wondered if this was how the Voice felt sometimes.

His body twisted around in a violent pirouette, altering his direction just before another bolt zipped through the spot where his old trajectory would have sent him. Smoke tickled his nostrils and with a jolt he realized his clothes were smoldering.

But as he angled upward toward the lord of thunder, his cloud began to retreat, keeping them out of reach as the lord sent bolt after bolt streaking at them.

The Voice sent them swerving left and right, up and down to avoid the flashing missiles, until he finally opened Leech's mouth and yelled in frustration. "Stay still!"

"Why fight the battle you want to fight?" jeered the lord and sent another jagged bolt of lightning at them.

"Think you're safe?" the Voice said defiantly. Leech's arm whipped around violently and sent the disc spinning in a blur toward the lord.

"Ai!" the thunder lord protested indignantly as he ducked.

"Next time I won't miss," the Voice boasted as he held out Leech's hand for the disc returning to them like a boomerang. That was something Leech had yet to learn how to do.

Electricity crackled from one wart to another on the thunder lord's bumpy skin until he glowed. His fists beat a quick tattoo on the drums as small bolts of lightning shot like a cloud of arrows.

The Voice sent Leech's body swerving to the right. Even as the lightning crackled by, it caught the disc, striking a tinging note. The disc shone as it sparked and fizzled with electricity until it buried itself halfway into the frozen lake.

*What do I do?* the Voice wailed in despair. *The disc is so full of lightning we can't touch it right away.*

Leech thought quickly. *Better let me take over. I work better with Bayang than you. We have to draw the thunder lord down near the lake where Bayang can reach it. Then we can leave the rest to her.*

*You can't trust her to do anything,* the Voice protested. *She'll let us die.*

His own family had killed Lee No Cha, so perhaps Leech could understand why the Voice didn't have faith in anyone.

*You may be a better flier and fighter, but I'm better at thinking,* Leech insisted. *It's your turn to trust me.*

*All right,* the Voice admitted reluctantly, and as soon as Leech had regained control of his body, he looked over his shoulder as he sped away. "Hey, Ugly. I bet you can't catch me," he jeered.

Even if the thunder lord didn't understand English, the nearly fatal attack had angered him. He rocketed after Leech, flinging one bolt after another. Leech was nowhere the accomplished flier that the Voice was, so he executed the Voice's instructions clumsily, somehow always managing to zig and zag just in the nick of time and avoiding being burned to charcoal.

Back and forth they went through the sky with the pursuit taking them lower and lower to the ground. All the while, Leech kept up a running string of taunts that made the thunder lord fume and curse.

Finally they were flying only twenty feet from the ground. Leech had planned to take the thunder lord even closer to the earth, but even if Bayang could not fly, she could still leap.

With a roar of *Yashe!*, she sprang into the air, paws ripping through the cloud as they reached for the thunder lord.

And grasped only empty air as the startled thunder lord hopped upward.

By now the Voice had grown shrill with frustration and attack. *Turn!*

Leech crossed his ankles and spun in an awkward pirouette that sent him darting back toward the thunder lord like a human rocket. If he could knock the thunder lord down to the lake, Bayang could take care of him.

The thunder lord was so surprised that his drumsticks paused in midair.

*Kill him*, the Voice shrieked.

Adrenaline pumped through Leech's body as he aimed himself at the lord's chest, but in the last moment the creature leaned backward. Leech missed him, but his fists struck one of the drums.

*Crack!*

As he shot past, he had just enough time to glimpse hairline fissures spreading across the body of the drum.

*Boom!*

The drum exploded in a huge fireball that sent Leech plummeting through the air into a drift of snow.

*Get up, get up!* the Voice screeched.

Rolling over, Leech shot back into the air.

The thunder lord was still alive but rising into the air. He'd dropped the bone sticks and was slapping at the flames that had spread to the rest of the drums around his body. There was a second explosion as another drum blew up. The next moment, the thunder lord rocketed out of the cloud of fire and smoke, trying to pull off the fiery drums.

He was still trying to do that as he disappeared above them.

# 5

## Bayang

Bayang found it faster to wriggle on her belly across the ice and snow than to try to walk as she made her way over to where Leech was hovering on his discs, struggling to tug his weapon ring free from the lake. The electricity seemed to have discharged, and though it was no longer hot, it was stuck in the ice.

As she neared him, the dragon noticed that the tips of his hair had been burned by lightning bolts, but at least he had survived yet another of Roland's traps.

"Let me help you get that," she said, relieved as she stretched out a paw. "You had me worried there. I can't figure out your flying. Sometimes you're as clumsy as an amateur and other times you're as polished as a dragon."

Leech's head jerked up, startled, and the faces of Lee's young victims flashed through his mind. In each re-incarnation, Lee No

Cha had looked different, and yet the fear in their eyes had always been the same.

Bayang's paw stopped halfway between them. She thought she had overcome his mistrust, but humans were such complicated creatures. What had she done wrong?

"Hey, buddy," Koko called from her back. "Did you get your brains fried?"

"I just want the ring," Leech mumbled and bent over again to pull at the disc embedded in the ice.

When Bayang heard the thunder, she looked up in alarm at the sky, but there was no sign of the lord of thunder. Then she felt the vibrations beneath her, followed by a volley of what sounded like rifle shots. She whipped her head this way and that trying to see the threat, but saw no one but her friends.

The girl in the gaudy robe began shouting frantically to them in the New Tongue, which had evolved over the centuries from the many different people and cultures in the empire. "Alarm! Alarm! Danger! Peril!"

A feline creature about twice the size of a cat shouted, "She means the ice is breaking! Get off it now!"

There was a loud crack behind Bayang. Twisting her head, she saw the snow fall into a crevice in the ice. The lightning bolt must have cracked the surface. The crevice snaked toward them almost as fast as one of the thunder lord's lightning bolts.

Bayang knew how important the weapon ring was to Leech. When he'd been abandoned at the orphanage, the weapon ring had been left along with the armband with the flying discs. "Get to shore," she said to Leech. "I'll get the ring for you."

But Leech went on tugging frantically as if he hadn't heard her—or didn't trust her. With an exasperated grunt, Bayang stretched her long serpentine body forward and grabbed the ring in one paw and Leech in the other.

The ice shattered as she yanked the ring free. The metal was already starting to freeze as she handed it to the hatchling. "What's gotten into you, Leech?"

Leech clutched the ring as if his life depended on it. "Nothing."

The lake was no place to argue now. "Take Koko to the shore. I'll get Scirye."

Bayang's sinuous body was already twisting around as Leech floated behind her. The next moment Leech sped through the air with Koko on his back. Bayang watched them as she wriggled toward the Kushan hatchling.

What *was* going on in Leech's mind?

# 6

## Scirye

As the ice crevice raced toward her, Scirye tried to shuffle toward the shore. Cracks had appeared all around her so that the lake resembled a giant white plate breaking.

Kles flapped his wings frantically as he tugged at her hand.

But it was like trying to run in an earthquake. When Scirye lost her balance and fell, she began to crawl forward on her hands and knees.

Behind her came the loud hiss of scales on snow. Bayang was heading toward her like a scaly locomotive, piling up the snow before her chest as she plowed along. As a dragon she was used to the cold depths of the sea, so the ice-cold lake held no terrors for her.

"Hop on." Bayang's claws, strong enough to puncture steel, closed delicately around her collar and hoisted her into the air. Kles fluttered next to her as the dragon deposited the girl upon her back. All around came groans and snaps as the ice fell apart.

At the lake's edge, the girl was still waving for them to come to her, but there was no sign of Leech and Koko. Scirye was wondering where they were when Bayang plucked her into the air again and reared up.

"What's the idea?" spluttered Kles.

As the ice gave way beneath them, Bayang plunged into the freezing water, but she held the girl safe above the lake.

Water rilled from Bayang's wet scales, which gleamed now like polished emeralds. Scirye decided that dragons were at their most beautiful when they were in their natural habitat of the water. "Do you understand now?" the dragon asked.

Kles attempted to recover his dignity as he fluttered by the dragon's head. "Ahem, yes. And thank you."

Chunks of ice bobbed against Bayang as she swam the rest of the way across the lake and then deposited her burden carefully on the shore.

When the teenage girl took Scirye's arm, Scirye immediately felt safe. "You've reached our haven, far traveler." She spoke English with a slight accent and then called over her shoulder. "Tute, bring blankets for our guests."

"I already thought of that," came a peeved voice from the gaudy wagon. A large feline creature padded down the steps at the rear of the wagon. The short hair on his head was as tawny as Kles's fur, but there were black spots along its back. His jaws stretched to breaking so he could carry several threadbare, folded blankets.

The girl turned to Bayang solicitously. "Oh, my, I don't think we have a blanket big enough for you though. Will you be all right?"

Bayang shook herself like a dog so that rain spattered all over. "Yes, I like a brisk dip. The temperature's no worse than the sea-floor."

"Then come with me, you poor little thing," the hospitable girl said to Scirye. "I have a comfy fire going in the cave." The friendly stranger treated Scirye like a fragile porcelain doll, insisting on supporting Scirye through the snow and up the slight slope.

All the way to the cave at the foot of the cliff, Scirye felt she was in a marching band as the little silver bells sewn around the hem of the girl's robe chimed, mixing with the jangling of the girl's many bracelets decorated with magic symbols.

Koko and Leech were already huddled by a fire inside, though Leech's flying discs hummed near his shoulder and the weapon ring leaned against his shin ready for use.

"I want a refund for this trip," the badger grumbled.

"I don't recall you ever paying anything," Bayang said.

"That ain't the point," Koko said, windmilling his arms for warmth. "It's the principle."

"You have no principles," Bayang retorted.

Koko scratched his head. "Oh, yeah. I forgot that I pawned them a couple of years back so I could buy a candy bar."

As the girl helped Scirye sit beside them, Kles looped elegantly in the air, finishing with a grand flourish of forepaw and tail. "You have our deepest gratitude, Lady...?"

The girl smoothed out her robe and then straightened, eyes glancing at the lynx as she cleared her throat loudly.

Tute dropped the blankets and rose on his hindlegs, but he was so unsteady that he almost pitched forward when he attempted a bow. "Ladies and gentlemen, I present to you the one and only, Māka the Magnificent, whose feats of sorcery make the very stars and planets halt and marvel."

Stretching out her arm sideways, Māka twirled her wrist. "At your service."

It seemed to Scirye that Māka was more of an age for an apprenticeship than grand titles, but the kindhearted girl had gone out of her way to make five strangers feel at home. Scirye liked her already so she returned the bow with one just as formal and grand. "Thank you, Māka the Magnificent."

Kles introduced their hostess to their company, adding, as he saw the shadow at the cave mouth, "And this is Bayang the dragon, of the Moonglow clan. Bayang, this is Lady Māka the Magnificent."

"You are most welcome," Māka said, spreading her hands as if they were sitting in her parlor rather than a cave. "Now you shall have a cup of nice, warm—."

The lynx was already swinging around to head back to the wagon. He had a perpetual air of being put upon. "Yes, yes, I know," he grumbled. "You want the tin of tea next." And then he left.

"If you would be so kind," the girl called after him and then wrapped a wool blanket around Scirye's shoulders that smelled of dried sage and thyme. As she draped blankets around Leech and Koko, she asked, "But who was that chasing you?"

And so Kles, with help from the others, told her their story. Māka's eyes grew wide as she heard about how they had chased Roland to Hawaii to retrieve the ring that Badik the dragon had stolen for him and how he had killed Scirye's sister during the theft. How the thieves had nearly trapped them there with the goddess Pele and stole a magic bowstring from her before they escaped.

The pursuit had taken them to the Arctic next, where they had failed to help a powerful spirit, Uncle Resak, protect the magical bow that had belonged to Yi the Archer. Again, Roland and Badik had gotten away.

Tute had come back with a basket about midway through their tale. He set it down on the cave floor, ears twitching skeptically. "And you say you're the chosen of the goddess?" he asked Scirye.

Scirye pulled back her glove to show the "3" glowing faintly on her palm. "She left this on my hand."

Māka shook her head in wonder and even the lynx dipped his head respectfully. "She must really not want Roland to get hold of Yi's bow," Māka said.

"And Roland's just as determined to stop us. He's set all sorts of traps like the thunder lord," Kles said. "The lord of thunder was only the latest."

"But how did he know you'd pass this way?" Tute asked.

Bayang shrugged. "He's rich enough to hire enough creatures to set traps along all the probable routes. This one happened to be guarded by the lord of thunder."

Koko shivered. "The hag was still a lot scarier. I get the heebie-jeebies just remembering her."

Of course, after that, they had to tell Māka and Tute about Scirye's battle with the hag. In the Arctic wilderness, Roland had hired the creature to capture them in a strange, magical sack, but before Scirye had trapped the hag inside her own bag instead, she'd taken the hag's belt. They hadn't been able to work out what power the other charms might have, but they thought the otter charm was what had let the wearer get free of the bag's hold. She now kept the otter charm separate in its own pouch around her neck with a charm from the goddess Pele.

"May I, Lady Scirye?" Māka asked, and when Scirye nodded, the sorceress leaned over to examine the charms on the belt.

Scirye tugged the glove down to hide the mark. "Can you figure out what some of them do?" she asked her hopefully.

Māka shook her head. "I can feel the power, but I'm not sure from which ones."

"Too bad," Leech sighed. "We need all the help we can get. We're not sure what Roland intends to do with the ring and the bow, but we have to stop him."

Falling on her knees, Māka hugged Tute. "I told you there was a reason why our show went wrong. The goddess wants us to aid Her chosen one." She paused dramatically. "It's Destiny!" Sometimes Māka spoke as if her words were on a theater marquee.

"The show went bad because you're one of the worst magicians in the world," Tute grumped.

Māka tweaked a furry, pointed ear. "I'll have you know my magic is good enough to astound the crowned heads of Europe and Asia."

"Only with how terrible you are." Tute closed his eyes. "Do these poor people a favor and leave them alone."

Māka leaned forward and pursed her lips as she scratched Tute between the ears. "Oh, did Mr. Grouchy Pants wake up on the wrong side of the bed?" she cooed.

Tute opened one eye. "Do not treat a powerful lynx like a common alley cat, missy!" Even so, his tail had started to twitch with pleasure.

Māka winked at the others as she continued to stroke the lynx. "Don't mind Tute. Some day his manners will match the size of his pride."

"That will happen long before your skills match your confidence," Tute murmured.

"Ha, ha." Māka laughed nervously. "Tute will have his little joke." But as she sat back, a small, palm-sized book dropped from her sleeve onto the stone floor. Before the girl could snatch it back up, Scirye read the title. *The Beginner's Grimoire: Easy Spells for Children.*

Māka hastily stowed the book back into her sleeve before she opened the basket. Inside it were a battered tin kettle and cups along with a small box of tea. As she scooped some snow into the kettle and set it on top of two large rocks that sat in the middle of the fire, Scirye couldn't help noticing odd red stains on Māka's skirt.

Koko sniffed the air. "It's funny, but I swear I can smell ketchup."

Tute's ear rotated and then pointed toward Māka. "That would be the hothouse tomatoes they tossed at her."

"Our audience was kind enough to share their humble repast with us," Māka tried to correct him.

"They threw it at you. Since when is that sharing?" Lifting his head, Tute explained to Scirye and her friends, "We'd been hired to entertain at a town banquet, but when Māka kept bungling the tricks, they flung vegetables at us."

"Their 'offerings' made a very nice soup that you were more

than happy to have." Licking a finger, Māka rubbed vigorously at a stain. "You need to look up the definition of 'tipping.'"

"You need to look up the definition of 'criticism.'" Tute placed his forepaws together in an earnest plea. "Either improve your magic or get so bad that they won't notice what they're grabbing and toss steaks instead. And in the meantime, leave these poor folk alone."

The last thing they needed was a clumsy sorceress and a grouchy lynx. Protecting Māka would only increase the risk for the rest of them.

Scirye eyed the others, hoping for help in refusing Māka's proposal of help. But Leech's chin was sunk against his chest as he thought about something. He seemed to be doing a lot of that lately. You almost had to give him a good shake to get his attention. Bayang was just as lost in thought and looking troubled. Only Koko looked as uncomfortable as Scirye felt.

It was up to Kles to politely decline the clumsy sorceress's offer. "Tsk, tsk. I'm afraid that audience etiquette is a casualty of modern times. On behalf of my companions, let me thank you for your warm and gracious offer to assist us, but surely you have other performances scheduled."

"Yeah," Koko said drily, "and more soup to make."

Māka's bells jingled and her braclets jangled as she shook her head. "When there is evil present, it is the duty of every follower of the True Path to fight it. It is Heaven's Will. Our public will just have to understand."

As the kindly Māka puttered about the cave and fussed over them, Scirye didn't have the heart to turn down her offer. Scirye had already come to like the magician too much.

When steam finally curled from the kettle spout, Māka dropped tea leaves into the kettle, measuring them out as if they were flakes of gold at first. And then with a smile at Scirye, Māka impulsively dumped in a double measure. "No sense being stingy. We want a proper cup of tea to toast teaching Roland a lesson."

"Let's just hope that vegetables is all he throws at us," grumped Tute.

Suddenly, over the crackling of the fire, they heard a faint howling sound.

"What now?" Koko groaned.

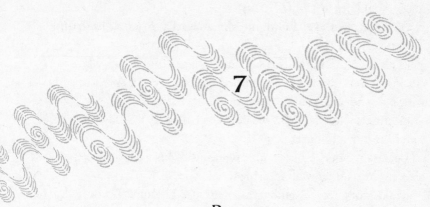

# 7

## Bayang

Leaning forward, Māka stoked the fire so that it blazed up even higher and hotter. "Don't worry. The fire should keep the wolves away."

The noise had brought Bayang out of her own dark thoughts. She leaned her head out of the cave and studied the surrounding mountains. "If they are wolves."

"Do you think Roland might have hired more thugs just like he did the thunder lord?" Scirye asked.

Bayang nodded. "We must really be bothering him. It's a compliment in a way." She dipped her head toward Māka and Tute. "I'm sorry for getting you involved."

"Don't be silly. As I said before, it was Fate that brought us together." With warm water from the kettle, Māka tried to wipe away a tomato stain from her skirt, but only succeeded in smearing it around more.

Apparently human fledglings like Māka were just as reckless as her own hatchlings, Bayang thought. "Scirye, if you'd be so kind as to send out Kles to scout?"

"Of course," the girl said, but she wagged a finger at the griffin. "Just be careful."

"I always am," the griffin said and hopped off her lap, his claws clacking on the stone as he bounded out of the cave. Spreading his wings, he shot out into the open air.

Getting to her feet, Scirye followed him to the cave mouth, watching him anxiously.

Leech shed his blanket and rose, pointing his weapon ring at the wagon. "You might want to bring in your horse."

Māka coughed in embarrassment. "Well, um, I would but she ran off yesterday."

"I told you the knot in the halter rope wasn't tight enough." Tute yawned. "But would you listen?"

"I just hope she's far away by now," Māka said.

Tute stretched, his claws clicking on the stone. "Probably. She was a lot more sensible than me."

"Too bad we can't say the same," sighed Koko. He drew out a glittering axe.

Tute's eyebrows rose. "And here I thought you were just your typical flying riffraff."

Koko plucked a hair from his paw and tested the blade. Though gold was soft, some sort of magic made the axe keep its sharp edge. "No sirree, we're riffraff with style."

Scirye leaned against the cave mouth, pulling the leather gauntlet onto one wrist while she scanned the sky anxiously.

"Don't worry, that furry parrot's too tough to die," Koko assured Scirye, but he watched for the griffin just as intently as she did.

Only Tute remained by the fire with Māka, who had surreptitiously taken out her pamphlet and was thumbing through it hurriedly.

Scirye had the sharpest eyes of the friends. "There he is!" she said, pointing and then leaving her arm up as a perch for her friend.

Finally Bayang saw the griffin as a dot darting over the snow. He was flying with head and body in a straight line like a bullet of feather and fur, and he had barely landed on Scirye's wrist when he panted, "*Lyaks* are coming. About a dozen of them."

Scirye stiffened immediately with Māka, and Tute got up.

"What are lyaks?" Leech asked.

"They're the hereditary enemies of the griffins," Scirye explained, cradling her friend against her. "Did they see you?"

Kles's chest heaved up and down still from the extertion. "No, but they have powerful snouts that could find us anyway."

"How big are they?" Bayang asked.

"About eight feet long," Kles explained. "They have throwing axes that might penetrate even your scales."

"Then I'll hit them before they get within throwing range," Leech said as he reached for the flying discs that still hovered near him. "I'm a smaller, faster target than Bayang."

She had meant to talk to the hatchling when they were alone, but there was no time for that now. "You seemed distracted when you fought the lord of thunder." The dragon set a paw on Leech. "Don't try to fly and fight unless you can give it your undivided attention."

The hatchling frowned. "I was just figuring out what to do."

"Well, the cave is a good defensive position so you don't need to fly anyway," Bayang insisted. "I can grow big enough to handle any trouble so you stay behind me and take care of anything that gets around me." She didn't give him a chance to object, pacing immediately to the mouth of the cave.

# 8

## Leech

*She knows I'm awake!* the Voice said in alarm. *She only spared you before because she thought you were alone. Now she wants to keep us trapped in the cave so she can finish us later.*

Leech felt not only scared but sad as well, because he had come to value the dragon's friendship. *She's just trying to keep us safe,* Leech insisted, or at least he hoped so.

He watched his friend spread her paws, her body bouncing up and down as she flexed her knee joints. He desperately wanted to believe her fangs and claws would harm only their enemies and not him.

Their visitors came down a pass across the lake, small dots slipping and sliding down the snowy slope. At first they fanned out as they searched, but then they smelled the smoke from the fire, and they began to howl as they crossed the lake, sometimes skidding on a patch of bare ice, but coming forward steadily.

Leech studied them as they drew closer. Their heads were long like a horse's with a single large eye in the center and a wide flattened nose. Their skin was as pale and moist as a slug's belly. They wore little more than furry kilts and vests, revealing chests and limbs almost as hairy as their clothing. Broad leather straps ran diagonally down from the lyaks' shoulders, and sheathed on it were several axes. Hanging from the belts at their waists were pouches and daggers.

They ran on all fours, but because their legs were longer than their arms, it gave them a peculiar humping gait. Still, they moved with a speed that suggested they could be quite nimble despite their clumsy way of running.

"Steady," Bayang said.

Scirye was standing behind her to her right with Māka and Tute while Koko and Leech had positioned themselves to her left. Kles began to growl, the sound reverberating in his chest, every feather and hair bristling, his eyes gleaming with a ferocious light. The griffin clans had fought the lyaks for thousands of years, and Kles was surrendering to a battle rage so old it was almost instinct by now.

Inside Leech's head the Voice was screaming, *What are you waiting for! Hit them now!*

His fingers tightened around the weapon ring, remembering that murderous fury that had filled him in his fights up in the Arctic. *No,* he told the Voice. *We can't go charging out there by ourselves. You're going to just get us killed.*

*So you'll let the dragon murder us instead,* the Voice argued but then fell into silence.

# 9

## Bayang

The lyaks' howls grew higher and more frequent as they excitedly straightened and began drawing their weapons, ambling toward them on just their hind legs now.

Bayang crouched, getting ready to spring out and swell in size when Māka's voice rose suddenly in a shrill chant. "Ñake!" Māka finished.

A bouquet of roses suddenly bounced off the head of the lead lyak. He stopped dead in his tracks and nudged it suspiciously with a paw.

"Well, that will work if he has hay fever," Tute drawled lazily.

Unfortunately, the lyak had neither allergies nor a sense of humor. Deciding that the bouquet was no deadly threat, he trampled it into the snow.

"Hmm. What did I do wrong? That was supposed to be a bushel of swords," Māka murmured.

Bayang could hear her rifling frantically through the pages of her pamphlet. It was just as her lynx had said, if only the sorceress's skill matched her grand title.

At least the other lyaks had stopped in surprise at the floral attack, and the dragon took advantage of it. She sprang from the cave mouth, muttering the spell and signing with her forepaws in midair.

Bayang landed in a shower of snow, now three times her former size and lashing out with a tail the size of a tree trunk. Three lyaks went down, but she felt something sting her shoulder. From the corner of her eye, she saw the axe with part of its edge embedded between two scales.

Pain on her left hind leg told her that another axe had struck her. The problem with being this big was that it was impossible to miss her. She spun on her legs, sweeping her tail out like a club. Two more lyaks went down, but the others were just as nimble as she had feared.

One of them managed to leap onto her back. *"Tarkär!"* screamed Kles. Casting aside all reason, he struck, becoming a furred and feathered lightning bolt aimed directly at the face of the lyak.

With a howl, the creature toppled off Bayang. And then she could hear Scirye shouting her war cry and Leech and Koko echoing her. *"Yashe! Yashe!"*

A lyak ran past screeching as it tried to pull Tute from its back, and then bouquets of roses began plopping everywhere as Māka must have panicked.

Bayang should have stayed in the cave, blocking the mouth with her body as she had intended. She was making one mistake after another. Not only was she in danger of losing Leech's friendship, but now she was going to get him killed.

Forget Māka's overconfidence. It was Bayang's own skills that didn't match her pride. She was just about to order the hatchlings to retreat when high above her, she heard a cry.

*"Tarkär!"* screamed a voice far deeper than Kles's.

More voices took up the call. *"Tarkär, tarkär!"*

Bayang risked a glance up and saw giant war griffins swooping down toward them.

# 10

## Scirye

While a lap griffin like Kles was small and lithe and graceful, these war griffins were large and powerful, capable of carrying an armored warrior—though at the moment they wore no riding tack and their backs were bare of riders. There were a half dozen of them, and each wore a large steel oval over their chest for protection while smaller metal pieces protected their broad shoulders. It took great strength indeed to flap their large wings, and their thick bodies and limbs were roped with muscle too.

Since they were chanting the same war cry as Kles, they must belong to his clan, the Koyn Encuwontse, which meant Iron Beak in the Old Tongue.

Immediately, the surviving lyaks whirled around and tried to race away, but the war griffins hunted them down mercilessly. Scirye knew the two species had been enemies for thousands of years, so she understood the griffins' ruthlessness in a way. Even so, she found herself looking away from the battle on the lake, searching for her own lap griffin.

The lyak whom Kles had been battling was trying to flee, but the little griffin swirled around the creature recklessly. Afraid the cornered lyak might hurt Kles in desperation, Scirye held up her gauntleted hand.

"Kles," she commanded. "To me."

But fighting an age-old enemy seemed to have brought Kles's battle fury to the point of madness, and the lap griffin, ignoring his own safety, continued to bite and slash at the lyak.

Koko let out a whistle. "Remind me not to get on his bad side anymore."

"I'll go after him," Leech volunteered from the air.

"No, if he doesn't come of his own will, she's lost him," Bayang said, voicing Scirye's own worries.

Scirye spoke even louder, using his formal name. "Klestetstse, I order you to come!"

The order nearly proved her friend's undoing, for when the griffin paused in a daze, the lyak nearly knocked him from the air. The only thing that saved Kles was a bouquet that suddenly materialized, ruining the lyak's aim.

"Kles, if you don't come this instant, I'll never speak to you again," Scirye said urgently.

Kles flew to her then with awkward beats of his wings as if the obedient part of him was struggling with the warrior part of him for control of his body. But he came, slowly, reluctantly, to perch on her leather-covered wrist as the mad light in his eyes slowly died.

Scirye instantly gathered him against her, stroking his ruffled feathers and fur. "You were so brave, Kles," she murmured. "You fought well." Remembering her manners, she looked over at Māka. "Thank you."

Māka the Magnificent was rolling up the pamphlet hurriedly so she could hide it in her sleeve. "The print is so small it's hard to get the spell right."

CITY OF DEATH 51

"Well," Bayang said, observing the floral bouquets littering the landscape, "at least the effort was there."

"Māka doesn't know when to quit," Tute agreed, "which is both a strength and a weakness."

"If the magic doesn't work out, you can always become a florist," Koko suggested.

"I would if they lasted very long," Māka said, blushing. Even as she said that, the bouquets began disappearing with soft puffing sounds.

Out on the lake, the war griffins were returning, looking almost cheerful from the battle. As they hovered before the cave, their powerful wings raised the snow in spurts with each beat.

Parts of their fur had been woven into braids, each griffin twisting the strands differently. Lumps of jade and raw golden nuggets were entwined within the strands as suited the fancy of each griffin. The braids of everyone, though, were held together at the tips by cylindrical beads of lapis lazuli. Around their legs were steel greaves and armbands in addition to the discs across their chest.

Their leader was a griffin whose braids held large coral beads. Encircling his thick neck was a golden torque cast in the shape of a serpent with scales of turquoise and large carnelian eyes.

"Why have you trespassed on the lands of the Koyn Encuwontse?" he demanded.

Kles squirmed out of Scirye's hold and stood up straight on her gauntleted wrist. "They are my guests."

The griffin leader squinted. "Ragtail, is that you?"

Kles cringed for a moment as if the war griffin had swatted him. But then the lap griffin lifted his head again. "It's been a long time, but I haven't forgotten you either, Kaccap."

"Captain Kaccap," the griffin leader corrected.

"Well, Captain," Kles said. He fluttered into the air and gave a grand flourish of paw and wing to Scirye. "This is my Lady Scirye—."

Kaccap bobbed up and down in the air as he roared with laughter.

"Since when does a lady dress like a court jester?" In her furs and coveralls, Scirye thought she probably did look like a clown.

These new arrivals had an attitude that reminded Scirye of the bullies she'd encountered in the various schools she had attended as she had followed her mother from embassy posting to posting. It didn't matter the country, they acted like little kings and queens of their domain.

These war griffins might be at the top of the roost in the eyrie, but in the greater world where Kles thrived, they would have been country bumpkins.

Kles shot forward, his claws stopping only inches from the griffin's head so that the war griffin flinched.

"You may say what you like about me," Kles growled, "but watch what you say about my Lady Scirye of the noble House of Rapañ̃e, daughter of no less than Lord Tsirauñe the Griffin Master."

At the mention of her father, the griffins instantly grew silent, and Scirye felt their eyes scrutinizing her. Her father was responsible not only for all the griffins at court, but also handled the relations between humans and the griffin eyries, which made him a powerful figure.

With great dignity, Kles indicated Leech and the others. "And these are her friends."

Kaccap dipped his head ever so slightly. "I humbly apologize, lay-dee." He spoke her title with obvious skepticism.

Even though he had rescued them, Scirye was developing a distinct dislike for the war griffin. She tried to adopt the manner and tone her mother used when facing down some low-ranking diplomatic bully.

Lifting her head haughtily, Scirye said in a voice that would freeze fire. "We have come a long way on a mission vital to the empire, Captain. You and your squad will take us to Riye Srukalleyis where we can finish our task."

Kaccap seemed startled by her destination. "And what would a young lady want in the City of Death?"

"I'll tell you on the way," Scirye said.

Kaccap stared at her doubtfully—well, she wouldn't have believed her if she were in his place either. But even if her hauteur had been a poor imitation of her mother, some of it seemed to have worked because Kaccap didn't speak his doubts out loud.

"We . . . were returning from patrol when we saw the lyaks," Kaccap said slowly as he tried to figure out what to do. "We must warn the eyrie first about the raid. They shouldn't have been able to sneak up this close to our home."

"Every minute counts, Captain," Scirye said, trying one more time.

"If the mission is so important, lay-dee," Kaccap said her title with a smirk, "then the Keeper of the Eyrie will want to meet you. I'm sure she will provide you with reinforcements."

Scirye sighed inwardly. With the straw wing gone, it had been worth trying to get the griffins to carry them to the City of Death. "How far away is Riye Srukalleyis from here?"

Kaccap tapped a claw on his beak. "About a hundred miles to the southeast for a griffin. For a human on foot . . ." He spread his forepaws. "Who knows? There are many tall mountains and deep chasms between you and the city. And it's winter so there is ice and snow."

"Ouch." Koko raised a hind paw and rubbed it for emphasis. "I don't think these tootsies can make it."

"It sounds like it would take forever on foot. If we can get help from the griffins," Bayang added, "it's worth a slight delay."

"Too lazy to fly yourself, dragon?" Kaccap demanded.

"My friend," Scirye said coldly, "injured her wing fighting the emperor's enemies."

"Indeed," Kaccap sneered.

Scirye glanced at Leech who shrugged. "I'm with Bayang and Koko. I say let's ask the Keeper for help."

"I can't leave my wagon behind," Māka said.

Kaccap eyed the shining wagon and chuckled. "Is this my lady's chariot?"

"This really isn't your battle," Bayang said.

"It is now," Māka said stubbornly. "Didn't I fight side by side with you?"

The last of the bouquets were disappearing. "I suppose so," the dragon admitted.

Scirye pointed at the cave. "Captain, have your squad pull Māka's wagon as far as it will go into the cave and then send someone back for it."

Kaccap opened his beak to protest but shut it with an abrupt clack. At least he hadn't refused out loud.

The snow swirled as five griffins settled on the slope. As they hid the wagon inside the cave, Bayang shrank again to human size.

When the griffins returned outside, they crouched on all fours. As Scirye climbed onto one, she felt the thick pelt. Their coats of winter fur made them appear even larger. When Kles shed his winter fur in the spring, she was always careful how she spoke to him because he grew touchy about his shaggy appearance.

Koko felt the fur of his griffin. "Whoa, it's like riding an over-padded sofa."

The next moment the badger had tumbled to the ground as the griffin reared. "Have a care, you overgrown weasel. You can either ride as a silent passenger, or you can be carried like prey in my claws."

Meekly Koko put up a paw. "Um, I vote for the first one."

So the griffin grabbed the badger by the scruff of the neck and slung him up onto his back, making a point to clean his forepaws with snow afterward.

"Squad up!" Kaccap ordered, and the griffins leaped into the air as one.

# 11

## Scirye

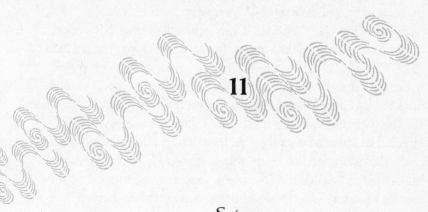

As far as Scirye was concerned, there was nothing to beat the elegance and power of a dragon in flight, but the griffins were a close second. And there was something to be said for warm fur rather than cold scales during a winter flight.

She had to suppress a giggle because Koko had been right. She felt like she was flying on a furry sofa.

She'd never ridden griffins bareback and without the proper tack before. Fortunately, Kaccap's shaggy coat gave her more to grip. It had been years since her father had given her riding lessons, but at least she remembered to try to keep her shoulders straight and parallel to her mount's shoulders. Her friends were doing their best to copy her but they were only barely managing to keep from falling off.

She had expected Kles to ride with her, but the little griffin had made a point of using his own wings. Kles might be the size of a parrot, but he had the heart of a war griffin.

Ragtail, his clan had called him. His full name, Klestetstse, meant Shabby in the Old Tongue. It was an odd sort of name that didn't fit the polished courtier she knew. And he had always passed his name off as a joke, insisting that he might have been shabby once but had grown into a magnificent specimen of griffinhood.

However, it seemed now that his own clan didn't agree with Kles's claims. His old acquaintances had treated him as some sort of joke.

As Kles struggled to keep up with his larger kin, Kaccap mocked him. "Still falling behind like when we were fledglings." And the captain brought his wings down in a powerful stroke that sent him shooting forward, and the rest of the squad copied him. The draft from their wings sent Kles tumbling, and by the time he had righted himself the distance between them was even greater.

Kles had always defended her against the bullies and enemies she'd encountered in embassies and foreign schools. Now she would return the favor.

"Captain Kaccap!" Scirye snapped, again trying to imitate her mother's commanding tone, "I expect all my party to arrive together."

Kaccap shot her an angry look, but he slowed and so did the other griffins. Panting, Kles caught up with them.

"Here," Scirye said, holding up her gauntleted wrist.

"I'm fine, lady," Kles said stubbornly and flew on.

By the time they entered a snow-filled pass, though, Kles's chest heaved with each breath and he beat his wings in a staccato rhythm.

She started to ask for a halt, but she saw Bayang, riding on the back of another griffin, shake her head. And she knew the dragon was right. It would hurt Kles's pride if the others stopped for him.

The kindly sorceress had also noticed Kles's troubles. "Let me try to calm the winds a bit," Māka said, a hand already beginning to move.

Tute, who was sitting with her, reached up a paw to grab her wrist. "No!"

But it was already too late. The beak of the griffin carrying Māka and Tute suddenly turned a bright violet. "My beak! What's happened to it?" he cried as she stared at it cross-eyed.

"Just give me a minute, noble steed," Māka said. She had taken out her book and was thumbing through it hastily. "Oh, that's where I went wrong."

The next moment, the beak changed in rapid succession from blue to a scarlet red with yellow polka dots.

The griffin dropped several feet as his wing strokes faltered for a moment. "Stop, stop," he screamed as he clutched his beak protectively. "You're making it worse."

Kaccap did a loop so that he was suddenly next to the sorceress. "By Oesho, why did you curse him?"

"I was just trying to help," Māka said, waving her book in the air.

"You must be the world's worst magician," Kaccap snapped. "Whatever made you think you could cast spells?"

Scirye expected sweet-tempered Māka to wilt under the war griffin's fierce glare, so she was surprised when Māka pressed a fist against herself. "I can't help it. The magic burns inside me. Right now it's a wildfire, but when I tame it, I will have a power that will light up the world and destroy the shadows. So I will never stop. To me, magic is like breathing."

Scirye was impressed by the other girl's desire, but she was as concerned as Kaccap about accidents. "Please, Lady Māka. We're not asking you to quit magic, just let it rest for a little while. What if, by some mistake, you shrank all the griffins' wings?"

Tute nudged her. "Yes, like she said. We won't help anyone but the vultures if we're just stains on the rocks."

Māka reluctantly dipped her head to Scirye. "As you wish, lady," she said as she tucked the book back up her sleeve.

*Am I any better at being a hero than Māka is at being a magician?* Scirye wondered to herself. So far, every time they had caught up with Roland he had gotten away. *Or at least I wish I could feel half the passion for this quest that Māka has for magic.*

They traveled along the pass without any more mishaps and emerged into a wide valley nestled between walls of black rock so sheer it was as if they had been cut from the mountain range with a knife. Though snow covered the ground like a fine sheet of fleece, she saw more war griffins sparring with dummies mounted on tall poles. When a griffin struck a dummy in the wrong spot, the dummy swiveled and the pole attached to the dummy hit the griffin and sent her spinning to the hoots and laughter of the other griffins.

Still other griffins were honing their agility by flying obstacle courses that contained not only hurdles on the ground, but nets suspended in the air with only narrow gaps through which to fly. And a third group was attempting to take a mock fort from a fourth group.

In the valley beyond, lean, sleek griffins darted around pylons over a snowy oval. "Are those warriors too?" Leech asked.

Scirye had seen pictures of them. "No, griffins come in all sizes for all sorts of purposes. Those griffins are getting ready for the great air races in the summer." She pointed to another group swooping and swirling. "And those griffins are practicing for aerial polo."

A forest of pines covered either slope at the end of the valley and here griffins about the size of collies took turns diving upon a dummy of a bird. Their shoulders were broad but their haunches were slender.

"Are they war griffins too?" Koko asked.

"Those are hunting griffins," Scirye explained.

As they flew over steep gorges sliced out of the mountain by the river and wide valleys, Scirye realized that Kles's eyrie was much larger than she had thought, for it included not only training grounds but pastures with sheep and goats eating from bales of hay. Fences separated the fields—resting under the layer of snow—and their bordering fences stitched the land like a patchwork quilt.

Though bare of leaves now, there were also row after row of almond and fruit trees waiting to blossom in the spring.

Everything suggested a prosperous and well-managed domain. In fact, Kles's clan believed that Oesho the wind god had created this lovely home just for them.

Leech let out an appreciative whistle. "The griffins have everything they need for the winter."

"It's not just winter that can cut the land routes off," Kaccap explained. "The lyak have invaded in the past to steal the gold."

Koko had been sitting hunched with fatigue but he perked up now. "Gold?"

"The eyries were placed here partly to guard the imperial gold mines," Kaccap said. "Lyak means thief in the Old Tongue."

"You wouldn't happen to have any samples around, would you?" Koko asked. "You know, sort of as a souvenir."

"Forgive the badger," Bayang said. "His mother dropped him on his head when he was a baby."

Two giant griffins had been carved from the stone at the mouth of the next pass. They stood, ever alert, unwinking eyes staring at the world. At the moment, though, snow covered their shoulders and icicles hung from their beaks.

When they burst over the next valley, Scirye saw numerous humans and wagons on the road leading to a sizable, prosperous town. Beyond it was another lake, but this one was as large as a small sea.

Kaccap explained that the miners, farmers, and shepherds lived here along with all the other humans who served the eyrie's needs.

From the way Māka pressed herself against her griffin's back as if trying to hide, Scirye suspected they were also overly critical of the entertainment hired for their banquets.

The ancient eyrie of Kles's clan lay at the end of the lake in the tallest mountain honeycombed with caves and tunnels. Here and there were areas where the gateways had been cut in even rows and at equal intervals, but many had been carved as needed over the centuries so that they were scattered about randomly.

Unlike the rest of the mountains, the snow had been tidily swept away from the openings as well as the ledges and platforms. On its peak, though, was a steel radio tower, a concession to modern times. Snow blew from the mountaintops, reminding Scirye of the white curtains of snowflakes dancing before the Arctic winds.

A river fell from the right shoulder of the eyrie's mountain, but winter had frozen the spray into icicles so that the resulting waterfall looked like a giant tower of crystal. Through the spike-covered walls, she thought she saw water continuing to rush downward. It was only at the waterfall's base that the water remained free, rippling in a large pond, before it slipped under the ice and into the lake.

From his ragged, clumsy flapping, Kles seemed to be on his last wings. It was no longer merely Scirye who was casting concerned looks at the little griffin. Leech and Koko too kept checking on their friend.

And yet when they were finally near their goal, Kles seemed to find some hidden reserve of strength. The beat of his wings became more regular and he lifted his head as if he were just out for a casual flight. Scirye couldn't have been prouder of her friend.

"Welcome to the Tarkär Eyrie, the home of the Koyn Encuwontse," Kles panted proudly.

Despite the frigid air, griffins of all sizes swarmed in and out of the eyrie. Some were flying in slow gyres as if they were sentries, but others were going about more peaceful tasks.

Several fledglings were even playing an aerial game of tag when they noticed Bayang riding a griffin. A dragon was such an unusual sight that they flocked about her.

A young racing griffin, lean as a whippet, boldly hovered in front of them. "What's a dragon doing here, and why isn't she flying on her own?" He gave a whoop when he saw the dotted beak of the griffin that Māka and Tute were riding. "And what happened to you?"

Kaccap clacked his beak in annoyance. "You'll learn soon enough if the Keeper thinks it's necessary." At a wave of his paw, his squad streamed past the inquisitive griffin.

"I'm sure I know what went wrong," Māka said to her mount. "So let me fix it."

"No!" came a chorus of voices.

By then they had attracted the attention of other griffins, including some older ones, until they were surrounded by griffins of all ages and all sizes. And their pace slowed from necessity.

A hunting griffin peered at them curiously. "Ragtail?"

Kles puffed. "You're looking a little moth-eaten, Yente."

"And you're out of shape," Yente snickered, and then over her shoulder, she shouted, "Hey, Ragtail's come home just as shabby as when he left."

That was too much for Scirye. "Excuse me, but we have urgent business with the Keeper, so I'll ask you to get out of our way."

Yente folded her forelegs. "And just who are you to give us orders?"

Kles seemed to recover some of his old spirit. "The Lady Scirye of the House of Rapañ̃e, and"—he raised his voice— "the daughter of Lord Tsirauñe the Griffin Master."

Yente looked as skeptical as the war griffins had, but Captain Kaccap made shooing motions with his forepaws. "So show some respect for the griffin master's daughter."

At the mention of her father's name, the griffins respectfully withdrew in all directions, forming a living tunnel now through which Scirye and the others flew.

"I always wished I had family," Leech said. "Now I'm sort of glad I don't after seeing how they treat Kles."

Scirye couldn't help wondering if the humans would welcome her any better than the griffins had Kles.

# 12

## Bayang

Kaccap took them to a circle about twenty feet in diameter. Carved in a wide ring around the opening were scenes with griffins—the dragon assumed they were scenes from the clan's history because the eyrie was featured prominently on several panels.

Fire imps burned upon niches in vessels of glass, casting warmth and light. Ruby eyes the size of rice grains watched them land. In the illumination, Bayang could just make out the occasional shadows of chisel marks still on the stone of the walls and ceiling of the cylindrical passage. But the floor itself had been polished flat by centuries of passing paws.

As his paws touched the rock of his home, Kles started to sag. Instantly, Scirye hopped off Kaccap and scooped her friend up into her arms. "Are you all right?"

"Yes, yes, now put me down." The lap griffin struggled to break free and then gave up.

There were a few snickers from the escorting griffins, but Scirye glared around so fiercely that none of them actually said anything.

Kaccap spoke quietly to a lap griffin with a chain of tiny golden bells about his neck. They jingled as the griffin flapped away.

While they waited by the entrance, human servants brought basins of warm water and towels.

Kles immediately roused. "We need to make ourselves more presentable too." He fluttered clumsily within Scirye's grasp to take a washcloth and dip it into the water. Then he was fluttering all around her head as he rubbed out the travel dirt.

She snatched the cloth from him, her face now red from the scrubbing. "I can do that myself, Kles. See to yourself."

As Scirye tried to clean the dirt from her face, the griffin tried to groom his feathers and fur, but between their travels and battles, his fur and feathers were matted with grime—and it would probably be easier to burn the hatchlings' filthy coveralls and furs than clean them.

Bayang contented herself with washing her paws and muzzle, as did Tute, while Leech and Māka cleaned their faces and hands. But the fastidious Koko went so far as to clean his fur as well.

By the time that was done, the lap griffin with the bells returned. "This way, Lady Scirye," he said with a bow.

Scirye set off with Leech and Koko flanking her and Bayang bringing up the rear. Kaccap and his griffins surged around them, keeping just enough space so that it was hard to say whether they were guiding or guarding them.

The dragon had been in many strange places but nothing like the eyrie, which seemed like a giant beehive. The walls of the passages were free of decoration except for lamps and markings in a flowing script that reminded Bayang of the writing on the antique flying carpet they had ridden when they had first begun their pursuit of Badik. She assumed the words were like street signs.

It was a different matter for the chambers that opened off the passage. Some had been hewn out of the stone like the passages, but sculptors had been free to ornament the rooms with patterns and pictures. Bayang noticed that in their ornamentation the griffins were fond of curves and spirals rather than straight lines—just as the walls of the eyrie itself.

Other rooms had been created by Nature. Glowing stalagmites reared from the floor while stalactites plunged downward like daggers, and water dripped down with plinking sounds. Over the centuries, the water had left minerals that now formed walls that dripped like cake batter while the floor undulated like a carpet that had been flung down hastily. Hot springs within the mountain kept even the upper levels warm and slightly humid.

Some of the rooms were offices, storerooms, or classrooms. Though there were tables and desks, there were few chairs or sofas. Rather, the griffins preferred to perch on wooden posts that ran from floor to ceiling. Projecting from the sides of the posts were perpendicular roosts.

One large cavern must have served as a nursery with nursemaid griffins making small neat nests of straw. "They're getting ready for the spring hatching," Kles explained.

"Yum," Tute murmured, licking his chops. "Omelettes."

Māka rapped him on the head with a knuckle and scolded him. "Mind your manners. It's not polite to eat your hosts' offspring."

"Especially when your hosts are so much bigger than you," Bayang added softly.

"Well, that vegetable soup didn't fill me up very well," Tute groused.

Koko glanced at Kles over his shoulder. "So who knew griffins were hatched and not born?"

"Don't be crude," the lap griffin frowned.

"I can't help being curi— Whoa!" Koko had been so busy chatting that he fell through the circular hole in the floor.

"Mind your step," Kaccap said as he caught the badger's paw.

Since the captain had spoken in the New Tongue, Koko blinked in angry ignorance.

"Who puts a doorway in the floor?" Koko demanded.

"It makes sense when all the occupants have wings," Scirye said and pointed at the ceiling a little farther ahead of them. A rectangular doorway had been cut into the stone, giving access to the level above. Even as they watched, a couple of lap griffins fluttered upward.

It would have been faster for the griffins to carry them through the openings, but it seemed they were being received formally, and etiquette required they be able to use staircases in the rear of the eyrie, also cut from the stone.

As Scirye mounted the stairs, she looked about curiously. "I feel as if I've been here before."

"Perhaps you visited with your father," Bayang suggested.

Scirye frowned as she searched her memory but then shook her head. "No, I think I would have remembered."

"Well, maybe you were in a kennel of wet dogs, because that's what it smells like to me," Koko murmured.

At last, they came to a huge cavern. On the three sides, griffins filled ledges cut into the walls that rose layer upon layer toward the ceiling, or they perched on wooden posts set horizontally into holes in the walls.

Each of the griffins must have been someone important, judging from the amount of gold they wore—though the styles varied from finished torques, armbands, and anklets to raw lumps of gold on chains. Red garnets and blue lapis lazuli and turquoise were sprinkled liberally among the jewelry.

All of the griffin castes were represented here and in a definite "pecking order," with the war griffins seated at the top with the hunting and sports griffins a little lower, and the lap griffins at the bottom.

The fourth wall was covered with banners, gold plaques, and huge medallions the size of trays that had been presented to the clan by past Kushan emperors as battle honors.

High above a hunting griffin with gray streaks of fur spoke, "The lyaks grow bolder and bolder. Each time they raid deeper into our lands. And if it is this bad in the winter, what will happen this spring after the snow and ice melt? The caravans with our gold must get through to Bactra. I say we take the fight to the lyak lands and end the menace once and for all."

Cheers of approval and raucous squawks of protest echoed from around the chamber.

"What's going on?" Scirye whispered to Kles.

"This is the Nest," her friend said in a hushed voice. "The elders must be holding a war council."

Protruding from the wall of battle honors was a golden tree branch. On it sat a single griffin. Her fur was silver with age and her wing feathers almost as white as the snow outside. In the light of the fire imps, they glowed like moonbeams. Around her head was a mesh of gold from which hung sapphires and rubies, but she wore no decoration and her fur, though brushed to a sheen, was left unbraided.

She carried herself with a natural authority that expected to be obeyed, and her beak bore a deep straight groove, perhaps a scar left from some battle-ax. Bayang had heard that the griffin clans were matriarchies.

"I believe Captain Kaccap has a report to make on this subject." The silver griffin motioned with her paw for him to come forward.

The captain strutted forward, bowing first to the silvery griffin. "Keeper." He then bowed respectfully in turn to the griffins on the other walls. "Elders. My patrol just destroyed a band of lyak raiders by the upper lake."

There was an uproar as every griffin tried to speak at once until the Keeper struck her branch with the steel-tipped claws of a forepaw. It rang like a bell and as the echoing notes died, she commanded, "Silence! I believe Elder Kacar had the floor."

"This is outrageous," the gray griffin said, flapping his wings irritably. "How long will it be before they begin attacking our very eyrie?"

Bayang saw a way of obtaining help for them against Roland. "My Lady Keeper, if I may speak?"

The Keeper looked at Kaccap. "Captain, are these the guests you mentioned in your note?" She craned her head forward. "Merciful Oesho, is that Klestetstse?"

Kles fluttered into the air, hovering at the same height as Bayang. "My Lady Keeper, let me introduce you to Lady Scirye of the House of Rapaññe, daughter of the griffin master, Lord Tsirauñe."

The griffins stirred all around them with whispers and a rustling of feathers as they all leaned down to peer at Scirye.

The hatchling bowed gracefully. "My Lady Keeper, will you hear my friend, Bayang of the Moonglow clan?"

The Keeper glanced at the gray griffin. "Elder Kacar, do you yield the floor?"

"We are all as curious as you," Elder Kacar said.

"We are pursuing thieves who stole the Jade Lady's ring in San Francisco," Bayang said.

"I heard of the theft," the Keeper said. "It was an outrage." She dipped her head to Scirye. "And I was sorry to hear about your sister, Nishke. When she was small, she accompanied your father several times on his visits here."

Bayang set a paw upon Scirye's shoulder. "Lady Scirye bravely chased after the thief, Badik the dragon, and we have helped her in her quest." The dragon nodded to Kles to continue.

It was silent within the Nest as Kles told the Keeper and his clan elders of their pursuit and how Badik led them to Roland.

"Roland is a rich and powerful man," the Keeper noted. "You do not pick simple enemies."

"The goddess Nanaia helps us in our quest," Kles said and nodded to Scirye, who pulled off her glove self-consciously and showed the mark glowing on her hand. The Keeper studied her palm as the elders rustled and murmured again to one another.

The lap griffin briefly told the gathering about their quest and when he was done, Elder Kacar said skeptically, "It's hard to believe a dragon could do all that, let alone human hatchlings and . . . and . . . a lap griffin."

Laughter from the other war griffins mixed with the protests from other lap griffins at that comment. The Keeper struck resonant notes from her branch until they grew quiet.

"Elder Kacar," the Keeper snapped. "I wouldn't want to think you were saying that war is more important than any other task." She indicated a beautiful golden disc of a scene of Nanaia riding upon her lion. Chips of lapis lazuli created a blue sky. "This was given to a courtier of our clan who negotiated the Treaty of Peking, saving many lives."

Kacar lowered his head stiffly. "Yes, Keeper."

"And he did it with no army backing him, only his eloquence and logic—but both of those were considerable," the Keeper went on. "I think that took considerable courage, don't you?"

Kacar bobbed his head again. "Yes, Keeper."

The Keeper turned her gaze back to Bayang and her friends. "And so you claim Roland is trying to reassemble Yi's magical bow?" the Keeper demanded.

"Alas, we were unable to keep him from acquiring the bow and the ring," Kles said. "What he needs is the arrows."

"Which are somewhere in the City of Death," Scirye finished. "We have to find them before he does. We were on our way there when the lord of thunder ambushed us. Roland had hired him to keep an eye out for us."

Bayang cleared her throat. "I also think Roland might have hired the lyaks to keep us occupied while he searched for the arrows."

The Nest burst into noise once more as every griffin began speaking until the Keeper silenced them with ringing blows to the branch. "My lord and lady elders, I suggest that I question our guests in detail before we discuss what to do about the lyaks. Captain Kaccap, if you'll bring them to my chambers?"

Then, spreading her wings, she spiraled gracefully upward and through a circular hole in the ceiling.

# 13

## Scirye

As soon as Scirye and the others mounted the griffins, the warriors rose into the air. Higher and higher they flew, past more trophies and honors, some so ancient that the banner cloths were disintegrating. Scirye felt as if she were rising through time itself.

Kles flew beside her, head raised high, his fatigue gone as the elders of his clan watched him soar through the air.

The hole in the ceiling was decorated with gold vines from which grew silver crescent moons, and they flew through it to a new level. Here the ceiling was only twelve feet high, and they flew down a corridor past offices and archives staffed with a mixture of human and griffin clerks.

At the end of the corridor was a stone oval door decorated with panels of human kings and queens receiving gifts from griffins. They were posed stiffly but rendered realistically.

"This door came from an ancient king of Babylonia," Kles boasted to her.

When Captain Kaccap knocked, a griffin servant answered. His beak was decorated with swirls of gold inlay. "Please come in," he said with a bow before he flew away with a note in his paw.

Kaccap and his patrol stayed outside while Scirye and her friends entered. The room was the first in the eyrie that she felt comfortable in. Plush, richly colored carpets covered the floor and the room itself was furnished with human chairs and divans as well as griffin perches. In a corner was an old-fashioned Victrola with a crank handle to power it and huge horn towering above it as a speaker. Scirye guessed that the Keeper entertained human visitors here.

Glancing at her own filthy clothes, Scirye hesitated to sit on the elegant antique furniture.

"Lady Scirye, please be at ease." The Keeper bounded easily onto a perch about four feet off the floor. Immediately, a human maid brought her a small golden plate filled with preserved dates and bread flat as a disc. "Your father and I are old friends and I hope that we will be too."

On the other hand, Koko didn't hesitate to make himself right at home, throwing himself onto a cushion-covered couch. "Yeah, this is more like the life I want."

The Keeper regarded the badger with amusement. "And from what jail did Lady Scirye recruit you, badger?" she asked in accented English.

Koko defended himself. "I was in a perfectly respectable museum, getting culture."

The feathers around the Keeper's eyes twitched in amusement. "Or picking out what to steal, but no matter," she said, wagging a date at him. "Just make sure you leave with no more than when you arrived."

Koko rubbed his paws together as more human servants brought in trays of food and set them on tables. "I'll settle for a square meal," Koko said as he watched a servant begin to slice meat from a haunch of venison. "Don't be chintzy now. Oh, heck. I'll take the whole thing." When the servant handed him the platter itself, the badger happily picked up the whole haunch and began to munch away.

Another servant brought over a tray of small cakes in the shapes of rabbits, deer, boar, and other game.

"My favorite," Kles said in delight.

"Yes, I remembered," the Keeper said, pleased with his reaction.

Though Koko had an entire venison haunch, he couldn't resist setting it down and snatching one of the cakes greedily. "Hey, this is pretty tasty. What's it called?"

"Honey cake with freshly ground mealworms," Kles said. "We're quite famous for them." As crumbs sprayed from the badger's lips, the griffin went on. "The minerals in the eyrie's water give the worms a unique nutty flavor."

The Keeper eyed the coughing badger and then turned back to Māka. "And I trust that you and your friend"—she inclined her head to the lynx, whose head was half-buried in the side of a roast pheasant—"will not be providing any more entertainment in our lands."

Māka lowered the pheasant drumstick in her hand. "You know about the banquet?"

"I wouldn't be the Keeper if I didn't know everything that went on," the griffin said.

"There will be no more performing until I help Lady Scirye complete her quest," Māka said. "I promise."

"Good." The Keeper swung her gaze to Scirye and her large black eyes seemed to bore into the girl. "Yes, I see the resemblance to your father, but even at his wildest—did you know we were hatchlings together?—he never dressed up like an Arctic pirate."

Her father was always so serious that it was hard to believe he ever did anything crazy. "My father was wild?"

The Keeper nibbled daintily on a date. "So he didn't tell you how he saved my life once?"

"How did he do that?" Scirye asked.

"Have you ever heard of skimming?" the Keeper asked.

"That's when you fly over the rapids of a river as close to the surface as you can," Kles explained. "But it's forbidden."

"Yes, and I'll punish any fool I catch doing that. But back then I thought it was some silly rule that old hens had made up. So he and I went skimming when the river was in full spring flood," the Keeper chuckled. "I got a little too low, and right away I found out that I wasn't as good a swimmer as I thought. Fortunately, your father swam like a fish and pulled me out." She fixed her eyes on Kles. "None of which should ever be repeated."

"Consider it forgotten, my lady," Kles said.

The Keeper purred her satisfaction briefly and then asked Scirye, "And you're pleased with Kles's services?"

"The eyrie trained him well," Scirye said politely.

"I think it's more the princess's doing than ours," the Keeper laughed. Kles had originally served Princess Maimantstse before she had sent him to Scirye. "Kles was always a feisty little thing. But then he had to be. The others were always picking on him."

"You knew, Keeper?" Kles asked.

"As I said, a good Keeper knows everything," the Keeper said.

"And you didn't help him?" Scirye couldn't help asking, indignant for her friend.

Kles answered for her. "She couldn't. At some point I was going to have to go where she couldn't protect me. I had to learn how to do that for myself." And he gave her a respectful bow. "And I thank you for that."

"There was no griffin more stubborn or determined than Kles," the Keeper said with an approving nod. "He made himself into a wise and able diplomat who served the princess well."

"And as he does me now," Scirye said, growing more comfortable with the Keeper. It was as if she had shed the regal manners and attitude with the signs of her office, and she was simply an old friend of her father's, happy to be reminiscing with Scirye.

The Keeper studied her claws. "I am not ashamed of the warrior's path—we must all do what we were born to. But when I was young, I dreamed of seeing the wonders of the world. So my size and strength seemed like curses to me." She nodded to Kles. "I envy you, Kles."

"Me?" the little lap griffin squeaked.

The Keeper gestured to Scirye. "You not only have the great honor of serving the Lady Scirye, but you have traveled from one foreign capital to another. But I doubt that anyone dresses in a costume as eccentric as your lady's." The Keeper rested her beak upon a forepaw. "I suppose there is a reason?"

So they told her more about their adventures, but Scirye noticed that the Keeper always addressed any questions to Kles. Scirye realized that the Keeper was doing more than satisfying her curiosity. She was also trying to restore Kles's pride.

When Kles was done, the Keeper dusted off her paws with a very humanlike gesture and motioned for the servant to take her plate of cakes and dates away. "So you think it's Roland behind our troubles as well, do you? But the City of Death lies outside our lands."

"He probably doesn't want you investigating if you hear any reports about activity there," Bayang said.

"So you'll help us?" Scirye asked eagerly.

"Roland's planned well. I don't dare leave the eyrie and the mines unprotected." The Keeper laced her claws together. "And I have obligations to protect the town that houses our human servants too."

"Even a few griffins would help," Scirye coaxed.

At that moment, someone tapped at the doors. When a servant opened them, a brown lap griffin darted inside. He lighted on a small branch next to the Keeper. In his beak, he had a note.

Taking the note, the Keeper began to read, gradually straightening with each new sentence. When she was done, she glanced at the servant. "Ask for confirmation," she said gravely.

The servant bowed. "We already did that, Keeper."

The Keeper crumpled up the note and threw it away from her as if it were polluted. "I'm sorry. I have been ordered to send you under guard to Bactra."

"Oh, dear," Māka blurted out. "The guild only threw vegetables. What will they throw at court?"

"Nothing we can make a stew out of. It'll be daggers most likely," Tute said. "So I hope all of you wore your iron underwear."

# 14

## Bayang

Bayang reared up in anger and disgust. She was surrounded by treachery. The first griffin who tried to touch her or the hatchlings would be sorry.

"I didn't take anything," Koko bawled. "Get me a lawyer."

"Yeah, we're the good guys," Leech said. "We've been chasing the thieves all around the world."

Scirye was sitting, frozen with disbelief, but it was Kles who had the presence of mind to spring from his chair and hover in front of the dragon and spread out his forelegs. "Don't do anything rash, Bayang. The eyrie is not Prince Tarkhun's caravansary."

Prince Tarkhun was a Sogdian prince they had rescued from an attack by Roland's men in the Arctic. Worried about their safety, Prince Tarkhun had tried to hold them in protective custody when they wanted to follow Roland into the Arctic wastes. Bayang had demolished a door and assorted furniture during their escape.

But Kles was right. This was not the same situation. For one thing, both of her wings had been healthy, so she could fly. For another, they had had a whole wilderness nearby in which they could hide. Here, they were in the home territory of griffins who trained for war. Even a company of seasoned dragon warriors might not be able to get free.

Bayang sank back down, but she eyed the Keeper coldly. "Why have you arrested us? I thought we were your guests."

"They didn't give a reason for the command. But I suspect you've become pawns of a court intrigue." The Keeper rested her beak upon a forepaw and then swung her gaze thoughtfully toward Scirye. "Your father is an important member of the reform party at the court. The conservatives are probably trying to strike at him and his cause indirectly by accusing you and your friends of some crime."

"My father?" Scirye asked.

"Yes, the Princess Maimantstse is the leader of the reformers and your father is her right hand," the Keeper explained. "You didn't know?"

"I don't get to see him much," Scirye explained. "He stayed in Bactra while I went with my mother when she was posted to embassies in other countries. When he visited us, he never talked about those things to me."

"He didn't want to trouble you," Kles said.

"I can accept that," Scirye said accusingly, "but how come you never told me about his situation, Kles?"

Kles shrugged apologetically. "I tried, but you always got bored whenever I tried to talk about current events. The only thing you wanted to hear about were the Pippalanta." The Pippalanta were a famous band of female warriors whom the Europeans and Americans insisted on calling Amazons. Scirye had developed an interest in them when her own sister, Nishke, had joined them.

Of all of them, Scirye seemed to be taking the arrest the hardest, but that was only to be expected. The girl lived her life by Tumarg, the code of honor by which Kushan warriors lived, and yet her father's enemies had still managed to accuse her of as yet unspecified crimes. A blow to one's faith was as bad as a blow to the head.

"But this isn't right," Scirye grumbled. "It's not—."

"Tumarg?" the Keeper supplied. "No, it isn't, but the conservatives often twist that word for their own selfish reasons. Just as they often manipulate the laws to get what they want."

"I'm liking these characters less and less," Koko declared.

"I have no love for them either," the Keeper said. "If they had their way, they would turn the clock back a thousand years. We griffins would not have the freedoms we have today."

Bayang had not survived this long without learning how to master her own fury. An emotional assassin was soon a dead one. "We have no choice," she said to the others. "We have to go to Bactra or give the conservatives even more ammunition against Scirye's father and his group."

"And do not underestimate the princess and Lord Tsirauñe," the Keeper advised. "They will right this wrong as they have others. And I will tell the court as well that this is a miscarriage of justice. And my opinion carries not a little weight in Bactra. But you yourselves are the best ones to convince them."

"And while we're telling the truth, Roland could be taking over the world," Scirye objected.

"Even if I could refuse my emperor, I cannot refuse my friend, your father," the Keeper soothed her. "In addition to the imperial order was a request from Lady Scirye's father that I send her to him."

"Oh, just great," Leech grumbled. Raised in an orphanage and then surviving in the streets of San Francisco, he'd never known his parents. Family obligations were just words to him.

Bayang understood though. "He's worried about Scirye, but it's an awkward time for that."

The Keeper nodded. "Yes, it's unfortunate. And now I am ashamed of what I have to do next." She clapped her paws together, and griffin mages with sashes emblazoned with stars and crescents entered.

Koko put a paw to his neck uneasily. "Nothing involved with chopping off heads, is it? I sort of like mine where it is."

"No, but I have been commanded to place wards on you, the dragon, and the magician," the Keeper said. "That's so the first two won't be able to transform, and the other cannot work spells."

"Oh, dear," Māka said.

"It's really a silly precaution," Tute snapped, "unless you have hay fever."

Bayang suspected that the ward wasn't necessary for Māka. All the Keeper really had to do was take away the fledgling's pamphlet. As a griffin mage applied a paper charm to her side, she said, "Can't you let Māka go? We only met her today so she couldn't be involved in any of the charges against us."

"My orders command me to send everyone." The Keeper spread her paws. "And after all, she *is* guilty of causing a riot in the town at least. But her only real crime is being inept. And I will tell the court that."

Māka swallowed, "Thank you, I think."

"Well, you know I'm as inept as they come," Koko wheedled. "How about putting in a good word for me too?"

"I think a muzzle would suit you better," the Keeper warned.

Koko waved a paw. "No, no, I don't want to be a bother."

When Bayang and the others had all received charms, the Keeper descended from her perch with a graceful flutter of her wings. "Come Lady Scirye and Klestetstse, I will walk with you as far as the entrance to our eyrie."

There was such a great difference in size between the Keeper and human hatchling and even more between the elderly war griffin and the lap griffin that Bayang might have laughed if she didn't know what a great honor this was. The Keeper was not only showing the eyrie how important her visitors were, but that she also disagreed with the order she'd been given.

Kaccap and his squad, who were waiting outside, realized it too as they fell in around them. As they marched along, they kept casting curious glances at Kles and his companions. And Kaccap looked uneasy over the way he had mocked Kles.

As they walked back the way they had come, griffins made way and bowed deep, fluttering their wings with a grand flourish.

It made Bayang smile to see how Kles lifted his head proudly as he flew alongside the Keeper's head and answered more of her questions about their travels.

*There'll be no living with the griffin now.* With a smile, Bayang turned to say something to Leech, but he looked away quickly, even falling back several paces as if he were avoiding her.

Maybe it was too much to hope that they had overcome their bloody past.

When they reached the entrance, it took her a moment to realize that the rigid shapes were not more stalactites but griffins standing rigidly at attention. The armor of these griffins was so plain that Kaccap's patrol seemed like peacocks in comparison. The steel of the new griffins seemed plain from the greaves and armbands protecting their limbs to the discs covering their chests. It was only when she got closer that she noticed that the steel was engraved with the silver likeness of some emperor or empress. Others had designs like lightning bolts or axes. Bayang guessed they were honors given after some great deed.

"I've ordered a company of my own guards to escort you, Lady Scirye," the Keeper explained with a gesture of her paw. "Everyone at court will see that the Tarkär Eyrie holds you in high esteem."

*Would their new escort be any easier on Kles than Kaccap?* Scirye wondered, but she bowed her head. "I thank you, Keeper."

The Keeper engulfed Scirye's hand in her large paw. "Come back in happier times, lady, and I will tell you stories about your father when he was your age."

Scirye bowed. "I would like that, Keeper. Thank you."

The Keeper released Scirye and motioned for Kles to rise into the air to the level of her eyes. It was another mark of respect, for instead of talking down to Kles as if he were a mere underling, she was treating him as if they were equals. "I know you should be at the vanguard, Klestetstse, but I hope you'll indulge me."

Kles dipped his head low. "Anything, Keeper."

Bringing her paw up underneath him, the Keeper carried him over to a guard wearing a golden torque and set the stunned Kles upon the guard's back. "Let Captain Warpamo lead while you ride with your lady upon one of my guards," the Keeper said. "She and your friends will need all your wisdom and skill when you arrive at court. And you won't be at your best if you fly under your own power all the way there."

*Had the Keeper watched their arrival?* Bayang asked herself. Perhaps, as she said, Kles did have a special place in her affections.

As she and her friends mounted some of the other dragons, Bayang stole a glance at Kaccap and his squad. They were positively goggle-eyed now and their beaks were open in amazement.

*Well,* Bayang thought with some satisfaction, *that should make the bullies think twice before they pick on another lap griffin again.*

"I have no gift of prophecy," the Keeper said, "and yet I know you have a difficult journey ahead of you, Klestetstse. Keep your lady and the world safe."

Kles swallowed as he sat on the saddle before Scirye. "I will, Keeper."

The elderly griffin waved good-bye to them as they rose into the air and eased through the entrance and out into the open. More squads were streaming out of separate openings and forming about them like a shell protecting the seeds at the center until they were surrounded in a globe of the finest griffin warriors.

And then they were off to Bactra, where poisonous court intrigues very well might make it the deadliest place they had ever faced.

# 15

## Scirye

True to his word, Kles rode with Scirye, sitting just before the pommel of the saddle. She rose slightly in the stirrups, knees bent, shoulders straight, head up, and Captain Warpamo twisted his head and gave her an approving nod. There was no bit to the bridle, unlike a horse's. This way the griffin could speak clearly. "You've ridden griffins before, lady."

Koko, of course, was more interested in the silver decorating his griffin's saddle, fingering it critically. "I bet this is almost pure."

"And it had better all be still on there when we arrive," Bayang warned the badger.

"Hey," Koko snapped. "Some folks collect postcards when they travel. Can I help it if I've got better taste than most?" But he put his paws upon the pommel.

"What do you think is going to happen to us?" Leech asked Kles.

The lap griffin waved a claw. "I think the Keeper is right. This is a way of striking at the princess. These petty spites happen all the time. They wouldn't dare to actually prosecute my lady or her friends. We should be able to prove our innocence quickly enough, and perhaps we'll even be able to obtain some help when they hear our tale."

With Kles pressed against her, Scirye could feel how excited he grew with each mile. He twisted his head from side to side as he gazed down at the rolling landscape below, which seemed to have as many mountains and hills as flatlands.

Just as in the eyrie valleys, the fields below were also lying fallow and the orchards bare of leaves. Whether they were hillside terraces or level fields, the land was well tended and orderly. The fences and low walls made the earth seem like the milky-white pieces of giant mosaic that spread from horizon to horizon.

Kles waved a paw to indicate a great canal, now frozen, from which many smaller channels radiated across the landscape. There was such an intricate network of irrigation canals shimmering in the sun that Bactra seemed surrounded by a lace of fine golden threads.

"Centuries ago this was just desert," he said. "But the Kushans transformed it into the richest farmlands in the world. They built hundreds of underground aqueducts that bring water down from the mountains in addition to what the rivers supply. And then they constructed thousands of miles of irrigation canals and ditches to carry that water to the fields and orchards."

It was the vastness of the waterworks, which stretched all the way to the horizon, that impressed Scirye—and she felt a flash of pride at how her ancestors had transformed this barren land into this paradise. Where there had once only been sand dunes there were now snug little homesteads scattered about like buttons on a snowy quilt, the smoke rising from their chimneys like stray threads. And the farther they went, the more homes they saw until they clumped together into whole villages and towns.

Leech looked over the side. "Is that the Silk Road?"

Below them, a truck chugged past a caravan of plodding camels.

It shimmered in the sunlight as if it were decorated with as many little mirrors and sequins as Māka's wagon.

Passing traffic had worn away the snow to reveal modern asphalt.

"The Silk Road is a term used for many routes across the land and sea," Kles explained. When he saw the boy's disappointment, he added, "But many roads follow the ancient tracks, so perhaps that was part of the Silk Road once."

"But why use a camel when you got a truck?" Koko asked.

"People need supplies even in the winter," Kles said, "when the snows have made it impossible for trucks to use roads."

Kles's small body was restless with happiness as he pointed out some landmark. After the first dozen, Scirye barely heard the litany of temples and bridges and historic forts, for she couldn't control her increasing unease. She didn't share Kles's confidence that her family's enemies would drop whatever charges had been made. Perhaps the Keeper had done too good a job restoring his pride.

There was no abrupt end between the countryside and the city. Rather, the fields and orchards became fewer and the number of buildings and roads increased, and so did the traffic. There were now as many glittering cars and trucks as there were mules and camels—all of them following a train of elephants outfitted in cloth of scarlet and gold, little huts called howdahs swaying on their backs—perhaps the entourage of royalty from India.

And even the sky became more crowded. Griffins of all sorts passed back and forth, carrying packages or passengers. The majority of the escort closed around them in a protective globe while others flew on all sides making sure their passage was clear.

"Make way, make way for the prince of the Khmers," chattered a flying monkey. Behind him came a palanquin carried by dozens of monkeys. Little bits of mirror and rhinestone festooned the brightly colored, complex designs of its sides, and little tendrils of smoke seeped from the enclosed box as if the prince were trying to keep warm with a brazier of coals.

Captain Warpamo narrowed his eyes, but before he could speak, Kles called in a voice that was both commanding and loud from such a tiny frame. "*You* make way! We are on the emperor's business."

The monkey's broad mouth drew up in a scowl but then he inclined his head toward the palanquin as if his master was speaking in a low voice. The next moment, he and the other flying monkeys descended lower to let them pass overhead.

The only time their griffin guards veered was to make room as a giant roc with wings as long as a city block began to descend to the airport with twenty or so passengers clinging to the netlike harness fastened around its body. The wind from its flapping wings threw even their mounts a bit off course.

Leech craned his neck to look down at the hangars that stood on either side of the concrete runway. "Maybe Roland's airplane is down there."

Bayang nodded. "We'll ask Scirye's father to make inquiries."

Finally Kles rose on his hind legs and spread his wings out as he crowed, "Now behold, Bactra, the Mother of Cities. People have lived here for four thousand years. When Paris was just a village of huts in the middle of an island, Bactra was already a city famous for its schools and temples."

Though she had been born in Bactra, Scirye had left the city when she had been very young, so her actual memories of it were fuzzy. She gazed down at the blocks of two- and three-story buildings that spread out like a grid from the main highway. Their walls shone pink and pale orange and peach in color. Sunrise colors, Scirye thought.

The roofs were all flat with wooden lattices running around the edge to provide privacy, so the city resembled a fleet of rafts floating above the avenues.

"When the summer's hot, families spend their days and even their nights on the roofs," Kles said. "People think of them as outdoor living rooms."

Even now, despite the cold, Scirye saw people gathered around large cylindrical clay stoves, cooking their meals behind the privacy of lattice walls. Others were tending some of the many dove sheds scattered across the rooftops.

"The roofs are different from San Francisco," Leech said, disappointed, "but the buildings themselves look pretty modern. I thought you said Bactra has been around for centuries?"

"That's because this is New Bactra," Kles explained. "Old Bactra was originally an oasis between two rivers, and as people settled there, it spread across the area between the two rivers." He pointed to a cream-colored smudge against the mountains to the south. "But late in the last century, King Kanishka IX built the dam that ensured a steady source of water throughout the year. And the city spilled over the banks into the surrounding countryside."

Ahead of them, factories and mills lined the right bank of a river, their tall smokestacks pouring smoke and steam upward and adding to the golden haze of the afternoon.

They passed directly over what must have been a steel mill, where sweaty trolls—looking like children from this height—moved about with steel beams while elephants pushed along hoppers of coal and iron ore.

Gaudy cars, trucks, and three-wheeled jitneys shared the road with camels, donkeys, and horses, flowing back and forth over a half-dozen bridges. And on the river a one-armed triton set his back against a loaded ferry to push it to the other bank.

"The river below," Kles said, "marks the eastern boundary of the Old Bactra just as the Bactra River marks the western side."

Scirye felt both a thrill and a little dread as they flew over the wall of tan-colored blocks that stood on the left bank. Long colorful banners fluttered from the spires of the East Gate towers, and they all gave a gasp, even Scirye. Kles had called Bactra the jewel of Asia, but it was more like a treasure chest of jewels had spilled over the land.

Brightly colored temples and shops squeezed in on either side of ancient mansions. And there were as many types and periods of architecture as there were people from Kushan's long history: a Hindu temple covered in statues stood next to a small open-air Greek theater with marble columns pale as ivory, shops in the rounded shape of tents from the northern steppes but with golden domes squeezed a scarlet and green Chinese pagoda from either side. The glazed tiles on the walls of the government buildings and universities made them look more like boxes decorated with emerald and sapphire chips.

"We're passing over the Krītam now," Kles said. "That's what Bactrans call the old bazaar, but it actually means 'amusement' in the Old Tongue. The area is said to be even older than the citadel."

The Kushan Empire spanned a vast amount of territory as well as time so that Kushan and Sogdian, Persian and Chinese, Indian and Mongol citizens surged through the narrow lanes, competing with honking cars, elephants, camels, and donkeys. Even the trolls carrying sedan chairs had trouble making headway through the crowds.

Koko scratched his head. "How do folks keep from getting lost? I haven't seen one straight street yet." The roads kinked to the left and then to the right in what seemed like random patterns. And in some places the houses' upper stories thrust out over the street, hiding humans, creatures, and vehicles alike.

Kles shrugged. "There was never any real plan for the original city. It just grew. But you'll still find streets of shops dedicated to one craft. The silversmiths will be in one area, the cobblers in another." The griffin pointed a claw at a long, winding path of shops with shining silver plates and vases hanging over the doorways in place of signs. "There's the street of the silversmiths." Scirye thought she could almost hear the *tink-tink-tink* of the silversmiths' tiny hammers. "And look, over there, it's the street of the weavers." He indicated another narrow road where the shops had carpets with elaborate designs. It seemed that every guild occupied a street in the Old City.

The noise level too became as dense as the buildings and the traffic, the voices of humans and animals surging upward in a tide of sound so that Kles had to speak louder. The noise didn't diminish even as they passed over a district of large mansions, all of them in different styles. The homes with fluted marble columns reminded Scirye of Greece, while the blue-and-green-tiled buildings seemed to belong to Persia. There were red-lacquered Chinese houses with green tiles next to sandstone buildings with carvings of Indian jungles. All the many different groups that made up the Kushan Empire were represented here.

Kles rose on his hind legs, waving a forepaw ahead of them. "And there is the palace."

The palace occupied the citadel, a tall hill that formed part of the city's western wall on the right bank of the Bactra River. The palace's buildings spilled over the broad hilltop, resembling carvings of fine aged ivory and stood in contrast to the newer homes that had spread out from the left bank below.

For four thousand years, the rulers of Bactra had occupied the citadel—though twenty-two hundred years ago, Alexander the Great and the generals who succeeded him had rebuilt the buildings like the ones at home. And when the Kushans had taken over two centuries later, they had kept them intact, but the friezes on the front were of Kushan gods in a mixture not only of Kushan but Greek, Indian, and Persian costumes as well.

Suddenly gun ports flew open all along the steep slopes and the muzzles of cannons and machine guns swung up to aim at them. Scirye realized then that the palace was more than just the top of the hill: it was the hill. Over the centuries humans had hollowed out the hill just as Kles's clan had carved out the insides of their mountain. Emperor Kanishka XII's home was as much a fort as it was a palace.

Then large portals opened like the yawning mouths of giants, and a hundred war griffins swarmed into the air.

They swept skyward, directly toward them.

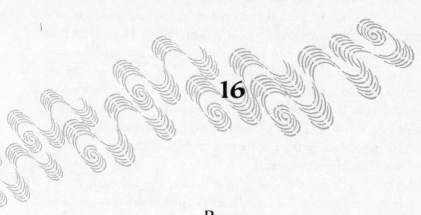

# 16

## Bayang

Captain Warpamo stiffened and he waved his paw tensely. "Skirmishers out." And a dozen riderless griffins shot downward to form a screen while thirty more riderless griffins separated into a roughly conical formation in front of the main party.

The bronze helmets of the human riders glittered in the sunlight. Their uniforms were a dazzling white with blood-red piping. The pennants of the riders' lances fluttered bravely in the wind.

Kles clacked his beak together angrily. "See the wolf insignia on their helmets? It's the the Wolf Guard, the personal regiment of the vizier."

"Is that bad?" Koko asked nervously.

"It's not good," Kles said. "The vizier leads the conservatives at court. They call themselves the Axe Bearers after the sacred symbols of the Kushans—though regular folk just call them the Choppers."

"Long ago, my lady's ancestors called themselves the People of the Moon, and it's said that Mao the Moon god gave the two-crescent-bladed axes to them to help them flee the Huns. The axes' glow led my lady's ancestors through the many dangers of that long trek and finally to safe pastures. Since then they've become a symbol of the imperial authority. If the Bearers had their way, they would turn the clock back eighteen centuries to what they insist were our glory days. But my lady's parents belong to the reform faction that wants to modernize the empire and forge new economic and cultural links to the outside world."

The vizier's guards hovered just beyond the skirmishers who were swirling around like angry bees. An officer with enough braid to be a hotel doorman hailed them. His bulbous nose reminded Bayang of a potato.

"We'll take charge of the prisoners now," he called. His long hair crept out from under his helmet and his black beard wagged when he spoke. His men were just as shaggy though their uniforms were all neat and tidy. The vizier and his supporters thought the long hair and beards made them look more like their revered ancestors.

"My Keeper has ordered me to deliver her guests to Princess Maimantstse, not to you." Captain Warpamo nodded to his companions and they began to descend toward the palace.

The vizier's guard hung in their path. "My Lord Vizier is also in charge of justice."

"Why would the vizier want us?" Leech asked Kles.

"It wouldn't be the first time he's trumped up charges to go after someone," Kles said.

Captain Warpamo continued to move downward. "As far as I'm concerned, I am simply escorting Lady Scirye and her friends home. They are not criminals so they do not come under your master's jurisdiction." At a nod, he and his escort began descending.

The dragon thought the two groups were going to collide in midair, but at the last moment the Wolf commander swerved aside. He circled about, watching in frustration as they passed and then barked out a sharp order.

The Wolf Guards below them began to descend at the same pace and appeared to be a white-uniformed wall.

As surreptitiously as she could, Bayang began to move her claws in a spell to increase her size a bit more, her lips barely moving as she spoke the ancient words. Almost immediately, she felt a searing pain where the ward was, as if someone had stabbed her with a dagger heated in flames.

The griffin mages had done their work too well and the ward held. She ground a paw against her leg. She was trapped in this size.

There would be no escape from the vizier.

## 17

### Scirye

A trumpet began sounding a fanfare, the notes trilling up and down excitingly. The vizier's men screened the musician from view, but Scirye saw how they looked at one another in confusion.

Captain Warpamo scowled. "What's going on?"

Suddenly, the Wolf Guardsmen beneath them frantically dodged to either side as a large white war griffin burst through their ranks. The griffin's feathered wings and shaggy winter hide made it seem more like an angry cloud than a creature. Upon his back was a rider in a leather riding outfit and helmet.

It took a moment to recognize Árkwi. Tall—nearly seventeen hands high—with a body that was powerful and yet still with some of the graceful lines of a racer, his dignity and wisdom made him the natural leader of all the imperial griffins—not just because he was the mount of the griffin master.

Scirye felt her heart skip when she saw the familiar features of the rider. "Is that father?" It was from him that she and Nishke had gotten their sharp noses and broad chins. She just hoped the features gave her the same air of strength that he had.

"It appears so." Kles folded his forelegs as a second rider followed close on the first. This griffin was jet black, the sunlight creating a sheen on its muscles. It could only be her mother's griffin, Kwele. "And that avenging angel would be Lady Sudarshane."

Scirye felt a lump in her throat. In trying to prevent the theft of the treasures, Badik the dragon had injured her as well as killing Nishke, Scirye's sister and her daughter. When Scirye had last seen her mother, she was lying injured on the museum floor. Had she done the right thing in leaving her there to chase after the dragon who had killed Nishke? "She ought to be in a hospital, not up here," Scirye said, feeling both worried and guilty.

The third rider wore a scarlet uniform with gold braid on the coat and stripes on the trousers. As he sounded the last notes of the fanfare, he banked to the side.

A plump woman rose at a more stately pace upon a tawny, golden griffin that looked as if a sun were melting. She was dressed in a quilted red and blue silk jacket and trousers and a tall, cylindrical furred cap from which a pheasant feather waved in the wind of her passage. Fixed to the front of the cap were the crossed axes of the empire.

"Ah, Captain Nanayor, how kind of the vizier to send an escort for my guests," she drawled lazily to the Wolf captain. "My dear brother, your emperor, and your master, the vizier, were worried about what to do with them, so I offered to take them into my custody until we can clear up this little misunderstanding."

Even if she hadn't seen the thick lips that was a mark of the imperial family, Scirye knew that the woman was Princess Maimantstse. Kles had served her before he had been sent as a tutor to Scirye. Next to her brother, Emperor Kanishka XII, and the vizier, she was the most powerful person in the empire.

"But—," Captain Nanayor began to protest.

"I'm afraid, though, that if you tried to land with us, you'd raise a frightful clamor and wake my brother from his nap. And we really can't have that." The princess fluttered her hand as if she were shooing away a pesky little puppy. "You are dismissed."

"But—," the Wolf captain tried to object a second time.

"Or do you think it's all right for you to disturb my brother?" Though her tone sounded gentle enough, there was a hint of steel beneath her words.

"Yes, I mean, no." Captain Nanayor circled nervously in the air as if he were having his griffin chase its own tail.

The princess smiled sweetly. "Then I suggest you stay right here and protect us from any menacing pigeons." A kick of her heels sent her griffin in a barrel roll that let it slip smoothly into position at the head of Scirye's group so she could lead them through their would-be captors.

The Wolf Guards didn't wait for a command from their captain but streamed out of the way, as if Scirye and her friends had suddenly developed the plague.

When the princess led Scirye and her friends past the dumbfounded guards, Scirye's parents and the trumpeter settled in at the rear.

Kles sprang into the air and did a loop of exultation. "You haven't lost your talent for tweaking the vizier's nose, your highness."

"Everyone should have a hobby." The princess held up a hand with a glove that covered her entire forearm so Kles could settle onto it. He took such obvious pleasure in her company and she in his that Scirye felt a twinge of jealousy. As if reading her thoughts, the princess looked over her shoulder at the girl. "Ah, and you must be Lady Scirye. I barely recognized you. Has Kles been behaving himself?"

"I couldn't live without him," Scirye blurted out. She couldn't keep the envy from her voice. "He's like my right arm."

The princess studied her, not without some kindness. Then,

waving her arm to dislodge Kles, she said regretfully, "Of course. He's indispensable. I didn't mean to deprive you of his company."

"I live to serve," Kles mumbled, but his head hung a little guiltily, like a man who'd been caught by his present girlfriend as he flirted with his previous one. And when he landed on Scirye's shoulder, he coiled immediately around her neck, draping himself over both shoulders as if to make up for the lapse.

"You rescued us just in time, Your Highness," Bayang said. "Thank you."

"My old friend, the Keeper, radioed me when you left, so I had my servants keep an eye out for you," the princess explained. "I thought the vizier might try something, so we got ready to fly, and when I saw his vultures take off, I knew I had to nip their mischief in the bud."

Scirye glanced with satisfaction at the vizier's guards milling about in a confused mass above them. Then she inclined her head toward the princess. "Your Highness, we really need to leave now to catch the true thieves." For Leech and Koko's sake, she used English rather than the New Tongue.

"We know all about Roland and Badik," the princess replied, switching to flawless English. "Your parents received a long telegram from Lady Miunai and they shared it with me."

Lady Miunai was the mother of their friend, Roxanna, whom they'd met when they'd chased Roland to the Arctic wastes.

"So you already know that it's urgent we reach the City of the Dead?" Scirye asked.

"That was the other thing I was debating with my brother and the vizier," the princess replied. "My brother agreed to dispatch troops."

"Then we can go home," Koko whooped.

"Roland and Badik still haven't been caught," Bayang said grimly. "Their airplane might be at the airport."

"I've already made inquiries and they're not there," the princess said. "They might have landed in some deserted area. But before we can deal with them, we need to get the charges against you dropped."

Leech bristled. "We're not thieves."

"You must be Lord Leech," the princess said. "I know you aren't." She smiled apologetically. "I'm afraid the vizier is trying to hurt me by hurting my friends."

"I could send him a rash," Māka suggested. "Just a teeny patch but in a very uncomfortable place."

The princess glanced at the sorceress. "That would hardly become a follower of the True Path, now would it."

Māka paled. "You know about me?"

"The Keeper warned me about you as well." The princess smiled.

As they descended, Scirye's other friends introduced themselves, though the princess already seemed to know a good deal about them as well. Between Lady Miunai and the Keeper, there didn't seem to be much that Princess Maimantstse did not know.

## 18

Scirye

They landed within a small courtyard of green and blue tiles that showed Salene the moon god in helmet and armor leading their ancestors, who once called themselves the People of the Moon, against their enemies, the Huns.

Graceful Greek columns stood at the front of Princess Maimantstse's palace, but the statues decorating it were a mixture of Greek, Kushan, and Indian deities.

As soon as Scirye climbed down from her griffin, she started to run toward her parents, but Kles fluttered in front of her. "Wait for the princess to give permission."

The princess waved her hand. "Of course you may."

"Thanks, Maimie," Lord Tsirauñe said, using the princess's affectionate nickname. "Welcome home!" And then he was engulfing Scirye in his strong arms and lifting her from the ground.

Hugging her father was like hugging a tree trunk, and she felt a momentary pride. The griffin master might be part of the court, but he was no soft courtier. Daily flying had kept him fit, though he flew not for the exercise but because it was as necessary to him as breathing.

When her father had set her back on her feet, Scirye put a solicitous hand on her mother's arm. "Are you all right, Mother?"

"That's what I asked her," her father grumbled as he stepped aside to let her mother have a turn.

Lady Sudarshane's hair fluttered beneath the edges of her leather flying cap as she embraced her daughter. "I'm not going to stay in a hospital like some porcelain doll when my daughter might be in danger." At the moment, she didn't seem like the poised, elegant diplomat that Scirye had always known but the hard-flying Pippal she had been before she had married.

Scirye searched her mother's face for some sign of pain, but even though there wasn't any, Scirye knew her mother had an iron will that could cover up any hurt.

"How did you get here?" Scirye asked.

"I flew home by plane," her mother said, "with Nishke."

Scirye thought of her brave, brilliant sister and felt as if there were a hole in her heart now that would leave her incomplete for the rest of her life. "I miss her so much."

"So do your father and I." Her mother caressed her cheek, comforting her daughter just as she had done when Scirye was small. "But at least we have you."

Guilt and grief rose up like a tide within Scirye. "I should have been at Nishke's funeral." She almost sobbed with remorse on the last word. "Or at the hospital with you."

Her mother squeezed her even tighter. "You were there in spirit."

Her father patted her on the shoulder as if soothing a yearling. "You were doing what Nishke would have done if she were alive—chasing after the thieves." Her father was a man of few words, more comfortable with his griffins than with humans, so this was a great compliment.

"If half of what Lady Miunai's telegram said about your adventures is true, you must have been terrified." Her mother tenderly brushed a strand of hair from Scirye's eyes.

"I was," Scirye admitted. When she saw the worry lines furrowing her parent's foreheads, she realized that while she had been feeling bad for neglecting her mother, Lady Sudarshane had been feeling the same about Scirye.

Clasping her mother's hand, Scirye tried to comfort her. "But I wasn't alone. And ... and I also saw such wonderful things." There were so many marvelous memories to share with her parents that the words came out in a rush. "I rode on a river of lava with Pele the goddess underneath the earth. And I wish I could show you the frozen sea up north with the winter moon shining on it. Or the dancers, oh, the dancers." She felt her heart ache at the very memory of the ribbons of light gliding to a tune only they could hear.

But there was only one part of her adventures that concerned her parents the most. "Lady Miunai wrote that you went into a coma after the goddess sent you a vision." Despite her best efforts, Lady Sudarshane's voice trembled slightly as she inspected Scirye for more signs of divine damage. "Are you feeling better now?"

Scirye felt her parents anxiety swell around her like a balloon, and she was sorry to upset them so much. "Yes."

Her father cleared his throat. "The Lady Miunai also said the goddess marked you with a sign of her favor."

Scirye pulled off her glove. "I guess you could call it that."

Her parents stared uncomfortably at the "3" glowing on their daughter's palm.

Lady Sudarshane cradled Scirye's marked hand as if it were a piece of delicate porcelain. "It looks like someone branded you. Does it hurt?" she asked, concerned.

Scirye slipped her hand away from her mother's and turned it over so the sign of the goddess's favor was hidden. "No, we think it's a clue. It might mean that Roland is looking for three arrows at the City of Death. We have to go there as soon as we can."

The princess had waited patiently while her parents had welcomed her, but she now interrupted. "First, though, we need to get these ridiculous charges dismissed. So, I'm sorry to break up your reunion, but I'm afraid I need to discuss strategy with your parents."

Scirye and her parents reluctantly broke their embrace. As she stepped away, Scirye bowed to the princess. "I'm sorry for all the trouble we're causing, Your Highness."

"I owe that much to a hero of the empire," the princess said and then turned to Kles's kinsmen. "We are grateful for all the aid you have given Lady Scirye. So let me offer you all the hospitality of the citadel after your long journey."

"Thank you, Your Highness," Captain Warpamo said with a stiff bow, "but with the lyaks roaming our lands, we need to get back."

They rose with great flaps of their wings that sent dead leaves and stray bits of snow swirling about. Árkwi and the imperial griffins accompanied them, separating from Kles's kinsmen after a hundred feet to bank away toward the imperial eyrie.

As they stood watching them disappear, a bearded, dark-skinned man in a quilted blue silk coat bowed low to the princess. "Your Highness," he said in the Old Tongue, "the rooms are being prepared for your guests just as you commanded, but the dragon's will take a bit longer."

Kles cleared his throat. "Please speak English as a courtesy to our friends."

The bearded man bowed to the lap griffin and answered in English. "As you command, Master Klestetstse."

His obvious respect was such a contrast to the attitude of his own clan that it was no wonder Kles preferred the citadel to the eyrie. Here his intelligence and learning gave him status in the human court, not his size and strength.

The princess smiled at Scirye and her friends. "This is my steward, Nanadhat. Just tell him what you need."

"Anything?" Koko squeaked with excitement.

"Don't drool on the floor, buster," said a badger dressed in a light green wool robe. "Someone has to mop it up, and that someone is usually little old Momo."

Wetting a paw, Koko hastily tried to slick down some tufts of fur. "Just how did a doll like you wind up here?"

"I was in a magic show." Lifting a paw grandly, Momo struck a pose. "I was Mademoiselle Fifi, the Girl with a Thousand Faces. But while we were in Bactra our scummy manager took a powder with all our dough. The show broke up and, times being what they were, I took a job here, and boy, was I glad of it. So what'll it be? Drinks? Snacks?" She sniffed the air and added disapprovingly, "Baths?"

"Momo"—Nanadhat frowned—"how many times do I have to tell you not to be so familiar with Her Highness's guests?"

"Aw, have a heart. I haven't seen another tanuki in a long time," Momo said. Tanuki was another term for badger.

The princess wrapped her arm protectively around the badger. "Let Momo be, Nanadhat. It's refreshing to have someone who gets to the point."

Momo grinned insolently at the steward and then tapped the charm that the griffin mages had placed on Koko. "Is this a price tag or what?"

Scirye took advantage of the princess's good mood. "Your Highness, are these anti-magic charms really necessary?" She indicated the paper charms on Bayang and Māka as well as Koko.

"No, of course not." The princess motioned to Nanadhat. "Send for the High Mage to remove them."

Scirye held out the stiletto the Kushan consul had given her to defend herself during Badik's raid on the museum in San Francisco. "Would you see that Prince Etre gets this back?"

As she took it, the princess smiled. "I'm sure he'll tell me to give it back to you, but it might be wise if you give me all your weapons."

Koko and Leech surrendered the throwing axes they had taken from the museum, giving them to a servant. But Leech said nothing about his armbands.

The princess raised her eyebrows when she saw the small throwing axes. Though the shafts were decorated with rubies and gold inlay, the blades themselves were of old steel. She knew them as precious antiques, but she said smoothly, "The Kushan Empire thanks you for returning their treasures."

Scirye wondered silently, *But will the vizier let the empire stay grateful?*

# 19

## Leech

 Leech watched Sciyre and her parents enviously. Abandoned as a baby, he had never experienced a family, only read about them. Was he a monster too like the Voice? Was that why no one loved him?

The Voice, however, was disgusted. *Look at the fool. She'll learn they don't mean it.*

*What makes you so suspicious?* Leech asked the Voice. *They love her.*

*There's no such thing as love,* the Voice said bitterly.

Leech, though, wanted desperately to believe there was nothing fake about what he was seeing. Koko was busy flirting with Momo so he turned to the dragon. "Was your family like Scirye's, Bayang?"

"Dragons express their love differently," Bayang explained. "They don't hug; they rub their necks against one another instead." Bayang's claw rasped as she scratched a scaly cheek. "But to be honest, I don't recall my life with my family very well. I was only a hatchling when I went away to train as a warrior. You, Scirye, Koko, and Kles have been more of a family to me than my blood kin. We've depended on one another when we were desperate, laughed at the good times, and shared what little food we had. To me, that's the definition of family."

So Bayang hadn't had much more family life than Leech. "Did you always want to be a warrior?"

Bayang's mouth twisted in a grimace, and as the boy listened with horror to all the suffering and death Badik's invasion had caused, he wanted to fling an arm about her neck to show his sympathy.

But the dragon was too proud to want a mere human's sympathy so he just stared at her as her mind wandered in another time and place. "After that, I made a vow to grow strong to defend my clan so it would never happen again.

"No wonder you want to kill Badik," Leech said.

*She's just trying to make you feel sorry for her so you'll let your guard down.* There was a childish, frightened tremor to the Voice.

Annoyed, Leech snapped at the Voice. *Stop being such a baby.*

*You're the baby,* the Voice shot back petulantly.

It was just the kind of interchange Leech had heard in the orphanage's nursery.

"Did I say something wrong?" Bayang asked. "Why are you frowning like that?"

"No, it's nothing you said. I was thinking of something else." Leech paused and added, "Just how old was Lee No Cha when he died?"

"Much younger than you." Bayang looked away guiltily. "But I had no part in that first death."

*Just in all the others,* the Voice complained.

So Lee No Cha had died at an early age and had stayed that way in all his lives. He had never been allowed to mature, to develop beyond a young child's fear of punishment.

Bayang's brow lowered as she scrutinized him. "Why this sudden curiosity about Lee? Once you heard about him, you were so horrified that you always avoided the subject."

*Now you've done it. She's sure I'm awake now!* the panicked Voice said.

"I just felt like knowing," Leech said with a shrug. Then, afraid he had said too much, he pivoted and went to watch a nymph pulling some vines away from a fountain basin.

## 20

### Scirye

A short while later a maid announced that the guests' rooms were ready. She was wearing a violet quilted jacket and green trousers.

Scirye's parents parted from her reluctantly, but they needed to confer with Princess Maimantstse on how to handle the charges against Scirye and her friends. So it was the steward, Nanadhat, who guided them into the east wing.

"And may I extend my personal thanks to you, lady, and your friends, for protecting Lady Roxanna," he said with a smile. "I, like all the House of Urak, am in your debt, and Princess Catisa wishes to thank you in person for saving her great-niece."

"You're Roxanna's kin?" Scirye asked politely.

"I am ____." He used a Sogdian kinship term that Scirye didn't recognize. "The House of Urak has its caravansary on the edge of the Krītam near the Eastern Gate. Just look for the sign with—"

"The two palms," Leech supplied.

Nanadhat dipped his head, pleased. "Just so, Lord Leech." He led them around a corner, indicating a room. "This is yours. And the badger may have the one next to you."

Koko jerked a claw at Leech. "I've been around this ugly mug so long that I couldn't get to sleep without hearing him snore. We'll take the same digs."

Leech tapped Koko's muzzle. "You're the one with the big schnozz. You sound like a trumpet."

"For that wisecrack, I get the bathtub first," Koko insisted. For all of his conniving ways, the badger was one of the most fastidious people Scirye had ever met.

Māka and Tute also elected to sleep in the same room, and it went without saying that Scirye and Kles would do the same.

Only Bayang would be alone, but the dragon could not wait to leave them. She had become as withdrawn and thoughtful as Leech, and Scirye wondered what was happening to her friends.

"Please let me know if you need anything else, lady." The steward gestured to the maid who had announced the rooms were ready. "Chin will be your maid during your stay."

Scirye smiled at her politely. "How do you do." Even as she turned toward her bedroom, Chin scurried around her and opened the door for her.

As Scirye stepped inside the spacious room, the tall latticed windows and high, elegantly arched ceiling made it seem as light and airy as a fairy palace. She suddenly felt out of place in her stained travel clothes.

"I think Koko had a very good idea, Chin," Scirye said. "I'd like a bath."

As the maid went into the bathroom to prepare the tub, Scirye took off the hag's belt and set it down on a table whose top was a chessboard with rows of ivory pieces standing ready for play. Maybe she'd challenge one of her parents to a game later.

As she began to take off her clothes, the maid gave a disapproving cough from the bathroom doorway. "Allow me to help, my lady."

Scirye was about to reply that she knew how to undress herself but hesitated when she saw the maid's disapproving frown. She was back at court now with all of its time-consuming protocols.

"Yes, thank you," Scirye said and felt like a doll as she stood with her arms held slightly out from her sides.

Chin's fingers twitched the moment she felt the grime on Scirye's fur jacket, but like a true professional, the maid hid any disgust she felt and drew off the garment and then the trousers and boots. The airport coveralls Scirye had worn underneath were even dirtier and smellier. Though the maid did not complain, she made her sentiments clear, though, when she asked, "Shall I burn them, my lady?"

Cheeks reddening, Scirye decided they were still the most practical clothes for her quest. "Try to get them as clean as you can. I'll need them as soon as we're freed." She almost giggled as the maid picked up the pile, because poor Chin was trying her best to hold her breath. For Chin's sake, Scirye hoped she did not have to carry them very far.

When Scirye entered the bathroom, she saw that there was a basin for Kles as well as a tub for her. The perfumed water had already filled the room with jasmine-scented steam.

Caution had made Scirye keep the otter and Pele's charms with her until she was safely alone with Kles. She hung the charms now on a peg meant for a bathrobe.

When she climbed into the tub, she luxuriated in the feel of hot water again. She stretched out her arms and legs, letting the bath ease away the aches that constant travel and battles had caused. As she floated in the warmth, Roland and magical arrows seemed faraway for the moment.

But then someone tapped at the door. "My lady, you have visitors," Chin said from the other side.

Scirye was about to tell the maid to send them away, but Kles asked, "Who is it?"

"The High Mage herself," Chin squeaked in a frightened voice as if she had already been changed into a mouse.

"We're not wearing any griffin charms," Scirye said to Kles. "What do you think the High Mage wants?"

Kles hopped out of the basin so fast that he nearly tipped it over. "I don't know, but the High Mage is one person you don't want to keep waiting." He began shaking himself like a dog and flapping his wings to get off the excess water.

Chin took that for permission to enter and while the griffin toweled himself dry, the maid fussed over Scirye, first with a towel and then a hairbrush, trying as gently as she could to get some of the tangles out, but without much success.

When Scirye had put the charms around her neck, she glanced at herself in a mirror. She looked more or less presentable now, but thank the goddess her parents had seen her bruises and cuts when they were half-healed or they might have taken a different attitude about her adventures, Tumarg or not.

In the bedroom, a robe of blue silk with red garnets about the collar lay across the bed while a pair of matching boots stood on the floor.

When she had dressed with Chin's help, the maid finally opened the bedroom door. "My lady will see you now."

Kles had brushed out his fur and feathers by now. "Better leave the talking to me."

Scirye was only too glad to follow Kles's suggestion when the High Mage entered the room with such small, mincing steps that she seemed to glide. She was a tall, stately woman, made even taller by the hat with the crown split into the twin spires of wisdom and foresight that added another yard to her height. Her robe was a dazzling white with small gold suns, moons, and stars forming intricate patterns as if she were a compact galaxy.

Behind her came a train of lesser mages as well as a freshly scrubbed Māka, still dressed in her tinkling robe. Tute padded after her, looking wary, but Māka seemed awed.

Kles fluttered into the air and gave one of his most elegant bows. "Your Wisdom, my lady apologizes for keeping you waiting. How may we help you?"

The High Mage turned her head, annoyed. "What is making that infernal racket?"

Tute simply gazed up at the High Mage insolently, but Māka bowed with a clinking of bracelets and chiming of bells. "I think it might be me, Your Wisdom."

The griffin waved a wing grandly at Māka and Tute. "This is Lady Māka, who also follows the True Path, and her companion, Tute."

The High Mage had a habit of tilting back her head so she seemed be looking down her nose at everything. She gave a skeptical sniff but was too polite to call Kles a liar. "Well, stand still, girl. I can't hear myself think with all the noise you make. And put your pet on a diet. No cat should be that fat."

Tute's ears flattened and his eyes narrowed. "I'm the right size for a lynx, and I'm no one's pet."

Māka immediately wrapped her arms around her friend to make sure he did not pounce on the High Mage. "Now, now, Tute. She's just concerned for your well-being."

Wanting to win some respect for their new friend, Scirye spoke up before the griffin could. "We would have failed in our quest if Māka and Tute hadn't come to our aid." She made a point of indicating them with her open palm so her visitors could see the goddess's mark glowing there, the reminder of Her favor.

It had the effect Scirye had hoped for. The High Mage cleared her throat. "Forgive me, Lady Māka. My devotion to the True Path occasionally causes me to neglect such things as courtesy."

Giving Scirye a warning glance to be quiet from now on, Kles smoothly asked, "How may we be of assistance, Your Wisdom?"

"We have heard of your many adventures and that my Lady Scirye has won a belt of strange magic unknown to us." The High Mage's eyes began searching the room until they fell on the belt lying across the chess table. "Yes! The spells are so crude, but they bubble with a raw energy." Excitement and greed sharpened her voice.

The High Mage's eyes devoured the belt the way Koko would have gobbled down a cake. She didn't realize that Scirye was wearing the otter and Pele's charms, and perhaps that was just as well. With a flutter of his wings, Kles half-turned so he could look back at Scirye.

At Scirye's nod, Kles said, "My lady took it as a prize after her victory over a monster named the Hag. But we haven't had time to study it. Would you be so kind as to examine it and then tell us its properties when you return it?"

"Of course." The High Mage floated across the room and scooped up the belt in both palms. She gave a curt nod to Scirye, a sniff to Māka, and then left with a swirl of robes, the other mages scurrying to keep up with her.

When Chin had closed the door, Scirye sank into a chair. "Thank the goddess they're gone. They make me nervous."

She started to reach for the remaining charms about her neck for reassurance, but Kles swept in close and set his paw on her wrist. "Better not," he whispered. "For all Chin knows, the things around your neck are personal souvenirs rather than magical objects."

Scirye glanced at the maid who was going into the bathroom to clean up. "She doesn't look like a spy," she murmured.

"You're at court now," Kles replied softly. "Everyone is a potential spy."

Māka put her fists on her hips. "How rude! I thought the High Mage would be a fount of wisdom, not some greedy old vulture."

Scirye and Kles exchanged nervous glances. "She thirsts for knowledge," Kles said.

And with Kles's warning about Chin fresh in her ears, Scirye asked, "Chin, would you bring us some tea and light refreshments?"

"At once, lady," Chin said. She dipped her head politely and then left Scirye's suite.

Kles fluttered to the door, peeking out through the keyhole to make sure she was gone. Then, returning to Scirye's shoulder, he cautioned, "We must be careful what we say at court, Lady Māka."

"She could have turned you into a toad," Tute said with a shudder, "or worse, she could have done that to me. And you know how I hate slime."

"But we are companions of a hero." Māka inclined her head respectfully to Scirye. "The High Mage would never harm us."

Scirye indicated a chair next to her. "I'm no hero. It's my friends who are brave. I was scared stiff the whole time. I just kept going because I didn't want to let them down."

"And yet you faced the danger instead of running away. So maybe that's what makes you a true hero," Māka said as she sat. "Your determination not to let your friends down provides a counterweight to your fear. There's a balance to everything: A beautiful soul inside makes up for an ugly face outside. A greater ability in one thing compensates for a flaw in another." She sighed wistfully. "Except in magic. It burns inside me, and I bungle every attempt to use it."

Scirye thought that Māka might be the one person among her friends who might understand what she herself was going through. "I feel like I'm botching things too," she admitted ruefully. "Roland's gotten away each time."

Māka sat back with the same look of concern she'd worn when she had saved them from the lake. If only the sorceress's magical skills could have matched her kindness. "So you have doubts too?"

"Just like you do." Scirye shrugged. "Or anyone else."

It was Māka's nature to want to help those around her. "I wish I could do more for you. All I can say is that I'll keep trying if you will."

"That's all any of us can do." Scirye held out her hand. "Shall we make a pact? As friends?"

"Friends?" Māka savored the word a moment and then solemnly pressed her hand against Scirye's. "I promise to try my best."

"And so do I," Scirye vowed.

She just hoped their combined efforts would be enough.

## 21

## Bayang

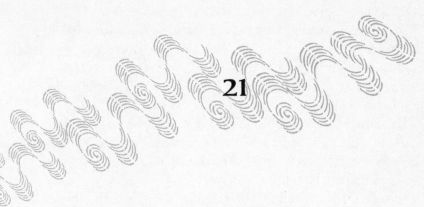

Dinner had been tailored to each of the friends' tastes and Bayang had made a meal of live squid and other marine creatures flown in at great expense and released into a huge glass bowl the size of a kettle drum, where the dragon could pluck them out one after another. Even the most human-hating dragon elder—and there were many of them on the council—could not object to the princess's treatment of Bayang.

Stuffed, the dragon had retired to her bedroom after dinner to think, dismissing the team of four maids who tended to her wants.

Despite the chancellor's accusations, or perhaps because of them, the princess had made a point of giving the dragon the largest chamber. Though the original human bed was large enough to accommodate a family of four, it was laughably small for Bayang in her preferred size. So a divan was knocked together quickly by the carpenters on her staff and then covered with silk cushions and quilts.

No, no one could doubt where the princess's sympathies lay, and Bayang was grateful to see such kindness and respect.

In the lamps dangling from the ceiling, the fire imps drowsed in a half-slumber, so they cast a dim light that was soothing for eyes used to the twilit regions of the ocean. There were even candles that gave off a rich bouquet of sea kelp and a hint of sea brine, making her feel at home.

She felt a twinge remembering she would probably never see her real home again. She had turned her back on her own clan because she believed they were wrong when they thought Leech was the reincarnation of a bloodthirsty monster.

Had she made a mistake? Had the killer been slumbering inside the boy after all? If Lee No Cha was awake, that would explain why sometimes Leech was so polished at flying and fighting and other times as clumsy as an amateur.

Badik and Roland were still the greater threat to her clan, and fighting them one more time might easily end in Bayang and Leech's deaths, but they had beaten long odds to get this far. Perhaps with the help of Scirye's goddess they might beat those odds again.

If that miracle happened, she would have to decide what to do about a newly awakened Lee. So far, he'd directed those murderous impulses against their enemies. But how long would it be before he turned his gaze upon Bayang and her kind?

She rested her muzzle upon her forepaws as she sprawled across the divan.

*What should I do?* Bayang puzzled. *I love him so I can't kill him, and yet I can't let a monster like Lee No Cha free to go on a rampage.*

Someone knocked at the door that moment and a cheery voice said, "Her Highness thought you might like some refreshment, my lady."

"Come in," Bayang called.

The door opened and Momo bustled in with a tray with a silver teapot and cup.

Bayang caught a whiff of an aroma that made her mouth water. "Kelp tea," she said in delight.

"Yep, boiled especially for you." Setting the tray down, Momo poured a cup and handed it to Bayang.

Bayang held it beneath her nostrils, savoring the rich smell. "I haven't had this since my last time at home." She again felt a small, quick pang of regret, but she shook it off.

The important thing was to enjoy moments like these and she sipped it appreciatively. "Wonderful," she sighed.

"I'll tell the chef you liked it." Momo grinned.

When the badger lingered, as if reluctant to leave, Bayang asked, "Yes? Is there something you want?"

The badger grew strangely shy. "I was just wondering if Koko liked anyone?"

Bayang almost said, *Only himself.* But she held her tongue. It might do the self-centered Koko some good if he could fall in love. "No, he has no serious attachments to anyone else."

The badger became her usual chatty self, asking more questions about Koko. And Bayang answered as best she could without shaving the truth too much.

But suddenly the room began to spin and the fire imps grew dimmer. "I feel . . . dizzy."

The cup fell from her paw with a clink on the floor.

As darkness closed over her, she heard Momo sigh. "Sorry, hon, but it's a wicked world out there and a girl's got to earn a living."

## 22

### Scirye

Scirye woke to the sounds of a city she had not heard in years, and though she had been born here, they seemed exotic. Yes, there was the rumble of trucks and cars as in San Francisco, but they mixed with the braying of donkeys and the protesting cries of camels and the trumpeting of elephants. Just a few feet away, she heard the cooing of doves nesting within the carved decorations on the walls. And from inside she heard the industrious servants' brooms whisking the hallways.

From the princess's kitchen came the mouthwatering aroma of bread baking fresh in the ovens mixing with the scent of incense burning in the princess's private shrine at first prayers, reminding her that the cooks and chaplains would have been up before dawn performing their duties.

She stretched within the coverlets, reveling in the sensation of silken sheets and a comfortable bed—as well as a clean nightdress. She had become so used to sleeping in her clothes on the flying wing with the straw tickling her cheek, or within the furs in a frozen igloo, that a normal bed now seemed strange.

So, despite the urgency, part of her welcomed the brief rest. After the days of stomach-twisting worry and fear, it was nice to leave the decisions to someone else for a while. Perhaps this is what they should have done from the first—assuming they could have gotten anyone to believe their charges against Roland.

Scirye twisted her head to find Kles. He'd already abandoned his silver perch for the windowsill, drinking in the sights of his beloved Bactra.

Some hardy songbird had endured the harsh winter night and had trilled a joyful hymn in praise of the sun. Kles listened for a moment and then lifted his beak from the glass panes of the wooden window frame carved in the shape of acanthus leaves and lotus flowers. With a flutter of wings, he tried to respond to the singer, but his singing sounded more like gargling.

Hiding her smile, Scirye rolled onto her back. Overhead, the ceiling had been painted with a scene of Oesho, the wind god, creating his beloved griffins from the clouds. Too bad he hadn't given them the gift of sweet music along with grace and strength and speed. But even if the griffin was off-key, she had rarely seen her friend so happy, and so she did not complain.

"Come in," she said. She had been expecting Chin, but it was her mother, dressed in a plain white robe over fawn-colored slacks. Her hair had been sensibly coiled and braided behind her head and she wore only lipstick. Her only jewelry was a traditional chain of small gold flowers and garnets that dangled from her hair. And yet an empress in gold robes and diamond tiara could not have looked more elegant or lovely.

Immediately Kles stopped singing as she entered. "We brought you some breakfast," she said and motioned for Scirye to get back in bed. "Let us spoil you this morning."

Her father followed her mother into the room in the bow-legged walk of a griffin rider, for good riders guided their mounts with the strength of their legs as well as their voice and the reins.

He'd given up his normal leather chaps and thick woolen shirt for a simple blue robe over brown trousers. But his old leather riding gloves had been thrust into his belt where they flapped as he moved. He might have looked like some stablehand dressed in his Sunday best except for the gold winged circlet of office around his head.

"How are you feeling?" he asked in his deep voice.

Scirye flopped her hands onto her lap. "It's wonderful to be home."

"It's good to be a family again," her father said.

Behind them came Chin with a lap tray that she set over Scirye's legs. It was heaped with slices of newly baked date rolls in the shape of flowers, fresh butter, her favorite jam, Sogdian plums, and basilisk eggs cooked just the way she liked them.

Her father stood with his thumbs hooked through his belt, but her mother sat on the bed, careful not to tip over the tray. "Let's enjoy your first day home. We thought we'd take you for a stroll and enjoy the morning."

"Am I allowed to leave Her Highness's palace?" Scirye asked, not wanting to get the princess or her parents into trouble.

"As long as you're with us," her mother said. "We already have permission."

Scirye knew what she would most like to see. "Then can we go to the imperial eyrie?"

Her father broke into a broad smile. "You haven't been there since you were a tiny thing. And bossy even then. You ordered the hands around so much they used to call you Little Duchess."

Scirye vaguely remembered the nickname as she spread her arms. "Then I order you to share my breakfast. There's more than enough for the four of us."

"Your wish is our command," her father said with a dignified bow.

As Scirye scooted over to make room, she pulled the tray into the middle of the bed so they could all sit around it. Since there was only goldware for one, they had to make do with their fingers. Even her mother, who could be quite fastidious about table manners, used her hands.

"We haven't eaten together for two years." Her mother buttered a flower-shaped roll and added jam before handing it to Scirye.

As Scirye ate it, she decided there was nothing as light and tasty as a sweet roll still warm from the oven.

"Not since my last visit to San Francisco. Right, Susu?" her father asked as he took a roll for himself. Susu was his pet name for her mother.

When they had finished breakfast, Scirye dressed in a sky blue wool robe with gold embroidery and lavender trousers and blue boots. It was strange to wear clean clothes again. And she stepped outside with a spring in her legs.

It was cold but sunny out. The wrinkles about her father's eyes crinkled. "It's the kind of morning when you could see for miles and miles on the steppes."

"I saw them when we were coming here," Scirye said. "It was just one big giant bowl of whipped cream with mounds and folds and all."

Her father nodded, glad to have something to share with his daughter. "Just so."

As they crossed the citadel, Scirye let the sunshine wash away the frightening memories and the even more terrifying prospects in the future. Below, the encircling city was busy with its own affairs. Here an elephant might be helping to lift roof beams up onto a warehouse being built. There, a car dodged around a string of camels. The smoke from kitchens rose like thousands of fine pale flowers from the rooftops of homes. But this high up, it seemed to have little to do with her. It was as if she were floating on a cloud.

After the uproar of yesterday, the citadel itself had lapsed into its usual routine. Lap griffins flew here and there, too busy with their errands to do more than nod to Kles. The sun flashed off the gold-inlay designs on their beaks, perhaps the latest fashion among their circle. Some of them were worse than peacocks with dyed fur and ostrich plumes to supplement their own feathers.

Channels intersected the citadel top in intricate geometric designs. In the summer, water chuckled through them to cool the hot air, but in the winter, they were unnecessary and lay dry as a platoon of fussy kobolds checked them for cracks and patched the chipped edges. But they stood up as one and bowed to them as Scirye and her parents passed.

A gnome, polishing a brass plaque on the pedestal of a granite statue of the Jade Lady, did the same thing.

Scirye dipped her head in acknowledgment to the gnome's courtesy and then gazed up at the Jade Lady's stern face. Yi's ring had been passed on through the centuries but the Jade Lady had been the last of its owners to be considered worthy.

"I'll get it back," Scirye murmured to the lady and added truthfully, "I hope."

Her mother set her hands on Scirye's shoulders and steered away. "We're supposed to enjoy the morning, not think about quests."

As they strolled on, Scirye was sorry that the water had been turned off in the fountains. Silvery naiads were busy scrubbing the basins with brushes and soap. And in the surrounding trees, dryads with green hair tied in ropelike braids stood upon ladders, shaping the branches. But both work crews also paused in their work to greet Scirye and her parents.

Scirye whispered to her mother, "I was so small when I left that I never noticed how much the citadel respects you and father."

Her mother took her arm and leaned her head in close to whisper, "Not us, darling. They're honoring you, my dear."

"Me?" Scirye asked, surprised.

On her shoulder, Kles puffed himself up. "And why not? Your exploits are worthy of a saga at least."

"Yes, I hear there are several poets already eagerly drafting epics already." Her mother playfully tugged a strand of hair. "With a little luck, they might even spell your name right."

Scirye was still digesting that fact as her father led them into an arbor. Thick, ancient grape vines entwined the lattice panels that formed the walls and roof. In the spring and summer, the grape leaves would provide a rustling green canopy and in autumn it would be a blaze of reds and oranges. But in winter, the leafless vines looked like twisted wire cables.

At the end of the arbor was a set of double doors that let light down a flight of steps to the first level of the eyrie.

The aroma of sweaty griffin mixed with their feed, hay, and leather, and Scirye realized why she had felt so at home at the Tarkär Eyrie. The odors there were the same as the imperial eyrie, the smell of her father when he came home from work, scents as familiar to her as her mother's perfume. She'd forgotten all about them, but her memories were awakening now and she felt as if she were three years old again—the age when she had left Bactra with her mother.

"Kles, will you do me the honor?" Her father had taken one of his leather gauntlets from his belt and pulled it on. He held out his left forearm now as a perch.

The little griffin hopped over onto it. Perhaps the large griffins teased the lap griffins here as much as they did at the Tarkär Eyrie. If that was the case, they would not dare mock a guest of the griffin master. And Scirye was grateful for her father's thoughtfulness.

She retained little memory of her life in the court, but she often dreamed about walking through the huge chambers where her father held sway. The stalls seemed so much smaller now. But, of course, she was much taller. Even so, the rooms were spacious enough for twenty griffins. Almost every place in the eyrie had some memory from her childhood. Until this moment, she hadn't realized just how much time she had spent here.

As at Kles's home, there were sleek, lithe sports griffins, hulking war griffins, and the hunting griffins whose bodies were larger than the first sort and smaller than the second. Grooms were busy brushing the tangles out of the griffins shaggy winter coats or trimming them or burnishing their claws. Still others bore buckets of food for their charges or rubbed lotion into the leathery pads of the griffins' paws, which had grown so hard they were in danger of cracking. Another group were either repairing or polishing the griffins' tack and gear.

Everywhere, they and their grooms bowed to her father—*and maybe to me too,* she thought with secret pleasure.

And as he sat proudly on her father's arm, there was no doubt in Kles's mind that the eyrie inhabitants were honoring his mistress—and himself too in her reflected glory.

The air grew chillier as they reached a doorway opening onto a wide ledge where a group of griffins circled in the sky.

Lord Tsirauñe gazed up with satisfaction. "Now that's the way humans were meant to fly, not in some metal box of an airplane. It takes centuries for Nature—"

"—to work out all the kinks," Lady Sudarshane finished for him and patted his arm indulgently.

A large white war griffin stood off to their right. It was Árkwi, her father's riding companion. Next to him was her mother's griffin, Kwele.

"No, no. Steady strokes," Árkwi shouted to a young brown griffin who was flapping his wings so frantically that he moved jerkily through the sky. He fluttered his own wings in illustration, creating a breeze that made Scirye's robe flap against her ankles. "You're not trying to put out a fire."

While Kles would always be her favorite and best of griffins, Árkwi would have been the handsomest.

"Look who came to visit," her mother said.

Árkwi sniffed the air. "I'd know that scent anywhere," he said and spun around. "Skee!" Skee had been Árkwi's pet name for Scirye.

When Scirye buried her face against Árkwi's massive chest, his smell seemed as familiar to her as hers had been to him. His huge paw covered a quarter of her back when he patted her. "I couldn't have been prouder of you than if you'd been my own hatchling." With his free paw, he gestured to a human groom who took a battered paper sack from his pocket and handed it to Árkwi.

Pinching the bag's top between his claws, the griffin presented it to Scirye. "There wasn't time for us to fetch it earlier. Here."

When Scirye took it, she shook out some lumps of jellied candy in the shape of stars and moons.

As Scirye stared at them blankly, her mother cleared her throat. "How sweet, Árkwi," she said, dropping a hint to her daughter. "You remembered Scirye's favorites."

Árkwi fluttered his wings pleased. "How could I forget?"

And Kwele laughed. "Scirye's cheeks were always bulging with them."

That had been so long ago. Scirye cautiously tasted one with the tip of her tongue. The flavor brought back a flood of memories and she popped it in. "Thank you."

Árkwi waved his paw. "Welcome home, Skee."

Kles's fur and feathers puffed out in irritation. "It is Lady Scirye." Was he jealous of Árkwi as she had been of the princess?

Árkwi blinked and regarded the little griffin. "Not to old friends."

"Even so," Kles argued, "nicknames aren't suitable for a hero of the empire."

Scirye reached over and stroked Kles's back as he stood upon her father's wrist. The little griffin's muscles felt very tense. He was a moment away from starting a brawl with a war griffin whose paw was as big as Kles himself. "It's all right, Kles. I don't mind if it's Árkwi."

"As you wish," Kles said stiffly, as his fur and feathers flattened again.

Árkwi nodded his head to Scirye. "Now if you'll excuse us, Skee, we have to see to the training of the new arrivals."

Though the griffin eyries sent only their elite to serve the emperor, none met Árkwi and Kwele's high standards.

"But when those foolish charges are dropped, perhaps we might go for a flight," Kwele added. Apparently, even the griffins of the eyrie kept track of the intrigues at court.

"I'd like that," Scirye said.

When they re-entered the imperial eyrie, her father took them off to the right, beaming as he pointed to a spot low down on a large wooden doorframe. "See that? That's the last notch I made before you left home." He slipped his knife from its sheath. "Stand against it so I can mark your height now."

Scirye smiled. "I'm too old for that."

The knife dangled in her father's hand as he gazed puzzled at Scirye. "Well, you may be taller, but that doesn't make you tall enough."

Her mother clasped Scirye's marked hand and held it tight. "I think what your father means is that you can go back to being yourself. You don't have to try to be a hero anymore."

"Yes, you're home safe now," her father said. "Leave this to older and wiser heads."

Scirye wanted to do just that, but she thought of her pact with Māka. She couldn't quit now. The mark on her hand felt hot, as if she were holding a warm cup of tea. "The goddess chose me. I can't stay. I made a vow."

Her mother caressed Scirye's cheek. "It was very rash, and you've been very lucky, my lare." Lare was "beloved" in the Old Tongue and only used for the special people in one's life.

"We may have been lucky," Scirye argued, "but we've also been very brave and very smart."

"I've already spoken with the goddess's priestesses and they release you from your vow," her mother said soothingly.

It would be so nice to stop the quest and let others take care of Roland and Badik. She thought of her conversation yesterday with Māka. If ever there was someone with less aptitude for magic, it was Māka—and yet she kept trying. With the world at stake, Scirye couldn't give up either.

"I wish it were that easy," Scirye said, trying to explain what she felt inside. "But this is between me and the goddess. Only She can release me."

"It's better not to meddle in heavenly matters." Her father frowned sternly. It was a look that made large war griffins bow their heads obediently. "We are not letting you kill yourself, young lady."

Her mother held up her free hand. "She's not one of your griffin hatchlings, dear."

Her father scratched behind his ear. "Yes, it's a lot easier to tell them what to do."

Kles rose from her father's wrist to land on Scirye's shoulder where he turned. "Lord Tsirauñe and Lady Sudarshane," he said, speaking for her as he so often did. "I know you would like to think Lady Scirye is still little so you can keep her from harm. But you cannot."

Scirye looked back and forth between her parents. They were treating her like a reckless child playing with matches, but she had fought monsters, escaped magical traps, and traveled vast distances. She was no longer small and helpless, and yet her parents were still treating her as if she were. They didn't want to accept that her adventures might have changed her.

Nor had they grasped an even more awkward truth: It was Scirye who was protecting them and not the other way around. And she would go on keeping them safe whether they wanted it or not.

She suddenly became aware of the gulf between her and her parents and it saddened her. Was this what growing up was like? And compared to battling Roland and Badik, it was silly to fight over measuring herself. Better to indulge her parents and enjoy what might be her last time with them.

"Yes, take my height for old time's sake," she said and set her back against the beam.

As her father scored the wood with his blade, Scirye felt guilty. The last thing Scirye wanted to do was to hurt her parents' feelings, but she knew she would have to leave.

And soon.

## 23

## Leech

Despite the luxurious beds, Leech had tossed and turned the whole night, wondering if Bayang knew about the Voice and what she would do. The strange thing was that he was more upset about losing her friendship than about losing his own life. After years in the orphanage and then the streets, he did not trust many people, so he treasured his few friends. Even when she had nagged him, he knew deep down that it was out of concern for him.

Leech was sitting by a window as the late-morning sun streamed through the glass while he tried to figure out what to do.

*You've got too big of a mouth,* the Voice whined. *Why did you have to make the dragon suspicious?*

For all of the Voice's skill at flying and fighting, Leech realized the Voice was still a young boy who let his feelings whipsaw him back and forth instead of controlling them. Could the Voice learn to master his fear and anger?

Who knew? Bayang had always cut that process short before that could happen in previous lives.

Leech tried to calm the hysterical Voice. *She promised not to kill me.*

*She gave that oath to you, not to me,* the Voice pouted. *She can claim the deal is off.*

Leech looked anxiously in the direction of Bayang's room. Just across the hall, the dragon would not have to go very far to hunt the Voice down. And yet even as that thought came to him, something else teased his mind just out of reach—something that lay beyond the obvious bond between Bayang and the Voice, the Hunter and the Hunted. But what?

He lost his train of thought when a miniature badger leaned against Leech's boot. "I'm going to get the hang of this if it kills me," he said in a tiny voice as he drew a paw across a furry brow.

Dozens more slumped against his feet, too exhausted to complain. He was actually ankle deep in little Kokos.

"Maybe you don't have the personality to change into a tiger," Leech hinted. The little badgers shimmered, merging together into a full-sized Koko.

"When you're in the main ring, you got to play it big." Koko threw himself onto a cushioned divan. "But this shape-shifting works up an appetite." Picking up a small bell from a nearby table, he rang it. When an Indian servant in a turban entered, the badger said grandly, "Jamir, bring me one of everything on the breakfast menu." He sniffed a foreleg. "And then maybe run another tub for me."

Jamir didn't blink an eye. "Sir, rose petals or jasmine blossoms?"

"Oh, what the heck. I deserve both," Koko said breezily.

When Leech caught a whiff of his friend, he fought back a sneeze. Koko had already taken so many perfumed baths that he reeked of scent. Cleanliness was even more important to the badger than his usual greed and gluttony, but Momo's comment about his aroma yesterday had driven him into a frenzy of soaping and scrubbing. "You're going to rub off your fur if you keep this up."

Koko brushed a foreleg. "Got to look good for dollface."

Since they had arrived, Momo was all that Koko talked about, which was making Leech feel a little jealous. But he quickly told himself to get over that. In all the time that Leech had been with Koko, he'd never met another badger until now. Perhaps Koko was lonely for his own kind.

In a little while, Jamir returned with a tray heaped with food, and after serving them, went into the bathroom to prepare a bath for Koko.

Leech watched Koko wolf down slices of roast lamb, lamb in a piece of flat bread, and then lamb covered in pomegranate sauce. "Slow down, will you? What's Momo going to say when you blimp out?"

Koko sucked the sauce from his claw tips. "She'll tell you that a badger's belly is his glory."

Careful not to get jabbed by Koko's fork, Leech took a hard-boiled egg. "Any more glory and it's going to take two griffins to carry you."

A gong began booming through the citadel. The very rock beneath his feet seemed to vibrate. Voices began to shout outside.

Hurrying to the door, Leech stepped outside. A male servant was running down the hallway, his sandals slapping the floor. He was in an Indian robe but the material was a green, yellow, and black plaid. "You'll come with me to your quarters."

Leech managed to snare the man's arm as he tried to pass. "What's going on?"

The man blinked as if he'd been so preoccupied that he hadn't noticed the boy. He babbled something in Kushan.

Leech looked around until he found Jamir had come to the bedroom doorway. Their servant looked as panicked as the man in Leech's grip.

"The axes," Jamir translated shrilly, "the axes are gone."

Leech blinked. "Axes? You mean the ones we took from the museum?"

"Sir, the sacred double axes never leave here. Anything you had were simply imitations of them," Jamir said. When Leech still looked blank, the servant struggled to explain. "The sacred axes are symbols of the empire. It . . . it is like kidnapping His Imperial Highness himself."

*Well,* Leech thought with relief, *I know Koko didn't take them.* The boy had been up all night listening to the badger snoring. *From all the uproar inside and outside the palace, someone was in big trouble. And for once, it isn't us.*

The servant Leech was holding gave the boy an exasperated push and started to run on even as the boy fell against one of Bayang's double doors.

The door flew open under his weight and he fell onto the floor of Bayang's room. That set off four maids crying out in surprise.

Embarrassed, Leech scrambled to his feet and looked about for his friend. "Bayang?" he asked.

One of them replied in accented English. "She is not here." The maid gestured to the bed. "That was cold when we came in this morning. Maybe she not even sleep here."

Leech had a bad feeling about this. Where was Bayang?

# 24

## Scirye

Scirye sat with the other companions in her room late that afternoon.

Koko folded his forelegs. "So where do you think that overgrown lizard's gone?"

Leech said nothing but sat with the distracted look that he so often had now, instinctively playing with his armbands.

"And what a coincidence that the sacred axes are missing at the same time." Tute stretched lazily. "How well do you really know Bayang?"

Scirye glanced at Leech for help defending their companion, but he was still lost in thought. She felt guilty for not asking him what was bothering him. What kind of friend was she? "Leech, are you all right?"

He seemed to come out of a dream. "Yes, what?"

Scirye frowned. "Tute was wondering if we could trust Bayang. Weren't you listening?"

Leech toyed with his armbands nervously. "Sorry. I was worried about Bayang." He turned to Tute. "We'd never have gotten this far without Bayang. She's saved our lives time and again."

Tute's claws ripped the expensive Persian carpet in frustration. "Maybe she was just keeping you alive so she could get into the palace."

"Have you got mange on the brain?" Koko snapped. "You've only been with us a couple of days so you don't know her like we do. She may be a grouch, but she's no thief."

The badger had voiced Scirye's own thoughts, though she wouldn't have put them in those exact words.

"Besides," Koko added, "if anyone was going to steal something and then take a powder, I would have said it was going to be me, not the big green lizard."

The lynx sat on his haunches. "Yes, I would have thought that too."

The badger glanced at him sideways. "You didn't have to agree with me so fast."

Māka tried to distract Tute by scratching him behind the ear. "The Lady Scirye is the chosen one. If she vouches for Bayang, then I trust her judgment."

But Tute twisted away from her hand. "Don't be so naïve, Māka. We just met them. We don't really know how loyal the dragon is."

Māka had begun to alternate squeezing a rubber ball in either hand. Scirye supposed that was to develop strength for her magic tricks. "Tute, if you say one more bad word about Lady Scirye's friend, you and I . . . we will no longer be partners."

Tute's ears stood up in shock. "You'd pick her over me? But I've got our best interests at heart."

"And the Lady Scirye has the world's," Māka replied firmly.

"That's the thanks I get for all I've done for you," the lynx grumbled but he fell silent.

Scirye didn't want their pact to break up Māka's friendship with Tute. "Māka, you really don't have to—," she said uncomfortably.

The sorceress turned to Scirye. "But I do," she said with such absolute faith in their quest that Scirye squirmed. "You are going to save the world."

*I just wish I could be as certain,* Scirye thought to herself.

# 25

## Leech

Leech was only half aware of the others as he argued with the Voice. He was tired of the tedious job, but he knew he had to convince the Voice of Bayang's innocence before the young brat that was the Voice panicked.

*She's left us holding the bag,* the Voice muttered. *When are you going to face the truth about her?*

*When are you?* Leech shot back. *She's my—our friend. She would never do that.*

Even though it was dangerous for Bayang to know about the Voice, Leech missed her. It amazed him how much his life was already entwined with that of the dragon's. Yes, she could be a nag and a worrywart, but her scoldings had been no worse than the orphanage matron's, and at least the dragon spoke the way she did out of concern rather than the matron's mean-spiritness. And Bayang took a great deal of responsibility upon her broad shoulders so it was unlike her just to run off, let alone steal a sacred treasure.

Suddenly there were angry voices in the hallway outside.

"Chin," Scirye said to the maid who had been kneeling on a cushion in the corner, "please see what that's all about."

Rising, the maid went to the door and opened it to reveal Nanadhat spread-eagled across the doorway, trying to make a barricade with his body. "You cannot enter the princess's palace without Her permission," he protested.

He tumbled onto the rug when Captain Nanayor shoved him. "His Imperial Highness has ordered that the vizier take custody of the dragon's accomplices in the theft of the sacred axes."

Scirye got off her bed and drew herself up, looking every inch the haughty noble lady rather than the girl who was Leech's friend. "Nanadhat, send word to the princess."

Nanadhat got up off the floor with Chin's help. "I already have, lady."

Scirye glared at the captain as he marched into the room with two Wolf Guards. "If we were accomplices in the theft, why didn't we leave with Bayang?"

"I'm no criminal mastermind, but maybe it was to scout out more treasures." Captain Nanayor pulled a machine pistol from the holster on his belt and made a point of clicking off the safety. His two guards did the same with their guns. "All I know is that you are now mine."

Nanadhat was outraged. "How dare you threaten her ladyship this way!"

Captain Nanayor ignored the steward when he saw Leech's hand on the flying discs. He motioned to the guardsmen, who immediately aimed their machine pistols at Leech. "I was warned those things let you fly. Put your hands up," he barked. He looked around the room. "All of you. Hands in the air. Your friend proved that we can't trust you. You're the vizier's now, not the princess's spoiled pets." He aimed a kick at Tute who sprang away with a hiss. "You barbarians will come with me."

"But I can't leave," Koko wailed in dismay. "I scheduled a massage for three."

"Pampering's over, beast," the captain sneered.

Māka had wrapped her arms around the growling Tute, but she stood up and obeyed. "Is it really necessary to bully us?"

The captain pointed his pistol at her. "This says I can do what I like. And next we're confiscating all magical items." He nodded to his guards. "Search them."

Tute crouched, ears low against his head as if he was ready to spring on anyone who dared to touch Māka. But it was Kles who went mad, launching himself from Scirye's shoulder before she could catch him.

"I won't let you lay a finger upon a lady of the House of Rapaññe," the griffin protested as he flew straight at the captain.

As the captain swung his hand at the griffin, Leech waited for the nimble creature to dodge, but he simply hovered, presenting an easy target for the backhanded blow that sent him flying.

*Crash!*

The small chess table overturned, spilling pieces everywhere.

"Kles!" Scirye ran to the prone griffin and, dropping to her knees, scooped him up into her arms. The griffin rolled over, shaking his head groggily, too dazed to answer. Scirye felt his limbs and body until she was satisfied nothing was broken. Then she narrowed her eyes as she glared at the captain. "You'll pay for striking my retainer."

*Crack!*

A bullet tore through the rug into the floor just before her. "Your title means nothing now. And when the vizier's done, your father will be stripped of his titles just like the princess."

Scirye held up her palm. The goddess's mark was burning an angry red. "We are engaged on a sacred quest."

The captain paused at the sight. Then he swallowed and said, "The vizier said you would try to fool us with that simple conjurer's trick."

Nanadhat cleared his throat. "If someone must search the ladies, let a maid do it," he suggested, heading off a deadly battle.
"Your master would tell you to show that much courtesy."

"Oh, very well," the captain said reluctantly and motioned to
Chin. "Go on," the captain said and indicated Māka with his gun.
"Start with her."

Chin approached Māka cautiously, making sure to keep the sorceress between her and the snarling lynx.

"It's all right," Māka said soothingly to her friend. "You're always saying I'm not much of a magician."

"But it's the principle of the thing," Tute grumbled, but he simply watched as Chin slipped the grimoire from Māka's sleeve and
then removed the belt with the star charms and the necklace with
the signs of the zodiac—and even the rubber ball Māka used for
strengthening her fingers. They made quite a respectable little pile
when the maid was done.

The captain wagged his gun at her wrists. "The bracelets too."

"They're just decorative," the sorceress said as she added them
to the pile at her feet.

Despite everything, even the Voice was impressed. *I didn't
think she looked strong enough to carry that kind of load.*

Next, the maid said something in Kushan that sounded like an
apology, and Scirye shrugged, submitting to the undignified hunt.
With a contrite bob of her head, the maid removed Pele's charm as
well as the pouch with the otter figure, which the captain immediately claimed.

"The animals too," the captain said to his guards. He purposely
held his pistol on Māka while a guard cautiously searched Tute
who growled and spat all the while.

The guard looked surprised when he felt Koko's fur.

"Heh, heh, how did that get in there?" Koko laughed nervously.

The guard pulled out a silver spoon. "Where do you keep it?"

Koko shrugged. "It's a tanuki secret."

Two silver forks, a knife, and even a small spatula were added to the pile along with Koko's charm from Pele.

"If I didn't believe you were thieves before, I would now," the captain gloated.

"Nice going," Tute snapped at the badger.

"What's wrong with a few souvenirs?" Koko said unrepentantly.

During all this, Kles had barely stirred as Scirye cradled the fragile body tight against her. She held out his limp body so Chin could probe the griffin's fur and feathers, finding only Pele's charm, which she took.

When he had put all the confiscated items into a sack slung over his shoulder, the captain turned at last to Leech. "And now we'll have those armbands of yours."

*You can't let this scum take them,* the Voice protested.

Even if his armbands weren't their last hope, he wasn't about to give them up. "You can have the charm for warmth," Leech pleaded, "but the armbands are all I have of my parents."

The captain aimed his pistol at Leech's forehead. "I'm tired of these games, boy. Lady Scirye is of noble blood, but you are simply gutter trash. It will be even easier to take the armbands from your corpse."

*Fight! Fight!* the Voice shrieked. The words pounded in his head so that Leech could barely think. He began to reach for the weapon armband.

"Don't shoot! Let me talk to him." Koko threw himself at the captain's arm, pulling it down so that a second bullet went into the floor.

The badger wasn't nearly as nimble as Tute. The captain's gauntleted hand caught him full across the muzzle.

Koko was as much upset at losing his hard-won privileges as his loot, so that the blow was the last straw. The badger, normally cautious to the point of cowardice, lunged forward. "They haven't built a hoosegow that can hold me." With a snarl, he bit the captain's wrist.

"Koko, let go," Scirye said.

His mouth full of Nanayor, Koko mumbled an indistinguishable reply but his tone was defiant.

Leech couldn't be sure if it was him or the Voice that took advantage of the distraction and began the spell to change the armband into a weapon. All he knew was this overwhelming desire to smash their enemies.

But one Wolf Guard had the presence of mind to put his gun against Scirye's head. "Stop whatever you're doing, or I'll kill her."

Scirye's spirit was as bold as ever even if her voice shook with fear. "Fight them, Leech," she urged. "Don't lose the armbands."

Leech struggled with the blind rage, the hate. It wasn't just these petty tyrants, but everyone who had ever bullied him. The toughs in San Francisco's streets. The bigger kids in the orphanage. The dragons . . . Was that him or the Voice?

But Scirye's life was at stake.

The spell died on his lips. His hand grew still, no longer making the magical passes. Instead, he forced his hands to take off the armbands and handed them over with Pele's charm.

As the captain added them to the sack, the Voice shrieked, *No, no.*

*We have to for Scirye's sake,* Leech replied and was relieved when the guard let his friend go.

"*Ptoo.*" Koko spat out the scrap of uniform that he had torn from the captain's sleeve. "You taste lousy anyway." He jeered at the man. "Time for your annual bath, stinky."

Despite the strong grip of his jaws, Koko's fangs hadn't been long or sharp enough to make more than two small puncture marks in the captain's wrist. But the sight of the twin drops of blood incensed the leader of the guards. "I'll show you how we deal with a wild beast."

# 26

## Scirye

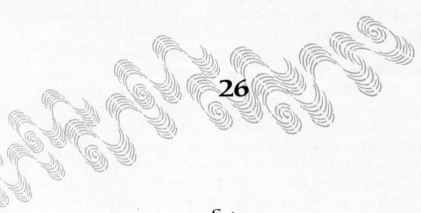

Captain Nanayor had no more than swung his pistol halfway toward Koko when Scirye flung herself forward, bumping the captain so that he staggered backward into the arms of his men.

"Enough!" Lord Tsirauñe thundered from the doorway. He looked worried at Scirye who had fallen to the floor. "Are you all right?" When she nodded, he said, "If you resist, you'll give them an excuse to really hurt you."

Lady Sudarshane helped her daughter to her feet. "Yes, don't make any more trouble, dear. We'll clear up the misunderstanding so just leave it to us."

"This isn't a 'misunderstanding,'" Leech protested. "It's a frame job."

Koko spat as if still trying to cleanse his mouth of the captain's taste. "Yeah, the fix is in." Sticking out a tongue, he swabbed it vigorously with a paw as if trying to wipe away any taste of the officer.

"Her Highness has already gone to object to the emperor. You won't be in the vizier's hands for long." Lady Sudarshane held out her hand. "So, Scirye, please return what you took from the captain?"

Confused and annoyed, Captain Nanayor began to search the sack. "What . . . ?"

"My daughter is prone to playing pranks," Lady Sudarshane explained, "and has developed a pickpocket's skills as a result."

Scirye looked at her mother, shocked by the betrayal. "While we're twiddling our thumbs here, Bayang could be killed."

"And Roland could be getting the arrows," Māka added.

"Please, do what your mother says," her father coaxed.

Scirye might have argued with her mother, but it was hard to refuse her father.

Reluctantly, Scirye handed the pouch with the otter charm to her mother. "Don't you believe us about the danger?"

"Of course, we do," Lady Sudarshane assured her as she gave the pouch to the captain. "That's why you have to leave it in our hands."

Scirye saw the glance that her parents exchanged. They were thinking, *Whatever happens to the dragon, at least our daughter will be safe.*

"It's . . . it's not Tumarg," Scirye said, upset by the injustice.

Her mother spoke in a conciliatory voice. "I know, but sometimes politics holds sway at the citadel rather than Tumarg."

Scirye was shocked. "But you always said—."

"You're old enough now to face facts," her mother said firmly.

"But not old enough for you to believe my warnings," Scirye said bitterly.

Her mother spread her hands. "Her Highness is already working on getting you back into her custody. Don't do anything to upset the negotiations."

"Trust us," her father said simply. "We'll make sure you're safe. I wouldn't let anything bad happen to our lare."

Scirye looked down at Kles who always gave her such good

advice. She felt so frustrated and helpless as he stared back at her silently. The sight of her dazed friend helped firm up her own resolve.

If her parents, blinded by their love for her, would not keep Tumarg, she would. She would escape with her friends at the first opportunity, find Bayang, and then stop Roland herself. And if that meant upsetting things at court and defying her parents, so be it.

When the captain ordered them from the room, she walked with her friends, refusing to look at her mother and father.

"Don't worry," her mother called after her. "We won't rest until we have our lare back with us."

Scirye knew that would be true, but she also knew that it was the City of Death and not the citadel that lay in her future from now on.

## 27

Scirye

The front of the vizier's palace was decorated with murals of scenes from the life of Hercules—of the Greek demi-god wrestling with the Nemean lion, and then of him newly clothed in the lion's pelt as he clubbed a hydra to death in its swampy home, and other inspiring scenes.

The foyer of the vizier's palace was tiled with cool blue and green tiles in a rectangle and star pattern. Servants were industriously sweeping at the base of a five-foot-high statue of a plump, bearded, long-haired man in a Hercules-like lion pelt pointing his club symbolically at the the future, but what in reality was the cloakroom.

"Whoa," Koko said, gazing up in lust and awe at the statue. "Is that eighteen karat or just gold leaf?"

"Show more respect for the vizier." A guard used the pistol barrel to strike Koko in the back.

The badger gave a grunt as he lurched forward. He would have fallen if Leech hadn't caught him, which brought him a blow of his own.

"Keep apart," the same guard snapped.

Koko scowled at him. "Do you get paid by the hour or by the bruise?"

"This is just a perk, beast." The guard sneered and hit Koko again.

Koko retreated out of reach before he jeered, "Your boss looks like a pawnbroker with a bellyache."

"Lady Scirye?" one of the servants asked. Like many of the Kushans, the red-headed woman was a blend of races, with dark skin and violet eyes but with the Asian fold at the corner of her eyes.

"Katkauñe?" Scirye gasped. She had been her sister's friend and one of the elite female guards called the Pippalanta by the empire and Amazons by the American newspapers. But when Scirye had last seen her at the museum in San Francisco, she'd been in an antique costume of armor and helmet, not in a servant's coarse brown wool robe and trousers. Even so, the garments couldn't hide her warrior's bearing.

"We heard you were alive," said a small woman with black hair and dark skin. Scirye remembered her name was Wali.

Scirye stared at them puzzled. "What're you doing cleaning the floor, Wali?"

The third Pippal was blond Oko, who had a barrel-shaped body and could lift a yearling war griffin. "This is our punishment for letting the treasure be stolen," she explained bitterly. "We've been given every lousy job in the citadel."

"But it wasn't your fault, Oko," Scirye protested.

"No more than you're a thief and a vandal," Katkauñe said. "And what are you doing here? You're supposed to be with Princess Maimie." That was what most folk fondly called the princess.

The captain shoved the pistol barrel into Scirye's back. "Get moving."

Oko took a step forward. "How dare you touch a hero of the empire."

"Get back to work, scum." The captain aimed his machine pistol at the Pippalanta.

The woman froze, glaring as the captain prodded his captives down a corridor into a private shrine. But the altar and the statue of Oesho with the club and lion pelt of Hercules had been moved aside. From the doorway below came warm, moist, stagnant air.

Every inch the daughter of the House of Rapañ̃e, Scirye turned to the captain. "What are we going to do in the shrine?"

"My lady, you do not get to ask the questions. I do," said a brawny man in a leather vest as he rose from a chair in a corner and strolled toward them.

Māka whipped around, her eyes wide with terror. "Run, lady, run!" she said to Scirye before the captain cuffed her hard enough to send her to her knees. With a snarl, Tute crouched, only to confront a gun muzzle pointed straight at his forehead.

When Scirye put her arms around her friend, she felt how the other girl was shivering. "The screams. They swirl around him like flies. And the blood. He's covered in blood," Māka murmured in a daze as Scirye helped her to her feet again. Worried, Tute rose clumsily on his hind legs on Māka's other side to support her as well.

Captain Nanayor sneered. "He should. He's the Questioner."

Koko looked at him skeptically. "He runs a quiz show?"

"He tortures people," Māka said in a small, frightened voice.

The Questioner seemed to swell even larger when he saw her fear. "I call it gathering information. I've had to ply my trade in makeshift rooms for the vizier, but he has decided to re-open the Chamber of Truth in your honor."

"The Chamber of Truth was declared illegal and shut down forty years ago," Scirye protested. Though she didn't know much Kushan history, that had been a major triumph for the reformers.

"The Chamber of Truth?" Koko asked.

Scirye stared at the Questioner angrily. "That's where viziers in the past tortured prisoners."

"Rather, the vizier has revived a fine old tradition and re-opened the place where I may pierce the veil of falsehood and deceit," the Questioner said.

Suddenly Scirye realized how wrong her parents had been. They'd been so confident of their place in court and the power of the princess that they had misread the situation completely. It had been a mistake to trust them to fix everything as if she were still three years old and their predicament was simply some broken toy.

"The vizier wants us to sign confessions that we helped Bayang," Scirye replied as she analyzed the situation, "and once we've done that, you'll kill us and claim that we escaped somewhere."

The Questioner regarded Scirye approvingly. "Fear brings such clarity and enlightenment sometimes."

"Everyone will know the confessions are false," Leech insisted.

"The vizier must be confident that he'll soon be so strong no one will challenge them," Scirye explained, suddenly feeling cold.

"Let me show you to your new accommodations, lady." Captain Nanayor prodded Scirye forward.

Silently, Kles flapped out of her arms and spread his wings like a small avenging angel.

As one of the guards pointed his machine pistol at the griffin, Scirye snapped. "Klestetstse, to me!"

Kles faltered in midair at the command and Scirye swept him back up in her arms, holding him tight and whispering to him, "As long as we're still alive, there's still hope."

But she felt precious little of that as she marched through the dark doorway.

# 28

## Leech

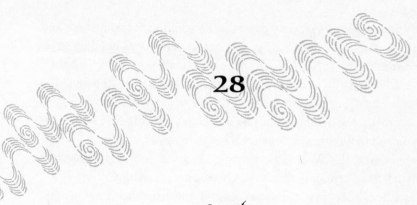

He had thought the orphanage had been a grim place, but it was nothing compared to the lower level of the vizier's palace. The passage was lit by fire imps of the lowest class. Barely larger than a match flame, they squatted dully within the iron lanterns, casting a dim, guttering light.

Water seeped through the cracks of the stones of the walls, dripping down through the patches of moss that looked like fuzzy green pancakes. Their footsteps echoed sibilantly on the dull flagstones as if a host of snakes were at their heels.

Tute was trying his best to support the faint Māka, but it was awkward for the lynx to move on just his hind legs. They would have both stumbled and fallen if Scirye hadn't held them both up.

The corridor turned at right angles and when they rounded the corner, Leech saw the iron door. As the Questioner took out a ring of keys, a woman behind them called out something in Kushan.

It was Katkauñe with Oko and Wali, and looking far more

dangerous with their brooms than the Wolf Guards did with their guns.

One of the Wolf Guards snarled something back at them and began to raise his machine pistol, but Katkauñe was quicker, striking the guard with the broom handle as she cried, *"Tabiti! Tabiti!"*

Kles had told Leech more about Lady Tabiti, also known as the Jade Lady. She had once led a nation of warriors and it was to her that a Kushan emperor had entrusted Yi's ring. She was so respected that Amazons now used her name as a war cry.

Even as the Wolf Guard dropped to the floor, Katkauñe had twirled the broom and sent the Questioner sprawling.

Captain Nanayor shouted angrily and began to draw his gun while the remaining guard jerked his machine pistol up to aim. Immediately Oko's broom handle shot out. There was a sharp crack of the captain's wrist bones breaking and his gun clattered on the floor. Wali used her broom to knock the pistol out of the second guard's hands, but not before he fired. The noise sounded like a cannon had exploded as the bullet ricocheted off the stones.

Then, with two almost simultaneous thrusts to the stomachs, the Amazons knocked the two Wolf Guards to their knees.

Throwing away her broom, Katkauñe snatched up the guard captain's pistol and aimed it at its former owner.

"Katkauñe, don't kill him," Scirye commanded. She swung her gaze to the quivering Questioner. "But feel free to shoot this fat worm if he doesn't tell us where Bayang is."

Apparently, the Questioner preferred to threaten rather than be threatened, and he began to blubber, "Don't hurt me. She's at the vizier's summer villa."

"You're going to repeat that to Princess Maimie." The red-headed Amazon spoke English with a thick accent.

From behind them in the corridor came the clatter of numerous boots. "Who fired that shot?" a man shouted to them.

The captain took advantage of the distraction to scramble to his feet. "The prisoners are loose!" And he bolted for his approaching comrades, the sack bouncing against his hip.

"He's got my armbands," Leech said as he started after him.

"You're blocking my shot," Katkauñe said.

Leech hadn't gone more than three steps before Tute darted in front of him. It was like tripping over a mobile hassock and the boy sprawled face forward. The next moment the lynx had pounced on his back. "You're running straight to the enemy and presenting them with a hostage."

"Well, my original plan was to make the Questioner testify to the princess, but that's not going to work." Katkauñe rubbed the back of her neck sheepishly. "No one ever said I was ever officer material."

"Yes, we always left the thinking to Nishke." Wali chuckled as she picked up one of the pistols.

Oko had gotten the third pistol. It looked much more natural in her hands than a broom. "So what do we do now?"

"We can't go back because of the guards." Scirye bit her lip. "So we'll have to go forward."

Even the battle-hardened Amazons hesitated. "Go into the Chamber of Truth?" Oko asked wide-eyed.

Scirye shrugged. "I don't like it anymore than you do, but Nishke used to say that when you have only one choice, you take it—no matter how awful it is." She nodded above them. "If the citadel's like any embassy I've lived in, gossip will spread like lightning. I'm sure the vizier's servants will spread the news to the servants of the other palaces. Eventually, the princess will come for us. We just have to hold them off until then." She rapped a knuckle on the iron door. "So wouldn't you rather have this between them and us?"

"See?" Katkauñe nudged Oko. "We've got Lady Scirye to figure things out for us now." Then she said to Scirye, "And please, my friends call me Kat, and I hope you'll consider yourself one of them."

"Then please call me Scirye," the Kushan girl said and, knowing the etiquette that the court demanded on formal occasions, "at least when it's informal like this." When she tried the door, though, it was locked. "Get his keys," she said, pointing at the Questioner.

Wali yanked the ring of keys from his belt. "There must be fifty of these things."

Booted feet were pounding rapidly toward them now. It would be a death trap to be caught between the locked door and the defenders.

"Then start trying them," Kat urged. "Maybe we'll get lucky and find the key right away."

Suddenly Kles's body began to jerk in Scirye's arms and he began to make gagging noises.

Scirye looked down, worried. "Kles, what's wrong?"

With a final cough, a slender white object fell out of Kles's beak and into his paw. He held up the otter charm. "It's smaller than the fish I used to swallow, but not nearly as tasty."

Leech recognized the otter charm. "But I saw them take it."

Kles winked. "Correction. They took away the pouch with a chess pawn in it. They couldn't see my paws making the switch as my lady held me because I had my back to them." His throat sounded a little sore after spitting out the charm. "Let's see if it works like we think."

"You clever thing," Scirye said as he climbed onto her shoulder.

As Kles wiped the charm on his fur and handed it to her, the Amazons shifted to either side, though they looked skeptical.

Putting one hand to the handle of the door, Scirye pulled. There was a click within the lock and the door began to creak open.

Relieved, Kat turned to her comrades. "Ha, leave it to Nishke's sister to find a way out."

There was a roar behind them and a bullet pinged off the metal. The Amazons turned and fired several shots at the guards in the corridor who ducked immediately behind the corner.

The Questioner and the two Wolf Guards crawled on their

hands and knees toward their comrades, shouting, "Don't shoot. Don't shoot."

"Inside!" Scirye yelled and ran into the chamber. As Leech followed her, he couldn't help wondering if Bayang was all right.

# 29

## Bayang

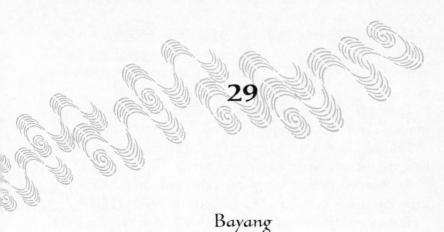

"Here you go, hon," Momo's voice said. "Have some water."

Bayang's eyelids fluttered open to see a badger's head the size of a hill. "How did you get so big?" she asked groggily.

Badik's laugh boomed in her ears like thunder. "We've stayed the same. You're the one who shrank—thanks to a potion the vizier gave our friend here."

Blind with rage, Bayang threw herself toward her enemy . . . only to slam against iron bars. She couldn't help crying out at the shock, as if lightning were coursing through her. Instinctively, she backed away only to hit more bars and receive more shocks.

"You can't escape, hon," Momo whispered. "There's a spell on the cage so it'll hurt everytime you touch it."

As she stood absolutely still on her hind legs, Bayang became aware of the painted metal bars that arched above her until they were welded to a circular plate at the top. The cage itself was suspended about the height of an adult human so it must be hanging from a chain.

"Drink up. You must be thirsty," Momo urged. She was holding a porcelain cup as large as a cauldron in her giant paw. From it was a straw the size of a sewer pipe that she had extended through the bars.

The shock made Bayang's lips feel half-frozen as she slurred her words. "The las-s-st dring you gave muh knocked muh out."

Suddenly, Momo was jerked upward. The cup crashed on the floor and the straw whipped through the air.

Badik looked as large as a green, scaly mountain as he held the struggling badger in his paw. "She gets nothing before I kill her."

The badger's paws thudded harmlessly against the iron band around the dragon's chest, her claws rasping over the metal surface. "I didn't sign on for any murder."

"My dear girl," Roland almost purred, "my contracts always have some fine print." The tall man with long blond hair was lounging in a chair in a khaki coat, jodhpurs, and boots. "You should have been more careful about agreeing to help me."

Momo gave up fighting and dangled like a furry sack. "Humph. And what would have happened to me if I'd said no?"

Roland chuckled. "You would have disappeared, but at least your conscience would have been clear—if *that's* what's so important to you." He took a sip from a goblet and set it down on a small table next to Pele's charm, which they must have taken from Bayang. "As for myself, I find consciences overrated." He jerked his head at Badik. "So kill Bayang and be done with it."

Badik's claw pointed at his scarred face. "No. She has to suffer for what her clan did to me. Her death is going to be slow." Years ago, Badik had invaded the territory of Bayang's clan and had only been driven out with great cost to both sides.

Roland made an exasperated sound. "We almost have the world at our mercy and you worry about some petty little revenge?"

Badik dropped Momo unceremoniously. "She will suffer as I have suffered."

A muscle twitched angrily on Roland's jaw. "Oh, very well, but it will have to wait until we come back with the arrows." It was more of a command than a statement.

Bayang's speech was improving fast as she woke up. "You won't get away with kidnapping me."

"On the contrary, I already have." Roland waved a hand toward two large battle axes dumped into a corner by a fireplace. Each was about a yard long, and though the wooden shafts had been decorated with designs in gold and silver inlay, the blades themselves were of old steel that still bore nicks in the blades from battle. "The vizier has made everyone think you've taken those little trinkets." He pretended to wash one hand with the other. "The vizier helps me get what I want, and in turn, I help him get the imperial throne."

*Does Leech believe I deserted him?* Bayang was so furious that she felt like she could have bent the bars, but she remembered the spell in time and remained where she was.

"Koko trusted you," Bayang said indignantly to Momo.

Roland steepled his fingertips. "Then he was a fool just like the rest of your pack."

On his finger was an archer's ring. Carved out of bone, a large triangle stuck out from the ring's side. It had belonged to Yi the Archer, whose bow had destroyed dangerous suns and monsters alike. Scirye's sister, Nishke, had died trying to prevent Badik from stealing it. Around his neck was the necklace he had stolen from the goddess Pele, destroying an entire island in the process. The string was the bowstring for Yi's powerful bow, and the staff leaning against his chair was the bow itself, which he had taken from a powerful animal spirit of the Arctic.

Bayang had to know the reason why Roland had caused so much misery. "Why do you want Yi's bow? Are you trying to get richer?"

"My dear, I have more money than I could ever spend." Roland laughed. "Power is far more precious than money."

"But you already have that," Bayang objected. "You meet with the leaders of the world."

"True," Roland admitted, "and for a while I was content to pull their strings, but puppets are such imperfect tools. They either fail to do what I want or even refuse willfully." He took a walnut from a bowl and cracked it between surprisingly strong hands. He picked through the broken shell for the nut itself. "But when I have Yi's bow, everyone will do exactly what I tell them to. And I'll straighten out this troubled world. Wouldn't you like a world where everyone's at peace and things run perfectly?"

"It would be *your* peace and *your* perfection." Bayang frowned.

"But of course." Roland popped the shelled nut into his mouth.

"And why is the mighty Badik listening to a mere human?" Bayang demanded from the other dragon.

Badik polished a claw against his chest. "Because I share the same ideas of peace and perfection. Roland will take the land and I will take the ocean."

"Who's the fool now?" Bayang snorted. "He's too greedy to ever share power with you." She added with a nod to Roland, "Or Badik with you."

Roland looked at her shrewdly. "You won't be able to stir up trouble between us."

*No,* Bayang thought to herself, *not while you have a common goal. But I probably won't live long enough to see you fall out with each other.*

Suddenly shouting came from the other side of the door, and then a sergeant in the white uniform of the vizier's Wolf Guard burst into the room. Every one of the whiskers of his black beard was bristling. "You are his lordship's guests, sir. You can't let these mongrels set up an altar to that . . . that abomination!" He jabbed a finger through the now open doorway at a makeshift altar in the hallway. A small portable statue of a many-armed goddess stood on one foot as if dancing, and the corpse of a chicken lay at her pedestal. Despite the heavy incense, Bayang caught a whiff of fresh blood.

In front of the altar were several Indians with quilted vests. Long pieces of cloth had been wound around their waists and legs so that they looked as if they were wearing baggy trousers.

Bayang had always taken a professional interest in other assassins so she recognized the yellow sash encompassing their stomachs. They were thugs, worshippers of the goddess of destruction and renewal, Kali. Once a thug had slipped the sash around the necks of his victims, he would grip the wooden cylinders on either tip and strangle them. Woven from the thread of a certain type of giant rare spider that lived in the Himalayas, the silk was tougher than steel.

In the past, bands of thugs would join caravans and even wedding parties and massacre the whole lot. The thugs claimed they killed in honor of the goddess they worshipped, though the loot they kept for themselves.

Roland looked amused. "Sergeant, Kali is as old as any of the deities you worship, and as for mongrels, Kushans are as much Greek, Indian, and Chinese as they are steppe nomads after two thousand years."

As the sergeant spluttered, one of the thugs in the hallway bowed and announced to Roland, "Master, the trucks are loaded and ready."

"And the lyaks?" Roland asked.

"They have sent word that their raiders will reach the griffin lands soon," the thug said. "It won't be long before the griffins will be too busy to notice what is going on in the City of Death."

"Excellent." Roland rose from his chair and picked up a furred cap and coat. "You can play with your toy when we get back, Badik."

Badik rudely shoved the sergeant out of the way. "I don't see what the rush is," the dragon complained. "The vizier is taking care of the brats."

"Because there are too many mountains for a plane or a roc to land in," Roland snapped, "so we have to drive the equipment in. And that takes longer."

"What are you doing to my friends?" Bayang demanded.

Roland paused on his way out and smiled maliciously. "It's all so delicious. When the vizier radioed me that you were arriving at the citadel, he had planned just to delay you. But I told him to kidnap you for my friend's pleasure and to take custody of those pesky children."

Bayang swallowed her pride. "Let the young ones go," she begged. "They're harmless without me helping them."

"Those pests have interfered with my plans once too often." Roland slapped his hat against his leg as if he were swatting some flies. "No one gets away with that. So as a sign of his goodwill, the vizier will take my revenge upon them. By the time he's done, they'll welcome death."

With a desperate roar, Bayang threw herself at the bars, grasping the iron in her paws and trying to pry them apart. The pain wracked her body but she kept on trying until she felt the blackness coming.

As she slumped backward, her last thought was of the hatchlings. How would they survive without her?

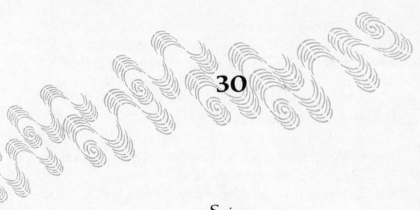

# 30

## Scirye

As soon as they were all through the doorway, Oko threw herself against the iron door and slammed it shut behind them—and not a moment too soon. Bullets spanged off the iron.

There was a little window on the iron door and Oko fired two shots through it. "The rats are scuttling back out of sight again." She chuckled. "I bet those toy soldiers out there have never been in a real fight before."

They were standing in a circular room some fifty feet in diameter with thirteen doors spaced evenly around the walls.

"These must be where they held the prisoners before questioning," Kles said in a hushed voice.

Māka started to pirouette slowly. "So much blood. Rivers of it pouring and pouring down into the dark."

And such was the power of suggestion that Scirye thought she caught a faint whiff of it clinging to the stones.

Tute nudged Māka with his shoulder. "Keep your imagination to yourself."

But Māka continued to turn in a daze until she stopped and faced the seventh door, which was directly opposite the entrance. "There. There the screams soaked into the floor with the blood."

"Blood and screams," Kles mused. "That sounds like the torture room."

"Yes, torture," Māka murmured. "So much evil."

Tute shoved his friend a little harder. "Snap out of it."

Māka started to stagger backward, but Scirye caught her arm.

"Does this happen often?" Scirye asked the lynx.

He shook his head. "This is the first time I remember."

After a moment, Māka straightened and rubbed her eyes. "I don't know what got into me." She gave Scirye a smile of thanks for catching her.

Koko shuddered. "I wouldn't want to have to sit in one of these cells listening to another prisoner being questioned."

No one pointed out the obvious: If they were re-captured, that would indeed be their fate. But it had to be in everyone's mind. Scirye tried to control her own trembling fingers as she tore a long strip from the expensive blue silk of her robe, fashioning a belt into which she tied the otter charm.

She thought of her mother and sister when they'd been battling Badik the dragon, trying to stop him from stealing the precious ring of Lady Tabiti, a treasure of her people. She had to be calm. She introduced her friends to the Pippalanta. Then, swiveling, she surveyed all the doors. "Are those all cells or is there another way out of here?"

"Not that I know of," Kat said. "What next, lady?"

Scirye was surprised and pleased that the Pippalanta were now looking to her to solve the problem as they had once looked to her sister. She just wished she had a solution.

"Quiet." Tute stood frozen, except for his ears, which turned this way and that, the tufts at the tips twitching.

"What—?" began Koko but shut up when Tute drew back his lips in a snarl that exposed his fangs.

When the badger fell silent, the lynx went back to listening, his ears rotating rapidly trying to pick up the strange noises only he could hear. Finally, he pointed his muzzle toward the third door from the entrance. "Yes," Tute whispered, "there's definitely someone inside that cell. But the Questioner said that we were to be the first prisoners to be questioned here in a long time."

Kat nodded to the door through which they had come. "But that's supposed to be the only entrance."

"Which means whoever's behind there has another way in," Wali said.

"And out," Tute grunted.

Leaving the Pippalanta to guard the entrance, they followed as silently they could while Tute stalked toward the mysterious sounds. The powerful muscles on his shoulders and legs rippled beneath the hide. Though the lynx was only as high as Scirye's knee, his compact body was heavily muscled. Scirye would not want to be his prey.

As Tute paused outside the wooden door, Scirye thought she heard crunching noises. Tiptoeing next to him, Scirye put her hand to the door while her other hand clasped the otter charm. The lock clicked at her touch and she yanked the door open.

Koko's eyes widened and he sniffed the air loudly. "Hey! Potato chips!" The tubby badger charged past the startled lynx and dove into the room. "Dibs!" he hollered.

There came a high-pitched squeal of terror and indignation, and the sound of Koko thrashing about with someone.

Scirye sprang into the room, ready to save her friend from a life-or-death struggle. Instead, she found Koko lying on the floor of the cell, hugging a green bag of chips like a drowning man clutching a life preserver. With his other paw, he was fending off a foot-high akhu.

Koko squinted as he asked, "Fenimore, is that you?"

## 31

## Leech

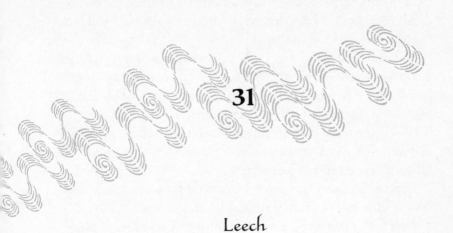 "Ah, good sir," the rat said in accented but good English, "Pärseri has a third cousin by that name who lives in America." Despite his friendly tone, the ratlike creature kept trying to reclaim his bag of chips. "How is he?"

Koko nodded. "Fenimore told me he had a big clan. He's doing fine on Alcatraz—that's a prison on an island in the San Francisco Bay where only the worst criminals get sent. Fenimore said the food may not be top notch but at least the garbage cans are full and there's no competition."

"Pärseri's heart overflows with joy and such moments are rare in this wretch's life," the rat said and dipped his head politely even as his paws flailed for the bag.

"My name's Koko." He nodded at Leech and the others as he held off the rat. "These are my buddies."

When Pärseri finally noticed them, he sidled over toward the bench, trying to block their view, but Pärseri would have needed to be as big as a hippo to screen all the food packed under the bench—candy bars, boxes of cookies, corned beef in tin cans, jars of pickled pigs' feet, and a whole ham.

"There are so many thieves about nowadays, and this place was always deserted, so I thought it would be safe to store my supplies here." Pärseri wrung his paws. "But apparently not. Might Pärseri ask what you're doing here in his chambers?"

"Well, the place is re-opening for business—with us as the first customers." Koko stuffed a pawful of potato chips into his muzzle. "But we were framed so we escaped."

"Excuse Pärseri's ignorance, but shouldn't you escape by *leaving* the Chamber of Truth?" Pärseri asked, puzzled.

"We're working on it," Koko said through a mouthful of chips.

"We're not hardened criminals," Māka assured him. "You're safe with us."

"But not Pärseri's property." The creature wriggled a paw at Koko. "He'll have his chips back, if you please."

The badger tipped the bag upside down and shook it to show it was empty. "Sorry. You should have spoken up sooner."

Pärseri stared mournfully at the now empty bag. "Oh, woe is poor Pärseri."

"Aw, what are pals for?" Koko wheedled.

"You are no friend of Pärseri's," the rat snapped, "nor of Fenimore's. His letter complained about a badger who never paid his I.O.U.'s."

Before Koko could get into a fight with the rat, Kles spoke up. "How do you get in here, Pärseri?"

Pärseri nodded to the drain in the center of the alcove. "That leads to the sewer, or as Pärseri's people like to call it, the Highway."

The drain was at most nine inches square. Kles would certainly fit, but the rest of them would have to stay behind.

"At least we'll have supplies for a siege," Koko said as he began to examine the contents under the bench.

The akhu stamped a hind paw. "No, no, no. They are Pärseri's!"

Kles sat on Scirye's shoulder as he studied the drain. "The cell's drain was probably used for the disposal of waste, but a torture chamber might need a much bigger drain, especially if several prisoners were being 'questioned' in the same session."

"We'll get lost in the sewers without a guide," Tute said, grinning at the akhu. "But I bet you know the sewers like the back of your paw, Pärseri."

Pärseri shook his head violently. "No, no. Pärseri will be much too busy taking his supplies to safety." He gave a shrill squeal when Tute's paw clamped around the back of his neck.

"Pärseri, if you don't show us the other way out of here," Tute said, almost purring, "you're going to treat me to dinner." The lynx leaned forward so that his whiskers brushed the trembling rat. "And guess who's going to be the main course?"

Pärseri groaned. "Oh, pity poor Pärseri, kind sir. What harm has he ever done you?"

Māka squatted next to Pärseri and said in a soothing voice, "Let's help each other. If you lead us, we'll pay you."

Pärseri perked up instantly. "Do you have chewing gum?"

"No, but you can use these to buy them." Māka indicated the bells on the hem of her robe. "The bells are silver."

"It's always wise to be kind to strangers." Pärseri beamed as he rubbed his paws together. "Especially when they're bigger than you are. But you must help Pärseri carry his treasures to safety too."

"Of course." Scirye remembered then what the princess's steward, Nanadhat, had said. "Do you know the way to the caravansary of the Urak? It belongs to the kin of a friend of ours, and I think they would help us. It's on the edge of the krītam near the Eastern Gate and it has a sign with two palms."

Pärseri was only too eager to help now. His head bobbed up and down. "Yes, yes, everyone knows the home of the great and mighty Urak. Long may their trash bins overflow. Pärseri can take you kind, generous people there."

With a nod of thanks to the akhu, Scirye turned to Māka. The bells were attached to a strip of cloth, and Scirye helped her friend tear it off. "Just a moment ago, you found the torture room. Do you sense things as well as cast spells?"

Māka folded up the strip with the bells. "Not as far as I remember. I really don't know what happened back there, but it was like the magic swelled inside me so I could suddenly hear and see and smell things much more strongly."

"Maybe we've finally found what you're good at," Scirye suggested.

"It's a gift I'd rather do without," Māka said with a shake of her head.

Scirye gave her a little apologetic smile. "I'm afraid you may be stuck with it."

Māka nodded sympathetically. "Just like you have to serve the goddess."

Under the akhu's watchful eye, they stuffed his worldly goods into their clothes. Leech suspected that Pärseri knew to the last cracker what each of them was carrying.

The Pippalanta were still keeping watch at the door, but Kat turned when she heard them, raising her eyebrows when she saw Leech and his friends appear with their clothes bulging with food. "I didn't know the chamber had its own market."

Scirye introduced Pärseri, explaining that they were carrying his supplies while he showed them another way out.

Oko shook her head in admiration. "You really do have Nishke's knack for getting us out of scrapes. And just in time too. They're looking for something to use as a battering ram."

"They ought to use the vizier," Tute observed. "His head ought to be hard enough."

Māka fell into step beside them as they headed toward the other door. They still had the Questioner's ring of keys, but Scirye thought the otter charm would be faster. Sure enough, Scirye unlocked it as easily as she had the other doors. But this time, she took several long, calming breaths before she opened it. Chains hung from the walls but the torture devices had been removed.

Leech thought he could smell the stale odor of blood and sweat that still clung to the walls, just as Māka had earlier. And it felt like his feet could also feel the stones vibrating with the prisoners' screams.

*No, no, I don't want to be here,* the Voice whimpered.

"This is still an awful place," Scirye said, echoing the thoughts of the Voice and Leech. She put an arm around the cringing Māka.

"But they also had the courage to stop such dark practices," Kles reminded her. "It's the vizier who wants to bring them back."

Tute circled around a square metal grate two feet on each side. A huge padlock held it securely in place. It was hard to tell if the reddish-brown splotches on the grate and lock were blood or rust. Even if they had found the right key on the Questioner's ring, the lock looked so rusty that Leech wasn't sure the key would have worked. "Couldn't we hold this fascinating discussion somewhere else?"

"Yeah, like maybe a hundred miles away from here," Koko chimed in.

The air that wafted up through the grate smelled of rot and decay.

Pärseri took a deep, satisfied whiff of the stench. "Ah, home, sweet home."

# 32

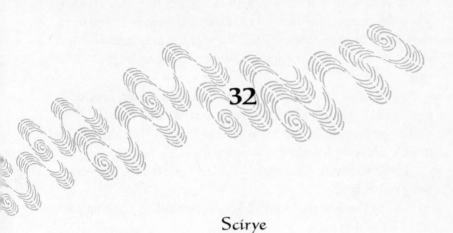

## Scirye

Scirye had been shaken by the torture room. It was the opposite side of all the heroic Kushan epics she'd read. She couldn't wait to leave this reminder of her people's dark past. Even so, she was reluctant to touch the padlock on the drain because of what must have flowed down into the opening in the past.

She glanced around and saw the others waiting expectantly. Ashamed, she told herself, *You can't be fussy when everyone depends on you.*

So she put aside her own feelings of revulsion and with one hand touching the otter charm, she bent over and grasped the lock in her other. The insides of the lock creaked as it slowly opened.

After that, Wali took Oko's place guarding the entrance so the big Pippal could help Kat lift the grate, but years of debris had cemented the grate in tight.

"It's going to take all of us to get it off," Kat puffed.

Scirye leaned over to help with the others, her skin crawling when she grasped the metal bars. From her friends' expressions, they didn't like the contact either, but together they began hauling at the grate. It took their combined efforts to heave the grate to the side.

As she gazed down at the noisome darkness, Pärseri pointed to one side of the hole. "Pärseri sees rungs on one wall of shaft."

The rungs were spaced for adult humans, but the akhu had no trouble dropping from one to the one below.

"Let Koko go next," Tute drawled. "He'll give the rest of us something soft to land on."

"You're the one that looks like an overstuffed cushion with legs," Koko shot back.

"If you're going to be so selfish," Tute sighed. With his usual grace, the lynx slipped over the edge of the drain and down a few yards. "Come on, Māka."

Māka seemed to have recovered some of her old spirit now that they were leaving the place. Lifting the hem of her robe, she lowered a leg. "Oh, dear," she said as her toes searched for the next rung.

Tute clambered upward until his forepaws could guide her to the rung. For all of his sarcastic comments to his mistress, deep down he really cared for her. "Now you've got it."

Scirye noticed the brown stains on the first rung. She hoped they were some kind of fungus and not dried blood. If she could, she would have gone down with her eyes closed. Kles rose into the air, hovering above her as she eased into the hole. She had to stretch her leg to find a rung.

As she descended into the drain, her hand reached out to grip the top rung. The very touch of the cold metal made her skin crawl, but she went on.

"These rungs were not made for badger legs," Koko complained from just above her.

By the time Scirye was six rungs lower, it was pitch black. Only the number 3 glowed on her palm. Still, it was comforting in a small way, as if it were a sign that the goddess was keeping an eye on her even here. Finally she joined the others at the bottom, standing in the stinking stream up to her ankle.

Above her, she heard the fluttering of Kles's wings. "Kles," she called up. "I'm right here." She heard the flapping of wings as her griffin groped for her and found her arm. Fluttering his wings, he followed her arm until he could settle on her shoulder.

"Ugh," Koko said as his paws splashed into the muck. "And I finally got clean."

Leech, Kat, and Wali joined them in turn. Oko was the last to enter the shaft, and Scirye heard the rasping sound as the big Pippal drew the grate back over the hole.

"Are you having any trouble?" Kat called up to her softly.

"It's easy without the grit gluing it in place," Oko grunted from above. There was a clanging sound. "There. It's back."

Pärseri had them follow him in a single line. With each step, their feet and paws seemed to raise new stenches. Their route twisted and turned through the labyrinth of sewer tunnels, the only light coming from the mark on her hand. And the longer she spent in the dimness, the more Scirye's imagination pictured all sorts of horrid things still clinging to the walls.

They splashed through the noisome sewer so long that Scirye did not think they would ever leave the stink and the darkness, but eventually they came to a spot where moonlight fell through a grate.

The akhu jabbed a claw over his head. "Up here is the caravansary you seek. And now, if you would be so kind, leave Pärseri's things on a ledge to your right." He pointed a claw at a ledge in a niche that was just visible.

When they had deposited the last of his supplies, Koko chuckled. "You might want to be choosier where you stash your stuff next time."

The akhu scurried up on top of his pile of loot where they could see his whiskers twitch in the faint light falling from the grate. "No one will ever find Pärseri's supplies again," he said, "especially lying, thieving, hungry badgers."

Tucking her pistol in her clothes, Oko climbed up the rungs along one wall of the tunnel and lifted the grate from the opening. Then she went through it.

"It's clear," she called down softly to them.

"Good-bye. Pärseri is devastated that we have to part," Pärseri said, but despite his friendly words, he sat protectively on top of the pile of his belongings.

One by one, they went up the rungs until they were all standing in their stinking, soggy clothes on the stones of a plaza, some of which were marked with the double palms of the Urak. Next to them was a small circular fountain into which Poseidon poured water from a large jar in his arms. He stood with a foot balanced on each of the strangest sea creatures. From the waist up, they looked like elephants but from the waist down, they had the scaly tails of fish.

The fastidious badger headed to it right away and began washing his fur vigorously. "I should've brought a towel along."

Scirye and the others soon joined him, trying to clean up but unfortunately with mixed results. The only real way to get rid of the stench would be burning their clothes and dipping themselves in a barrel of soap bubbles.

Koko jerked a paw at the sea creatures. "Are they the latest in shoes?"

"They're water creatures called makara," Kles said. "And just hope you never meet one. They have tempers worse than a rhinoceros."

As Scirye looked around, she saw that the plaza sat in the center of a two-story building of mud brick with narrow slit windows and numerous doors, including several large enough for an elephant to use. "Does this remind you of any place?" she asked the others.

Leech caught a whiff of spices that reminded him of the Sogdian caravansary where they had stayed in the Arctic. "The materials are different, but it's laid out like Roxanna's caravansary," he said. Their friend's home had been part warehouse and part fortress, just like this one.

Suddenly a gong began to sound from a watchtower.

"Protect Lady Scirye," Kat ordered.

Oko immediately seized Scirye and placed her behind her as Kat and Wali closed in to form a triangle about her.

"This is bad," Tute said as gun barrels began sliding out of the slits, "very bad."

# 33

## Leech

Instinctively, Leech reached for the armbands—was it himself or the Voice guiding his hand? But his fingers closed on only cloth and skin. He felt helpless, then angry that they had been taken away.

*Why did you give up the armbands?* the Voice wailed. *We can't fly out of this trap. You're just another snotty punk without them.*

Deep down, Leech thought that was all too true, but as the Voice went on complaining, Leech ignored it as he hunted desperately for something he could use as a weapon. He was starting to learn how to focus on the task at hand and treat the Voice like background noise.

*Even if we had them, I wouldn't leave my friends,* Leech said to the Voice as his eyes hunted desperately for a weapon.

*You can't trust anyone,* the Voice insisted.

*Don't you have any friends?* Leech asked.

*I thought I did,* the Voice said sadly, *once, but they were quick to turn on me.*

The Voice spoke no more and Leech found himself feeling sorry for it.

Māka started for the drain from which they had climbed. "Hurry. Back to the sewer."

But a voice warned them softly, "Don't move." From a door came a large, handsome man with pale brown skin. He looked to be about thirty with all of the hair shaved off except for a long blond topknot that hung all the way down his back. He was wearing a kilt and vest of brocade, and his yellow linen shirt had lace about the collar and cuffs. "Usually only akhu come out of that drain."

"We're friends of Prince Tarkhun," Scirye said quickly. "And we're here to see Princess Catisa."

His thin, wispy voice didn't match the man's bulk. "And how would you know Prince Tarkhun?"

"We had the pleasure of saving His Highness's life," Kles said. When they had been traveling the Arctic, they had rescued the prince from bandits. The griffin tactfully avoided mentioning that they'd almost gotten his daughter, Roxanna, killed while she had been guiding them during their search.

"Ah, so you're the heroes," the man said. "Her Highness has been expecting you—though not quite in this manner." He waved to the unseen guards. "It's all right. They're friends of the clan."

Leech breathed a sigh of relief as the rifles slid out of sight, and then the man led them through a second doorway and up a staircase. The smells of spices was stronger here and the bright fiery colors of the walls and furnishings on the second floor reminded him even more of Roxanna's home.

The man ushered them into a large room where the walls were hidden by rich tapestries showing strange cities and creatures, and on the floor were carpets of rich hues, artistic designs and a weave so plush it was like walking on springs. Against one wall was a dais about eight inches high and the man told them to sit down on cushions laid out before it.

A little while later, a woman entered from a side door. She wore a short tan robe of a light but strong cloth and her thick yellow trousers were stuffed into her black boots. Robe, pants, and footgear were studded with designs made from small pale white stones. Despite the cost of her clothes, she was no hothouse flower, for her skin had been burned a rich nut brown by the sun. She held her head up with the same air of authority—like someone used to being obeyed instantly—that Roxanna had had.

"I am the Princess Catisa, the great-aunt of Prince Tarkhun. And this is my faithful servant, Nandi." When she motioned toward the man, the bejeweled gold bracelets on her wrists jangled together. Leech had never seen so much jewelry in his life. Every one of her fingers was covered with rings and dozens of necklaces hung from her neck. Several pair of earrings hung from her ears and dozens more pendants dangled from her thick crop of gray hair. All of her jewelry held more white stones of different sizes. He wasn't sure how the woman could move with so much jewelry. "I welcome you in the name of the House of Urak."

Fluttering into the air, Kles bowed deeply. "On behalf of my mistress, the Lady Scirye of the House of Rapañńe"—the griffin gestured to her—"I offer you a thousand and ten thousand greetings, O Mighty Princess."

The elderly woman's lively, curious eyes reminded Leech of Roxanna. "And a thousand and ten thousand greetings to you, oh wise griffin. When I'd heard the vizier had you, I thought it would be a long time before I saw you."

Kles gave a discrete little cough. "Yes, well, only a few know we've left the vizier's hospitality."

"Yeah, our escape was a do-it-yourselfer," Koko added.

"The vizier kidnapped our friend, Bayang, and made it look like she stole the axes," Scirye explained.

"Ah," Princess Catisa said shrewdly, "the vizier stole the axes himself and then kidnapped your friend so everyone would think she did it. That way he could discredit his political rivals."

*Including Scirye's father*, Leech thought. He liked Scirye's parents and the princess and hoped they were all right.

Scirye introduced her companions and then they took turns with Kles telling the princess about their adventures from the theft in the San Francisco museum to their escape from the citadel.

The Princess questioned them every now and then before finally concluding. "My great-nephew was right when he said you were both brave and clever."

"With a little luck thrown in," Leech added.

"That never hurts," Princess Catisa agreed, "but my great-nephew said that Lady Scirye was the chosen of Nana." Nana was the Sogdian name for Nanaia.

"I just hope I can keep my end of the bargain." Scirye stared at the goddess's mark on her hand. "I remembered the pictures on the walls of the shrine in Roxanna's home. And I saw what happens when people don't keep their promises to Her."

Princess Catisa clapped her hands together. "Ah, but if you must honor your word to the goddess, She must honor her word to you."

"Then I wish She'd tell us what we have to do," a frustrated Scirye complained.

"I'm sure She's already been helping you during your journey," the princess said.

"Scirye told me that the goddess sent a dream that saved everyone from the hag in the Arctic," Māka replied helpfully. When they had been chasing Roland in the northern wilderness, a hag had put them to sleep but Scirye had woken just in time.

Koko winced. "Don't mention that dame again. Just the thought of Her gives me the heebie-jeebies."

"And perhaps you're not aware of all the other ways She's aided you." The princess shrugged.

"Lady Miunai said that maybe it's probably as hard for Her to communicate with us as it would be for us to communicate with ants," Scirye recalled.

"It's probably even more difficult because we think we know everything." Princess Catisa rapped a knuckle against the side of her head. "And we have such thick skulls that it must be hard for a message to get through to us."

"You mean look for omens?" Māka asked, taking a professional interest.

"Those too," Princess Catisa said, "but I meant favors She's actually done for you."

"So maybe if I try to be more aware of my surroundings, I'll find clues about how She's helping us," Scirye said hopefully.

"Yes, they might be right under your nose," the princess said and then cautioned, "but we can't expect Her to do everything for us."

"Or we'd become spoiled," Māka agreed.

"Hey, there's nothing wrong with being spoiled if it's like Princess Maimie's palace," Koko protested, but he shut up when Leech elbowed him savagely in the side.

"Our friend Bayang is being held captive at the vizier's summer villa so we're heading there to get her," Scirye explained. "Every minute counts. Now that the vizier knows we've escaped, he'll go to his villa and kill Bayang so there won't be any witnesses. We'd appreciate it if you could provide directions to it and some supplies. And then we'll be on our way. We wouldn't want you to get into trouble on our account."

The princess rested her chin upon her palm as she studied them. "My great-nephew sent me a telegram that spoke highly of all your characters, the dragon included. His judgment's good enough for me. If you say you must go, then we will help you."

The man called Nandi cleared his throat. "With all due respect, Your Highness, wouldn't it be wiser to let the authorities save their friend?"

The princess sat up regally. "You forget, Nandi. The House of Urak always pays its debts. We don't let the authorities do it for us."

Nandi dipped his head apologetically. "This Bayang must be quite a person to inspire such devotion. I hope to meet her one day."

"I think you will, Nandi," the princess said. "I've decided that you shall guide our guests to the vizier's summer villa and help them save their friend."

"As you command, Your Highness." After another bow, Nandi began pulling on his ponytail, and it was as if he were yanking on the threads of a sweater so that it unraveled. His clothes collapsed onto the carpet and the threads began to wind themselves into a large cloudy globe—like a giant ball of golden yarn.

"I thought Nandi was human. But he's an ifrit?" Scirye asked the princess.

Two silvery eyes blinked at her from the cloud. "I'm Upach's little brother. Ifrits can take human form, as I do. It serves me well when I carry out my errands for the princess. But my sister is a purist who likes to keep the shape she was born with."

Koko rubbed his paws together. "Boy, if I could do that, I'd never have to pay bus fare again."

"When Upach transforms, she just dissolves into mist," Scirye said. "Is your magic different, Nandi?"

Nandi laughed, his misty body swirling into a tangle of cloudy ribbons. "I like to think I have more showmanship than my sister, but perhaps it's merely my vanity."

"You may indulge your vanity all you wish as long as you accomplish your tasks," the princess said. "And once they are done, return to me."

The cloud bobbed up and down slightly in assent. "As you desire."

"No, it is not my desire," the princess said sadly, "but my duty to send children into that serpent's lair. I wish it were otherwise."

# 34

## Scirye

Kat bowed to the princess and then to Scirye. "I think the ifrit will be worth a hundred Pippalanta, so if I may, I will take my leave now, lady. Between Nandi, Wali, and Oko, you should be fine."

"Where are you going?" Scirye asked.

"I'll tell Princess Maimie and your parents exactly what happened and where you're going," Kat promised.

"You're going back to the citadel?" Leech asked.

Kat chuckled. "They're searching outside the citadel, not inside."

Wali gave him a wink. "Only an idiot would go back there."

"Which certainly applies to me." Kat grinned. "Don't worry. I'll lose myself among the servants."

"What if one of them turns you in?" Leech wondered.

"We weren't the only ones who were angry over the way we were treated," Oko explained. "We have many friends among the staff. They'll protect Kat."

Scirye stroked Kles's leg as she thought for a moment. "I agree with you that it's vital the princess and my parents know the truth," she finally said. "So all three of you should go."

"I think Wali and Oko should go with you," Kat insisted.

"This is not a request," Scirye said firmly. "This is an order."

The red-headed Amazon stared at her defiantly for a moment but then sighed. "Your sister used to look at me just like that when she was telling me to do something I didn't want to do."

"I suppose she looked at me just the same way," Scirye admitted.

"I still think—," Wali began but Kat elbowed her.

Kat glowered at her friend. "Didn't we say we'd leave the thinking to her?"

"Well, that was then and this is now," Wali grumbled but she fell silent.

"And tell my parents that I'm alive and well and . . ." Scirye hesitated, knowing it would be dishonest to say that she would be all right. They were facing too many unknown dangers for that. "Just tell them that I love them and that I'm carrying out the task the goddess has set for me."

By the time they got the message, Scirye would be beyond their reach so they would not be able to command her to stay with them.

Oko took out the pistol. "Here, lady, you should take this."

The two other Pippalanta offered their weapons as well and the princess offered to supplement those with more guns, but of the friends only Scirye had used one.

"And I didn't hit the target much," Scirye said.

"Using a gun in a real fight is different from practice," the princess observed. "So perhaps daggers would be more useful to you."

Scirye was impatient to leave, but she had to wait while the princess's servants gathered up supplies and weapons for them. When they had been outfitted, they trooped after the princess and Nandi back to the open plaza at the center of the caravansary.

While the Pippalanta stood a little apart, Scirye and the rest of her friends stood in a line with Kles inside Scirye's robe. Then, raising one arm, Princess Catisa held the forearm just before her mouth as she began to murmur a spell. The next moment the bracelets began to jiggle as if they had come to life.

Tissue-thin wings sprouted from the moonstones and they suddenly exploded from the settings in the bracelet, fluttering about like pale butterflies as they swelled to about four inches long.

They hovered about the princess like the shimmering snowflakes in a blizzard—and Scirye shivered because that was like the magical trap that Roland had set for them in the Arctic. They had barely escaped with the help of some creatures of light called the Dancers.

Raising her other arm, the princess summoned more of the luminous insects until she was almost hidden in the cloud. Still more appeared so that the cloud seemed to expand until it had filled the tent.

The moon butterflies—which Scirye decided was as good a name as any—brushed her cheeks as if a breeze was planting baby kisses on his face, and the beating of thousands of wings made tiny clicking sounds.

"Oh, wonders of my heart and delights of my soul, take them where Nandi leads," the princess called. As the moon butterflies began to settle on Scirye's skin and clothes, their legs tickled like thousands of baby eyelashes and yet were cool and soothing to the touch.

The butterflies felt more like a second skin than armor because she could move her arms and legs. More important, they left spaces over her mouth and nostrils so she could breathe. Because they also covered her ears, she only dimly heard Nandi say, "Come."

The next moment she felt herself rise into the air, though she wasn't sure how high because the butterflies also covered her eyes. She floated slowly at first and then picked up speed as she angled upward.

She needed to see so she began blinking rapidly, trying to force the butterflies away, but they were just as determined to stay and kept fluttering back, each time blanking her vision. Still, she managed to glimpse the ground far below them.

In desperation, she tried to rub her eyes, but that only seemed to make it worse as confused butterflies switched from her fingers to her eyelids and vice versa.

"Let her see," Nandi instructed, finally noticing her troubles. "Let them all see."

The butterflies drew away from her eyes so she felt as if she were rimmed by shining goggles, but she was finally able to glance at her friends. Their bodies were encased in butterflies, glowing faintly as the moon overhead. Perhaps because he'd gotten used to aerobatics, Leech looked the most at ease, experimenting with a cartwheel and then a somersault. He looked the happiest and his friend Koko the most miserable. He floated along like a sack of potatoes, his forelegs and hind legs dangling beneath him.

"This is wonderful!" Māka said as she raised shimmering arms, and Scirye was glad her friend could experience such marvelous magic firsthand. Maybe it would encourage her to keep trying on her own.

"Lynxes were never meant to fly," groaned a miserable Tute, who looked like a second potato sack.

Scirye had flown upon a straw mat, a dragon, and a griffin, but nothing had prepared her for this. She felt as if the moonlight were passing through the butterflies into her body itself, filling her insides until she glowed herself . . . until she was a moonbeam herself.

"Don't worry," Nandi assured them. "You'll be all right flying with me. I must answer not only to the princess, but also to my sister, Upach, if anything happens to you."

"Whom do you fear more, Nandi?" the princess asked, a smile teasing the corners of her lips.

"I pray that I shall never have to find out." Nandi extended a tendril. "Now please follow me," he said, more to the butterflies than the children.

They rose like balloons out of the plaza, bodies shimmering all silvery and restless under the pale moonlight. Then Nandi extended a tentacle and swept it toward the east before he flowed in that direction, and the butterflies followed him.

From far below, Scirye could hear the princess praying in formal Sogdian. "And may I remind thee, O Nana, that she is a mere child and will need more help than we adults."

It seemed that even Sogdian prayers were in the form of business contracts, and the princess was more worried about Scirye than she had let on.

They swept quickly over the wall of the old city and across the shining ribbon of the river. Below them, the city lights sparkled like gems cast onto black velvet and Scirye's throat caught at how lovely the city looked at night. All too soon they were zooming over the irrigation canals beyond the city. They looked like lace draped over the snow-covered fields.

On and on they sped, following the gleaming cloud that was Nandi as he led them deeper into the darkness.

# 35

## Leech

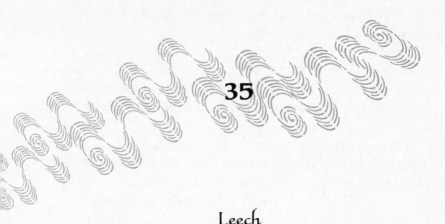 As the stars swept past overhead, Leech said, "These bugs are almost as good as the discs!"

"Once we find Bayang and stop Roland, I swear we'll get your armbands back," Scirye assured him.

Koko grinned as he nudged Leech. "And you know how Lady Scirye keeps her promises. So don't worry, buddy."

Leech rubbed his arms. "When I don't have my armbands, I'm just one more piece of gutter trash. So I don't know how much help I'll be."

When Scirye shook her head, the butterflies encasing her head fluttered agitatedly. "Don't ever say that about yourself again. We've gotten this far because of you, not your magical trinkets."

Kles's voice came muffled from within the layer of butterflies. "We need you just like you need us. We are stronger as a team than as individuals."

*I think they really mean it,* the Voice said wonderingly.

Leech thought back to the time when he had just run away from the orphanage. He'd been just as amazed when a stranger named Koko had helped him.

In some ways, the Voice was like the little brother he'd never had, so as the older brother Leech had to explain things and help the Voice mature. *You just haven't met good people before this,* Leech argued. *I didn't trust other people either until I met Koko.*

*Him?* the Voice scoffed.

*Okay, not the best example,* Leech admitted, *but at least he tries to be a friend. And what about Scirye, Kles, Māka, and Tute? They've already risked their lives over and over for us.*

*They've surprised me up until now,* the Voice conceded.

*It's nice to have people you can trust and depend on, isn't it?* Leech asked the Voice. *They're our friends. And friends are better than family because we choose them and they choose us.*

*Yes,* the Voice said softly.

*And even Bayang has been trying to make up for what she did.* Leech said, and knew he had pushed too far when he heard how angry the Voice became.

*Yes, she has. But I can't forget how she came for us all those times before,* the Voice said bitterly. *You'll never convince me she's changed.*

*This is a different time and a different place,* Leech snapped. *She's not the way she was and neither am I. Or at least I hope I'm not.*

*So you think I'm a monster too?* the Voice asked hurt. *Is that why you keep fighting with me?*

*I just meant that people change over time, and that includes Bayang and us,* Leech tried to explain.

*Yeah, you're a lot dumber than the original,* the Voice snapped.

Leech tried to reason with the Voice, but it had lapsed into a sulky silence.

# 36

## Scirye

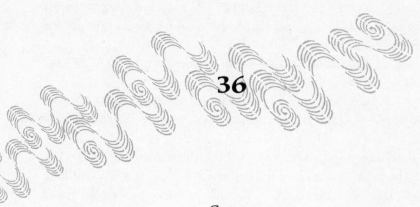

After several hours, Nandi said, "We're near the vizier's summer palace so we must be silent from now on."

They followed him downward until they were barely gliding a few feet above the ground, dodging around rocks and trees. An "ouch" from Koko indicated that he'd had a little less success at that than the others.

Several hundred yards ahead of them, gleaming in the moonlight, was a ten-foot-high wall that stretched to the left and the right as far as she could see. Here and there patches of plaster had fallen, revealing rows of mud bricks. Behind that wall, some large beast roared hungrily. Another creature screeched in answer. That touched off a chorus of howls and shrieks from more denizens.

Scirye drew her eyebrows together. "That sounds more like a zoo than a rich man's villa."

"It's a paradise," Nandi whispered.

"A what?" Leech asked, coming up on them.

"Paradise is what ancient Persian rulers called their own private parks," Nandi explained. "The vizier has stocked it with all sorts of exotic wild animals that he hunts. In the center is a lake and on the lake is an island with his villa."

That explained all the commotion from beyond the walls, and all the creatures sounded as nasty as their owner.

"I would have thought they'd be patrolling the walls," Scirye said, studying the place. The breeze felt good on the bare skin of her face.

"His paradise is the size of a city so the wall that encloses it has to be even vaster. He would need a regiment to man such long walls, and even then there would still be gaps where someone could sneak across," Nandi said grimly. "The beasts of his paradise are his best defense against intruders. He'd only need a token body-guard at the villa itself."

With Nandi in the lead, they flew over the wall, barely inches from the spikes at the top, and then into the paradise.

Compared to the orderly farmlands over which they had flown, the paradise was a lush place of weed-grown meadows, dense thick-ets, and sprawling stands of evergreen trees. There was a timeless-ness to the landscape, as if some enchantment had preserved a bit of the world when it was originally created.

They skimmed over the treetops, sometimes brushing a tip so that it rustled. The paradise, as seen at night and from above, seemed like an ocean of shadows that had been frozen into billows and crests and troughs. It made her feel as small and insignificant as the vast Arctic wilderness had.

She felt even more helpless as something crashed through the treetops, branches shaking as if something heavy were jumping on them. She looked below at the tangle but she could not see the crea-ture stalking them.

Tute began glancing from side to side and sniffing the air, his ears twisting and turning, trying to find a clue as to what was fol-lowing them. Within her robe, Scirye felt Kles's fur ruffle with tension. She reached for the dagger the princess had given her, but she could not grab it through the coating of moon butterflies.

Suddenly she jerked to a halt as her ankle snagged on something. When she looked behind her, she saw a hairy apelike paw clutching her boot. A foxlike head with long ears thrust out of the branches to snarl at her. Its fangs looked incredibly sharp.

She kicked at the creature's wrist, but its grip was unshakable.

Within her robe, Kles began thrashing about, trying to break through the layer of butterflies.

On the tree next to her, another creature rose, its hind paws clinging easily to the swaying treetop as it stretched long, long limbs toward her.

Nandi struck her captor, flowing downward through the branches on the right like a silvery avalanche. There was a startled squeal and the creature let go. Branches snapped and broke as the creature and Nandi plummeted.

Suddenly butterflies sprayed from around her throat and she dipped at the sudden loss of buoyancy.

"*Tarkär!*" Kles cried as he emerged from her robe. He dove at the second predator and both disappeared within the tree.

Scirye hovered anxiously as the tree shook violently. Māka, Tute, Koko, and Leech circled around her. It was hard to simply float there while her best friend in the world might be fighting for his life.

Then, from beneath her, she heard a howl cut off abruptly, followed by a shriek from the first creature. There was the sound of more branches crashing and then a pair of heavy thuds.

The next moment Nandi emerged like a tattered golden flag, his body trailing in tatters. And then a battered Kles struggled into the air.

Scirye held out an arm, and the griffin fluttered onto it, his claws clicking on the butterflies scaling her skin. She hugged him tightly against her. Even through the layer of butterflies, she thought she could feel how wildly his heart was beating. Kles had all the courage and pride of a war griffin packed into his small body, and she loved him all the more for it.

Nandi pulled his shredded body into a compact ball. "We have to hurry. The scent of the blood will draw other predators." A tendril gestured at the fluttering butterflies that had left Scirye and they resumed their positions on her.

Flattening himself into a disc, Nandi began to speed forward and Scirye, with Kles flying beside her now, followed with the others. After a while, he slowed and extended a tendril, gesturing for them to go down into the tree canopy.

Scirye was a bit nervous about entering the forest, but nothing was stirring as she flew among the branches.

Nandi flitted like a golden wraith, but Scirye and her friends made more noise, knocking through the tree limbs until they came to the edge of the wilderness.

Beyond them was a lake where water lapped gently at the pebbly shore. A graceful bridge arched high across the lake to the large island in the middle. It reminded her of pictures of Chinese bridges, but it had been built out of stone rather than wood. Willow trees edged the island's shore, their leafless branches hung like long curtains of hair. Beyond the trees they could make out empty flower beds marked by shrubs cut low like thick walls. And in the center were several rectangular marble buildings. Like the citadel, they were decorated with panels of brightly colored tiles.

The order of the island contrasted sharply with the wild chaos of the paradise. *The villa would look lovely in the spring and summer,* Scirye decided. And even though the villa was lying dormant in the winter, it looked too harmless to be a prison for their friend.

Even as she studied the island, a shadow passed before the moon. A rider was landing on a griffin within the villa. Was it a messenger?

"There's a guard on the bridge," Tute said, his lynx eyes appearing to glow as they gathered in the moonlight.

Scirye stared at the marble statues decorating the ends of the bridge and realized that one of them was a man in the white uniform of the vizier's guard. He'd set his bronze helmet on the bridge railing against which he was leaning.

When they scanned the island, they saw only a single guard strolling along on the shore of the island. He looked just as bored as the bridge guard.

"We'll fly close to the surface," Nandi whispered. He held up a tendril, watching the guards intently. When the island guard had left and he'd made sure the bridge guard was still daydreaming, he waved them forward. "Now."

They glided at an angle until they were skimming just above the lake. The air was chillier here and Tute jerked up and down erratically, obviously hating the notion of getting this close to water.

When they reached the midpoint, Scirye began to believe they were going to sneak onto the island successfully. But then she heard a bubbling sound off to their left.

"Someone please tell me that's their stomach growling," Koko begged.

The water fountained upward and an elephant head reared up from the water, long snout wriggling as it shredded the mist. It rose from the water higher and higher as the huge body leaped into the air, revealing the glistening scales of an armored fish.

It was a makara and from the way it stabbed its tusks at the cloudy ribbons, it was in a foul mood.

## 37

Bayang was having trouble standing up. The cage thwarted any magical spells, even her duplication magic, so the only solution was brute force. She had made several attempts to break the bars of the cage and each time had left her wracked with pain. Now her hind legs trembled with fatigue, but slumping down would only bring her into contact with the bars and more pain.

And yet the thought of the hatchlings—her hatchlings!—in the clutches of Roland's henchman made her gather her strength for another try. She was just about to reach for the bars again when she heard the deep, sonorous voice outside in the hallway.

It was the kind of voice that could sway thousands, but there was also a peevish quality to it, a hint of a perpetual grievance, as if there was always a tack sticking the owner in the foot.

"This is an outrage, an outrage!" the man thundered. "Who built this altar here?"

"It was Roland's thugs," a second man replied. "We tried to stop him, but he told us to leave them alone."

"And you obeyed him?" the first man demanded. "You're my guards, not his. Take this thing away and burn it."

"At once, lord," the second man said.

Bayang suspected the vizier himself had come. Had he brought the hatchlings with him?

The bearded Wolf sergeant opened the door. The statue of Kali was gone, but her makeshift altar had been left behind, bloodstains and all. A second guard was taking it apart so he could bring it outside and destroy it.

Bayang expected the vizier's build would match his grand voice, but instead of a tall man bulging with muscles, a short pudgy man strutted into the room in a leather riding outfit that made him look like a giant football. His long hair and beard were curled and glistened with oil. And his puffy cheeks made his eyes seem small and piglike.

He stopped dead when he saw the axes dumped into a corner. "And this sacrilege"—he jabbed a horrified finger at the sacred battle-axes—"is beyond comprehension!" Yanking off his gloves, he gave a grunt as he picked up the first one—as if he was not used to having to lift anything heavier than a pen.

The sergeant had followed him into the room. "Allow me, my lord."

The vizier nodded curtly for the guard to get out of his way. "No, this is my personal penance for allowing hooligans to treat sacred treasures like empty bottles." As the guard took up a post by the doorway, the vizier set the axes reverently on a long table against one wall. "The hatchlings," Bayang said, "what have you done to them?"

The vizier's eyes shifted uneasily, but he intoned, "I swear by my ancestors that those young pests will meet the fate of all those who try to oppose me."

The vizier seemed so agitated that Bayang suddenly felt a flicker of hope. "The children rarely cooperate with others' schemes for them. Did they escape?"

"This mess is all Roland's fault!" the vizier spat out the name. "I told that idiot that I would delay the bunch of you with a long, drawn-out trial while he found the arrows. But no, he insisted on destroying all of you. So I had to rush and improvise and they got away. And now everything's falling apart. Well, I'm through with that maniac."

Bayang thought smugly, *The hatchlings are free!* She could endure anything now. "You should be fleeing the empire instead of chatting with me."

"I'll catch the brats soon enough," the vizier snapped. "No one will ever see them again, and once I get rid of you and Roland, I can get everything back on track."

"Roland has Badik and the thugs," Bayang said.

The vizier paused and threw back his head for a deep laugh. "The emperor was ever so grateful when I offered to post most of my Wolf Guards there. Once I send a messenger there, they'll dispose of Roland, Badik, and their thugs. If that idiot hasn't already found the arrows, I can take my time searching for them myself. I put up with that pompous peacock strutting and screeching about how he was going to rule the world when everyone knows I'm the only one fit to do that."

Bayang suspected that the vizier had planned some form of double-cross all along. "You're as mad as he is."

When he heard shots outside, the vizier frowned and gestured to the bearded sergeant. "See what's going on."

The sergeant immediately pivoted and hurried down the corridor.

But Bayang thought she knew who was creating all that commotion. It could only be those foolish hatchlings who were coming for her instead of going on to the City of Death.

Bayang wanted to seize the cage's bars and break them, but she could only stand there helplessly.

# 38

## Leech

Spikes shot outward all over Nandi's misty body so that he looked like a giant mace. Nandi extended a tendril that motioned them to go on to the villa. "I'll take care of the makara," he said as he shot upward.

Leech's body suddenly lurched to the right and he fought to swing it back on course. *Stop trying to take over!* he told the Voice.

Leech's body was like a favorite toy that two brothers were trying to share.

*We should head away from the dragon, not to her,* the Voice objected.

*Bayang's my friend, even if she's not yours. And I'm going to save her,* Leech warned the Voice. *So don't try to stop me or you'll kill us both.*

*You're too weird to understand. So I guess you really are different from me,* the Voice declared sullenly. *Well, I'm not going to lift a finger to help you. How do you like that?*

*What's it going to take to make you forgive her?* Leech asked, frustrated.

*Let her die as many times as I have,* the Voice said.

Before he could make peace between the Voice and Bayang, he reminded himself, he had to rescue the dragon first.

When the ifrit struck the makara's head, his body flattened around it, oozing over the creature's eyes and blinding it. Nandi's spikes were not solid enough to penetrate the monster's hide. Instead, they snaked into the monster's ears, nostrils, and mouth.

The makara jerked its head about as it tried to stab its attacker with its tusks and whipped its long snout to knock him from its face. The great mouth opened for a howl, but there were so many of Nandi's tentacles down its throat that it only came out as a choked sound. Suddenly the makara plunged into the only safe place it could think of—the lake. The splash sent large waves rippling across the surface and the tallest washed over them.

The startled butterflies managed to keep them aloft but they slowed, and their luminous butterfly coatings made them easy targets. The bridge guard shouted the alarm. The next moment, there was the crack of a rifle shot and the water sprayed upward a yard away from Leech.

Leech knew that all he had going for him was speed, so he zoomed on. "Hurry!" he urged both his friends and butterflies with a wave of his hand.

They started to surge forward, but by now Nandi's underwater battle with the makara churned the lake so that it resembled a giant pot of soup coming to a boil, and another rogue wave smacked against them.

When the butterflies lost speed once more, Leech kicked himself upward above the waves. Alone of the group, he was used to flying on his own so he would have to take the lead. "We have to go higher," he instructed the others.

As they picked up speed again, the rifle cracked a second time. But this time the shot hit several yards behind him.

As the wind began to brush his face from the speed of his passage, for an instant, he forgot about his worries for Bayang and his own fears. Nothing could beat flying. This would always be his first love.

"Oh, no," Scirye said as she bobbed up beside him. "They'll kill Bayang now that they know we're attacking the island."

"Is that what we're doing?" Koko said, rising next to them. "You could have fooled me. I thought we were rushing into a trap like we usually do."

They were almost to the shore when the guard on the bridge returned to the island. At the same time, the second Wolf Guard returned double time. When he saw them, he raised his rifle to his shoulder.

"I need to sink my teeth into someone," Tute growled, "so leave this pair of nitwits to me."

"I'll help," Māka offered.

"Your stupid card tricks aren't going to scare them away. I'll handle this alone," he said, and he veered toward the second guard.

She gave Scirye an apologetic smile. "I may not be able to help Lady Scirye as a magician or a seer, but I can do this much." Skimming low, she snatched up a branch to use as a club and headed for the guard running from the bridge.

"Good luck," Scirye called as they passed them.

The last thing the second guard had expected to see was an overgrown, glowing cat hurtling toward him like a missile. He gaped for seconds before he recovered his wits enough to raise his rifle. By then, it was too late.

"You bugs let go of me," Tute commanded. Immediately, the butterflies flew away in all directions in a shimmering white cloud. Out of it burst sixty pounds of snarling lynx.

The guard fired without aiming, and his shot went wild. And then Tute had ducked under the rifle and struck him in the belly. Lynx and frightened man tumbled together over the ground and into a tall rhododendron shrub.

Māka's landing was less dramatic, stumbling forward a few steps before she got her balance and then dispersed her own butterflies. Before the cloud of departing butterflies could hide her from view, the determined sorceress's hands were already raising her club.

"Māka's got guts," Leech observed as he, Koko, and Scirye darted over a flower bed that was just a rectangle of dirt until the spring planting.

"Even if she's short on common sense," Koko agreed as the trio arched over the bordering hedge like dolphins leaping from the sea.

Hedge leaves brushed their stomach as they skimmed over the hedge itself. "She thinks we're heroes so she's trying to be like us, I think," Scirye said.

They whizzed through a pavilion with fluted columns, scattering dirt and debris in their wake. The noise of their friends' struggles echoed underneath the marble dome. Upon the floor was a large mosaic of a well-muscled Hercules. Canvas tarps had been tied over something in the middle—most likely a bench. Leech figured that the villa was meant to be used in the summer so the furniture had been covered up until the spring.

The pavilion stood at the south corner of a square garden with elegant buildings boxing the garden's four sides. Their second-story balconies were supported by slender columns, giving shade and shelter to anyone on the ground.

In the center of the garden, a statue of Hercules dressed in a fur pelt leaned on his club as he gazed down from his pedestal at the twigs and leaves gathering in the basin of a large fountain that had been shut down for the winter. Apparently the vizier was a devotee of the Greek demi-god.

The griffin twisted his head from side to side. "Where should we look first?"

Suddenly Leech heard a scream off to their left. "There would be a good start," Leech said.

"That's Momo!" Koko cried and immediately veered toward that building.

"Careful," Leech warned. "She's working for the vizier."

Koko sped on recklessly. "I bet it wasn't her choice. Old Potbelly forced her into a life of crime," he called over his shoulder.

It wasn't like his friend to lead the way into danger. *Koko must like her a lot if he'll make up a flimsy excuse like that,* Leech thought. *He's good at fooling other people. I just hope he's not fooling himself.*

Despite his own misgivings, Leech swerved after his friend and Scirye and Kles were right by his side. Perhaps because their slimmer bodies were more aerodynamic, or simply because they weighed less, they caught up with the badger just as he reached the marble steps leading to the building's entrance.

The next moment, a net dropped down on them, pinning them to the floor beneath a mesh of heavy steel wires.

# 39

## Leech

The butterflies clinked against the metal wires as they tried to heave off the net, but it was too heavy.

Fighting down his own panic, Leech suggested, "Let's try to lift up one side and crawl out." But strain as they might, they could not raise the net one inch.

"There must be a magical spell to hold it down," Scirye panted.

Leech felt the cable strands press against him as if the net were pulling them harder against the ground. "Is it my imagination or is the net tightening?"

"I think it is too," grunted Scirye. "Which means it won't be long before the mesh begins to cut through the butterflies into our skin."

"No one's going to slice me up like a hunk of baloney," Koko said, and then he said to the butterflies, "Scram, bugs." When they didn't leave right away, he hunted for words they would understand. "Hit the road, vamoose." Exasperated, the badger tried politeness. "Pretty please with sugar on top, go away, butterflies."

Immediately a cloud of butterflies floated away from the badger and upward through the mesh to float a couple of yards overhead.

It was hard for the badger to move his paws under the net but somehow he managed to make the magical signs of his spell. Finally, his shape began to shimmer, and the next moment hundreds of tiny Koko's crawled through the interstices between the mesh.

"Ah," Scirye said appreciatively, "very nice."

"Yeah," the tiny Kokos chorused as they stretched. "I've never done this many of me or this small."

"A victim must have to be a certain size for the trap to trigger," Leech said thoughtfully. "Otherwise it would be trying to catch a passing mosquito."

"So how do I get you out of the net?" Koko wondered.

"I don't think the villa was ever intended to be a real prison, so Roland had to improvise some extra magical defenses." With difficulty, Scirye turned her head to look around. "Over there by the doorway. See the paper with the writing in red ink? Try tearing that up."

The air began to shimmer again as the Koko's ran together. "That tickles a lot," he giggled. Slowly the glowing area expanded until Koko was whole once more. Quickly he went to the doorway and stretched up a hand and grabbed the yellow strip.

As soon as he tore it in half, the net's strands began to soften and then shrink until they were simply a lace of paper strips.

When Leech sat up, the strands tore and fell away. Flying into the mansion with its narrow spaces filled with furniture was too hazardous, so he said to his own coating of butterflies, "Release me."

They dispersed, and next to him Scirye freed her own butterflies. Together, the butterflies joined the swarm glowing over their heads.

Kles rose after the butterflies. His fur and feathers were tangled and matted with sweat, but he still managed a dignified bow. "I apologize for any doubts I had for your magic, Koko."

"Too bad it's my only trick," Koko sighed.

"Kles, go on," Scirye instructed. "Bayang may need your help."

"As you wish, lady." With a wave of a forepaw, the griffin shot into the building.

# 40

## Bayang

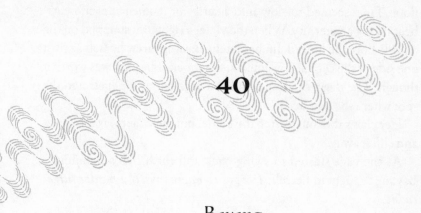 The vizier had begun pacing back and forth impatiently, checking the corridor every few seconds for his guards to bring him news. But the only one who came was Momo.

"It's payday, my lord," the badger said with a bow.

The vizier backhanded the badger across the muzzle and she gave a shrill cry of surprise. "You're too much of a chatterbox to leave around." And he drew a stiletto from a sheath on his belt.

"Mama warned me there'd be days like this," Momo said as she darted toward the doorway.

The vizier tried to block her way, but the badger nimbly dropped to all fours and scooted between his legs as if she were used to eluding taller, bigger humans.

He took a step after her but caught himself and turned back to the cage. "Well, at least I can get rid of you."

Bayang balanced on the balls of her hind paws when the vizier raised his dagger to shoulder level with the blade parallel to the floor. Time seemed to slow into a series of moments, each heartbeat taking an eternity. When the vizier's right foot stamped on the marble floor, he lunged. Immediately, Bayang threw herself against one side of the cage and grunted at the shock. The pain was worth it though. The dagger's point scraped a cage bar as it penetrated the spot where she had been.

Her claws shot out to grab the blade, but the vizier was too quick and slid it away.

As the cage started to swing back and forth like a pendulum, Bayang thought to herself, *I've got to make myself a harder target to hit.*

She began to slam against the bars, making the cage rock from side to side violently and ignoring how much it hurt.

"Hold still," the vizier said petulantly. He reached out to steady the cage.

"You'll be sorry if you do that," Bayang said.

"I can suffer anything if I can sit on the throne at the end." The vizier smiled.

*I hope this hurts him more than it hurts me*, she thought savagely. As soon as his hand was in contact with the cage, she spun, jabbing her tail hard through the bars to strike the vizier's hand.

She timed the blow perfectly. The vizier cried out and hopped back, wringing his hand. "You foul creature!" A wicked smile spread across his face when he noticed the fireplace. "You'll wish I had stabbed you when I roast you alive."

As the vizier walked toward the fireplace, Bayang said to herself, *Maybe I can twist the cage off the chain.*

Heedless of the pain, Bayang began to throw herself back and forth and from side to side so that the cage began to spin crazily as it swung. *If I could only break a link on the chain.*

The vizier carefully took a burning branch from the fire and held it up like a torch. "Let's see how you like this." He held the torch up so the cage would swing into it.

Within the cage, the torch looked like a blazing wall. Bayang instinctively began to cringe. Fire licked at the bars, heating the metal so it was red hot, and then, as the cage passed through them, the flames reached for Bayang hungrily.

*I'm sorry, Leech,* she thought. *I meant to do so much more for you.*

Suddenly she heard a familiar voice cry, *"Tarkär, Tarkär!"*

She saw Kles dart through the doorway like a thunderbolt of fur and feathers heading straight for the vizier.

## 41

## Scirye

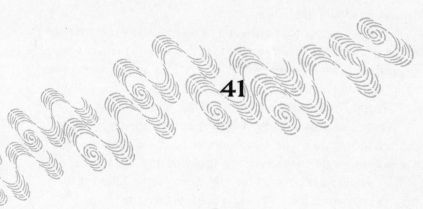

When she heard the hollering, Scirye dashed forward, not caring if there were any more traps. Dodging around furniture and tripping over rugs, she followed Kles's furious battle cries and the wailing of a man in terror and in pain. Panting, she paused in the doorway long enough to see Bayang in a tiny cage suspended by a chain from the ceiling. The dragon was no bigger than a parakeet and shouting encouragement in a shrill, high voice to Kles.

The griffin flapped his wings as his claws raked at the vizier's arms, which the man had thrown up protectively over his face. From the way Kles's feather and fur had puffed out, battle madness must have taken over the griffin. She knew that, seized by the rage, a griffin would keep attacking until he or she dropped from exhaustion.

Taking out her dagger, she crossed the room until she was only a couple of yards away. "Kles, this is your mistress, Lady Scirye," she ordered in a loud, firm voice. "Stop."

It took a moment for her words to register, even more for the griffin to understand them, but he rose shakily into the air.

Free of his attacker, the vizier lowered his arms and snarled. "You! Roland said you were pests."

"Give up," Scirye said, raising her dagger threateningly.

"Never," he growled and, whirling around, he threw himself through the window. The wooden frame and glass panes shattered beneath his weight and then he was sprawled on the lawn.

Kles would have pursued the vizier, but Scirye called again to him. "Kles, stay with me. Bayang is our first concern."

Kles drew a shaky breath. "Then we'd better do it soon, lady." Already, they could hear the vizier bawling for his guards as he scrambled away.

"What happened to Momo?" Koko puffed as he stumbled into the room.

"She ran away when the vizier tried to kill me," Bayang said.

Koko glared. "I ought to knock his block off."

"You can settle with him later. He got away." Scirye pointed her dagger at the broken window as she stamped out the fiery torch that the vizier had dropped.

"We have to escape ourselves," Bayang said. "Roland and Badik are already on their way to the city, but they're taking equipment that's so heavy they have to drive to the City of Death in trucks." The dragon added bitterly, "If only I could fly, we might beat them there."

"Roland's heading into a trap. The emperor has sent troops there," Leech said.

"Yes, but the troops are the vizier's own guards," Bayang said. "They're probably under orders to cooperate with Roland."

Koko let out a whistle. "That's like sending chickens to stop a fox."

Scirye studied the cage intently. "First things first, let's get you out of there."

"Don't touch the cage or you'll get a shock," Bayang warned. "And the more force you use, the greater the pain."

The dragon was standing in the same pose that Scirye had seen originally, standing erect on her hind legs, hunched forward slightly to keep her head from brushing the top, her forelegs dangling in front of her, tail coiled around her stomach.

The position looked uncomfortable, and from the way the dragon's body trembled, it didn't seem like she could keep it up for much longer. This was one more score to settle with Roland and Badik as well as the vizier.

"How do we get Bayang out?" Leech wondered.

"Could you shrink some more?" Kles asked the dragon.

The dragon was shaking with fatigue now. "There's a second spell on this cage that keeps me from working magic. They must have shrunk me to this size while I was out and then put me in here."

Koko closed the door and braced a chair underneath the doorknob. "Well, you better come up with something fast."

Scirye bent over so she could peer up at the underside of the cage. The bars arched from a ring at the top down to a wider ring at the bottom. The cage's floor was screwed on to the lower ring. "I bet we can loosen the base."

"No, don't touch the cage," Bayang said, worried.

"We've come too far and done too much just to leave you here." When Scirye set the tip of the dagger against the first screw, she felt a shock. *Bayang put up with a lot worse,* she told herself, and trying to ignore the pain, began to turn the screw counterclockwise.

Her hands were aching by the time the first screw dropped out. "Let me do the next one," Leech said, taking out his dagger.

There were four screws in all, and Scirye spelled Leech with the third one. Though it was slower, she used her left hand this time.

When the third screw fell away from the cage, there was a slight gap between its base and the bottom ring. Scirye began to massage her hands, feeling the ache leave quickly.

Licking his lips, Leech began to work on the last screw, but he had no more given it several turns when Koko called softly from the doorway. "Someone's coming." From the hallway, they could hear the guards' booted feet thudding on the floor.

"I've had enough of this," Leech said. Sheathing his knife, he grabbed the cage with one hand and the base with the other. He cried out with shock and began to shake.

"Are you mad?" Kles asked anxiously. "Let go."

"Yes, get away while you can," Bayang urged.

"Not without you," Leech said. Gritting his teeth, he pulled at the base. Crying out as metal screeched and the gap widened.

"That'll do," Bayang said. Letting go of the perch, she thumped against the bottom of the cage, writhing in agony at the contact. And yet her claws didn't stop scrabbling toward the gap until she slithered through.

Scirye was ready with outstretched hands, catching the dragon neatly. Gently, she cradled her pain-wracked friend against her stomach.

Bayang looked over at Leech and then up at her. The dragon was more concerned by her friends' injuries than her own. "Are ... are you all right?" she asked.

"My hands are just a little sore," Scirye said.

Leech was flexing his fingers. "Same here."

"Then set me down on the floor," Bayang said as she sat up on Scirye's palms.

"But you're hurt," Scirye protested.

The dragon flinched when she tried to shrug. "What's a few more aches and pains if it can keep my friends alive?"

When Scirye had obeyed Bayang, the dragon began to move her paws in the magical gestures, but it was without her usual grace and speed. And she was panting by the time she began to shimmer at the finish of the spell. The iridescent cloud swelled.

"Out of the way," Koko said as he backed up hastily. Running to Leech, Scirye helped him get on all fours so he could scramble away in a half-run, half-crawl.

The next moment, the cloud solidified into about ten feet of very solid dragon. "Ah, that's better," she declared as she knocked tables and chairs over with loud crashes. "Koko, get the axes."

The badger fetched the sacred weapons, and after everyone had climbed onto her back, they all crouched low as the dragon slithered through a hole she had made in the wall.

As they slipped out into the cold night air, the door crashed open behind them. "Shoot, shoot," one of the guards shouted.

Bullets spanged the dirt behind them as Bayang began to gallop toward the lake.

# 42

## Scirye

As Bayang limped along a path past the shrubs and toward the lake, Māka and Tute raced toward them across the empty flower beds. Māka's gaudy robe was torn and muddy and the lynx's ear was notched by a cut. "So you're still alive," Tute called. The lynx seemed genuinely surprised.

"I'm glad I can say the same thing about you," Scirye said, giving the sorceress a hug. "So your spells worked?"

Māka blushed. "No, but my club did the trick."

Bayang swung her head around at a loud splash and stared at the roiling surface of the lake. "What's going on?"

"It's Nandi," Scirye said.

The dragon scratched her cheek with a rasping sound of claw on scale. "Who or what is Nandi?"

Suddenly the makara burst out of the lake, wagging its head from side to side, but Nandi was still wrapped around it like a silvery scarf.

"Nandi's the guy acting like a blindfold," Koko said.

"He's Upach's brother," Scirye explained. "Prince Tarkhun's great-aunt, Princess Catisa, sent him and the butterflies to help us. He started fighting the makara so we could rescue you. He must not be strong enough to kill it, but he can confuse it."

"Princess? Butterflies?" Bayang asked and then raised a paw. "Never mind. You better tell me later. But this is going to be some story."

Bullets pinged against the path's flagstones from the mansion. "First, I'll get you all to safety," Bayang said. "Then I'll help this Nandi." Bayang tried to gallop, but her stiff legs only managed a shambling trot.

Shots sent dirt spurting up from the flower bed next to them. A squad of guardsmen were aiming their rifles at them.

"I'll distract these pests," Kles said, wheeling around.

"No, Kles, it's too dangerous," Scirye called.

"I can't let them shoot you," he said as he flew back toward the guards on the path.

She consoled herself with the fact that though his fur and feathers were ruffled, they weren't puffed out, which meant he wasn't lost in his battle rage. "Then don't be a hero. Leave as soon as we're safe."

She felt a lump in her throat as her friend dove toward the guards' heads, disrupting their aim. *Was there ever a braver griffin?* she wondered to herself. Unable to shoot the griffin when he was right among them, two of the frustrated guards swung their rifles like clubs. Kles dodged their blows as he clawed at faces, bit hands, struck stunning blows with his wings, and created havoc wherever he could.

All she could do now was face forward as Bayang swung her wings over them protectively and surged into the lake.

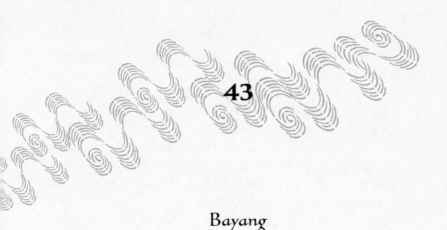

# 43

## Bayang

The lake was cold, but Bayang was used to the chilly depths of the sea, so the waters seemed like a warm bath that eased some of her aches away. She was free now and back with her hatchlings and she would never lose them again, and that determination refreshed her spirit just as the lake renewed her body.

She thought again of Leech's face as he tried to rip the bottom from the cage. He had been in such pain that she felt guilty for thinking that Lee No Cha had woken up. Lee would never have sacrificed himself for a dragon that way.

Churning up the lake's surface, the makara was shaking its head back and forth like a metronome with Nandi's silvery body wrapped around its head like a thin scarf. From the island, she could see the guards running onto the bridge, followed by the vizier. "Hurry, set up the machine gun," the vizier ordered shrilly.

Bayang's heart sank when she saw a pair of guards lift up a long weapon, resting the bipod near the gun muzzle on the bridge balustrade.

"Time to play submarine," Koko urged.

Before Bayang could submerge, though, the vizier began shouting, "Go way!"

She twisted her head around on her long neck to see him waving his arms frantically at the makara bearing down toward him.

The monster shook its head in frustration, and Bayang saw that Nandi's misty tendrils were pulling at the makara's nostrils just as a bull was led by a ring through its nose.

Waves rose higher and higher before the makara's body like an ocean linger plowing forward relentlessly.

"Never mind the trespassers for now. Everyone shoot at the makara!" the vizier cried.

The guards turned their rifles on the beast and soon the machine gun was chattering away, sending a rain of bullets at the makara. Mist spurted up where they entered Nandi and then sprayed up again as the ricochets from the makara's hide exited again through the ifrit.

The makara shook and shuddered from the hail of bullets, but goaded by Nandi, the monster churned on. Scirye couldn't see blood, but the bullets must have stung like insect bites because the monster was bellowing in rage.

Just before the makara reached the bridge, the cloudy ifrit shot skyward, leaving the furious beast to crash into the center of the bridge. Mortar crumbled and heavy stones flew about like toy blocks. As the bridge fell apart beneath them, men cried out in fear as they plunged into the icy water.

The makara towered above the lake for a moment, stunned by its sudden freedom and the silence and then lunged forward, wanting to take out its revenge on the nearest target.

Unfortunately for the vizier, he happened to be the closest as he splashed desperately for his island.

He had just enough time to holler, "No, go away. I'm your master."

But the great jaws closed around him, and his scream ended in a gurgle as the makara dove toward the depths of the lake, taking its latest victim along with it.

## 44

### Scirye

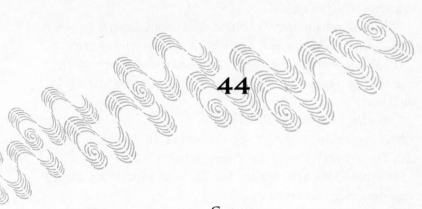 The exhausted dragon's paws slid in the mud on the far shore, so she reared up out of the lake instead and threw herself onto the slope, crawling on her belly like a humble slug behind a clump of bushes.

Scirye and the others slid off the dragon's back. Though Bayang had tried to keep them dry, their legs were wet, but even though Scirye was shivering a little, she was more concerned for her friend. "You need to rest."

Bayang sighed as she wriggled her shoulders. "There's an undersea volcano with these wonderful healing mud pits back at home. What I wouldn't give to soak in the ooze."

Scirye felt a little twinge, remembering that poor Bayang could never go there again. In disobeying her orders to kill Leech, the dragon had become an outlaw in the eyes of her clan.

"The main thing is that you're alive," Scirye said, hugging the dragon. "When this is over, we'll find you a whole health spa with mud baths and massages—though I'm not sure how you massage a dragon through her scales."

"Try a sledgehammer," Koko said. "And don't forget your other promise when we're finished. I finally get to eat everything I want."

Despite everything, they were all feeling cheerful because they were together again. "Maybe not everything," Scirye laughed, "or you'll burst."

"But what a way to go," Koko said.

Kles came skimming low over the bushes, fresh from his skirmish. Scirye held up her arm. "Welcome home."

He brushed his head against her sleeve in answer as a silvery cloud descended next to them.

The dragon raised her head wearily. "How do you do? You must be Nandi."

"And you must be Bayang." The cloud rippled with amusement. "Do the children always get you into so much mischief?"

"They've gotten me into a lot worse than this," Bayang chuckled.

"Yes, I heard about the volcano," Nandi said and suddenly began to rise. "Can you fight, dragon? It looks like the vizier has reinforcements coming."

Tilting back her head, Scirye saw five griffin riders dropping in a vee formation out of the sky. At the apex was a great white griffin that could only be Árkwi. And that meant the rider could only be her father, and mounted on the black griffin to his right would be her mother. Oko flew to her right while Wali and Kat formed the left side of the vee.

"Wait, Nandi," Scirye said. "They're friends."

Snow billowed upward from the griffins' great wings as they landed gracefully, but Scirye was already running through the spray of snowflakes.

Lord Tsirauñe kicked his feet free from the stirrups and jumped down beside her. "You certainly make life interesting, girl. *Oof!*" he said as Scirye wrapped her arms around him.

Scirye pressed her face into her father's leather riding coat. For the first time in many hours, she felt safe.

After a minute or so, she felt the rumble of her father's voice. "And who is this?" he asked.

Scirye turned to see Nandi floating politely behind her. He'd taken the form of a sphere. "Father, this is Nandi the ifrit who's been a big help to us. Princess Catisa sent him."

"I thank you and your mistress then," her father said with a bow.

With the same grace that she brought to everything, Lady Sudarshane swung her leg over her saddle and slid off Kwele to the ground. Her flying suit made her look more like a rough-and-tumble pirate than a diplomat. "I hope our daughter hasn't been making too much trouble for you?"

The globe of mist bent over almost double in Nandi's own version of a bow. "Judging from her character, it was probably no more than usual."

Lord Tsirauñe folded his arms as he regarded Scirye. "You've scared us half to death, young lady."

"I didn't mean to," Scirye said in a small voice.

Her mother tapped Scirye on her nose. "Innocent intentions are no excuse. Most of the guard and the garrison have been turned out to hunt for you."

Bayang gave a polite cough. "With all due respect, the accusations against me were false."

Scirye shifted her feet uncomfortably. "And anyway, we really shouldn't have been taken to the Chamber of Truth since it was illegal."

Lord Tsirauñe exchanged guilty glances with his wife before Lady Sudarshane said, "It's our fault. We should never have let the vizier's guards take you."

"Thank Nanaia you escaped," her father said and then scratched the tip of his nose. "You know, when the Chamber was operating legally, no one ever broke free from there? How many parents can brag that their daughter not only escaped but was the number one criminal in the empire?"

Lady Sudarshane wrapped her arms around her husband and daughter. "We're not supposed to be proud of that, dear."

Lord Tsirauñe laughed. "Well, we always hoped Scirye would leave her mark on the world, but I wish she would've done something safer—like knitting the longest scarf in the world."

Scirye returned their embrace just as fiercely, but she couldn't help wondering if she would ever get to do this again. Only the goddess knew.

Finally, her mother said, "When Kat informed us of the vizier's treachery, the princess thought it would be better if we got you first. Once you were safe back at the citadel, she could tell His Highness what the vizier had done. She was afraid that if she told His Highness right away, he would send an expedition, which would be bound to have some of the vizier's assassins."

Kles understood court intrigues. "Who might arrange an unfortunate accident that would remove inconvenient witnesses like us."

Bayang looked at the rescue party. "But she sent only five of you?"

"Five are more than enough," Kat replied, "if it's the griffin master and three Pippalanta and one former member."

"True enough," the dragon gladly conceded.

After Scirye had introduced Bayang to the Pippalanta, Lady Sudarshane glanced around. "Now where is that weasel of a vizier? I want to wring his neck." Her mother made a choking motion with both hands.

"The vizier is dead," Scirye said. "He was killed by a makara in the lake."

"I suppose it's only fitting that his pet should take care of him." Her father clapped his hands together. "So now we can take you home."

Scirye tensed, suddenly dreading the next moment. "I need to go on to the City of Death with my friends. Roland bought the loyalty of the vizier's guards here, and I bet he's done the same with the ones sent to protect the city."

Remembering their argument in the stables, Scirye cringed and waited for an angry confrontation—or worse, some condescending remark—but her father simply frowned thoughtfully.

Bayang added, "And Roland will have his hired thugee too."

"Thugee?" Lady Sudarshane looked as if the very word were disgusting. "The man's shameless."

"The news gets worse and yet," Lord Tsirauñe regarded his daughter, "you mean to go on?"

Scirye tried to look him in the eye to show her determination. "Yes."

Her mother studied her as if she no longer recognized her daughter. "I didn't want to believe the tales about you, but you've changed. Perhaps this is the goddess's doing."

"Excuse me, my lady," Bayang said, "but I think Scirye's heart was always this strong. It was just hidden until the attack at the museum cracked the shell."

"She's grown up," Lord Tsirauñe admitted and smiled sadly. "Even if it's better for the world, I still wish it could have taken longer."

Her mother gazed at her with fierce pride. "Scirye, whether it's your choice or the goddess's, we'll help you."

Scirye stared at them in surprise.

Lady Sudarshane put a finger to Scirye's chin and gently shut her open mouth. "Back at the citadel, your father and I were trying so hard to avoid the truth. Going to the city is Tumarg."

There was no need to explain further. Her parents had taught her, just as they had taught Nishke, that honor came before even personal safety.

Her father nodded. "Many talk about Tumarg, but few follow it. We're very proud of you."

Scirye felt a warm glow as her mother added with a shrug. "Anyway, your father and I were talking about doing more together as a family—though I had hoped it would be a picnic."

When her mother glanced over at the Pippalanta, Kat spoke for them. "Count us in too. We have a score to settle with this Badik and Roland." Oko and Wali grinned as they nodded.

As Kles hastily adjusted her clothes and hair, Scirye turned to the golden cloud that had been hovering nearby. "Nandi, can you take a message back to Princess Maimantstse at the citadel?"

A hole appeared in the mist that curved upward at the ends like a smile. "I think that would come under my mistress's instructions to help you."

Her parents gave a description of Princess Maimantstse's palace and then said, "Please tell her that we will not be coming back with Scirye because Roland will be at the city soon and the vizier's guards will probably help him, not stop him. Ask her to bring every warrior she can muster and join us there." Her father finished with a bow. "If you tell her that, the House of Rapaññe will be in your debt."

Nandi's misty tendril waggled back and forth. "Consider it partial payment from the House of Urak and from myself."

Then he began to glide upward until he was ten yards above their heads. Extending a dozen tendrils, he waved toward the paradise. A moment later, a shimmering cloud rose above the roofs of the island and sped toward him. As it neared, Scirye saw the butterflies flittering through the air in a horde.

She watched them and Nandi speed toward Bactra. "Good-bye and thank you." She kept waving until they were out of sight.

As her mother watched the ifrit with the long train of glistening butterflies behind him, she murmured, "Your father and I can't wait to hear the rest of your tale."

Koko began to brush some of the dirt from his fur. "Just think of it as a picnic with guns and monsters instead of mosquitoes and ants. Do we have fun or what?"

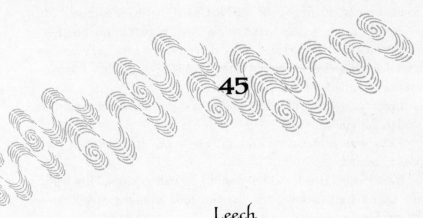

# 45

## Leech

*Her parents came for her.* The Voice sounded amazed and sad.

"They must love her a lot," Leech agreed.

He hadn't realized he'd spoken out loud until Koko punched him lightly in the arm. "What do you expect? She's got a pedigree. She's not a mutt like you and me."

Leech hadn't been able to take his eyes away from Scirye and her family. "That's the way parents are supposed to be, isn't it? I mean, not abandon them or kill them, actually protect their children," he said wistfully.

"Are you thinking about your own parents or Lee No Cha's?" Bayang asked thoughtfully.

*Careful. If she thinks I'm here,* the Voice sounded frightened but defiant, *it won't matter that you're different from me. As long as I'm inside you, she'll have to kill you too.*

Leech felt his stomach flip-flop, but he forced himself to look right back at the dragon. "I don't know anything about my own folks so I've been wondering about Lee No Cha's. They were so cruel."

"I was curious too so I read our records as part of my briefing for my mission," Bayang said. "The dragon elders gave Lee's family a choice: kill Lee or we would exterminate the entire clan. It was a choice no parents would want to make."

Leech cringed inside. *No wonder you don't trust anyone,* he said to the Voice.

*I dare you to ask your "friend" about the other killings,* the Voice taunted.

Even though Leech did not want to, he had to know. "But with the later reincarnations, you dragons took over the executions. Wasn't his first death enough?"

Bayang looked away in embarrassment. "The elders didn't want to take the risk."

And so Bayang had become the Hunter and Lee No Cha the Hunted.

But again Leech sensed there was something beyond that bond between Bayang and the Voice. And then the boy remembered what Bayang had said about her own youth and her reasons for becoming a warrior. "How old were you when Badik started his war?" the boy asked.

"About the equivalent of a six-year-old human," Bayang said.

"I bet you were too small and weak to fight against grown dragons," Leech said.

"Unfortunately, that was all too true," Bayang admitted.

Leech touched his arm, feeling for his missing armband. "But what if you'd had a powerful device back then and you had met Badik?"

"I'd have broken every bone in his body," Bayang replied without hesitation.

Leech felt as if he were acting as an interpreter for both Bayang and the Voice. "So maybe Lee was just as scared and just as angry when he killed the dragon prince."

"I would never have made a belt out of Badik's hide like Lee No Cha did with his victim," Bayang snapped.

*I thought if I gave it to father, he wouldn't get mad,* the Voice insisted.

Leech tried to convey the Voice's thoughts to the dragon. "Maybe he panicked. He was only a kid after all. Maybe he was more afraid of what his parents would say than of the dragons. So he thought if he gave his father a gift, he wouldn't be so angry."

Bayang arched her neck so her face was in front of Leech's. Her eyes bored into his as if she were hunting for Lee hiding inside him. "Do you think he eventually realized it was wrong?"

Leech took a step back before that penetrating gaze, and he heard the Voice give an involuntary whimper. *It was a bad thing to do,* the Voice confessed. The shame was plain in his tone.

"Yes, I think he . . . did," Leech said to the dragon and added for the benefit of both the Voice and the dragon. "We can't undo the bad things we did, but we can try to do good things to try to balance things out. I mean, you were an assassin but then you became my bodyguard."

Bayang folded her forelegs, tapping a claw against her scales as she thought a moment. "And I hope I'm your friend too."

"And what about Lee if he was alive?" Leech asked. "You're like each other in a way."

Suddenly they heard Momo call down from above them. "Look out below."

Leech leaned his head back to see the badger riding on a sleek thoroughbred griffin. It might have even been the one that had carried the vizier to the villa.

A sack plummeted toward the ground, and the Amazons, who'd been tending their griffins, shoved their mounts away as they themselves jumped back before the bag thumped down in their midst with metallic clinks.

"I found this stuff while I was taking my severance pay from the vizier's baggage," Momo hollered. She pointed to the large bundle still tied behind her on the griffin's back and then pointed below. "I thought you might need your things back."

Leech ran to the sack immediately and opened it to reveal Pele's charms, the pouch with the chess piece, and Leech's armbands—the hag's belt must still be at the citadel being studied by the mages. Māka's zodiac necklace and belt of star charms were there, though, and so, unfortunately, was her grimoire.

"My armbands," Leech said, holding them up lovingly.

"And my book," Māka said, hugging it to her.

Tute rolled his eyes. "There's always some bad news to balance out the good."

Koko cupped his paws around his mouth to form a megaphone. "Okay, doll, I forgive you."

"That's nice," Momo shouted sassily, "but who asked you to do that, handsome? Maybe I'll bump into you again somewhere some-when and we can chat again."

"Count on it, doll," Koko promised.

At a kick of Momo's heels, the griffin banked and then began flapping toward the south.

Koko set his paws on his ample hips. "Now there goes a badger after my own heart."

"She turned out to be nice after all," Leech said.

Koko grinned. "Nice-schmice. Did you see the size of her sack of loot?"

He was still shaking his head in admiration as Momo vanished into the sky, griffin, stolen treasure, and all.

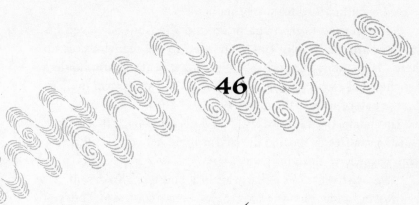

# 46

## Leech

Leech couldn't wait to mount the flying discs once more. As he rose into the air, Lord Tsirauñe gazed at him. "So it's true."

Aware of all their eyes on him, Leech skipped through the air like a stone over a lake.

Tute butted Māka's hip. "Now, if you could work that kind of magic, we'd actually get to finish a performance."

"I'm afraid these are one of a kind," Leech said as he glided back to them. He swung his arm, pleased at the familiar weight of his weapon armband.

"Don't forget this. You may need it in the mountains even with the clothes Princess Catisa gave us," Scirye said, holding out one of Pele's charms to Leech.

"What about your parents?" he asked.

Lord Tsirauñe waved a hand to include not only his wife but the

Amazons. "We have a warming charm written on the inside of our traveling outfits. So don't worry about us."

Scirye started to tie a charm around Kles, but he waved his paw toward Māka and Tute. "I'm used to the temperatures up here. They'll need it more. As long as one of the charm holders touches those who don't have it, they should stay warm too." So Scirye passed it on to the magician.

Tute bumped her leg. "At last, you've got some magic that works."

Māka sniffed as she tied the charm about her neck. "A little encouragement wouldn't hurt, you know."

"I just wish there was a charm against monsters," Koko said.

"Roland and his monsters scare me," Scirye confessed, "but you know what frightens me even more? Dealing with the goddess."

Leech watched enviously as Lady Sudarshane slid an arm around her daughter. "We can help you carry out your mission but not with Her. I wish we could though."

Her father hooked a thumb in his belt. "All She wants is the arrows, right?"

"I think so," Scirye admitted. "But I can't be sure. She's never been clear about what She wants."

"It's really frustrating, isn't it?" Leech sympathized.

"Hmm, maybe She's just as frustrated," her mother said. "Just imagine if you were trying to talk to a spider? Your words would just be meaningless sounds to it. And even if it understood your language, it wouldn't have your knowledge and memories, so it still wouldn't understand." Lady Miunai had said much the same thing to them when they had talked to her about the goddess.

They made camp there and Bayang told them of her adventures after her kidnapping, and they told her about theirs.

Then Scirye turned to the Pippalanta. "Did you have any trouble getting to my parents?"

Kat and the other Pippalanta looked like walking arsenals with their swords hung in sheaths slung diagonally across their backs, daggers hanging from their waist, and rifles slung over their shoulders—and that didn't include the lances they had left in the saddle sheaths. And yet, despite all the weight of their gear, they looked far more comfortable than they had when they only had brooms.

Kat slapped her thigh with a laugh. "Who pays attention to servants? We just walked right into the citadel like we figured we could."

Oko grimaced. "Though it made me grind my teeth to have to ask as meek as a mouse."

It was hard, Leech thought, to see how anyone could ever mistake Oko for a mouse, no less a meek one.

"Among other things, the princess will demand our reinstatement," Wali said. "We'll be Pippalanta again."

Kat nodded to Bayang. "So you're Bayang."

"We've seen each other before. I was at the museum too, but in disguise," the dragon explained. "I was the elderly woman with the chain."

Oko chuckled. "I was wondering how San Francisco bred such strong old folk."

For the few hours before dawn, they tried to rest while each of them took a turn keeping watch. Leech, though, was too excited to sleep and kept touching his armbands to make sure they were still there.

The next morning they breakfasted on cheese, dried fruits, nuts, and some dried bread, and then they mounted again. Leech, of course, mounted his flying discs.

Even if it meant a delay, they circled around the paradise because of the rifles of the vizier's guardsmen. When they had found the old dirt road to Riye Srukalleyis, Bayang gestured for them to go lower and they descended so they could all see the numerous ruts. When they landed, the tread marks were unmistakable.

"Roland's caravan must have made those," Scirye said. "I hope he doesn't find the arrows before we get there."

"He's not the goddess's friend," Māka said simply.

Leech glanced at her to see if she was being sarcastic, but she looked perfectly confident.

Scirye squirmed. "I'm nothing special."

It was like his friend to be modest—or perhaps uncomfortable with her role. "You've gotten us this far," Leech assured her.

"We've done it together," Scirye insisted.

Soon the land began to rise as they reached the foothills of the Astär Mountains. They were about twenty miles to the west of the Tarkär Eyrie and no one wanted to delay to go there for help. Nor did they want to deplete their small party even further by sending a messenger there. So they continued on in a straight course.

Most of the rolling land was wrapped in a dense skein of leafless vines like brown ropes that Lord Tsirauñe said were the former vineyards of the Greeks who had lived here before the Kushans. The veterans of Alexander the Great's army, they had been just one of the many groups who had settled here. "These hills were special to them," he explained, "because their god, Dionysus, was said to have been born here."

Leech thought of Princess Catisa's warning. "He sounds dangerous."

Lord Tsirauñe studied the land below as if looking for the god. "I'd be careful what I said about him, especially here. And above all, always show him respect."

Here and there, groves of wild pistachios, almond, and redbud trees struggled out of the tangle like swimmers trying to crest a wave. Leech tried to imagine what it would be like in the spring. "The hills must look like the green waves of an ocean."

"And in the autumn, they burn yellow and red like fire." The griffin master looked over his shoulder at his daughter. "When we were courting, your mother and I used to come here all the time to picnic."

By afternoon, the grape vines disappeared, and the pistachio and redbud trees gave way to what Māka said were forests of junipers. Though there were still some almond trees even at the higher altitudes, these were wild ones so they were of a smaller, scragglier size.

It was here that Leech began to have trouble flying. He dipped when he meant to fly level and strayed into the path of a griffin when he intended to go straight.

*I thought you could handle the flying discs,* the Voice complained.

Nothing escaped the griffin master's watchful eyes. "The air's thinner at this altitude," Lord Tsirauñe explained, "so it makes flying trickier. The griffins grew up here so they're used to it, but you're not."

Leech's chest heaved in and out as he took several large breaths. "But I can still breathe okay."

"There must be a breathing spell that's part of Pele's charm then," Kles reasoned. "It did let us breathe while we were surrounded by lava." That had been when Pele had taken them up through a volcano.

"Take your time and allow more space for maneuvering," Lord Tsirauñe advised.

"But sometimes the wind shifts quickly," Leech said.

"Sometimes you can find clues before that happens." Lord Tsirauñe pointed at puffs of snow blowing off a cliff face. "That tells me the winds are going to change and what way they are going to move."

The griffin master had other tips about flying that Leech drank in thirstily.

Even the Voice was impressed. *I thought I knew a lot, but he knows more.*

*He's a true lord of the air,* Leech agreed.

Leech tried his best to put the lessons into practice, but it was during one of his many failures that he found the first sign that Roland had passed this way. Though he scanned the sky and land diligently for hints about the wind's intentions, a sudden twist of the capricious winds sent Leech plunging downward.

He pulled out safely at about thirty feet above the ground, and as he leveled off, he spotted the dark shape off the side of the road. Remembering to do things slowly and carefully, he circled around to see that it was a truck tumbled on his side.

When he called the others' attention to it, they spiraled down to the ground. Tute immediately jumped off the griffin he was riding to examine the road.

He pointed to a huge hole in the middle of the road that was full of rocks and gravel and then swung his claw toward the truck's broken front axle. "*That's* what wrecked the truck. It must have been in the lead. When it lost an axle, they dumped it off to the side"—he indicated the numerous footprints and the skid marks—"and then filled the hole with the debris around here so the others could get by."

He padded back and forth studying the tracks. "I'd say this happened two days ago."

"So they're not that far ahead," Leech said.

The whole company's spirits rose at the news and they flew on eagerly as the foothills gave way to the steep slopes of the mountains themselves, not even the hardiest trees could find enough space for their roots. The only plant life were weeds poking up through the snow on narrow ledges or out of crevices. The road itself snaked back and forth up the face of the mountainside like a long snow-covered ribbon.

The nearly barren mountains, their shoulders dusted with snow, towered over them like monsters waiting to crush them. Leech felt as if he were a bug flying around over their toes.

They found more evidence that trucks were a poor choice for a caravan. In one spot, a landslide obliterated the road and down at the bottom of the cliff was the burned-out hulk of a truck that must have gotten caught in it.

Roland's expedition had to dig a path over the rubble so the other trucks could get by. A few miles on, they found another truck with a broken axle—this one caused by a huge rock. Roland even had to begin jettisoning supplies because there were fewer vehicles to carry them. They also found several cairns of stones that hastily covered a body. With his typical ruthlessness, Roland was pushing his men and machines to the breaking point.

Lord Tsirauñe frowned as he saw Leech bob up and down in the air like a cork in a stormy sea. Despite Leech's best efforts, it was all he could do to stay upright.

"For now, I think you'd better ride with Oko again," Lord Tsirauñe ordered. When the boy opened his mouth to object, the griffin master held up a hand. "We'll need you when we meet Roland so we can't afford to have you break a leg or worse."

Somehow Leech managed to right himself. "I'm okay." Almost immediately, he was turned sideways and sent rolling along.

"This is no time to be proud, boy," Lord Tsirauñe insisted sternly and turned to the blond Amazon. "Oko."

Oko swung out of formation, angling beneath Leech and then, careful as a mother hawk with a fledgling, rose slowly to meet him.

*He can't treat us like a baby,* the Voice fumed.

Even though the dragons had been wrong abou Lee's motives, they had been right about his hot temper.

*It's tough enough feuding with all dragon-kind. Now you want to pick a fight with Scirye's father?* Leech asked. *Did you know about all those ways to tell shifts in the wind?*

*Well, no,* the Voice admitted.

Leech could sense the Voice beginning to pout. *I have to treat him like the kid he is,* Leech thought to himself and then to the Voice he said, *You know a lot about flying, but Lord Tsirauñe knows more. If we don't listen to him, we might not live much longer.*

Leech sensed a hunger in the Voice. *I want to do all the things I never got to do. If he can help us, then I say, "All right."*

As Leech carefully banked toward Oko, the Amazon caught him with one arm and slung him up behind her, all in one smooth motion.

Bayang yelled, "I wish you could teach me how to get him to listen to me."

"I will when I get my stubborn daughter to do what I say," Lord Tsirauñe shouted back and then squirmed. "Don't tickle me," he scolded his daughter.

Scirye smiled politely. "I was merely adjusting my grip."

*My father would have hit me if I'd done something so disrespectful*, the Voice said.

*At least you had a father*, Leech said.

*Yes, but I might have lived longer without one*, the Voice said.

As Leech rode behind Oko, he thought over what he had just sensed from the Voice. The Voice could be so selfish sometimes, but that's what you had to expect from a small kid. And when the Voice said some of the vicious things it did, it wasn't because it was a cruel monster but because it was a small, frightened person who was desperate to live.

But how much could he tell Bayang about his suspicions? And how would she react?

Leaving the flying to Oko, he had a chance to think about what to do. He was still pondering the matter at sunset when they heard the voices moaning.

"Wazzat? Wazzat?" Koko demanded, twisting his head this way and that anxiously.

"We're nearing the Maenads' Pass," Kles said.

"Those were the crazy woman who followed Di...Di...," Leech struggled with the god's name.

"Dionysus," Kles said.

"The one Princess Catisa warned us about," Leech said.

Koko's eyes widened. "Is that the maenads' ghosts wailing?"

"No, the wall of the pass is honeycombed with the eyrie's tunnels," Kles explained. "That's just the wind whistling through the passages."

"Turning it into one big flute," Māka said, nodding her understanding.

"Well, I would have put it more elegantly, but in effect, yes," Kles agreed.

The higher they climbed, the louder the moaning grew. Leech kept telling himself that it was just the wind, but he couldn't help thinking that it sounded too mournful to be just a natural phenomenon. At any moment, Leech expected crazy-eyed spirits to leap out at them.

*I don't like this place*, the Voice whimpered.

Leech thought of the Voice as a small frightened boy, crouching in the darkness. He wished he could have given him a hug, but all he could say was, *None of us do*.

## 47

## Scirye

The pass was about a half-mile wide, and as different as could be from the steppes, and yet the bleak terrain made her feel just as lonely and insignificant.

Seen from above, the snow-covered floor of the pass looked like a frosted cake, except for the ragged gash where Roland's men had dug a path for his truck convoy. And despite their prayers to Oesho, the winds tugged and pulled at them as if determined to unseat the riders. Sometimes the winds felt like invisible serpents coiling about them and then trying to yank them aloft.

It took all of the griffin master's skills to keep them more or less on course, and even he could not keep the griffins from veering the wrong way or plunging up and down as if on a roller coaster.

The howling wind intensified until the griffins were straining just to keep from being blown backward. Her father listened to the panting of the griffins and saw the irregular, awkward strokes of their wings. And despite Pele's charm, Scirye's cheeks felt numb from the cold. She could only imagine how her parents and the Pippalanta were managing in just their flying gear.

"This is no good," her father finally announced to the company. He motioned at the floor of the pass. "We'll have to camp here and hope the winds slacken in the morning."

The pass answered him with a deep moan followed by wails from other caves. Even though Scirye knew there was a logical explanation for the sound, she could not shake an eerie feeling.

Roland's men had shoveled a path across the floor of the pass, but on either side the snow rose to six feet high. When they landed on the trail and Koko got off, he gave a little hop. "Yikes! There's someone there."

Readying his weapon armband, Leech jumped from Oko's griffin and aimed at the spot where the pale face peered through the snow on the right side. He squinted at it a moment and then stood up. "It's a statue, you idiot. The eyes aren't blinking."

Curious, Scirye high-stepped through the snow to where Leech was hovering. Squatting down, she scraped the snow off to reveal a head broken off some statue.

The full-fleshed lips were smiling at some secret prank being played on them, and the eyes seemed to mock them.

"There's the rest of him," Kles said, pointing at the torso that stuck up from the snow on the side.

Scirye looked at the head and then leaned against the snowbank to examine the torso. "It's pitted all over with bullet holes."

"The holes are new too," Kat observed with a professional eye.

"Maybe Roland's guards used it for target practice," Koko said.

Kneeling, Māka studied the head. "It looks Greek. To think it survived intact all those centuries until those modern barbarians damaged it for sport."

"And in his own home too." Bending over, Scirye began to dig through the snow toward the statue. "It's not Tumarg to do this to something this old."

"What are you doing, lady?" Wali asked.

"I'm going to put this head back on the statue." Scirye kept fling-ing handfuls of snow to the side until a few minutes later, Kat joined her with a collapsible shovel.

"Allow me a turn, lady," Kat said. The Pippal made short work of digging a trench to the statue. Straightening, she called to her friends, "Wali, Oko, bring the head here."

With a boost from Kat, Scirye managed to lie on top of the snowbank next to the statue. As Oko and Wali lifted the heavy head, Scirye cleaned the snowflakes and bits of ice from the cheeks and nose and then tried to position it on the neck. Some bits must have been lost from the neck because it tilted slightly off center.

"I'm sorry," Scirye said to the statue, dusting the snow from her palms. "I'm afraid that's the best we can do for now. But when"—she made a point of using *when*—"we get back, I'll make sure it's done right."

As the Pippalanta helped lift her from the snowbank down to the trail, her father scraped enough snow away from the torso until he revealed the pedestal on which it stood. Bending over, he read the inscription on its plaque. "This is Dionysus himself," Lord Tsirauñe gasped and stepped back.

Lady Sudarshane nodded. "You'd expect to find a shrine to him up here. The Greeks claimed He was born in these very moun-tains. They loved Him for His wine and wild songs—and feared Him for what his gifts did to humans."

"Dionysus sounds like a dockworker on payday," Koko ob-served. "It's always a good idea to give one of them a wide berth."

Lady Sudarshane shook her head. "You don't understand. He filled normal women with such ecstasy that they lost all control and did terrible things. Maenads, they were called, and they would chase down wild animals, tear them apart, and devour them raw. Once, under Dionysus's spell, a queen killed and ate her own son."

"Is he still around?" Leech asked with a shiver.

Lord Tsirauñe scratched his throat. "I've always thought they were just traveler's tales, but one man claimed to have found the prints of a giant tiger like the one that He rides."

"And I met a man once," Kat said in a hushed voice, "who said he'd seen the lights of His maenads flitting across the hills at night. They were calling something like this." She threw back her head and made a ghostly whisper from the back of her throat. " '*Euoi. Euoi.*' He left everything—camel, tent, trade goods—and ran for his life."

Cautiously, Scirye retreated several steps. She hoped she hadn't done anything to annoy him.

Only Māka remained by the statue. "Roland's fools have just condemned themselves," she said as somber as a judge delivering a death sentence. "The land will rise up against them now." She placed a palm upon the statue as she gazed up into Dionysus's blank eyes. "But as you carry out your vengeance, lord, please also remember the kindness that Lady Scirye did you."

By common consent, they made camp farther along the trail, out of sight of the statue. The walls of snow on either side gave them shelter from the fierce winds of the pass, but not the keening from the passages of the dead eyrie. No one, not even Koko, felt much like talking and they turned in after a quick meal.

All too soon, though, Scirye felt Wali shaking her shoulder.

"It's midnight, lady. Time for you to take my place at keeping watch," whispered the Pippal.

Scirye became aware of herself lying on a blanket on the ground with her arms around her griffin and his foreleg around her. Carefully, she tried to disentangle herself, but Kles woke up anyway.

"Go back to sleep, Kles," she whispered as she sat up.

"I'm awake anyway," Kles said. His beak clacked in a big yawn.

As Wali lay down, Scirye said to Kles, "You don't have to take my turn with me. After all, you don't expect me to stay up when you do it."

The griffin crept up her arm to her shoulder. "I'll make sure you keep awake." His paws began to groom her. "And your hair's in a frightful mess again."

Scirye wrapped her blanket around them, submitting to the soothing rhythm of his claws. It wasn't long before she noticed that his paws slowed and then stopped all together. With a smile, she gently lowered the snoring griffin onto her lap.

As Scirye listened to the others sleeping, she suddenly felt very protective of them. They trusted her while they were in such a helpless state. Well, she wouldn't let them down.

She was startled by a puff of warm, moist air on the back of her neck and jerked around. A tiger as big as a bull stared down at her. Tilting on the tiger's head—almost hanging from one ear, in fact— was an ivy wreath. The tiger's large eyes glowed like green coals as they regarded her.

She opened her mouth to warn the others, but the tiger's rider leaned forward so that his chest rested against the tiger's great head. He wore a tunic of red and gold silk, cut in the style of the antique costumes that the Kushan men had worn when the exhibit had opened at the museum in San Francisco. Small gold pendants shaped like clusters of grapes dangled from his curly hair.

The rider's face was the same as the statue's, but every strand, every detail of the face, the very pores of his perfect skin, seemed sharply etched while everything around him seemed blurred in comparison, as if Dionysus were the most real thing here, far realer than his statue or Scirye or any other living creature.

Scirye couldn't move. All she could do was gaze upward into eyes that glittered like sparks whirling above a bonfire with wild and energetic and unpredictable joy.

Scirye was so frightened that her voice came out as a raspy whisper. "Wh-what do you want, l-l-lord?"

Dionysus smiled as if the two of them were sharing a private joke and then he beckoned to her.

Suddenly she was no longer in the pass but on a hillside on an autumn night among rows of vines climbing up stakes, their clusters of ripe, round grapes silvered by the moonlight. Leaves rustled everywhere, making a sound of distant surf, and the air was filled with a heady, sweet smell of ripening fruit.

And she was throwing herself recklessly through the grape vines in a headlong plunge down a hill, feet pounding the earth as if it were a giant drum. Girls and women were singing and laughing all around her, laurel wreaths entwined in their hair in time to the beating of tambourines and jingling sistra and notes of reed pipes.

Though she did not recognize the words of the song, she cried out the chorus as loudly as everyone else, *"Euoi! Euoi!"* The syllables were like drops of honey to her tongue. The earth itself pumped its energy into her each time the soles of her bare feet pattered against the dirt so that she felt like she could dance forever.

Were these the maenads her mother had warned her about? But these were no wild hunters. These were people who were enjoying being alive.

"Euoi!" Scirye said.

"What did you say, lady?" Kles asked as if from faraway.

Scirye felt as if she had forgotten something important that she had to do. And her hand burned as if she were holding a red-hot coal.

"Euoi-euoi-euoi!" The singing and the music became louder and more frantic, and caught up in the frenetic rhythm, Scirye told herself that the errand could wait for tomorrow. Right now, she was enjoying herself too much.

"Lady?" Kles called again. She felt something light, soft blows on her chin like dry raindrops.

And suddenly Scirye remembered the arrows.

She sat up, panting to see that her griffin had reared up from her lap and was using his paws to pat either side of her jaw. The mark on her hand shone with a fierce light.

Heart still pounding, she looked about. She was no longer dancing through the autumn hills but was once more sitting in a wintry mountain pass.

Suddenly she felt so empty, so dead inside—gone was the energy and the joy and the laughter. And she began to cry.

Kles surged up to her shoulder so he could stroke her head and coo to her as if she were a frightened hatchling. "Sa, sa, it's all right, lady. Your Kles is here."

She leaned her forehead against his as she did when she was confessing her innermost secrets. "I had a dream. No, I met Dionysus and joined His maenads. And it was so wonderful." Even now, she felt an itch in her legs that she could only satisfy by dancing.

"Perhaps He was inviting you to join Him because you tried to fix His statue," Kles suggested as he wiped her tears away with the soft back of his paw.

She raised a hand and pressed him closer. "If you hadn't woken me when you did, maybe I would have gone too deep into that dream and never have come back." Even now, she felt regret that the griffin had roused her.

"I'm beginning to think that Dionysus isn't as cruel as I thought," Kles said. "The problem is that He doesn't understand humans very well, so He can't see that some of His good deeds can harm mere mortals."

She thought of the maenads. At least Nanaia had never filled her with such a hunger as Dionysus had. "So maybe it's better if the goddess doesn't change things for me. I've got to do it myself."

"There's a fine line between helping and interfering," the griffin observed. "Perhaps this is why the goddess gives you hints rather than getting involved directly," Kles said. "She's so powerful that when she came to you in a vision, just that slight bit of Her knocked you out for an hour. If she were to appear right now to tell you what to do—."

"I might go into a coma for years and years," Scirye said. "Or maybe I wouldn't wake up at all." The new insight didn't erase all the frustration she felt, but at least it helped.

"Bayang warned you about getting mixed up with gods and

goddesses," Kles reminded her. "Speaking of which, it's her turn to keep watch."

When they woke Bayang, Scirye told her what she had seen and heard.

Bayang gazed at her a moment, the golden orbs of her pupils almost gleaming. No human had such eyes, only a dragon.

"Maybe I'll take the rest of the watches," Bayang said. "Dionysus holds no sway over dragons."

Scirye did not dream again of the maenads and she felt a little sad when she woke up the next morning. Apparently, you could not expect more than one invitation from Dionysus to join the dance, and she had missed her chance.

But as she sniffed the cold air, she smelled the sweet, heady scents of her dream, and she sat up. The dragon was lying coiled in the snow, casually popping grapes into her mouth from a basket as she gazed at the sleeping Leech. She'd been doing that a lot since Leech had become distracted, as if she were trying to figure out what was happening inside their friend's mind.

"Where did you get grapes in winter?" Scirye gasped.

Bayang held a grape up between her claws. "I was keeping watch and as I turned my head—poof!—the basket was right next to you."

Scirye plucked a grape from the cluster. It was about the size of her thumb and greenish gold. When she bit into it, her mouth was flooded with a golden warmth like a summer sun. Maybe this was Dionysus's way of encouraging her—a sort of consolation prize.

She watched Kles take a grape between his paws and begin to nibble it enthusiastically. "I've never tasted anything this good," he said.

Bayang held a claw up to her muzzle. "Listen. What do you hear?"

Scirye's ears strained in the hopes of catching the sound of drums and reed pipes again, but it was silent. The air was still and the pass was no longer wailing.

"I don't hear anything. The winds have died down. Do you think Dionysus calmed the winds for us?" Kles asked.

Scirye wrapped her arms around her griffin as if he were an anchor. "I think He did. He's helping us along and not bearing any grudges because I didn't join His maenads."

"I'd better wake up everyone else, or I'll eat all the grapes," Bayang said and began rousing the rest of the company.

Scirye had to agree. It was hard to stop with just one.

When they were all awake, Scirye told the others about what had happened last night.

Kat nodded when she finished. "Dionysus has blessed you— and us."

But Māka was actually annoyed. "He had no right to claim you because you belong to Nanaia."

"You might want to keep your voice down," Tute warned.

"A follower of the True Path must scold even a god when he misbehaves," Māka said indignantly as she got to her feet.

Scirye tried to pull her friend back down. "I think He was offering me a gift, and I was free to turn it down."

Māka, though, was determined to protect Scirye. Māka balled her hands into fists and defiantly faced the direction of Dionysus's statue. "Scirye has been chosen by Nanaia already," she scolded. "She cannot be yours."

Koko cringed as her voice echoed from the frozen walls. "Now you've done it."

No one moved. No one said anything. They hardly dared to breathe as they waited for hordes of vengeful maenads to attack.

When nothing happened after several minutes, Māka began to look sheepish. Scirye reached up and tugged at her sleeve. "Thanks for defending me, but why don't you sit down and enjoy the god's gift?"

Koko helped himself to a handful of grapes. "Don't scare me like that. I almost lost my appetite."

But as each of the Pippalanta took their share, they dipped their heads respectfully first to Dionysus and then to Scirye, much to her surprise and discomfort. Even her parents regarded her thoughtfully as they sampled the grapes.

*Back in the palace, I resented that they treated me like a little girl,* Scirye thought sadly. *Now I wish they would.* But as she ate another grape, she felt a new energy wash away any sadness. Anything, even getting the arrows, seemed possible this morning.

She hoped so.

# 48

## Bayang

Refreshed, they soared through the pass with all the ease of a holiday flight. And as they neared the end of Dionysus's pass, Scirye turned around and called behind them, "Thank you."

As they left the pass, the winds became strong again as they roared up the steep slope. Angling downward, Wali's griffin bobbed up and down and swayed from side to side as if drunk. Even so, the Pippal and her griffin remained as calm as if they were out for just a little exercise.

Though Bayang would usually have preferred to be flying on her own, she was glad to leave it to Wali right now. Her body still ached from the torture at the villa, and though she had slept well, she would still need many more hours of rest to make up for what she had lost. Even a dragon's iron constitution had its limits.

As they descended, they paralleled the frozen waterfall that looked like a tower of ice had fallen on the slope. Fringes of icicles decorated the sides, and judging by the waterfall's width, the river must be impressive in the spring thaw.

Snow lay in crevices and on ledges in cottony lumps as if the mountains had just been pulled from a giant box and the packing was still clinging to it. Here and there a scrawny, leafless tree twisted out of some crack in the rock as it struggled to survive.

The base of the mountain ridge thrust out in a series of wider shelves that descended to the foothills below.

The next ridge was lower than the pass, but steepness of its barren slopes gave them an impression of greater height. Wingless because of her injuries, Bayang was glad she was riding a griffin rather than trying to climb the sheer sides with just her paws. She could just make out the snowy road that snaked up the ridge and a wrecked truck lying off to the side. It would be amazing if Roland got any of his vehicles through.

But it was Leech who dominated her gloomy thoughts. The clever hatchling had obviously been arguing not only with Bayang but with Lee No Cha as well. That meant that Leech was still in control of his mind and body and not the monster Lee. But how long could the human hatchling hold out against a strong-willed killer like Lee?

*Wait. Leech had been trying to get me to look at things as a human, not as a dragon.* She owed that much at least to the hatchling who had saved her life.

It would not have been easy for most dragons whose lives were bound by tradition, but as an assassin, she had taken pride in her ability to disguise herself in posture, thought, words, and actions as well as in costume. To pull that off, she'd learned how to cast off her dragonness and think like the character she wanted to become.

So she tried to see things through the eyes of a human almost newly hatched facing a dragon prince in all his righteous indignation—the large, strong body; the sharp claws and fangs. She would have used her most powerful weapon to smash the threat too.

And afterward a hatchling's primary concern would be avoiding his or her parents' anger and might not be aware of what other dragons would say if he or she mutilated the corpse.

At least Bayang had been able to grow up and become a warrior who never again had to feel so afraid and helpless. The Lee that was trapped inside Leech had remained that terrified hatchling whose inexperienced mind believed violence was the answer to any threat.

She remembered how frightened and angry she had been during Badik's invasion. What if her mind had remained forever locked as that scared hatchling, never to mature, never to escape?

Shame washed over her. And what if Lee had been awake in some of the reincarnations when Bayang had come? She shut her eyes in shame as she remembered the face of one terrified hatchling after another—two hatchlings if Lee had also roused. No wonder he thought she was the monster instead of him.

She glanced at Leech who was clinging to a Pippal on her griffin. If Bayang could not convince Lee that he was safe, he could again become a deadly threat to dragon-kind.

Could she allow that to happen? Or could she break her promise to Leech? Either way, the dragons and Lee would be trapped in the ancient cycle of killing or being killed. The madness had been going on for centuries, acquiring the ponderous weight of tradition so that no one looked for another solution.

Until now.

There had to be another way to end this craziness. But what?

## 49

## Scirye

They passed over one desolate ridge after another until, on the afternoon of the fifth day, they reached the inmost circle of foothills with level after level of terraces cut into the sides. Scirye could see the outlines of walls under the snow like someone had drawn the parts of a jigsaw puzzle with vanilla icing on a giant white cake.

Her father signaled to the other riders to fly lower so sentries would have a harder time seeing them, but not so low as to raise a curtain of snow with the downdraft of the griffins' wingbeats. They finally landed upon a broad ledge upon the western side of a hill.

When Scirye slid off, she heard an odd clack beneath her boots. With her foot, she scraped away the snow and dirt to reveal bits of brown and yellow tile that formed the head of a mosaic lion.

She glanced around until she saw the odd bumps that must have marked a wall. "I think we're on what's left of a house."

Leech pointed up the slope to the hilltop, which had split down the middle so that the two halves stuck up like horns. "Did that happen in the battle?"

"Probably," Kles said, fluttering nearby. "Since there were no survivors from either side, we don't know what really happened, but it must have been powerful magic unleashed that day."

"Well, for once no one can blame that on me," Koko said, waving a paw at the destruction.

"Just remember that the defenders sacrificed themselves for us," Lady Sudarshane said. Taking a pair of binoculars from a saddlebag and hanging them about her neck, she began to climb the slope.

"Guard the griffins," Lord Tsirauñe instructed Oko and Wali, and then fetching his own binoculars from his gear, he trudged with Kat after his wife.

Scirye started after them. After all, her parents had not told them to stay put, and she was curious about what Roland might be up too.

Her friends must have felt the same strong urges because they fell in behind her. When he heard them coming, her father looked as if he were about to order them to return to the griffins when her mother put her hand on his shoulder.

"This is really their quest, not ours," she whispered to her husband.

Lord Tsirauñe gave a reluctant nod and then, putting a finger to his lips for silence, resumed his journey.

Several yards from the hilltop, her father got down on all fours along with her mother, who motioned them to do likewise. When they had obeyed, her parents began to crawl upward, creeping on their bellies until they had reached the cleft in the hill. Then, with great caution, they peered down at Riye Srukalleyis, the City of Death.

Below them, surrounded on all sides by steep hills and mountains, was a basin that had been formed by a great river—the outlines of its banks showed like a jagged scar cutting the ground into halves. The east bank had been farmland, fields still outlined by what was left of the boundary walls.

The west bank was full of what looked like glassblower's rejects. Scirye decided that the long, rolling burrows must have once been the city walls. Here and there, the snow had been blown away to reveal a surface like melted wax the color of dried blood. Within the walls, the buildings and towers had been reduced to large mounds. Snow covered half their relics, but their exposed lee sides were as slick as glass with browns, blacks, greens, and reds fused together like poorly mixed cake batter. The city hadn't so much been destroyed as melted in the final battle, and she couldn't even begin to guess what titanic magic that had taken.

"Who did this?" Leech asked in an awed voice. "Was it the invaders? Only they got caught in the backlash?"

"It might have been," Kles said. "Or it might have been the defenders in one last desperate bid to stop the invaders. No one knows."

"Oh, the poor people," Māka murmured and began to weep. "Can you hear them? They're still crying."

Now that Māka had pointed it out, the breeze did sound like folk wailing in the distance.

Tute patted her awkwardly with a paw. "It's just the wind."

But Māka lay her head down on her arms and began to cry. A kind soul like hers would be vulnerable to such suggestions, especially if her magic amplified her senses. If that was true, then her gift was also a curse, and certainly not one that Scirye would want.

A hundred yards away from the ruins, the rows of tents of Roland's camp billowed in the wind. A rider in a white uniform coat rose on the back of a griffin and began circling like a vulture. More of the vizier's guards in heavy white overcoats and with rifles slung over their shoulders marched in front of the slick walls. She wondered if any of them had any doubts about their master, now that he had let a stranger violate this holy site.

She tried to imagine the city before its destruction, when its streets would have teemed with pilgrims and camels and griffins and the mounds were actual buildings, but she couldn't picture it. The city had been dead too long, and its twisting lanes were a rabbit's maze. It would take an army to search all the ruins, not the few members of her party. And they would have to dodge Roland's men at the same time. And even if they found the right spot, how did they dig through solid glass? No wonder Roland had wanted to bring heavy equipment.

*Boom!* A cloud of dust, snow, and shiny fragments plumed upward, and even as the cloud settled, they could hear the glassy lumps shattering.

"They're using dynamite," her father said.

Shocked, Māka raised a tear-streaked face. "That's sacrilege!" She started to rise but Tute clamped his strong jaws on her sleeve and yanked her back down.

Lady Sudarshane was perplexed. "But why would they do that? They'll destroy the arrows along with priceless artifacts."

A dragon directed turbaned men to the remains of the mound where a convex slick disc now lay revealed. Even at this distance, Scirye could see the bright yellow sashes around their stomachs, which must be the murderous sashes that Bayang had told her about. A moment later, they heard the roar of a generator and then the *rat-a-tat-tat* sounds like machine guns firing. Scirye ducked, but her parents, Kat, and Bayang remained where they were.

Lord Tsirauñe adjusted the focus on his binoculars. "The dynamite removed the debris that had piled up after the destruction of the city. The thugs are using jackhammers now on the city level." The glassy layer broke like dozens of plates shattering. "I suppose they'll dig right through to Yi's time, before the city ever existed."

"The dragon in charge is Badik," Bayang said grimly.

Scirye felt her stomach tighten. They'd caught up with the creature who had killed her sister and Leech's friend Primo, as well as terrorized Bayang's clan.

Leech rolled onto his side and looked at Scirye. "So where do we start?"

As everyone's eyes turned toward her, Scirye pulled the glove from her marked hand. The "3" pulsed slowly but she didn't have any idea where to search first. *I guess I always hoped that You would tell me what Your mark means once we got here. Please, please give me a sign,* Scirye pleaded silently with the goddess. But Scirye's mind remained a blank. For the hundredth time, she tried to remember the details of the vision.

"I don't know," she confessed. "I'm sorry."

Māka sensed Scirye's frustration. "It's all right. Just try to remember any helpful details from your vision."

Scirye drew her eyebrows tight together as she tried to recall. "Let's see. I was in this old temple when She came." Her eyes opened. "It was on a mountainside."

"I read that the Archer's temple was on Mount Kemshap. It means 'The earth is cursed' in the Old Tongue. I always thought it was given that name after the war, but maybe it dates from before that—all the way back to the Archer." Her mother aimed her binoculars on the tallest mountain. It lay to the west of the city. "I see a ruin there. Could that be it?"

Scirye pulled the glove back on and took the binoculars from her father, directing them at the same mountain. Once she had them in focus, she saw the three giant, treelike columns from her vision, but she almost didn't recognize the rest of the temple.

Roland had nearly as many men working there as in the city. Crews were dismantling the temple stone by stone and dumping the debris by the columns. Already the ornate pillars and arches on the sides had been taken down—presumably to see if the arrows were hidden inside them.

More crews were digging around the temple grounds, using camp stoves with fire imps to warm the soil first for their shovels. Steam rose in ribbons from the damp earth, and the area looked as if a colony of giant moles had their homes there.

Scirye bit her lip when she saw the armed guardsmen on sentry duty. From the looks each group gave the other, there was little love lost between them.

"I recognize the three big columns at the rear. And right across from it was a mountain shaped like a lion." She swung the binoculars in a slow arc until she found a lion-shaped peak. It was on the other side of the city directly opposite Mount Kemshap. "Yes, I think the temple's where She wants me to go."

Lord Tsiraũne scanned the large, steel-gray clouds rolling in from the north. "I'd say we're in for some snow this evening. The griffin patrols will stay on the ground and the work crews will probably return to their camp. If there are any sentries, they won't be expecting trouble."

Koko sighed. "Sure, what idiots would be out on a night like this?"

"What are we going to use to dig with?" Leech asked.

"We all have fold-up shovels as part of our camping gear," Kat explained.

"We'd better get back out of sight before the griffin patrol spots us," Lady Sudarshane suggested.

"I'll keep watch," Bayang volunteered, so they left the dragon near the broken hilltop while they went down the slope to where the Pippalanta had set up camp behind some boulders.

They didn't dare start a fire, so the Pippalanta unpacked food from the saddlebags, but when Kles trotted over to her with flat bread and some cheese, Scirye shook her head. "I don't feel like eating."

"You must eat something even if you're nervous," Lady Sudarshane insisted.

Scirye nibbled at the bread. "What do you think the goddess has planned for me?"

Her mother touched her forehead to Scirye's lovingly. "I don't know, dear. But you can count on this: Your father and I will be there with you."

But Scirye took small comfort from her mother's words. She was leading her parents and her friends into the deadliest of dangers on only a hunch.

# 50

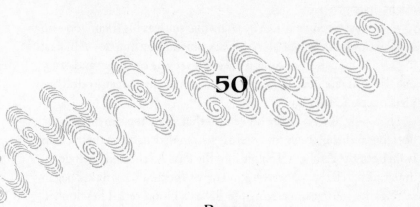

## Bayang

As Bayang kept watch on the hilltop, she shifted her body, trying to find a more comfortable position for her aching limbs. She found herself fighting back the fatigue that tried to claim her; she couldn't give in to it. Not only did she have to be on guard, but she had to think about her dilemma. She often had nightmares about her past victims. She couldn't live with herself if she added Leech's death to her crimes.

On the other hand, she couldn't leave Lee No Cha awake and in Leech's body, not with weapons powerful enough to kill a dragon.

She was actually surprised that Lee No Cha had not taken over yet. Was it proof that Lee No Cha was not a monster after all? Or was there another reason?

Did he feel as lonely as she once had? Was he also enjoying this new experience of having friends even if Lee No Cha could only do so indirectly?

You might not take a friend's advice but at least you listened.

And you thought twice about doing anything that your friends might disapprove of.

If she could convince Lee No Cha that she was his friend too—no small task when she had been the assassin hunting him down in past lives—she might be able to stop the endless cycle of killing and carry out the ultimate goal of her mission: to end the threat to dragon-kind once and for all.

She was still wondering how to do that when the sun neared the horizon and the crews and sentries streamed back to their camp from both the Archer's Temple and the city. As she slid back down the slope to tell the others the good news, the first snowflakes began falling, the setting sun edging the flakes a blood red. They looked like little circular blades whirling about. She hoped they weren't an omen.

As day gave way to night, the snow fell heavier. It wasn't the blinding blizzard that Roland had set up as a trap for them in the Arctic Ocean, but it was like being inside a pillow stuffed with cotton. The winds had picked up, sounding even more like wailing ghosts just as Māka had sensed. But fortunately human ghosts held no terrors for a dragon and she kept slitherng on. Only able to see a few yards ahead of her, Bayang nearly missed their camp.

"The snow's falling so thick we could miss the temple alto-gether," she said when she was finally sitting among them. "We might want to let the snowfall thin out a bit more so we can see better." And perhaps she'd have a chance to talk to Leech.

Lord Tsirauñe glanced about at the white curtain engulfing them. "I agree. It might be more sensible to wait."

Māka rose and turned as if sleepwalking, and her eyes had taken on that faraway look. "I can guide you there." Her voice was so low that it was hard to hear her.

"This is no time for your experiments," Tute hissed.

Māka turned to appeal to Scirye. "Trust me as I trust you. You're not only the Chosen One, but my friend. Let me keep my part of our pact."

As Scirye looked uncertainly between Lord Tsirauñe and Māka, Lady Sudarshane warned, "This decision is not about pleasing your father or your friend. It's too important for that."

"Are you really sure about this?" Scirye asked Māka.

"*This* is the reason why I'm here," Māka said and took both of Scirye's hands in hers. "I was sent to be the needle for your compass."

Friend or not and pact or not, Bayang would not have given in to the bumbling sorceress. She'd heard the stories about how Māka had sensed the Chamber of Truth and the torture room, but those could have been lucky guesses.

But after hesitating a moment longer, Scirye nodded her head to her father. "We'll let Māka lead us."

Though Lord Tsirauñe still looked doubtful, he said, "So be it." Then, turning on his heel, he looked at his wife. "Since Māka is your passenger, you and Kwele will take the point."

When he had climbed into the saddle, he leaned over and held out his hand to help his daughter up. But grasping the rear part of the saddle, Scirye tried to pull herself up—only to find that she could only manage halfway, which left her with her legs dangling. No one laughed, though, as Lord Tsirauñe grabbed her belt and hoisted the "chosen of the goddess" the rest of the way up. Everyone's thoughts were on the dangerous task ahead.

Making peace with Lee No Cha would have to wait.

As Kles flew to Scirye's shoulder and coiled like a furry, fuzzy collar around her neck, Bayang hid her own frustration at not being able to talk to Leech and mounted again behind Wali. Leech rode with Oko, and Koko with Kat. Grumbling that cats were never meant to fly, Tute joined Lady Sudarshane and Māka.

The griffins had used the delay to prepare for the coming battle and had pomaded their fur into spikes so that they looked twice as fearsome now. They rose into the air with great strokes of their wings that sent the snow whirling in sheets about them. The riders had covered any bits of metal with strips of cloth to keep them from jingling. There was only the creak of leather harness and the howling of the wind.

As they flew upward, curtains of wet, cold, white beads swept one after another over them. It was all Bayang could do to breathe, let alone hold on to Oko. And she, at least, had the benefit of Pele's charm to keep her warm, but icicles were already beginning to form in her griffin's fur and the fringes of her flapping cloak.

Lord Tsirauñe had taken a position to his wife's right, but the griffins flew almost wingtip to wingtip and even then kept contact with one another more by the flapping sound of their wings than by what they could see. Nor was it easy for them to keep formation in the strong winds that kept Wali's griffin constantly fighting to stay level.

Bayang's eyes were used to the dark depths of the ocean, but as they went on, even she became disoriented in the tumbling world of snowflakes. There were only Māka's shrill shouts to guide them on.

Soon enough, the beating of the five griffins' wings deteriorated from a steady rhythm to an irregular one. An experienced flier herself, she knew it meant that the griffins were tiring.

Lord Tsirauñe sensed it too. Bayang could make out his shadowy shape leaning forward as he began stroking Árkwi. And as his gloved hand touched his griffin's fur, the icicles fringing the tips tinkled together. "On, my noble ones, my joys, my loves," he encouraged, his words not just for Árkwi but for the others as well. The griffin master's words acted like a tonic on the griffins and they began to flap their wings with a steady rhythm once more.

After a half hour of misery, Bayang heard Māka announce, "We're here. Land now."

And Wali's griffin like the other riders followed Kwele down.

Bayang did not see the ground, only felt the impact as the griffin landed clumsily, his legs buckling beneath him.

Bayang immediately slid from the saddle onto the snowy slope and then made a point of stepping in front of the griffin so she could bow. "I thank you. You're truly a hero among griffins."

Wali's griffin returned the bow politely, the icicles, now covering both fur and feathers, chimed together softly. "We each have a part to play. Now do yours, Lady Dragon, and help Lady Scirye find the arrows."

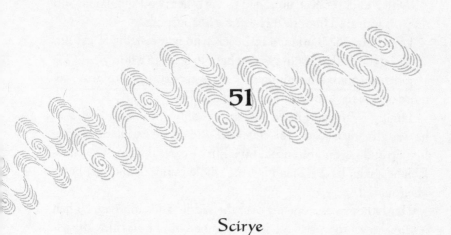

# 51

## Scirye

The winds whirled around her, shrieking like people in pain, and at first, Scirye could see nothing through the swirling snow. And then in a brief moment when the wind whipped the flakes away, she saw the three columns dimly.

"Well done," she said softly to Māka.

Ice had formed along the sorceress's eyebrows and even the tips of her eyelashes. "The magic feels stronger than ever in me." Māka's voice was hoarse from shouting, but her delight was plain. "I feel like I'm ready to explode."

Scirye was glad for her friend. "You've kept your part of the pact. Now it's my turn."

But her father held up a hand. "Wait," he said to her and then called in a low voice, "Pippalanta, to me."

A dismounted Kat appeared at Lord Tsirauñe's side then. Behind her were Oko and Wali, also on foot. "Lord?"

Lord Tsirauñe pointed to the temple. "Take care of any sentries."

With a nod, the Kat motioned to the other two Pippalanta, and they disappeared into the night with grim purpose.

Lord Tsirauñe motioned to Leech who was starting to get off. "Stay on the griffin just in case we have to leave in a hurry."

For fifteen anxious minutes, Scirye's ears strained to hear any noise beside the wind, but she heard nothing.

Finally, Wali came back. "There was only one sentry, lord, and he was already asleep." She chuckled. "So all we had to do was tie him up and gag and blindfold him. But be careful where you walk. Roland's men have dismantled the whole building and dug holes all around it."

Her father swung one leg over the saddle and stood up. "Then it's time to get to work." As Scirye climbed off, he was already getting a folded-up shovel from a saddlebag.

There were four more shovels in all with Wali carrying hers as well as Kat's, and the griffins would dig with their paws.

Snow lightly dusted the ground, which had already frozen, making footing slippery, and in the dark it was hard to skirt the recently dug holes and trenches, as if the mountain had been attacked by giant gophers. Each of them had fallen at least once by the time they met Kat standing by piles of stones.

It was a miracle, Scirye thought, that none of them had broken an ankle.

"This is the temple, Lady Scirye," Kat said and looked about. "What's left of it."

Roland's men had been thorough, removing the roof and all the walls but a few courses of stone at the rear just beyond the three columns. The stones had been dumped into piles on the sides. And all that marked the temple was its floor, which stood now like an almost empty platform.

"So where do we begin?" Leech asked.

*Well?* Scirye asked the goddess, aware of everyone's eyes watching her, the Chosen One. But there was only the sound of the relentless winds.

Their task seemed hopeless—as hopeless as Māka facing the guards at the vizier's villa or guiding them through the storm, but she had succeeded. So Scirye had to try at least.

With a sigh, she pointed at the temple. "Well, let's start there." Maybe Roland's men had missed something.

A section of the floor had been removed from the center as well and a hole had been dug down to an earlier shrine. Bayang lowered her into the hole, and as soon as Scirye's boots felt the ancient stones, she thought she heard a wisp of chanting and drumming. She yanked the glove from her hand. The mark was still pulsing. But that was all.

And after being lifted out of the hole again, they all probed different parts of the temple but found nothing. After an hour, they left the temple and began to explore the area around it. Scirye was about to examine a shallow trench when she saw a large silhouette on her left about thirty feet from the temple.

*Who's wandering away like that?* she wondered.

Scirye was just about to call out when she noticed the peculiar way it shambled along. And then she remembered where she had seen just such a gait before. It was a lyak. Roland must have hired some of them to patrol the area while he and his thugs concentrated on his treasure hunt. And it was just their bad luck that one such patrol was passing by the temple.

Then she heard the lyak take a long, deep breath and then another. She remembered the broad nostrils she had seen on the others. Did that mean it had a good sense of smell?

Apparently so. Snuffling loudly, the lyak began to head straight toward her.

As quietly as she could, Scirye slid the dagger from its sheath.

Scirye felt a hand on her arm. Wali gave a little shake of her head and then pointed at herself to indicate she would take care of the intruder. She'd already left her carbine and shovel back with Oko. Sliding out her own dagger, she moved silently to intercept the intruder.

Suddenly there was a second silhouette. Then a third, and then more and more.

"Mount up, mount up," Lord Tsirauñe ordered.

Kat and Oko slipped past them, stuffing their shovels into their belts as they unslung their carbines.

"Come on, Skee," Árkwi said as he picked Scirye up and deposited her on the saddle. Around her, she saw that the other griffins were doing the same with her friends as they got ready to escape into the safety of the skies.

The next moment a huge head with one eye seemed to materialize over her. More lyaks were leaping at them from a totally different direction. Scirye realized too late that the lyaks had smelled them long before, using the first group to distract them while the second snuck up behind them.

Scirye had her dagger out in an instant and aimed straight at the lyak's chest.

The large eye blinked, startled, in a face almost as pale as the snow as the creature's own weight drove it down onto the knife point. The lyak howled in pain and Scirye was pulled from Árkwi's saddle as her attacker fell.

As she lay on the frozen ground with the lyak on top of her, his stench was thick in her nostrils. His blood felt warm against her chest as she squirmed against the frozen ground, worming her way out from underneath him. She heard Kles flapping overhead, frantically trying to tug the lyak up.

Stunned from her fall, Scirye sat for a moment.

*"Rapañne! Rapañne!"* the griffins called as their claws slashed and their deadly beaks bit the snarling, howling lyaks.

Her parents and the Pippalanta were firing their carbines at a quick but deliberate pace, so that each bullet knocked a lyak down, but despite the toll that the sharpshooters took, the lyaks were focusing all their attention on the griffins.

Nor did the lyaks seem to be in any hurry to kill their ancient enemies, thrusting their spears and chopping their axes only at the griffins' wings.

With a shock, Scirye realized the lyaks wanted to trap all of them on the ground first, like a cat that breaks the wings of a bird before it begins a cruel game of torture.

*And now,* Scirye thought, *everyone's going to die because of me.*

## 52

## Leech

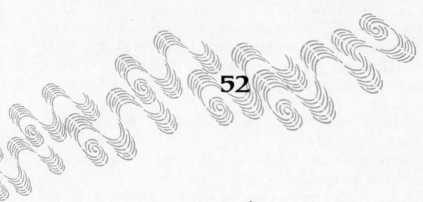

The griffin that Leech was on pivoted and twisted, her paws lashing out at her tormentors. It was all Leech could do to cling to the saddle. *Now I know how a cowboy on a bucking bronco feels,* he thought.

As the world whirled around him, he looked for his friends. Bayang had leaped off her griffin, who had reared up on her hind legs to defend herself. Māka was half off her mount while Tute, clinging to the saddle with his hind paws, did his best to haul her back up. But there was no sign of Scirye, Kles, or Koko.

*I want to go home. I want to go home,* the Voice wailed.

The Voice sounded like any small child now and not a warrior with powerful magic. *But there's no home to go to,* Leech said with brutal honesty. *That China's long gone.*

His griffin suddenly swept her powerful wings down, knocking several lyaks to the ground. But that was a mistake because immediately several lyaks jumped upon the wings, chopping at them with their axes.

Leech felt the shudder pass through the griffin's body even as she screamed. Her legs buckled beneath her, pitching him forward.

He rolled over the hard ground straight into a lyak's legs. With a snarl, the creature raised a spear to take care of the annoyance.

*Clong!*

The lyak dropped like a stone beside Leech, but his comrades took no notice of the boy.

"You okay, buddy?" Koko asked. He'd picked up a shovel that one of the Amazons had dropped.

Leech nodded mutely. There was no time to transform the flying discs, but he would need his weapon ring. When he was done, he expected to see his mount dying, but she had managed to raise herself halfway up again. As vulnerable as she was, the lyaks were only targeting her wings.

Leech and Koko would make them pay for their mistake.

"If there's one thing I hate worse than pigeons"—Koko gave a grunt as he swung the edge of the shovel's blade against the back of a lyak knee—"it's lyaks."

Leech brought his weapon ring down with a thunk on the lyak's head. "I thought you hated pigeons the most."

"I just demoted them," Koko said and, lifting his shovel over his shoulder, brought it down hard on a lyak's skull.

*Clong!*

The creature dropped instantly to the ground.

By then, a lyak realized what they were doing and turned with a snarl. Koko thrust his shovel forward, ramming the tip of the blade into the lyak's belly. When the creature doubled over, Leech's ring knocked him on the head and finished the job.

"It's just like being back in San Francisco," Leech said. "I mean, you and me fighting together against some gang."

"Except they didn't have spears and axes." Koko grunted as he struck another lyak so hard the shaft of his shovel snapped. He picked up an axe from the ground. "And at least the gangs in San Francisco take a bath every now and then."

They only managed to clear a small space in front of the griffin on her left, but that was enough for the griffin who only had to defend her right side. Her paws lashed out, bowling those attackers over.

She said something in Kushan to Leech and Koko, and when she reared up, Leech thought she must have told them to cover her exposed chest and stomach. Though it must have hurt her terribly, she reached over her shoulders and tore her torturers from her wings, flinging them right and left. But she now had several great gashes in the wings and a dozen smaller ones at least.

*The griffin's going nowhere,* the Voice screamed. *Use the discs and get away!*

Leech ignored the yelling Voice. "Take her left," he called to Koko and took up his station on her right near her wings.

Leech ignored the screams of the Voice as he fought for his and Koko's life.

It couldn't have been more than a few minutes, but it felt like hours as Leech fought.

Leech heard some of the griffins shout, *"Rapañ̃e! Rapañ̃e!"* He was relieved to hear Māka's voice too, repeating the war cry.

His griffin was fighting her way to the other griffins, who had formed a defensive ring around Scirye. Scirye's parents and the Amazons were firing, and with each shot a lyak screamed and fell over. Bayang, Māka, and Tute fought as well. Kles was circling overhead, swooping down to help anyone who might be in trouble.

Suddenly, there were no lyaks in front of them. Instead, they were backing away.

"That's right, run, you chickens," Koko jeered. He'd picked up a second axe so he now had one in each paw. He waved both of them over his head now in triumph.

But the lyaks looked satisfied rather than afraid, and when Leech saw the maimed and broken wings of the other griffins, he realized the lyaks were retreating because they'd accomplished their goal: Leech's friends were trapped on the ground.

All the lyaks had to do now was wait for Roland to come with reinforcements and then it would be all over.

*Not for us,* the Voice said. *We can fly away.*

*Would Scirye run off and leave the fighting to us?* Leech demanded.

*Um, no,* the Voice said. *It wouldn't be—what's the word? Tumarg?*

*Yes,* Leech said hopefully. *And you know Koko, Kles, Māka, and Tute wouldn't desert us either.*

*Of course,* the Voice said indignantly. *Don't you know your own friends?*

*Sure,* Leech said, *but I also know you like them too.*

The Voice sighed. *I suppose I do.*

*Then you'd feel rotten if you left them to die while you saved your own skin,* Leech pointed out.

*I guess,* the Voice admitted. *Besides, Roland's hurt so many people. I don't want him in charge of the world. He's worse than any dragon.*

*So do you still want to run away?* Leech asked.

*No, that stops now,* the Voice said, determined.

## 53

## Leech

 Kwele and Wali's griffins were so badly wounded that they collapsed where they stood.

Koko slumped against a pile of rubble and waved his paw feebly. "The next time you guys hold a picnic, do me a favor and leave me off the invitation list."

Tears began to roll down her cheeks as Scirye looked around. "I'm so sorry, everyone. This is all my fault."

Wali had gotten a medical kit from one of her saddlebags. "Lady, you only need to apologize when you ask us to do something that's *not* Tumarg."

Kat smiled and then dipped her head. "It's an honor serving you, lady." Then she turned and waved a hand at everyone else. "And it's an honor fighting with all of you."

*She meant you too*, the Voice said enviously.

*She meant us*, Leech assured him.

*I'm still afraid though*, the Voice said.

*So am I, but I'm just as afraid of letting down our friends,* Leech said.

*I think I am too,* the Voice said. *But what do I do? I'm not as brave as them.*

*All we can do is try,* Leech said, *just like they are.*

While Wali took care of the riders' injuries, Lord Tsirauñe had gotten another medical kit from his saddlebags and was tending the wounded griffins. "Leech, can you fly in this weather?"

Leech glanced at the snowflakes that had begun to fall even heavier than before. *Can we?* he asked the Voice.

*I don't know,* the Voice said uncertainly. *I guess we could try.*

"I'd be willing to attempt it," Leech said.

"Then take my daughter away from here," Lord Tsirauñe said and put up a hand to stifle Scirye's protest. "You have to carry out your mission from the goddess, but if there's time, Leech might be able to ferry your friends out of here."

"I'd be willing to try to take the grown-ups out too," Leech offered.

Árkwi was lying on his stomach, waiting his turn for his master to help him. "With all due respect, my lord, the lyaks would hunt Lady Scirye down, snow or no snow. Or anyone else who left here. We're better off staying together."

"I'll fight anyone who tries to make me leave," Scirye said firmly.

Lady Sudarshane was sewing up a gash in Kwele's side with thread and a huge needle. Though it must have hurt each time the needle pierced the invalid's hide, the griffin trembled but did not cry out. "It's no use arguing, dear," she said to her husband. "She gets her stubbornness from you."

Lord Tsirauñe eyed his defiant daughter for a moment and then shrugged. "All right. Then we'd better try to improvise a fort with the stuff around here."

They climbed back onto the temple floor because the raised platform would give them a slight advantage. Then they used the remaining wall even if the columns might get in the way of the defenders and brought stones up to build three other walls against part of it until they had a square with each side about ten feet long and five feet high.

"Do you suppose Nandi delivered our message?" Māka panted as she waddled with a rock over to a wall.

Kat grunted as she hefted a large stone to fill a gap. "Well, ifrits can be funny creatures, but he seemed like the responsible sort. So Princess Maimie is coming with every warrior she can muster. We just have to hold out until then."

Tute's body arched as he shoved a rock along with his head as well as both forepaws. "And what will we do when the storm ends and the guardsmen can fly again? They'll pick us off from above."

"You look nimble enough to dodge the bullets." Kat laughed as she added a slab on top of the other stone.

Koko rubbed his belly ruefully. "Maybe I should've just kept it to five meals at the palace."

Leech struggled to lift a stone into place. Carved on it were nine crows in a tree. Suddenly large paws suddenly took it from him and set it in position. As she spoke in a low voice, the dragon adjusted the rock on the wall. "Back at the vizier's summer villa, you asked me if I could be a friend to Lee if he were alive. And I couldn't give you my answer until now."

You didn't see the proud dragon embarrassed very often, but she was now. "I think I finally understand why he acted the way he did. And I realize now my missions were all part of a tragic misunderstanding that's led to more killings that still haunt me in my nightmares. Those other reincarnations weren't Lee any more than you are."

*So she has nightmares too?* the Voice asked in surprise. The next memory sounded painful. *Sometimes I remember the dragon prince's face too. He was so frightened at the end but I couldn't stop hitting him. I knew it was wrong. I guess I'm as bad as Bayang.*

The dragon still didn't look at Leech as she went on, perhaps afraid to see how hostile he was becoming. "If Lee No Cha was with us now, I would tell him that all my previous missions were tragic mistakes. I should have realized that he was a small, frightened hatchling and not a monster and that we are both very much alike. And if I could not earn his friendship, I would try to gain his respect, not by words but by my actions."

*Even if we could become friends, what would happen if some other dragons came after me?* the Voice wondered.

When Leech repeated the question to Bayang, the dragon shrugged. "It's not a matter of 'if' but 'when.' I'd try to make them understand, but if I couldn't, I'd fight them."

"Even if they were members of your own clan?" Lee asked.

"You are my clan now, not them," Bayang said.

*Ah* was all the Voice said.

Leech glanced at Koko and then at Scirye and Kles. "We've made our own family, and I think our ties are stronger than just blood."

The dragon clasped her paws together, intertwining her claws. "Our destinies may be tied together, but let's carry the destruction to our enemies and not one another."

*I'd like that*, the Voice said.

Leech said, "I think if Lee No Cha were here, he'd be willing to try to be your friend." The next moment he flinched when a bullet chipped a marble fragment that faced the downward slope. Through the snow, Leech saw the silhouettes of men and griffins. Apparently, no one had been willing to risk flying through the storm as they had, but they had been willing to walk.

The badger sighed. "Just for once, I'd like to outnumber the bad guys."

Leech understood what his friend meant. Desperate struggles were all too familiar. So was the stomach-twisting fear.

Roland called up to them, "Surrender and you won't be harmed." A guardsman, probably acting as an interpreter, shouted something in Kushan right after that.

Koko hoisted himself up to the top of the wall. "What makes

you think we'd trust a jerk like you?" he jeered and blew a raspberry.

"You pests!" Roland swore in the darkness. "You're harder to kill than cockroaches." His tone became more thoughtful. "The vizier sent word to me about the crazy claims that the girl was making. At first, I thought it was just the superstitious ravings, but if you've managed to get this far, maybe you can help me find the arrows after all." His voice grew harsh as he commanded his men. "There's a girl with red hair and green eyes. Don't harm her, but you can kill the others."

The Voice chuckled. *I guess I'm just meant to die young.*

*We're not dead yet, but if that happens, you won't die alone,* Leech said.

*Yes,* the Voice said.

# 54

## Bayang

Bayang called to the Wolf Guards below. "The vizier is dead. The emperor knows about the whole plot and troops will be here soon. If you help Roland now, you'll be branded as traitors."

As the men hesitated, a giant silhouette rose up. "What are you doing here?" Badik asked.

The sight of her ancient enemy washed away all of Bayang's soreness and fatigue.

"The vizier came to kill me, but we took care of him instead," Bayang said. "What more proof do you need that I'm telling the truth?"

When the guardsmen remained where they were, Badik roared angrily. "The vizier's still alive at the citadel, you idiots. I'll kill anyone who listens to her lies. Now advance!"

After hesitating a moment, the guardsmen came on again.

Bayang had always known their adventure might end badly,

which was why she had tried so often to get the hatchlings to quit. When the goddess had shown that Scirye was her favorite, though, the dragon had begun to hope for success. But where was the goddess now when they needed her the most?

Bayang could have pounded her paws in frustration, not because they would fail in their quest, nor even because her personal enemy, Badik, would triumph. It was the hatchlings for whom she was afraid. They were too clever, too brave to die like this.

Twisting her head, Bayang looked affectionately at her companions. From their positions at the four walls of their improvised fort, Scirye's parents and the Pippalanta had risen to a crouch and begun firing. Māka had her dagger in one hand while her other leafed through her pamphlet as she hunted for some spell that might work. Tute was growling and Kles's fur and feathers began to puff out, preparing to fight. Scirye had her eyes closed as if she were begging the goddess for help. Even the usually cowardly badger was holding a lyak axe in both paws, ready to defend her.

Last, her eyes fell on a frightened but purposeful Leech mounted atop one of his discs and doing knee bends to loosen up, which made the discs bounce up and down as if he were a basketball.

It was time to live up to her bold words to Leech . . . and Lee No Cha. Bayang couldn't make up for all the wrongs she had done, but at least she might increase their chances of survival a little bit by taking out the biggest threat.

"Leech," Bayang called to the hatchling and then looked about, "and everyone. I love you." Then, turning her back on them, she balled a forepaw and raised it defiantly toward the giant silhouette. "Badik of the Fire Rings, fight me if you dare. Or will you keep hiding behind Roland like his pet dog? Coward, slimeworm."

And then English was no longer adequate so she switched to the dragon tongue. For there are no insults like a dragon's because dragons live a long time and so their hatred ferments for centuries until it becomes a brew so potent that it burns the mind like acid eating through steel.

The venomous words almost burned her throat as she flung them at her ancient enemy, the first ones making Badik so furious that he could not even speak, only hiss.

"Badik, stay where you are," Roland commanded angrily.

But Bayang's insults had made Badik go berserk. As he began to charge up the slope, Bayang shouted, *"Yashe!"* and vaulted over the crude wall.

She worked the growth spell as she galloped downward and immediately the world began to shimmer around her as she swelled in size. As she did the snowflakes seemed to shrink to the size of pinheads.

"Light the lanterns," Roland yelled, "and kill her."

Light suddenly flared in dozens of lanterns as shutters were opened to reveal the fire imps inside burning intensely.

She lowered her eyelids slightly and tried not to look directly at any one lantern so it would not blind her. Lyak spears and axes bounced off her scales. Bullets pinged against her sides. But she paid them no heed. Revenge was her one desire.

Badik was dashing toward her, eyes wide, strings of saliva dripping from his mouth, paws skidding recklessly in the snow.

Twenty yards on, he met her. He was wearing iron plates across his chest as armor.

With a little hop, she sprang at him with all four paws, and with a jump of his own, his paws met hers. Instantly, Bayang thrust her head forward and Badik barely pulled his throat away from her snapping jaws—only to be stunned by a blow from her flapping wings. She ignored the pain from the wound on one wing and swept her tail, knocking Badik on his back.

The sheer ferocity of Bayang's attack overwhelmed Badik at first, but he still managed to trip her with his tail so that she fell over on him.

The two dragons wrestled in the snow, grasping paws as they tried to avoid each other's fangs and clouts from their wings.

Then Badik's head shot up like a battering ram, his hard skull thudding against the base of Bayang's throat and her windpipe. Choking and wheezing, Bayang fell onto her side. Immediately, Badik's head shot out like a cobra's, but Bayang rolled, and though fiery pain raced along her back, she spread her injured wing clouting Badik on his head.

Her chest heaved as she tried to draw air through her bruised windpipe, and the dazed Badik struggled up on all fours, his drooling jaws and a forepaw slashing viciously at her. All she could do was try to shield herself with her wings, but as he shredded them, she wondered if she would ever be able to fly again—but then, given the odds against her, she would never live long enough for them to heal.

She thought of her old instructor, Sergeant Pandai. Bayang thought she'd almost had the wily veteran pinned when she suddenly found herself flat on her back. As the sergeant had helped her up, she'd said, "Remember, you can use your enemies' own eagerness as a weapon against them."

She lowered her wings as if she were helpless to control them, no longer trying to hide the agony the motion caused her.

As Badik's jaws lunged at her with a triumphant hiss, she raked a paw across his cheek.

Blinded in one eye, he tilted back his head and roared in agony. Immediately, she stretched out her hind paws and caught one of his hind legs. He tried to stagger away, but she yanked hard and he spilled onto his back in the snow.

Her head shot forward on her long neck and the moment her jaws clamped on his throat, she bit down hard, felt her fangs crunch satisfyingly through his armored scales, tasted his blood, felt his breath trying to pass in vain along his throat.

She used her tail to fend off his twitching body and the paws that, even in his death throes, were trying to rip her open. And then Badik, the greatest enemy the Clan of the Moonglow had ever known, lay still.

## 55

Scirye

There was nothing as majestic or as terrifying as dragons in their full wrath, and for long moments it was silent on the battlefield, except for the wailing of the winds. Scirye was just about to give a cheer when Roland shouted, "Kill that dragon! Kill her!"

Finally, a guardsman recovered his wits and fired. Soon all the guns were blazing away at Bayang as she struggled to rise.

"Cover her," Kat said, and the Pippalanta began to fire in the quick but deliberate rate they had used before.

Some scales must have been torn off in the fight with Badik, for Bayang quivered every now and then when a bullet found an exposed spot where a scale had been turn off. But she kept limping back to her friends.

"Hurry, please hurry," Scirye murmured. Blood dripped from several wounds and down her beautiful scales.

Leech cupped his hands around his mouth like a megaphone. "Shrink. So you won't be such a big target."

Scirye added her voice to his. "Shrink."

The others joined them and somehow Bayang heard them through the roar of the guns. Her outline shimmered and dwindled until she was only as tall as a human.

Still, some bullets hit her. Ten yards from the fort, she staggered and fell to her knees. Even so, she kept crawling forward.

Five yards. Then three.

She reached out a paw as if to touch the fort but with a last shudder pitched forward.

## 56

## Leech

"Bayang," Leech sobbed.

*Is she dead?* the Voice asked sadly.

Leech felt an ache inside as terrible as when his friend Primo had died. *Yes.*

*She really meant it when she said she loved you,* the Voice said in amazement.

*She said it to us. She had stopped thinking you were a monster,* Leech pointed out.

*It's too bad,* the Voice said regretfully. *Maybe we could have changed things between us if she could have lived.*

"Charge, charge!" Roland shouted, and the Wolf Guards and thugs cheered as they began to move forward. Perhaps Roland had forgotten about the lanterns in the excitement, or was so confident in the success of their numbers that he didn't care about casualties, but he didn't order the lanterns to be shuttered again. His men began falling to the defenders' bullets.

When the lyaks heard them and saw what was happening, they began to howl as they surged toward the fort as well.

As the others hurried to their posts, Leech got on his flying discs but took one last glance at Bayang.

And that was when he thought he saw the dragon wink.

# 57

## Scirye

Leech hovered a few inches in the air, clutching at the east wall. "Bayang?" he called.

"Come on, buddy," Koko said, taking his arm. "We got to get ready."

"But I saw her wink," Leech said.

Wishing desperately that was true, Scirye looked over the stones at the dragon, but her eyes were shut, her body lifeless. "It must have been some trick of the light," Scirye said. The lanterns gave off a flickering light as their bearers moved, casting shadows that danced about the slope.

"I guess so," Leech sighed and reluctantly pivoted and moved with his friends to the center of their little fort.

Kat and her griffin had taken the south wall, which faced what remained of the temple platform, and the excavation just in front of it actually made it even more difficult for attackers. Wali was defending the west wall with Tute and Māka, who had armed herself with a lyak spear. Oko and her griffin would guard the north wall with the columns standing behind it. The big Pippal had also stuck the imperial battle axes into her belt for close combat. As big and heavy as they were, she could swing each in a hand. Scirye's parents and Árkwi had remained at the east wall to face the guardsmen.

Scirye, Kles, Leech, Koko, Kwele, and Wali's griffins were the reserve, ready to react to any attacker who got over the walls. And considering how few defenders were on the wall, that would probably happen very quickly. Leech on his flying discs and Kles would be the strongest part of the team as the two invalid griffins, though determined to fight, could barely move.

The Pippalanta and Scirye's parents were firing steadily now, empty cartridges clinking on the stone as they fell and the cold air was thick with the smell of gunpowder.

Kles curled himself from her left shoulder, around her neck, to her right shoulder so that he could squeeze her with all the strength and fierce love in his small body. And then he dropped away, fluttering his wings so that he rose upward until he was overhead.

Even through the stones of the platform, she felt the pounding of many feet—as if the mountainside had turned into a giant drum. And the howls and shouts merged into one loud, thunderous roar, as if tidal waves were crashing down upon them.

With no time to re-load their carbines, the Pippalanta had picked up their lances, which they were using to deadly effect. On the west and south walls, the two griffins were screaming their battle cries as they raked attackers off the walls. On the east wall, her parents had abandoned their carbines for their lances as well, and Árkwi was battling a griffin who had fluttered up on the parapet. A sudden sweep of her mother's lance caught the attacker in the side and he toppled backward.

Suddenly she heard a dragon shout, *"Yashe!"*

And Bayang rose in all her glory—and rose and rose as she swelled in size. She had too many wounds to move with her usual grace and speed, but she could still use her tail, claws, and fangs to deadly effect.

Leech's elbow nudged her. "I told you she was alive."

"I've never been so glad to be wrong," Scirye said.

On the north wall, Oko was swinging the great battle-axes as easily as if they were small hatchets, and on the west Tute was snarling and spitting from the top of the wall as his claws struck at the lyaks. Māka held her spear in her left hand while darts of fire flashed from her right as she shouted spells with a strong, confident voice. Her magic couldn't have improved at a better time.

"It's our turn first," Leech said. There was a wild look to his eyes as he sped forward, raising his weapon ring.

Koko, with a lyak axe, ran after him.

Scirye's heart swelled with pride at her companions' bravery, but she reminded herself that her job was to help the others, so she forced herself to look for another trouble spot. To the east she saw two Wolf Guards rise into the air on griffins, but the winds were blowing harder than before and a sudden gust slammed them together in midair and they fell out of sight.

The columns partly screened off Oko and the attackers at the north wall. But as the big Pippal fought two lyaks at once, a third climbed up and began reaching for a throwing axe in his belt.

Scirye took a breath. It was up to her now.

"Let's go," she said to Kles as she charged forward.

*"Tarkär, Tarkär!"* The little griffin was in his full battle fury, fur and feathers puffed out, eyes wild, as he shot forward like a tawny missile.

Out of the corner of her eye, she saw the two invalid war griffins try to follow, but the best they could do was a stumble.

"We'll take this," she said to them as she ran forward. "You wait for the next problem." The dagger felt slippery in her sweaty palm and she scolded herself for not wiping it on her clothes first.

As the lyak got ready to throw the axe at the unsuspecting Oko, Kles struck him full in the face. He pitched forward with the small, berserk griffin clinging to him. The fall stunned Kles and the lyak snatched the griffin away from his head as he sat up.

Scirye was so afraid for her friend that she did not stop to think about what she was doing. She simply lunged forward with all the force she could muster in her dagger arm.

The next thing she knew, the lyak was at her feet and she was cradling Kles in one arm and a bloody dagger in the other.

"Lady!" Oko yelled.

Looking up, she saw that another lyak had mounted the wall and was about to thrust at her with his spear.

As the triangular spearhead shot toward her, she instinctively jerked her dagger up. Metal rang on metal as the blades met, her arm tingling at the contact. Then the dagger flew from her fingers when the lyak twirled his spear.

With a howl of triumph, the lyak leaped down from the wall and lunged at her with a spear.

Scirye glimpsed a sacred axe whistle through the air and into her attacker as she dodged backward. When she bumped into something hard, she realized she'd forgotten about the broken temple columns

Despite the leather covering her palm, she felt the marble go instantly from icy cold to warm against her palm, and her gloved hand began to burn like a lantern. The column began to vibrate beneath her touch and she was blinded by a flash of scarlet light.

The next moment, she was holding a slim, long cylinder.

Puzzled she brought her hand back in front of her and saw the arrow. It was almost a yard long and fletched with white feathers at the end. At the front was a wicked arrowhead with four barbed prongs. But this was no fragile antique. The wood of the shaft wasn't brittle but as strong and supple as the day it had been carved, and the bronze arrowhead gleamed brightly without a hint of the green patina that came with age.

Still holding the arrow, Scirye used her teeth to pull the glove from her right hand. The mark of the goddess was glowing on her palm. The "3" had been a clue all along, but the arrows had not been inside the temple, they were the temple, disguised as marble pillars. She'd mistaken the feathers for the palm leaves of a capital.

"Get back!" Oko shouted as she shoved Scirye away. When the column had transformed, it had left a gap in the wall and a lyak had already jumped into the breach. Even as the giant Pippal swung her axes, the ground began to shake.

Not only did the hastily constructed walls of their fort begin to tumble down, but the temple platform as well.

# 58

## Bayang

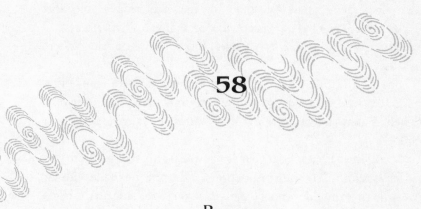

Bayang had managed to keep her balance during the earthquake. She already knew what she would see when she twisted her head around. Her friends now stood exposed with their former walls scattered about their feet and paws.

She wheeled around, swinging her tail at about a yard above the ground. It was like sweeping an area with a telephone pole and guardsmen and thugs went flying.

Her great size would be as dangerous to her friends as to her enemies, so even as she climbed onto the temple platform, she began to shrink.

Some guardsmen and thugs had snuck around her on the north and south and were joining the lyaks surging onto the platform. Her friends' griffins had disappeared under swarms of lyaks. Kat and Oko were standing back to back, surrounded by a circle of foes. Wali was backing toward them as she battled two thugs with curved knives.

Lord Tsirauñe spun around with a cry as a bullet hit his shoulder. Lady Sudarshane fell clutching her right side. A bleeding Árkwi stood over them protectively, screaming his defiance.

There was no sign of Scirye, Kles, Koko, Māka, or Tute. Where was Leech?

She tossed a guardsman to the side then a thug. She did not bother to grab a lyak who tried to bar her way but simply ran over him. Then she saw Leech spinning in the air as a lyak grasped either ankle.

"No!" she shouted as a guardsman thrust his rifle's bayonet up at the hatchling. He spun just in time, deflecting the blade with his weapon ring and then knocking his attacker to the side on the backswing.

As she tried to gallop to his aid, four enemy griffins charged full tilt into her left side. It was like being hit by a truck and she toppled over onto her side. She grunted when her many wounds smacked against the stones.

And then lyaks, guardsmen, thugs, and griffins were piling onto her.

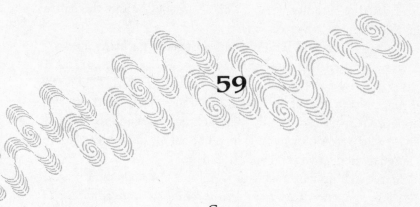

# 59

## Scirye

The temple floor had collapsed into piles of rubble so she lay on her back on the still trembling ground. As a thug held his dagger against her throat, she felt the grief rise in her like a dark, choking tide. First Nishke and now her parents and her friends. Poor Kles was awake again, but a lyak knife was pressed against his neck too. Her own dagger was gone.

When she saw thugs and guardsmen dragging Māka and Tute over to Roland, she shouted, "Let them go!" The lyak snarled something and pressed the blade closer against her skin and she stopped.

*Nanaia, where are you?* Scirye called in despair.

Another lyak pried the arrow from her hand and trotted over to present it to Roland. He was wearing his stolen treasures. Strapped to his back was Yi's bow, which Uncle Resak had used as a staff. Around his neck was the bowstring that had been part of Pele's necklace, and on his finger was the pointed archer's ring.

When the lyak barked something in his own tongue, a guard officer acted as an interpreter. "This thing says he saw the entire marble column change into this."

Roland slapped his forehead with a laugh. "That's why these arrows were called monster slayers. They grew larger as they traveled through the air." He gazed at Scirye and then the "3" glowing through her glove as if the leather was transparent. "So the stories about you are true. You really were picked by the goddess. If you'll change the arrows for me, I'll forget about all the trouble you've caused me and let you and your friends go."

Scirye's natural instinct was to refuse, but then she thought, *Bayang got her revenge. Now it's time for me to do the same . . . if I can just get close enough to that pig.*

So instead she said, "Only if you promise to let us go afterward."

"Of course, my dear." Roland smiled with all the fake sincerity he could muster.

"No, lady," Kles protested.

"We have no choice, Kles," Scirye said.

"Release her," Roland said and when a Wolf colonel translated, the lyak lifted his knife away.

Getting up, she marched straight toward the column on the left, the thug keeping pace with her. A guardsman backed out of her way. Her fingers should have been numb without the glove, but the glow seemed to be keeping them warm.

She had no trouble slapping her hand against the column, closing her eyes against the flare of blinding scarlet light. With her eyes still closed, she whirled around and then opened her eyes again as she ran toward Roland.

As she'd hoped, he and his men were dazed momentarily by the light.

She was five paces away, but it was hard to get traction in the snow and frozen dirt.

Then three yards.

She swung the arm with the arrow back for a thrust, gripping it just behind the bronze head. It was finned on all four sides and with a tip as sharp as the day it was made. She couldn't use it as an arrow but she just might use it like a dagger.

At two yards, Roland began to shake his head as if trying to clear it.

One yard.

Even as she began to stab the arrow at Roland's neck, the ground began to tremble again and she heard a rumbling sound as if a locomotive were charging straight at her. Then the ground tilted sharply underneath her and she fell to her knees.

The earlier tremor had been over in a few seconds. This one went on and on, shaking more and more violently with each passing moment so she stayed on all fours. The whole mountain pulsed with a strange red light that washed over them in waves.

She only dared to breathe when the shaking stopped and the red light faded away.

Suddenly a guardsman swore. "What kind of witchcraft is this?"

He took several steps back from Māka. A golden light burned within her as if her body were a paper lantern holding an immense candle, a candle that grew brighter by the moment until flames burst from her shoulders and began a flickering dance, the fiery tips taking the shapes of swords and arrows that waved about before collapsing back and then shot out again. Snowflakes did not melt when they touched the strange fire but spun away instead. It was the armor that Nanaia the Avenger wore.

When Māka-Nanaia sat up, her eyes blazed as if from an inner sun, and wherever she glanced men and griffins sank to their knees in fear and awe. Only Roland remained on his feet. "Shoot her," Roland yelled to his men as he pulled his own pistol from its holster.

"Fool, haven't you done enough harm?" Māka-Nanaia's words rasped like steel on a whetstone. She flung up an arm and flame leaped from her fingertips.

With a cry, Roland dropped the pistol. The red-hot metal hissed against the frozen earth. A moment later, he got down on his knees in sullen submission.

Māka-Nanaia's fiery eyes searched the cringing mob until she found Scirye. "Child of Destiny, you called to me when you were hurt and in need. And I've come at last."

So Nanaia hadn't deserted her after all. In fact, she'd been with Scirye this whole time. Kles landed on her shoulder and squeezed it with his hind paws so that she remembered to kneel. "But why did you disguise yourself as Māka?" she asked.

When Māka-Nanaia smiled, she still looked like her friend, the bumbling magician.

"I was as frustrated as you were whenever we tried to communicate. The dream and vision seemed to confuse you more than explain things, so I thought if I became human, it would be easier to talk to you." Māka-Nanaia gestured at her forehead. "But I went from working in many dimensions to just three, and the brain of my human form couldn't hold all of my thoughts."

If it hadn't been so irreverent, Scirye would have said it was like squeezing a size-ten foot into a size-two shoe. But the goddess seemed to be able to read her thoughts.

When Māka-Nanaia laughed, Scirye heard faint echoes of hammers on steel. Even when she was happy, Nanaia never stopped being the Avenger. "It's a more graphic way of putting it, but yes. I lost most of my memory, including that of my true identity, so I mistook my disguise for my real self." As She kissed Scirye, a warmth wrapped around the girl like a mother wrapping her baby in a quilt. "But that let me find a friend as well as a champion."

"Well, I'm never doing this again," Tute rumbled. "People were always trying to pet me." Since he had now grown to the size and shape of a giant lion, Scirye doubted he would have that trouble anymore.

The both of them must have been vulnerable in these forms, and yet they had been taking risks right beside her. Scirye felt her spirits lift. If Māka-Nanaia was willing to do what it took, so would she.

"So your magical spells—?" Scirye began.

"Were my power trying to find a way out, but my human form was too clumsy to use it well," Māka-Nanaia finished. She became sad. "I shall miss you."

"You're leaving?" Scirye asked in dismay. "But I need you."

"Alas, my full magic is too powerful for flesh. It's dissolving this body even now," Māka-Nanaia said. Her light had grown so bright that it was becoming difficult to make out her features. "So I must hurry and tell you what you need to know. When Roland sent the dragon, Badik, to steal the ring, I could see that it would set a certain chain of events in motion, so I needed my own champion to save the world."

Scirye squinted at the intense light reflecting from the goddess. "But why me?" she asked. "Kat and Wali and Oko were there too."

Māka-Nanaia's light was almost painful now, like the flame of a candle that was too large for the lantern. "*You* were the only one who opened your mind and heart to me. And *you* were the only one who was willing to chase the thief." Scirye remembered that the survivors of the attack at the museum had been pretty dazed. "Sometimes a champion is the one who is ready to act, not the strongest or the bravest. You instinctively knew what had to be done. And you have taught me lessons about heart and courage, so I love and honor you all the more for that."

"So what do you want me to do now?" Scirye asked.

"Once there was a monster born of the very earth so the ground continually renews its vitality," Māka-Nanaia replied. "As it roamed the world destroying whole nations, terrified people gave it many names, but the Kushan's ancestors called it Kemshap. Finally, the emperor of China sent his champion, Yi the Archer, to stop it and he tracked it all the way here.

"The only way to kill Kemshap is by piercing its heart. Though Yi the Archer was the greatest bowman who ever lived, he could not send arrows deep enough through all the thick layers of mud and dirt that make up Kemshap's hide. But he did manage to wound it so badly that it fell unconscious. So the monster has slept through the ages since then, becoming undistinguishable from the hills and mountains about it. And Yi's arrows became the columns and the surviving humans built a temple to honor them—though over the centuries and in the great cataclysm that followed, humans forgot the original purpose of the arrows or that this mountain was ever more than earth and rock."

"So by transforming the arrows and taking them out of this thing, Kemshap, I let the monster wake up?" Scirye asked in horror.

"And the goddess and me as well," Tute said. His voice resonated like a gong. "We must've gotten caught by residual effect when Kemshap awakened. So I thank you for that."

"And now, my champion," Māka-Nanaia said, "it's time for you to complete Yi's task."

"How do I kill a monster who's almost immortal?" Scirye asked.

Māka-Nanaia's shape disappeared in a sphere of cold, pure light—as if the candle flame had finally burned through the paper walls trying to contain it. Brilliant, untouchable, ageless, She seemed more like a star. "The arrow still in its side saps much of Kemshap's strength and makes him sluggish. So you must..." And then the bodies of the goddess and Tute dissolved into a thousand motes that swirled about.

Scirye stretched out a hand. "No, wait!" She felt cold and alone again.

"Too late. She's left the human plane," Kles said in awe.

Suddenly a jumble of images flooded urgently through Scirye's mind—so many that she felt as if she were trying to piece a picture together out of swirling snowflakes. But she thought she heard a single word, "Outside." What did that mean though? They already were outside. Did the goddess want Scirye to lure the monster inside something? But what? The monster was the size of a mountain.

"Lady, lady." Scirye became aware of Kles upon her shoulder. His paw gently patting her cheek. The last thing they needed was for her to go into a coma like she had when the goddess had sent a vision to her in the Arctic.

The whole world might end because Scirye was too stupid to understand Her instructions. Desperately, Scirye turned this way and that, calling to the motes of light that were already beginning to wink out. "What do I do?"

Suddenly, the slope began to tilt, swinging from a thirty-degree angle to sixty degrees or more. The temple ruins disintegrated into chunks of marble, and with a roar, a chasm opened at the base of the mountain. Dirt and snow and boulders cascaded into it.

Scirye tried to jab her fingers and kick her heels through the snow, but she could not break into the frozen earth to get a good grip. So she began to slide downward toward the yawning canyon.

# 60

## Leech

Leech slid down the slanting slope as the ground shook beneath him, flinging off humans and lyaks like a wet dog ridding itself of drops of water.

The last thing he remembered was the lyaks trying to yank the discs from his feet, but the magical devices had seemed glued to his soles. When he tried to hit the thieves with the weapon ring, someone had swung a spear shaft against his head and he'd blacked out.

When he heard the familiar hum of the discs, he kicked against the earth and bounced into the air. The weapon ring was still in his hand. But the lyaks were scampering in panic.

A boulder rumbled by, catching an enemy griffin as it struggled to rise into the air. He soared higher as the rock and the shrieking griffin sped underneath him.

"I hate roller coasters," screamed Koko.

Leech wheeled about and darted toward him, saw his friend scrabbling desperately in the snow and dirt for some kind of paw-hold.

Crouching, he gripped the weapon ring in both hands as he swept in. "Grab hold, buddy."

"You're worse than a roller coaster," the badger said, but he stretched up both paws to grasp the ring.

Leech strained to lift Koko. "I wish you'd skipped a few meals at the citadel," he panted.

"If I could have seen the future, I would've stayed in the Chamber of Truth," the badger snapped.

It took all of Leech's skill to keep his balance while his friend switched his grasp to the boy's legs and then clambered up onto his back.

"Need a hand?" a familiar voice asked.

"N-no thanks. I don't hitchhike with ghosts." Koko kicked his heels against Leech's sides. "Let's get out of here."

Leech looked up at Primo's grinning face. Leech blinked. It couldn't be. Badik had killed him at the museum when the dragon had stolen the ring.

But he couldn't deny that it looked like Primo. The man above him was of medium height but with a solid build that made him seem bigger. He was dressed in a khaki jacket and trousers with cloth strips wound around his ankles and calves. He was standing on a lavender cloud, fluffy enough to be cotton. Despite the strong winds, the cloud remained as stationary, as if it had been nailed to the sky.

*Big brother?* the Voice asked softly, sounding even younger than usual. Leech felt the Voice's amazement surge through him.

*Who?* Leech asked the Voice.

*He's my— I mean, our older brother,* the Voice said.

*How come you didn't recognize him before?* Leech asked.

*I wasn't awake yet,* the Voice replied. *That only happened when you started to use the magical armbands.*

"Don't worry, Koko. I'm not a ghost, just a human with a few dents," Primo assured him. "Before the monster fell on top of me at the museum, I managed to work a spell that let me whisk away into the next gallery," he said. "But it took awhile to recover from my injuries. I've been looking for you everywhere, but then this morning a voice whispered to me to come here."

Leech wondered if the voice had been Dionysus, trying to repay Scirye's kindness.

"You never told me you could work magic," Koko said.

"I thought I was giving Leech enough to handle already without adding that," Primo said.

Leech could feel the Voice's sullen anger smoldering in him like a red-hot coal, and it affected his own mood. Or was it the Voice talking through him now? "Who are you, really?" Leech asked.

Primo looked sad. "Someone with a guilty conscience. Someone who should have stood up for you when the dragons first made their demands. Why do you think I call myself Primo?"

"Because you think you're the best," Leech said, as mad as the Voice now.

"That may be true enough until you grow older," Primo said with a slight grin, "but I was also our parents' firstborn. You're not the only one who can be re-born, you know. I've searched for you in many lives, but assassins always beat me to you. And then I got word about you from a friend at the citadel." He added, "We were all sorry for what we did back at that earlier time, especially father."

"I don't believe all this talk about brotherly love. It took all this time to find me," Leech said furiously, "and you think an apology's going to make up for it?"

"No," Primo sighed, "but let's discuss this later. Right now we have some people to rescue." A murmured spell and a pass of his hands and his cloud began to extend. "Hop on, Koko."

The badger gripped Leech tighter. "No thanks. That doesn't look very strong."

"My cloud would support an elephant." Primo jumped up and down in demonstration. "See?"

"We haven't got time for this, Koko," Leech said. He was also so furious that he needed to get away from Primo. "So everybody ashore." Pivoting, he leaned backward and let go of the badger's legs, spilling the badger onto the cloud.

Koko sat up, spluttering and spitting out wisps of purple mist. The protest died on his lips. "Hey, this would make a pretty good bed at night. How many of these could you make?"

Even as he crossed his ankles and pirouetted in the air, Leech could hear the Voice weeping. *Are you okay?* Leech asked.

Within the shadows at the back of his mind, Leech heard the Voice sob, and he felt the tears sting the corners of his eyes. Were they the Voice's or his—or both? *He was sorry. He came looking for me.* Gone was all the bloodthirstiness. More than ever, he sounded like a small boy.

*For all your power and all your skills, sometimes you're still a little kid,* Leech said wonderingly, and then he saw Scirye, skidding down the slope, her heels kicking up sprays of snow as she tried in vain to stop. Kles was flapping just above her, straining to pull her up with all four paws, but even his great will could not compensate for his lack of size.

As Primo said, they would have to talk things over later. Right now there were people to rescue.

Crouching, he sped toward her. Twenty yards ahead of Scirye, Badik's body tumbled into the yawning chasm.

"Scirye!" he shouted and, squatting, held a hand out, felt her clasp his wrist as he gripped hers. She kicked herself from the ground even as he lifted his arm. When she set her feet on top of his right foot, he lost his balance and they wobbled so much that she was almost tossed off. Desperately, she flung her other arm around his neck and he saw the arrow she was still holding in that hand. And then she was clambering onto his back and they were rising safely into the air.

When they turned around, Leech saw that Primo had managed to rescue Scirye's parents and the Amazons as well as dozens of unarmed guardsmen, lyaks, and thugs who had been drafted to carry Kwele and his friends' griffins onto the cloud—for the loyal griffins had fought until their injuries would no longer let them even stand, let alone walk.

An angry Roland was there too, but stripped of all his weapons and magical treasures. His belt had been used to bind his arms and he lay on his belly, and at the moment Koko was using him as a convenient sofa.

"Do you see Māka?" Leech asked, searching the crowd still on the mountain. The nearby ones were struggling to reach Primo's cloud but more were simply sliding down the slope on a side away from the chasm. With or without riders, the griffins of the Wolf Guard were struggling into the air, only to be scattered about by the winds.

"You slept through a lot, didn't you? She was Nanaia," Scirye said and then explained about Yi the Archer and his arrows and Kemshap.

The news was almost more than he could assimilate. First Primo and now this. But pure joy replaced all his confusion when he saw Bayang limping down the slope toward the waiting cloud. Over her shoulder was Árkwi.

What would Primo do to the dragon when he saw her? Probably nothing, because Bayang had been in a different disguise each time she had hunted Leech down.

Even so, as soon as he had let Scirye off on the cloud, Leech sped toward the dragon. "Bayang, you're alive."

She was bleeding from numerous wounds and there were raw patches of flesh where whole patches of scales had been torn off, and one eye was nearly half-shut. "I'm glad I can say the same," she said.

From the corner of his eye, Leech saw Scirye hugging her parents, and then he waved to Primo. "Primo, this is Bayang." He made a point of saying, "She's our friend."

Primo stared at the dragon suspiciously. "Have we met somewhere before?"

"That's always possible," Bayang said carefully. "I've spent a lot of time in the human lands."

They studied each other intently, and Leech had the feeling that if they ever fought each other it would be to the death. He just hoped it wouldn't come to that.

Suddenly the mountain stirred again and boulders began rolling in an avalanche of dirt and rocks. When the cascade stopped and the cloud of material dissolved, a huge cavern gaped at the top of the mountain. Inside, stalagmites and stalactites formed of iridescent rainbow bands gleamed at them. Suddenly, with a loud rumble, the hole closed, and when it opened again, streams of mud slid down like drool.

Leech realized that the glimmering pillars were actually Kemshap's fangs.

A hill next to Kemshap began to rise until it became a leg with a huge irregular-shaped disc as a foot. A new chasm snaked from the hole through the city so that the glasslike ruins fell with the sound of all the dishes in the world shattering.

Kemshap's peak swung back and forth, and then it pulled its other leg free.

"And now," Primo groaned, "Kemshap can destroy again and there's no one to stop it."

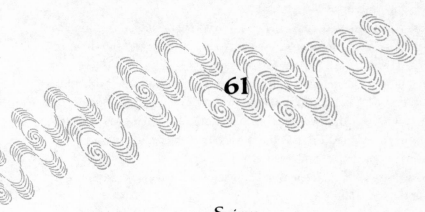

# 61

## Scirye

"I can," Roland said from underneath Koko. "I've trained for years with the best archery masters. Give me the bow and arrows."

"Why should we trust you?" Scirye demanded.

"Because," Roland said, "I don't want this world destroyed anymore than you do. What's the point of ruling a wasteland?"

Scirye looked at Bayang who shook her head. "I never had need of a bow." When the dragon shook her head, the Kushan girl turned toward Primo who was sending his cloud speeding away from Kemshap. "Primo?"

"I'm afraid not," he said, glancing back at the monster of earth and stone.

"We've used one for a few days in training," Kat confessed, "but I doubt if any of us could string one, let alone hit what we were aiming at."

Lord Tsirauñe, his shoulder newly bandaged, looked at Scirye.

He was deferring to her now as their leader, which made Scirye feel strange and uncomfortable.

What did the goddess want her to do? She waited a second for inspiration to come, to be given some divine clue, but as usual, there was only the frustrating silence.

If only Nanaia had been able to stay in human form long enough to instruct her. Her first instinct was to let her parents decide, but she realized that wasn't what Nanaia had wanted. And it wasn't what she wanted either. The goddess had chosen her to find the arrows, so ultimately the responsibility was hers.

"Hurry," Roland snapped and grunted when Koko bounced up and down on him heavily.

"Uh-unh. Mind your manners," the badger scolded.

The storm was ending, so she could see Kemshap clearly. The monster seemed to fill half the sky now. It took a single, ponderous step, but that step covered half a mile, obliterating anything underneath it.

The last marble column still protruded horizontally from the monster's side. Seen from that angle, the column looked more like a huge arrow. It was just as well that it made Kemshap sluggish, but for how long? Could it pull it out somehow?

Everyone was watching her as they waited for her decision. She just wished she had more time to think, but she would just have to go with a hunch. "All right, Roland, but you only get one chance." When Roland opened his mouth to protest, she frowned. "No arguments. String your bow."

"Are you sure about this?" Bayang asked.

Scirye pointed at the column. "I'm hoping that the weather's worn away some of the dirt so Kemshap's hide is thinner." She glanced at Oko. "But if Roland aims at anyone else but the monster, hit him."

The big Pippal still had the imperial battle-axes. She took one of them from her belt and reversed it to use the blunt side as a hammer. "With pleasure."

Roland nodded at her. "I underestimated you, my dear."

Kat undid the belt from around Roland's arms and Wali returned the parts of the magical bow to him while Oko stood ready to swing the axe.

The bowstring had been disguised as a necklace. Quickly he undid the knot to reveal loops on either end of the cord. Puka shells fell into the cloud as the string writhed and curled like a long, slender worm.

"The bow's so thick," Bayang said, already reaching for it. "Do you want me to bend it?"

Roland slipped Yi's ring onto his thumb. Carved out of bone, a triangle projected horizontally from the top like a pointed ledge, with the apex aimed away from his body.

"This will give me all the strength I need to use the bow," he boasted.

Oko raised her axe, ready to end the experiment immediately. "You mean, it makes you superhuman?"

"No, you fool, just when I handle the bow," Roland snapped, but he was sensible enough to freeze while he waited for Scirye to make a choice.

"Go on," she said.

Roland fastened one loop to the top of the wooden shaft. Then, setting the bow behind one calf, he pulled the top down, and the thick wood bent as if it were a straw. So it was easy to fit the second loop over the other end of the shaft. Roland's face was flushed and excited as he held it up. "The energy! The power of this bow!"

The string, now taut, sung a low, eager note, almost as if it were humming.

Kles fluttered in the air, ready to attack Roland too. "The bow must sense its ancient enemy."

And so had Kemshap. Ponderously, trailing piles of debris, Kemshap turned and began to stomp toward them.

## 62

Scirye

Roland placed himself at the front of the cloud and then called over his shoulder to Primo. "Take a bearing on that column sticking out of the monster and get me within a hundred yards, and then hold this thing as steady as you can."

Primo frowned at being ordered around by the villain, but he swung the cloud around in a wide arc. The cloud was so large and heavy with passengers now that, even though it still moved swiftly in a straight line, it was as ponderous as a barge in turns.

As soon as they saw the cloud returning to Kemshap, one of the prisoners shouted, "Are you crazy?"

Wali had armed herself with a rifle and aimed it at them now. "Shut up." And the prisoners lapsed into a sullen, frightened silence.

Like birds hypnotized by a snake, they stared in fascination as the monster loomed larger and larger in front of them. Even Oko couldn't help shifting her gaze momentarily from Roland to Kemshap.

Pivoting, Roland swung the bow hard against Oko's temple. Even as Oko's knees buckled, Roland had hooked the little triangular point on the side of the ring over the string. Then, fitting the arrow to the string, he pulled the string back with the help of the archer's ring and aimed the arrow at Primo. "Take us away from here," Roland commanded.

"I knew we couldn't trust you," Bayang growled.

"Take one step toward me and he dies," Roland warned and the dragon stopped.

"I thought you cared about what happens to the world?" Leech demanded.

Roland shrugged one shoulder. "By the time that monster demolishes Asia, I should either have worked out the secrets of this weapon or I'll have found some remote island where I'll be safe."

Even as the cloud veered away slowly, Kemshap began to shrink in height. Huge knobs popped up from the surface. Then the knobs burst, lengthening into monumental spines that shot outward with the speed of an express train.

Helplessly, Scirye watched the stony spikes rushing to impale them with thunderous grinding noises.

Roland spun about to meet the new threat. "Don't come near me," Roland yelled at Kemshap.

"We're still out of bow range," Kat said.

But the panicked Roland had already released the string. As the arrow sped from the bow, it grew longer and thicker with each passing second until it was twenty feet long, and the wooden shaft hardened into marble.

"Please, please," Scirye murmured as it shot like a rocket toward Kemshap.

The bronze arrowhead shattered one of the spines, its pointed tip vanishing in a puff of dust, and then bounced off a second and then a third, clattering about as it bounced downward from one remaining spike to another.

Roland wheeled around, raising the bow over his shoulder in

both hands like a club. "You, boy, give me the flying discs," he snarled at Leech.

Leech started to speed backward. "Never."

Roland swung Yi's bow in a vicious blow but missed the boy. The motion threw the man off-balance. Terror filled his eyes as he flung the bow away and raised his arms to try to right himself.

Bayang stretched her long body toward him to catch him, but her paws just missed.

Roland screamed as he went over the side.

And Scirye watched helplessly as the bow and Roland disappeared below. There was still one arrow in Kemshap's side, but it might as well be on the moon now. That left only the arrow she had, but with no way to shoot it, there was no way to stop Kemshap from destroying the world.

# 63

## Scirye

As the giant spikes rumbled toward them, Primo tilted the cloud skyward, knocking Scirye from her feet. Desperately, she dug her fingers into the cloud for handholds, but only grasped mist. Suddenly she was sliding across the cloud, her shouts drowned out by the thunderous rumbling of the oncoming spikes.

And then the cloud was bucking up and down and from side to side as if it had become a wild bronco, bouncing Scirye about. Beneath her, the cloud thinned so it was like looking through a murky window as the dirt-and-rock spires roared beneath them, skinning enough of the mist from the bottom of their craft so that she could see through it.

A moment later, Primo leveled off the cloud and sent it racing forward, away from Kemshap. And the cloud's surface became opaque as it thickened again.

"*Whoo-ee,*" Koko panted. "I've never had a near collision with a mountain before. I'd hate to see what he's like when he doesn't still have an arrow in him."

Scirye glanced about. Her friends and parents were still here and picking themselves back up, but some of the prisoners had fallen off. Even if they were her enemies, she still felt sorry for them.

Kles fluttered about her, adjusting her clothes. "Are you all right, lady?"

Scirye didn't answer as her mind raced. There was probably dynamite at the camp, but she was willing to bet Kemshap could replace whatever the dynamite blew up. Even if they had enough dynamite to fill a cargo freighter, that still might not be sufficient.

Anyway, that hadn't been what the goddess had been trying to tell her. Desperately, she tried to recall all the things that Nanaia had said as Māka, some inkling of Her plan that might have slipped out of Her human form unawares.

"He's trying to hit us with the spikes," Kat shouted.

Kemshap had shifted his feet so that he could swing his spikes at them. Immediately, Primo sent his cloud up, but not at such a steep angle this time, so they were able to keep their balance.

Balance!

Scirye remembered what the goddess as Māka had said about how things balanced out. Nanaia was powerful as a goddess but a bumbler as a human. Strengths in one thing compensated for flaws in another. The good evened out the bad. She ran through the vision again, keeping Māka's words in mind and remembered the goddess reversing her cape.

Scirye had the answer, feeling as sure as if the goddess had written it out for her: the Inside equalized the Outside. Weakness matched strength. And as frightening as the solution was, it was also almost a relief after wondering what she was to do for so long.

She remembered how Nishke had faced a dragon with just an antique weapon that was liable to break at any moment. She couldn't do any less with Kemshap.

With Kles on her shoulder, Scirye crossed the spongelike cloud, kicking up wisps of mist as she went. When she had reached Leech, who was standing with Bayang, she whispered, "I need a ride. We're going to give that monster a little surprise."

Leech's eyebrows knit together in puzzlement as he said in a low voice, "We don't have the archer's bow anymore."

"I'm going to deliver the arrow personally to Kemshap's heart." She twirled her hand, motioning for Leech to turn around. "That's what the goddess meant when she reversed her cape in the vision that she sent."

Leech was even more confused. "You're supposed to switch your clothes around?"

"No," Scirye said. "She was trying to tell me that the inside was more important than the outside."

Bayang nodded. "Pele's charm should let me breathe inside that monster just like it did when we were submerged in lava. I'll go."

"No, I will," Leech said as he held out his hand.

"The goddess chose my lady," Kles said sternly, "not you."

With the memory of Nanaia's shining form still fresh in their minds, neither the dragon nor the boy argued.

As Leech turned around and squatted, her mother finally took notice. "Where are you going?"

"To do my job," Scirye said as she clambered onto Leech's back.

Ignoring his own safety on the slippery cloud, her father actually began running to intercept her. "You stay right here," he ordered. "I'm not going to lose my other daughter."

Scirye wrapped her arms around her friend's shoulders. "The world's more important than us," she said, but could not help feeling guilty. Though before this, she might have twisted and bent her parents' commands to her own liking, she had never openly disobeyed them. "It's what Nishke would do."

From somewhere, she thought she heard her sister laughing. "Yes, I probably would."

And then Leech was soaring away from the cloud with Kles next to them.

"Where to?" Leech asked her.

"Straight to Kemshap's mouth," Scirye said.

# 64

## Leech

Leech's heart was pounding as he raced toward the peak that was Kemshap's head. "You and your Tumarg," he said to his friend.

"I'm sorry for getting you into this," Scirye said, gripping him tighter.

"You've got a lot to live up to, and I've got a lot to live down," Leech said. "And maybe this will make up a little for what I did in that former life."

"There's nothing to make up for," Scirye said. "Lee No Cha was Lee No Cha, and you're you. And the Leech I know is a good person."

Scirye's title meant little to a street rat like Leech, but he'd come to respect and even admire her during their time together, so her praise meant something to him. "You really think so?"

"I know so," Scirye said. Once the Kushan girl made up her mind, that was that.

"Well, I think we're all better for having met you." Leech couldn't help laughing. "Even Koko."

He angled downward a little more sharply as the monster started to shrink once more. Knobs began erupting all over its face like dirty pimples and became spikes that shot outward in all directions as Kemshap's head became a giant pincushion—and the pins kept growing and growing.

Leech felt the muscles on his legs twitch as if the Voice were trying to gain control again. *Of all the crazy things we've done, this is the craziest*, the Voice said.

Leech resisted the Voice's efforts. *If anyone has a chance of stopping Kemshap, it's Scirye*, Leech insisted. *If that creature is roaming around, the world won't be safe.*

*It's not the world I knew, but let's give everyone a fighting chance*, the Voice admitted. *Just like Bayang tried to do for us. So let me take over.*

For a moment, Leech hesitated, but then he forced himself to surrender control. *Okay.*

There had been times when he felt the Voice had seized control of his arms and legs. So it was strange to feel again like a passenger in his own body. It was even odder to feel the Voice looking through his eyes, like being in a tiny room with one window. Or to have someone else make his legs bend a little more so he had better balance.

But he also felt himself swept along on a tide of confidence and the sheer joy of flying.

*Do you see Kemshap's mistake?* the Voice asked eagerly. He didn't wait for Leech to answer. *The longer the spikes become, the more they spread out.*

Finally Leech understood. *Which leaves a gap for us.*

"Hold on," the Voice said to both Leech and Scirye as they raced onward.

# 65

## Scirye

Scirye's teeth clacked as they bounced off one spine and toward another. "Down," Leech ordered.

The humming of the discs rose to a whine when they hit the second spike, but instead of ricocheting off it, Leech squatted down and Scirye copied him as they skimmed along its length as if it were a road with a curved surface. The spikes, though packed densely together, still left a space of several yards between each of them.

It was like entering a giant thornbush, and Scirye clung to him, trusting in her friend's skill. They'd traveled this far, defeated powerful opponents, and fought through traps because they'd learned how to depend on each other. She wasn't about to stop now.

As the discs grated along the spike, Leech let out a whoop of sheer joy, and Scirye felt her own blood begin to race like a horse across the steppes, like a maenad dancing through vine-covered hills.

"Euoi," she murmured.

Kles was coiled around her neck to keep a low profile. "Excuse me, lady?"

"Nothing." She laughed, feeling the wind rush against her face until her cheeks were numb. She was a Kushan and steppe and mountain and desert and now the sky were her playroom.

Suddenly they began to strike little bumps along the irregular surface that knocked their heads against a spike above. Then she started to hear clunks and clacks behind her. She risked a glance in back of her and saw foot-long thorns begin to sprout from the sides of the giant spines. Kemshap had figured out what they were doing, but it was too late.

They shot out of the thicket of spikes and Leech halted their momentum by pirouetting quickly in midair. He'd become a good flier in the short time she had known him, but she'd never seen him fly with such authority before.

As they hovered in front of the cavernous mouth. Scirye swallowed as she stared at the stalactites and stalagmites with their iridescent bands. They looked so huge when you were up close. And the stench from the creature's mouth almost made her gag. It smelled of rot, like the water in a stagnant marsh.

Despite all of her noble speeches, she hesitated. If her plan didn't work, it would be the nightmare of nightmares— swallowed alive, trapped in the damp darkness of the monster's gullet.

Kles brushed his beak ever so lightly across her cheek. "Live in glory and honor and joy, my lady, for you are my lare."

The next moment she felt a small paw tug at Pele's charm around her neck. She gave a jump when it came away in his claws.

"What—?" she began to protest, but the small griffin had unwrapped himself from around her neck, snaking down to snatch the arrow from her belt. Then, with the arrow in one paw and the charm in the other, he launched himself into the air.

As he flew straight into the yawning maw, Kles cried defiantly, "*Tarkar!*"

And then he was gone.

# 66

## Leech

The cry was torn right from Scirye's heart. "Kles, why did you do that? I'm the one who's supposed to go."

The Voice was already turning to escape. *What's wrong? She ought to be glad someone else is doing it.*

Leech sensed the Voice's confusion. *She loves him, and he loves her.*

*I don't understand love,* the Voice said.

*Neither do I really,* Leech admitted.

*But Primo was searching for me . . . I mean us,* the Voice said. *Does that mean Primo loves me?*

*It's got to count for something,* Leech said.

Though the griffin would be a gnat in comparison to the monster, Kemshap was all too aware of the arrow Kles was carrying. If it was possible for a living mountain to looked worried, he would have said that was what Kemshap was doing, because it had stopped dead in its tracks. Even its spikes remained stationary as it ignored them.

*That thing seems distracted, so I guess it's safe enough if you take over*, the Voice said. *I can handle the flying but not her. You're still better with people.*

Wanting to comfort his friend, Leech reached behind him and awkwardly patted her on the shoulder. "Kles didn't want you to get hurt."

Scirye gave an anguished sob. "I wasn't going to get hurt. The otter charm would have given me a way back out."

Leech glanced over his shoulder at her. "You can't be sure. Maybe Kles was afraid it wouldn't work on Kemshap like it did on the hag's bag or a prison lock."

"I've got to go after him," Scirye insisted. "You said it was hard living with the guilt over what Lee No Cha did. Well, I won't be able to live with the guilt if something happens to Kles because he's doing my job."

*What do we do?* the Voice asked Leech.

*We've got to help her*, Leech replied.

As he swung around, he took off his own charm from Pele and gave it to Scirye. Instantly, he began to feel the winter cold. "Here. It's the latest fashion for diving into monsters."

# 67

## Scirye

 They zoomed up over a wide, curving cheek toward the giant pit that was its mouth, but Kemshap ignored them as they drew near. Instead, it seemed to be concentrating all its attention on its insides. Rocks and mud oozed down from the corners of its mouth like drool, and the stone formations in its mouth swayed as the walls of its mouth convulsed.

The cavernous mouth opened and shut, spraying rocks and dirt about each time it closed. And when the mouth widened, Scirye could see the stalactites and stalagmites rocking and swaying as the monster's throat spasmed, trying to cough up the invader.

The stench made Scirye choke, but she did not complain. Somewhere within the blackness was her oldest and dearest friend fighting for his life. When she found him, she was going to give him the biggest hug he'd ever had—and then she'd pluck out every one of his feathers and hairs for scaring her like this.

"Careful. I think Kemshap's trying to gag," Leech warned.

Touching the otter charm for good luck, Scirye got ready to jump. *Don't think about the smell. Don't think about the danger. Just think about the people who are dear to you. Think about the whole world.*

They'd all worked so hard and sacrificed so much just to get her to this point in time. For a moment, her heart was full of love, and she regretted that she couldn't tell anyone else but Leech.

Scirye gave him a quick peck on the cheek. "Thanks for being my friend."

"Thanks for being mine too, but don't make it sound like we'll never see each other again." Leech slowed down as they passed over the void. "Good luck."

"You too." Letting go of his neck, Scirye jumped into the wide fissure. *"Yashe!"* she cried.

She'd meant to land in the space between two stalagmites, but they were rocking so violently that she hit one of the slippery columns instead, bouncing face-first into the muddy soil that formed the inside of Kemshap's mouth.

The earth clung to her so zealously that she had to strain to push herself away from it, and large patches of it oozed down the front of her clothes. She wiped her face with her sleeve, which was so dirty she thought she might have made herself even messier. All the epics she had read had not prepared her for this. It was more like being back in the sewers. Even a poet would have had trouble putting this into a heroic light.

The stinking mud clung to her ankles at every step as she headed toward the shaft that served as the monster's throat. The passage walls heaved in and out even more than Kemshap's mouth. But she'd been afraid that Kemshap's insides would be a solid, impenetrable mass. At least this gave her a possible route to her griffin.

"Kles?" she shouted down into it. Her voice echoed back to her, but there was no sign of her friend. All she could do was hope as she slid down the damp gullet. The dirt that formed the throat had an oily feeling, and as she moved along it, she felt the greasiness soak her clothes and skin. She wondered how many baths it would take before she felt clean again—assuming she survived.

Down, down she slipped, the only light coming from the glowing mark on her palm. She lost all sense of time and distance. She only knew that the smell was getting worse.

Suddenly her boot soles slammed against something. By the dim light from her palm, she saw that she had landed on dirt poles about the thickness of broom shafts, but unlike the throat and mouth the soil was hard as concrete.

Had this tangle always been there or was it a trap that Kemshap had created just now for Kles? The monster had probably never met such a tiny threat as the griffin before and must be frantically improvising defenses.

For a moment, pride for her friend drove away her own fears. Touching the pouch containing the otter charm, Scirye eased a leg between a narrow opening. The dirt poles writhed, widening the space so she could lower her other leg.

"Kles?" she called.

"Go away," came the faint voice. "You weren't supposed to follow me."

He was still alive! Scirye almost laughed with delight as she continued to climb down. "You're getting to be as much of an old grump as Bayang."

"It's from associating with a willful mistress who's determined to throw her life away," Kles shouted back.

"Well, that's what you get for trying to throw yours away instead," Scirye scolded. "I won't allow it. So wait for me."

Kles gave an embarrassed cough. "I ... um ... don't seem to have much choice in the matter."

For the first time since she had jumped, Scirye was enjoying herself. "Oh, so you got stuck without the otter charm, did you? That's what you get for not taking me along."

She could just imagine the griffin squirming wherever he was. "Humph, a polite person wouldn't tease another's misfortune."

"You've called me an unmannered savage a lot of times," Scirye reminded him.

"Only when you do things like use the tip of my tail as a paintbrush," Kles huffed.

When Scirye reached Kles, he was caught in a cage of twiglike sticks formed from dirt. Kemshap seemed to have kept decreasing the size of the shafts until he'd filled his throat with a dense mesh that had finally snared the invader.

Scirye's fingers parted the bars of the cage. "Oh, Kles, promise me you'll never do that again."

"Then promise me that you'll stop fighting legendary monsters," the griffin retorted. He was gripping the precious arrow in one claw as he crept through the opening. "I'm too old to be diving down throats." He pressed himself against her cheek. "But thank you for rescuing me."

She hugged him back. "Now for the hard part. We have to find Kemshap's heart."

Kles held up the arrow. "But this knows. I can feel it quivering like a hound that's caught the scent."

Scirye touched a finger to the arrow shaft and felt the electric tingle. "Then let's go."

The griffin eased up onto a shoulder and wrapped around the back of her neck in his favorite position.

The dirt bars became finer and finer until they were like a web, and even began to grow sticky with some gluelike substance, but nothing could stop them.

Finally, Kles tightened a paw on her arm. "The arrow's tugging me toward that passage to your left. Take it."

The tunnel was about four feet wide and angled up gently, the wrinkly walls pulsing as she began to climb up. Suddenly her hands and feet began to slip as the surface became oily. She would have slid backward if she hadn't shoved her feet out on either side between the folds.

Though it was hard to grip the greasy dirt with her hands or find purchase with her feet, she slowly began to climb. The walls vibrated in a rapid, regular rhythm, and she became aware of how warm it was getting.

By the time they reached the chamber, she was sweating and Kles's fur and feathers were also matted with perspiration.

By the dim, blue-ish light within the chamber, she saw a black crystal the size of a house suspended between what looked like hoses of mud. Through the murky material, she could make out something spinning inside with wide, flat blades like the agitator of a washing machine. As it whirled and whirled, it sent fluid pulsing back and forth through the giant hoses.

"Here, take the arrow," Kles said, holding it out. His paw shook as if he were having trouble holding the arrow now that it was so near its prey.

"Let's do it together," Scirye said as she wrapped her fingers around the arrow shaft just above his paw. It seemed like a puny twig compared to the giant heart.

"Look out!" Kles said.

Just in front of them, a column of dirt shot up from the floor with the force of a pile driver. Two more columns descended to thud against the floor.

Scirye hopped to her left and then jogged several steps, zigging and zagging, trying never to be predictable. She almost fell into a hole that opened suddenly in front of her but managed to jump over it.

"I'll draw its attention," Kles said.

She grabbed his tail and held on for dear life. "No! You're never leaving my side again. It . . . it hurt too much when I thought I lost you."

Kles freed his tail from her grip. "Very well," he agreed and then yelled. "Watch out! On your right."

They barely ducked under the spikes that shot out from the wall.

Scirye had no time to think, letting instinct twist her body and make her dodge and jump. But finally they reached the heart.

There wasn't time to pause. "Now!" she said, and she and the griffin lunged forward, shoving the arrow together into the heart. Even though they had thrust with all their might, the arrow didn't penetrate more than a few inches.

So her guess had been wrong and all this effort had been wasted.

But then the arrow began to wriggle as if alive. Startled, she and Kles let go and watched it expand as it carved its way another inch. The heart began to convulse.

"Yi's magic must have been as powerful as his arm," Kles said.

All about them, the chamber began to shake as if in an earthquake. One more inch deeper. Then two. Then an entire foot, and with each second the arrow grew wider until it was nearly a foot wide.

A chunk of the ceiling crashed down on the left. A fissure cracked the floor on the right. Then a hose burst, spraying a purplish ichor all about.

Still, the arrow burrowed like a snake, biting into Kemshap's heart until it was up to the feathers at the end. Finally it disappeared out of sight.

Cracks began to snake across the surface of the heart as if it were shattering.

"We did it, Kles," she said, too tired to cheer.

"Well done, lady," the griffin answered, trying to brush the dirt away from her face with a gentle paw.

A piece of the heart broke off and thudded against the floor, and then another and another until there was only a pile of rubble. A feathered shaft protruded from one piece. It had shrunk back to its former size now that its task was done.

"This is too dangerous to leave lying around." When her hand closed around the arrow, she felt it quiver and her palm grew warm and began to glow. When she yanked it free, the arrow began to tug at her arm.

*It must still want to fight Kemshap even though the monster's dead,* Scirye thought to herself.

Forcing her arm to stay at her side, she turned toward the passage through which they had come. But it had aleady collapsed. There would be no return journey.

Scirye wrapped an arm around Kles. She was glad she wasn't alone right now. "I love you, Kles."

The griffin's small paws circled her neck. "And I love—" he began, but then the floor gave way beneath her and the ceiling dropped, burying them completely.

## 68

## Leech

Lady Sudarshane, Lord Tsirauñe, and the Amazons were weeping, and even Koko was snuffling as they stared at Kemshap. Below them, the monster had collapsed in a hodgepodge of hills and its spikes had become huge burrows of dirt and rock.

And somewhere in that debris, Scirye and Kles were buried alive. Koko sank down on his knees in the mist. "Geez, what a way to go."

Leech felt tears stinging the corners of his eyes. Scirye was the most opinionated person he had ever met, but she had also been the most decent, honest, and reliable human he had ever known. So Leech had wanted to measure up to her own high standards, and even Koko had tried to be a better badger.

*I'm sorry she's gone,* the Voice sympathized.

Bayang put a paw on his shoulder. "So, do we need to settle anything between us?"

Leech knew the dragon was speaking not to him but to the Voice. *Well?* he asked the Voice.

*You're right, Leech,* the Voice said. *The times are different, and I have to change to live in them.*

Leech turned slowly on his heel so he could face the dragon. "You're different. We're all different. So let's try to be friends."

Bayang looked relieved. "Good. Because we have more important things to do than fight a feud that should have ended a long time ago."

"Important things like rescuing Scirye?" Leech asked.

"We're going to dig right there." Bayang pointed at the broken marble column protruding from the hill, all that was left of the third arrow, the one that Scirye had not transformed back to its original shape. "I figure that marks where Kemshap's heart should be."

And for a moment, next to the marble stump, Leech glimpsed Māka in her gaudy robe standing next to an impatient lynx, but then they were gone as soon as he blinked. "I get it. The old arrow is probably near the heart where Scirye and Kles are."

Bayang turned and waved to Primo. "Will you take us to Roland's camp so we can get pickaxes and more shovels?"

"Gladly," Primo said and he began to swing his cloud about.

# 69

## Leech

The storm had passed by the time they returned from their scavenging trip to Roland's camp. The wind and the snowflakes seemed to have scoured the dust and impurities from the air so that everything he saw on the moonlit ground seemed sharply etched on his eyes.

Since he had given Pele's charm to Scirye, Leech had taken a coat from the camp to wear over his robe. Even then, he still felt cold, but his discomfort vanished when he spotted Roland's body. "We don't want any more bad guys getting hold of the ring," Leech said as he rose on the discs and left the cloud.

As he sped toward Roland, he saw the bow a few yards away. Circling around, he hovered while he squatted in midair and picked it up. The wood seemed to pulse against his palm and the string hummed. As he slung it over his shoulder, he felt the vibrations pulse through him.

He went on until he reached Roland, who was lying facedown.

Roland's hand was already cold and Leech was afraid the archer's ring might be frozen on the finger, but it slid off easily into his palm.

He gazed down at the jewelry carved out of bone. It seemed like such a harmless thing, but it had started all of them on this strange journey. It was too bad that Scirye wasn't here to share the moment.

When he had reached the cloud again, he handed the ring to Kat. "Here. I think Scirye would want you to return this for her."

Tears appeared at the corner of the tough warrior's eyes. "Now Nishke's spirit can finally rest."

Oko hefted a shovel to her shoulder. "Not until we find her little sister."

Primo landed them upon the hill that was all that remained of Kemshap. A team of prisoners wrestled a portable generator off the cloud while a second team carried the lights that Roland had used on calmer evenings. All of them were volunteers, some seemed genuinely moved by Scirye's sacrifice while others, realizing they were technically traitors, were trying to curry favor by cooperating.

Even though they were as impatient as Leech to begin digging, Scirye's parents had to wait for the lights to come on.

But a dragon is used to finding her way in the lightless depths of the ocean. As they stepped off Primo's strange craft, Bayang pointed to the broken column. "We'll dig there," Bayang announced to the other rescuers, "but since we can't be sure this is where Kemshap's heart is, the rest of you should explore elsewhere."

As they climbed up the slope, Koko munched a cookie that he had found in the mess tent. "I bet we hear Kles long before we see him," he said, trying to lift his friends' spirits.

"He'll be giving a lecture on internal organs," Bayang agreed.

Leech chuckled. "There's one person who likes the sound of his own voice." All three of them wanted to cling to the faint hope that their friends had survived.

Bayang said a growth spell and her body shimmered in an iridescent mist until she was three times as large. "Be careful not to get behind me," she warned. Then the dragon began to dig, her large paws breaking up the frozen dirt into clods that she cast behind her. Soon she was digging in a steady rhythm like a scaled steam shovel.

As he watched the mound of discarded earth rise behind Bayang, Leech was sure they'd find Scirye soon. Going to a spot on the other side of the shattered arrow, Leech swung a pickaxe. The cold ground was like iron but he worked determinedly until there was a small pile of rubble, which Koko lifted away with his shovel.

Soon, despite the cold, he was sweating. A little distance away he heard the generator cough into life and light suddenly flooded the slopes. All about them, people began digging.

*And we won't leave until we've found our friends*, the Voice said.

*No, we won't*, Leech promised.

# 70

## Bayang

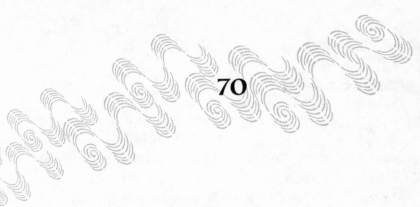

By sunrise of the next day, the hill was pitted with holes and Bayang had personally excavated a crater. Even her great muscles ached and Leech and Koko were moving as stiffly as zombies.

By common consent, they joined the others for breakfast, for Wali had brewed a vat of hot tea to go with the cheese and hard cakes she had liberated from Roland's camp.

Bayang had little appetite for food, but she had welcomed the tea and had returned to the hill to sit by herself as she warmed her paws on the tin cup. As she inhaled the aroma from the tea, she remembered warm summer days floating in the ocean among the kelp. She felt a pang that she would never see her home again, but she put that aside. She had made her choices. She would live with them now.

She sighed. It would be a shame if Scirye would not get to enjoy any more sunny afternoons. But the hatchling had made her choice as well, a very noble one. All Bayang could do was try to save her now.

When the pebbles began to rattle, she stood up hastily and looked about. Was Kemshap coming to life, or was this some sort of aftershock after his death?

But the rest of the slope lay still.

Curious, she looked at the spot again and saw that the ground had risen to a small mound several inches high. And then a bronze arrowhead thrust out of it, followed by the hand clasping the shaft. The next moment, the dirt cascaded aside and a familiar but very dirty red head followed.

Scirye grinned up at the dragon. "You need a bath, Bayang."

Bayang was so surprised that the only thing she could think of to say was, "So do you, young lady." Instinctively, she extended the cup in her paw. "Would you like some tea?"

Scirye blinked the dirt from her eyes and sniffed appreciatively. "It smells wonderful, but would you mind giving me a paw? I feel like I'm one big bruise."

Bayang set her cup down. It was only then that she remembered to shout to the others, "Hey, I've found her."

Scirye grinned up at her. "What do you mean? I'm the one who found you."

Laughing with relief, Bayang began to dig with both paws until she had freed Scirye's shoulders and arms. Seizing the hatchling's wrist, the dragon hauled her out of the hole. "Up you go."

A very bedraggled griffin clung to her back. He let go, falling with a plop on the ground.

As she hugged the hatchling, Bayang reminded herself that despite having just heroically slain a gigantic monster, Scirye was still a human with fragile bones.

Even though Bayang tried to be as gentle as she could, the hatchling laughed. "Ouch. Not so hard."

Tenderly, Bayang lifted Kles in her paw and repeated his battle cry in a soft, loving voice. "Tarkär, friend. Well done."

Tucking the arrow into her belt, Scirye had tried to pick up the cup in one hand and almost dropped it. It was only then that Bayang noticed her fingers were so raw and bleeding from scraping against rocks that she had difficulty holding anything. Gripping the cup clumsily in both her hands, the hatchling drank thirstily, then lowered it.

"Here, Kles. I saved you half," she said.

As the dragon held the griffin, Scirye lifted the cup to the griffin's beak.

As Kles settled back against Bayang's paw, he croaked, "For our next adventure, could we read a book? Preferably something boring—like how to grow carrots."

Scirye had turned her face up toward the sun, letting it warm her cheeks. "I thought you liked all this excitement."

"Sometimes you can have too much of a good thing," Kles said, and sighed.

By then the others had stumbled over the uncertain footing of the slope toward them, and there was another round of hugs with some tears mixed in.

When everyone had had a turn with Scirye and Kles, they sat down. "Did you just burrow through a whole mountain?" Kat asked, staring at the hole.

Lord Tsiraûne scratched his cheek. "I don't recall anyone in the family being part gopher."

Kles was sitting up now, but leaning against his mistress for support. "I think it was the arrow's doing, my lord."

Scirye held up it up. "The arrow just began knifing through the dirt. I'm just glad I was able to hold on."

"So are we," Lady Sudarshane said, smiling as she began to cry again.

## 71

## Scirye

Scirye was taken to Roland's camp where she was comfortably installed in a tent with a portable stove. Kles had coiled himself about her neck and shoulders and was chirruping in a low voice that was his equivalent of a cat's purr.

As he sat with his friends, Koko gave a deep sigh. "So it's finally over."

Scirye glanced at her hand. The mark was fading, the outlines of the "3" hard to see. Suddenly she felt sad, realizing that the end of the adventure meant that her friends would now be going their separate ways. "I suppose you'll be heading home to San Francisco with Primo," she said to Leech and Koko. A new thought hit her and she looked at Bayang. "But what will you do?"

The dragon lifted her head with all of her old dignity. "I'll go home and ask for a meeting with all the representatives of the different clans. Since I did kill Badik, they'll have to honor my request and come. Then I'll try to convince them that Leech is no threat. After all, he did help save the world."

"Will they believe you?" Leech said, worried.

Bayang shrugged and winced at the pain in her injured wing. "Probably not. We dragons can be a pretty hardheaded lot."

Leech looked distracted for a moment, as if he were listening to someone, and then he asked, "What'll they do to you?"

Bayang looked away from Leech and twisted her head to check the scars on her wing. "The dragons will put me to death for disobeying their orders."

Leech paused as if he were listening to someone and then he said, "Even Lee No Cha would say that's wrong."

"And if he were here," Bayang said carefully, "I would thank him, because he would now be my friend and not my enemy."

"You could stay with us and Primo," Leech offered.

Bayang shook her head. "Primo and I could never feel comfortable with each other."

Koko gave a cough. "Scirye, couldn't you ask the princess to work out a deal with the dragons?"

Bayang folded her wings again. "Even a princess of a vast empire is still a mere human to the dragons. My people will only listen to one of their own kind."

Scirye pulled the blanket tighter around her shoulders as she glared at the dragon. "I never thought I'd see the day when you would break a vow."

"I beg your pardon?" Bayang said stiffly.

"Didn't we promise to return the staff to Uncle Resak and the string to Pele," Scirye demanded, indicating the bow in one corner.

The dragon scratched the tip of her snout. "Hmm, we did do that, didn't we?"

"And you don't want to break an oath to a goddess," Leech chimed in eagerly. "So you can't go back to your clan just yet."

"They'll just have to wait." And Bayang laughed.

"And while we're traveling, we'll figure out some way to convince your clan to forgive you," Scirye suggested. It seemed like a remote hope but then so had been stopping Roland.

"Sure," Koko said. "We're bound to save the world a few more times on the way to Hawaii. Do that enough times and even dragons will have to forgive and forget."

"What about Primo?" Scirye asked Leech.

Leech shrugged. "He'll just have to understand that you're my family too."

It was Kles who played the spoilsport. "How do we leave though? We don't have the straw wing anymore."

Leech waved a paw at the tent around them. "We can build a wing out of canvas and poles."

"But how do we launch it?" Kles asked. "Bayang can't fly yet."

They all lapsed into silence, trying to figure out how to make that happen. Suddenly, Scirye felt a warmth wrap itself around her as if Nanaia were with her again.

"What are you smiling about?" Leech asked her curiously.

All of Scirye's doubts and worries vanished mysteriously. "I don't know." Scirye shrugged. "I just feel like it."

Then a familiar voice boomed from above them. "Ho, lumplings!"

They heard a puzzled Kat shout. "Who's that talking? I can't see you. And no one calls me a lump of anything."

The tent boomed and the ropes creaked as a stray draft from Naue tried to tear it free. "Have you seen my friends?" he asked, cheerfully ignoring Kat's questions. "They look odder than you and they're much more entertaining."

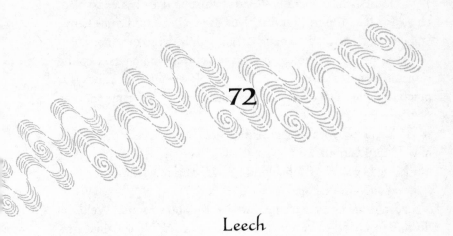

# 72

## Leech

Mounting the discs, Leech rose through the air as all eyes in the camp watched him. The Voice did not speak but he could feel his elation added to Leech's own.

Below him, Scirye, Bayang, and Koko were waving their hands to get Naue's attention. Flapping his arms as he rocketed upward, Leech shouted, "Naue, here we are."

Leech felt a thin gust of air circle around his waist as if Naue had extended an invisible tendril. Playfully, the wind spun him around and around as if he were a top. "Oh, such great joy! Such rapture! You're alive, half-lumpling. Naue feels like singing. And he will."

Before Naue could begin one of his long hymns of praise to himself, Leech said quickly, "And we're glad to see you managed to pull yourself back together."

"How can lightning destroy Naue the Invincible?" Naue demanded as he stopped twirling Leech.

"How did you find us?" Leech asked.

"One of Naue's many admirers whispered in his ear." Naue paused as if confused. "Or did Naue dream he should come here?"

Leech wondered if Nanaia had guided the wind to them.

In the meantime, though, Naue shook off his momentary confusion and began to swirl around Leech. "No matter. Isn't it always so much fun when Naue is with you lumplings? What game shall we play next?"

As Leech fought to keep his balance, he managed to say, "We have to build another wing somehow."

"Naue is generous," the wind declared. "He will wait for your signal. You know the one?"

Leech remembered seeing flares in Roland's camp. "We'll put flowers in the sky," Leech said. That was what Naue called fireworks.

But Naue was too impressed by his own kindliness to pay attention to the boy. "Lovely is the friendship of Naue, Great Naue!" the wind sang in a booming voice. "Grateful are the lumplings, for who else is so kind, so gracious, so understanding?"

He was still singing as his voice faded into the distance.

*If he had legs,* the Voice observed, *he'd be strutting right now.*

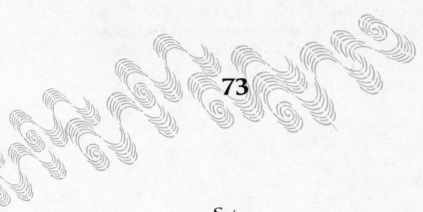

## 73

## Scirye

When Leech brought them the news, Scirye was sure that the goddess had done her one last favor. Or was it some last bit of Māka still in Her? Was the memory of being human part of Her now?

*Thank you*, she said silently to the goddess and her friend, for she would never be able to think about the one without the other.

Bayang was busy using charcoal from the brazier to draw a crude diagram of the wing on one end of a wooden table. And on the other end, Leech was busy making up a list of what they will need.

"We'll need supplies too," Koko said, serious for once. "Lots of them."

Scirye looked at the excited faces of their friends. "This is the way it should be," she murmured to Kles who had coiled himself around her neck.

"Yes," the little griffin agreed, "the five of us racing to a new adventure together."

As she felt his warm body vibrate as the griffin began to chirrup contently, Scirye was ready to purr with him.

# Afterword

This series began when my editor, Susan Chang, told me she was interested in the Caucasian mummies that had been found along the Silk Road, some of which dated back 3,800 years. The dry climate had preserved their bodies so it was possible to see that they had red hair and Caucasian features and had been buried in cloth with a weave distinctive to the Celts of Europe.

I'd been just as fascinated by the mummies and how they came to be in what is now China. DNA tests showed that they were of both Near Eastern and Asian ancestry, suggesting that people were already traveling back and forth upon the trade routes we call the Silk Road.

It was more than people and jewels; spices and other goods also moved back and forth across continents, and ideas as well. The goddess Nanaia was a combination of the Mesopotamian goddess Anahita and the Greek goddess Demeter, with some overtones of Indian deities as well.

Many authorities believe that the descendants of these mummies became the Kushans, whose empire sat astride the Silk Road for several centuries. They were a flexible people who were adept at blending ideas and concepts, including commissioning the Buddhist statues of Gandhara. Buddhist themes were sculpted in classical Greek style to create a haunting and serene beauty.

When I began the series, I had no idea that the Asian Art Museum in San Francisco was going to bring in an exhibit that featured Kushan art and jewelry, and I had a chance to see it twice. If you are curious about these treasures, you might want to look at the exhibit's catalog, *Afghanistan: Hidden Treasures from the National Museum, Kabul.*

The Old Tongue in this series is Tocharian, and I'm embarrassed to say that I found I had mispronounced some of the names of the Kushan characters, so I've corrected it in the guide.

Finally, I want to thank the readers for following the adventures of Scirye and her companions. I hope they had as much fun on this journey as I did and that, by the end, they could also smell a hint of spices carried on the dry wind.

---

These are some of the sources consulted for this book:

Adams, Douglas Q. *A Dictionary of Tocharian B.* Amsterdam: Rodolpi Bv, 1999.

Asarpay, G. "Nana, the Sumero-Akkadian Goddess of Transoxiana," *Journal of the American Oriental Society* 96, no. 4 (October–December 1976): 536–542.

Ball, Warwick. *The Monuments of Afghanistan: History, Archaeology and Architecture.* London and New York: I.B. Tauris, 2008.

Cribb, Joe, and Georgina Herrman, eds. *After Alexander: Central Asia before Islam.* Oxford: Oxford University Press, 2007.

de la Vaissière, Étienne. *Sogdian Traders: A History.* Translated by James Ward. Leiden: Brill, 2005.

Ghose, Madhuvanti. "Nana: The 'Original' Goddess on the Lion," *Journal of Inner Asian Art and Archaeology* 1 (2006): 97–112.

Hiebert, Fredrik, and Pierre Cambon, eds. *Afghanistan: Hidden Treasures from the National Museum, Kabul.* Washington,

D.C.: National Geographic, 2008. Note the original French edition has more material on the actual excavations.

Juliano, Annette L., Judith A. Lerner, and Michael Alram. *Monks and Merchants: Silk Road Treasures from Northwest China*. New York: Abrams, 2001.

Mair, Victor. *Secrets of the Silk Road: An Exhibition of Discoveries from the Xinjang Uyghur Autonomous Region, China*. Santa Ana, Calif.: Bowers Museum, 2010.

Mani, Buddha Rashmi. *The Kushan Civilization: Studies in Urban Development and Material Culture*. Dehli: B. R. Publishing, 1987.

Michell, George, Marika Vicziany, and Tsui Yen Hu. *Kashgar: Oasis City on China's Old Silk Road*. London: Francis Lincoln, 2008.

Rosenfield, John M. *The Dynastic Arts of the Kushans*. Berkeley: University of California Press, 1967.

Thakur, Dr. Manoj K. *India in the Age of Kanishka*. 2nd rev. ed. Dehli: Worldview Publication, 1999.

Video:

*Lost Treasures of Afghanistan*, National Geographic, DVD, 2006.
*The Silk Road*, NHK, Central Park. DVD, Media, 2000.
*The Treasures of the Silk Road: Mysteries of the Taklamakan*, SBS, DVD, Madman, 2005.

*Reader's Guide*

## ABOUT THIS GUIDE
The information, activities, and discussion questions that follow are intended to enhance your reading of *City of Death*. Please feel free to adapt these materials to suit your needs and interests.

## WRITING AND RESEARCH ACTIVITIES
**1.** Go to the library or online to learn more about the Kushan Empire. Create an informational poster including a labeled map of where the key places in the Kushan Empire would be located today, and a border of illustrated informational paragraphs describing the influence of Greek, Chinese, and other cultures on Kushan language and ideology.

**2.** Although *City of Death* is a fantasy novel, a note at the beginning of chapter 1 tells readers this is an alternate December 1941. Go to the library or online to learn what was happening in real-world history in December 1941. Use your research to make a timeline of actual historical events for the month. If desired, include key events from the years 1939–1945.

**3.** Informed by your research from activities 1 and/or 2, above, write a short essay describing how you perceive the influence of the Kushan Empire era and mid-twentieth-century history and culture has inspired Laurence Yep's heroes and villains, human and nonhuman characters, or other elements of the novel.

**4.** Create a PowerPoint or other type of software-based presentation that offers a tour of the fictional Bactra in *City of Death*, explaining the architecture, the types of beings living in the city, and the political situation, including people in key leadership positions.

**5.** Natural land formations, such as mountains, and elements, such as wind, play critical roles in *City of Death*. Using descriptions from the novel, create a drawing, collage, sculpture, or other visual artwork representing one of these formations or elements. If desired, create a display by combining your work with that of friends or classmates.

**6.** In the voice of Māka in chapter 20, write a journal entry describing your understanding of your magical power and why you feel such a strong loyalty to Scirye.

**7.** In the City trilogy, Roland, with the aid of Bayang's dragon nemesis, Badik, is trying to assemble the lost treasures of the Emperor Yu. In the voice of the character of Roland, write an order to Badik explaining why he must obtain the Archer's arrows and how he should deal with Sciyre and others who try to stop him.

**8.** Research famous lost treasures, such as the Imperial Fabergé eggs or the Crown Jewels of Ireland. Inspired by your research, create a description and history for a fictional lost treasure of your own invention. Share your "lost treasure" information with friends or classmates and together create a brainstorm list of historical figures or fictional characters who would be best fit to search for the treasure.

**9.** Throughout the novel, Leech and the Voice engage in many conversations and debates. Dramatize one or more of these dialogues for friends or classmates. Consider how you might costume a "Voice" and how you could stage the conversation so that one realizes that it is, in a way, an internal dialogue.

**10.** Who (or what) is Kemshap? In the voice of Pippalanta or a Kushan elder, write and present a short speech answering this question, explaining the threat Kemshap presents to the world, and sharing your thoughts about Roland's role in this chaos. If desired, wear a costume to present your speech.

**11.** Kles (Klestetstse) is Scirye's best friend, loyal servant, and advisor. Write an essay describing a moment in your life during which you could identify with Kles, such as how you acted as a teacher to a younger sibling, what you provided as the shortest player on your basketball team, or how you stuck with a friend through a crisis. Use quotations from the novel, along with your own experiences, to complete your essay. Conclude by surmising what Kles might think of your actions.

**12.** In his afterward, Laurence Yep tells readers he hopes "they could also smell a hint of spices carried on the dry wind." Can you? Write your answer to this question in the form of a poem or song lyrics.

## QUESTIONS FOR DISCUSSION

**1.** As the novel begins, Scirye and her friends are riding on a magical wing. Why do you think the author chose to begin the story with this action scene? What do you learn about the "wing's" riders and their relationships in the first three chapters of *City of Death*?

**2.** Like the previous novels in the series, *City of Death* is written from three points of view: Scirye, Leech, and Bayang. How do you think each of these characters brings an important perspective to the story? How do you think reading a story told by multiple narrators affects your experience as a reader?

**3.** Who is Māka? Do you believe she has magical power at the beginning of the novel? Had you been one of Scirye's friends on this adventure, would you also have trusted Māka?

**4.** Throughout the novel, Leech argues with another being, or spirit, trapped within him: the Voice. Describe their relationship.

Do you think there is some sort of voice inside each of us? Explain your answer.

**5.** On page 198, Leech says to the Voice, "It's nice to have people you can trust and depend on, isn't it? . . . They're our friends. And friends are better than family because we choose them and they choose us." Do you agree or disagree?

**6.** What roles do geography and landscapes play in the novel? How do they help characterize the situations in which the friends find themselves? What might this tell readers about the connections between people and their environments?

**7.** Name several characters from the novel that have the ability to change form. If you could choose to have the powers of one of these characters, which would it be and why? How would you use your abilities in your modern-day life?

**8.** When Scirye is tempted by Dionysus, she wishes for Nanaia's help, then thinks, "Maybe it's better if the goddess doesn't change things for me. I've got to do it myself." (page 261) Soon after, Lord Tsirauñe tells Scirye and her friends to stay back while he investigates Roland's activities, but Lady Sudarshane disagrees, reminding him "This is really their quest, not ours." (page 270) How are these two statements related to Scirye's evolution as a hero and to her journey from childhood to adulthood?

**9.** Throughout the novel, Scirye grapples with the risks of endangering herself and her friends to find Roland, and to honor the code of Tumarg. What is Tumarg? Why is it so important? Do you follow a code of ethics you learned from your family, faith, school, or community? Compare and contrast your own set of principles to your understanding of Tumarg.

**10.** On page 336, Scirye considers Māka-Nanaia's insight about balance, realizing "the Inside equalized the Outside. Weakness matched strength." Is the notion of balance, both literally and metaphorically, the central motif of the novel? Explain why, or make your case for another organizing concept in *City of Death*.

**11.** What is the "City of Death"? Why is it so named? What type of leadership must Scirye exhibit to lead her friends to victory over the many types of opponents in the city?

**12.** Where is Scirye at the end of the novel? Do you believe Bayang and Primo can ever truly reconcile? If so, on what terms? If there were to be a fourth City novel, what title would you like it to have, and why?

# About the Author

LAURENCE YEP is the critically acclaimed author of more than sixty books for children and young adults, including two Newbery Honor Award winners: *Dragonwings* and *Dragon's Gate*. In 2005 he was the recipient of the Laura Ingalls Wilder Award from the American Library Association for a substantial and lasting contribution to literature for children. Mr. Yep lives with his wife in Pacific Grove, California.